'Cassie?' With a gentle bold Jack turned her to face him—and found himself even closer.

Near enough to feel the warmth of her body, to see the gold rim sparkle in her eyes, and smell the essence that was pure Cassie. His lips were a breath away from hers.

'Conversation won't answer the questions keeping me awake at night'. He slid his hand around her neck. 'Like how will it feel to have you crushed against me?' He tilted her chin up with his thumb. 'And are your lips as delectable and sweet as I imagine?'

He lowered his head and covered his mouth with hers in a tender exploratory kiss. Her body stilled, then melted into his, causing an instant physical reaction. His heart flipped, and then soared when she didn't pull away. His fingers caressed and firmed as his free arm encircled her waist, binding her to him. His chest expanded and fire flared in his stomach, rapidly spreading to every extremity.

Cassie's arms snaked up and around his neck, her fingers tangled into his hair and he trembled. There was no awareness of time. It was an instant or a lifetime until necessity for air forced his lips from hers barely long enough to gasp and let a possessive male growl escape before settling again. He heard her contented sigh mingle with his low rumble.

Yet suddenly Cassie wrenched free; slamming onto the workbench and sending him stumbling away, almost falling over the dog.

He took a step forward, hands held out in appeal. 'Cassie, what's wrong? Tell me what I did.'

'It's wrong. We can't...we mustn't'. Her hesitant words were muttered against her palms as she dropped t

CAPTIVATED BY THE ENIGMATIC TYCOON

BY
BELLA BUCANNON

First Published in Great Britain 2017
By Mills & Boon, an imprint of HarperCollins*Publishers*
1 London Bridge Street, London, SE1 9GF

© 2017 Harriet Nichola Jarvis

ISBN: 978-0-263-92322-3

23-0817

Our policy is to use papers that are natural, renewable and recyclable products and made from wood grown in sustainable forests. The logging and manufacturing processes conform to the legal environmental regulations of the country of origin.

Printed and bound in Spain
by CPI, Barcelona

Bella Bucannon lives in a quiet northern suburb of Adelaide with her soulmate husband, who loves and supports her in any endeavour. She enjoys walking, dining out and travelling. Bus tours or cruising with days at sea to relax, plot and write are top of her list. Apart from category romance she also writes very short stories and poems for a local writing group. Bella believes joining RWA and SARA early in her writing journey was a major factor in her achievements.

To my own special hero,
who understands my struggle with routine
and being organised.

To Flo and Victoria
for their support, advice and guidance.

And to everyone who knows I am a hoarder
and couldn't believe I understand decluttering.

CHAPTER ONE

JACK RANDELL GRINNED at the sound of Strauss, his Aunt Mel's favourite composer, as he reached the back door. Hopefully this meant her feisty spirit was resurfacing as she'd rarely listened to any music she could dance to since the accident three months ago.

Although she was technically his great-aunt, he could never envision her as being that extra generation older. She and Bob had given him unconditional support during his teenage years when understanding between him and his parents had seemed irretrievable. This house had become his sanctuary, still was even at the age of twenty-eight.

His spirits lifted in anticipation that she'd also begun baking again, and that the kitchen would be filled with mouth-watering aromas. He automatically inhaled as he stepped across the threshold.

No tempting smells and no sound of human activity. He wasn't surprised at the lack of heating; Mel rarely turned it on until the sun began to set. While he'd been visiting his parents in Brisbane, he'd thought July's bitterly cold days in Adelaide might have changed her mind. Another reason to believe she was active again and didn't need it.

After glancing into the kitchen, disappointingly neat and clean, he was about to call out when he heard a scraping sound from the family room on his right. He walked in and stopped, breath caught in his throat and heart skipping intermittent beats.

An enticingly filled-out pair of denim jeans occupied the space in front of the heavy coffee table now placed in the far corner. Definitely not Mel, who declared denim was for the young. *His* tightened as the pleasing form leaned in further, angling past the bookcase that had been pushed almost to the table, partly blocking the window.

He heard a triumphant *huff*, followed by a pained, 'Ow.' The taut bottom jiggled, and he became decidedly uncomfortable. Mesmerised and immobilised, he watched as the wriggling continued towards him.

A long-sleeved navy woollen jumper appeared, followed by a cap of cropped black hair. The woman snaked onto her haunches, holding up a small object. Her light harmonious laugh rippled through him as she rubbed a spot on the top of her head.

'Got you. I'll sew you back on later.'

'Cassie, coffee time. I'll… Jack, I didn't expect this early surprise!'

Fixated on the figure in front of him, Jack didn't react to his aunt's voice. He was spellbound as the head spun, dark hair flew and a hand hit the floor to prevent toppling over. Scrambling to her feet, she twisted towards him and he found himself fighting for air again.

Walnut-coloured eyes framed by long black lashes widened as a delightful pink hue tinted her cheeks. Natural red, not quite symmetrical lips parted as she sucked in a deep breath and glared at him as if he'd been the cause of her injury.

Holding her gaze, he suddenly jerked back as Mel's face loomed into his vision, eyebrows raised, perceptive smile in place. A great improvement since he'd said goodbye sixteen days ago.

'Remember me?'

He wrapped her in a bear hug and kissed her cheek, thankful she'd regained her normal happy disposition.

'Great timing as always. Coffee in the lounge, and you can tell me how your parents are. Oh, by the way, this is Cassie Clarkson. Cassie, my great-nephew, Jack Randell.'

She walked out with a slight hint of a limp, paying no heed to his dropped jaw. Who the hell was Cassie Clarkson, and what was she doing here when Mel had family who'd willingly come any time she needed help? Had she provided references for whatever she did, and had they been checked?

Hadn't his aunt learnt from previous attempts to cheat her, two of them by so-called friends? An older woman on her own was considered an easy target by unscrupulous people. Even he had been duped by an attractive friend of his sister. He'd lost unpaid rent, plus his own time getting the damaged property fit to let again.

The young woman who was pinning whatever she'd picked up onto a coat hanging on a clothes rack—he now became aware of it, plus two by the window—was delightfully curved and a perfect height to nestle her head cosily on his shoulder.

Which he really should not be imagining when he had no idea who, why or what as far as she was concerned. Good looks and toned bodies might attract but they could also mask a desire for the lifestyle and prestige marrying into a wealthy family offered. Hard lessons learnt weren't easily forgotten.

Ignoring the acceleration of his pulse and the warmth spreading through his body despite the cool air, he stepped forward. She looked up, and he had a hankering for warm Christmas brandy heated by the glow in her eyes. Instantly tempered by his self-imposed wariness of mere physical attraction. He took another pace and held out his hand.

'Hello, Cassie.'

She wiped hers on her thighs before accepting.

'Dust. Hello, Jack. Mel's mentioned you a few times.'

She kept their touch brief, barely polite, and removed her hand smoothly so she couldn't have felt the *zing* that shot through him. Neither did she sound as impressed as he'd like her to be, though there was no reason for him to care. Or for his fingers to involuntarily try to hold on. He definitely liked the slightly rough edge to her voice.

'And you don't approve. Any particular reason?'

She laughed again, triggering the same response. 'I never make hasty judgements. I admire the way she portrays you, your siblings and cousins as paragons of virtue; I'm just convinced she's oblivious to your faults.'

He suspected she was baiting him, didn't rise. 'She brings out the best in us. Who exactly are you and what are you doing here?'

'I'm a declutterer.'

'A what?'

Cassie wasn't fazed by his bewilderment, and quite liked the baffled expression on his handsome rugged face. Payback for not letting her know he was observing her ungainly exit from under the table. She'd caught her breath as they'd made contact and wondered if he'd felt the same electrical spark that zapped up her arm.

'I help people sort out and downsize their belongings.'

'Mel's not a hoarder.' Quick and sharp.

'No, she's not, and she's expecting us for coffee.'

She walked past him and went to the kitchen to wash her hands. The tingle on her nape told her he'd followed. She dismissed it, refusing to gush over cowboy hero features and eyes the colour of buffalo grass after spring rain. Or to surrender to the urge to finger comb his ruffled light brown hair. Even if his voice was deep and smooth like the old-time crooners on her mum's CDs.

'So she's hired you. Why keep it quiet?'

His sharp tone irked. Counting to fourteen before turning rather than the universal ten was her safety valve. Failing to get any employer's relative onside could backfire on her.

She enjoyed her work and satisfied customers spread the word, ensuring she rarely had to advertise for clients. He was the first of Mel's relations she'd met, though a niece had visited prior to her arrival this morning, and there'd been a few phone calls.

At her interview, Mel had explained her family regularly checked up on her since she'd insisted she no longer needed a live-in carer. Her hairline fracture had healed with minimal after-effects, and she took care moving around. She still slept in a made-up room downstairs and never went to the second storey when alone.

Today, as they'd worked, she'd chatted about the younger generation, and the way they fussed over her. Cassie's heart had clenched at the thought of having numerous relatives who cared.

Running her hand over her hair, she turned to find Jack almost within touching distance.

If one desired physical contact. Which she did not.

Legs apart, hands tucked into rear pockets and eyes narrowed with suspicion, he appeared to be spoiling for a confrontation.

She met his unblinking stare with confidence, regarding the ripples in her stomach as natural under the circumstances. Showing him she wouldn't be intimidated, she began a slow scroll down his face, noting the high forehead, the wide generous mouth and the strong stubbled jaw. Sculpted biceps and pecs were clearly defined under a fawn work shirt, unbuttoned at the neck and folded at the wrists, revealing tufts of fine brown hair.

Unfortunately, it was *her* pulse quickening and *her* temperature rising as her gaze slid over firm blue denim-clad thighs and past long legs to black tradies' boots. Keeping tight control on the speed, she made the journey up to a gratifying flush and a very masculine scowl.

'I wasn't aware she hadn't told you.' She heard the hitch

in her voice, hoped her features didn't betray her reaction. 'If you'll excuse me, I'll see you in the lounge in a few minutes.'

She walked towards the door, head held high, shoulders rigid.

He moved aside. 'It will be my pleasure.' A tone or two deeper than his last remark, with a definite hint of cynicism.

Upstairs, in the bedroom Mel had invited her to use, she slumped against the closed door, shaken by the encounter with her employer's handyman nephew. The guy wouldn't be out of place on the pages of the celebrity magazines Narelle, her best friend, avidly studied. She could imagine those full, firm lips...*no!* She would not.

Cassie had escaped from him to gather her thoughts, and wasn't sure she'd succeeded even after brushing her hair until it shone. Not for him, she told herself as she went downstairs. Being neat and tidy was a matter of pride.

Her career choice had been a natural progression after assisting the woman she'd called Mum all her life help different friends prepare for the move into retirement villages or homes. At first she'd been fascinated by the variety of, to her teenage eyes, useless items, some not even decorative. There were always old postcards and souvenirs, hardly used presents, and so many photographs in albums, boxes and drawers.

Talking to these people at this crucial moment in their lives, she'd empathised with their anxieties and their pain at having to let go of items that defined their lives. Growing up with no relatives except Mum, she'd found the differences in family interactions intriguing. She'd also discovered she had a talent for sensing the emotional reasons behind the spoken need to cling to certain pieces. The appeal of working in the same building every day, no matter what the job, had diminished in comparison.

* * *

Jack's baritone was audible as Cassie approached the lounge room door, though the actual words were indistinguishable. Their combined laughter triggered a yearning for the closeness she'd shared for twenty-three years with Julie, her maternal aunt, to her, now and for ever, Mum.

At two days old, her birth mother had brought her to Julie then left for America. She'd made spasmodic short visits while Cassie was very young and occasional telephone calls after. There'd been no contact for fifteen years.

The cancer that had taken Mum four years ago had been short and aggressive, but thankfully there was no heart-wrenching guilt for missed opportunities. Every memory was precious, any reminder, however painful, evoked grateful thanks for the time they'd had.

Hearing Jack's voice again, she closed her eyes, pressed her open hands to her lips and breathed in and out twice. Channelling her inner strength, she walked in.

Jack's expression was inscrutable though his lips curled a little as their eyes met. He'd taken the huge armchair in the corner, body at ease, legs stretched out. She'd tried it when they'd had morning tea, felt lost in its size and preferred a corner of the family-sized sofa. Sam, Mel's medium-size, scruffy mixed breed dog, was curled up on the rug in front of him.

'Jack's been enjoying the Queensland sunshine,' Mel explained as she poured a cup of coffee and handed it to Cassie. 'He makes it sound very tempting.'

His velvet tongue would tempt the devil into a trip to the Arctic. Cassie bent to select a chocolate biscuit from the long, low table then sat, arching against the big comfortable cushion. Who needed pricy gyms when they bent, stretched and lifted all day? She worked hard and slept soundly.

'He's a little testy because I hired you without consulting the family first, Cassie. As if I can't decide for myself.'

'Not what I said, Aunt Mel,' he interrupted, eyebrow quirking. 'I asked why you've hired someone when you'd get all the help you need from us.'

Being fit and healthy, he wouldn't understand his aunt's wish to regain independence after relying on her extended family's care and attention for so long. This was a major step in her rehabilitation.

'And I appreciate it, dear.' Her employer grinned at Cassie. 'I can also detect censure. It's the *Aunt* Mel. If he's really cross I become *Great-Aunt Melanie*.'

Her affection was so clear Cassie smiled then swung in Jack's direction as he burst out laughing. It was a rich crackly sound, generating an image of a campfire in the Outback. Bizarre, as she'd never had the experience.

'Guess who I learnt that from. I knew I was in big trouble whenever you called me Jackson Randell in that quiet, resolute tone guaranteed to have any of us kids confessing every misdemeanour.'

'*Jackson?*' Never ever would Cassie have visualised him with such a distinctive name. All she'd heard and seen— apart from his movie star looks—said regular working guy who'd had normal teenage disputes with his parents. Yet now, as she studied him, she became aware of an innate assurance that tested her ever-present caution. Evidence of well-to-do family and a private education.

'Only ever used on official documents or by aggrieved mother and aunts.' His eyes sobered, locked with hers. Straightening up, he put his coffee mug down and leant his elbows on the chair arms. Sam crept forward, laying his head on Jack's boot.

'Mel insisted you be present when she explained what's going on, Cassie.'

Although he pronounced it like everyone else, his timbre as he said her name triggered tingles across her skin.

She detected a slight undertone, a hint of warning and was glad Mel spoke first, causing him to turn her way.

'I've had a lot of time to think lately about life, and being dependent on people, Jack. It's made me realise I'm not as resilient as I've always believed. I need to get my home and affairs in order before I become doddery and senile.'

Jack shook his head and chuckled, and the image of a wide plain and starlit sky flared again.

'Mel Frampton, you're one of the brightest, sanest people I know, and I'm grateful to be part of the same gene pool. I also have every intention of leading you onto the dance floor at your centenary celebration.'

'It's a date. Right now, not being game to access the top floor without help is frustrating. I decided to begin with a cull of my clothes and shoes. Apart from my bedroom walk-in, I have two wardrobes full of garments, most of which no longer fit.'

'You were never overweight.' Jack's forceful exclamation surprised both women.

'No, but it's crept on over the years. Not good for an inactive middle-aged woman. Eating more salads and limited baking means I've lost some. Now it's time to get rid of anything that doesn't suit me or fit comfortably. My accident was a reality check.'

'Okay, it doesn't…'

'Cassie, you explain how it works.'

Gee, thanks, Mel. Now I have to confront him and pretend I'm not affected by his piercing green eyes.

The owner of those disturbing eyes shifted in his chair, aligning his body to hers, his posture challenging. He flexed the fingers of his left hand on his thigh. Convincing his sceptical mind that her employment was the better option required tactful honesty.

It wasn't unusual to have relatives question her motives or trustworthiness. There were so many dodgy crooks trying to take advantage of older people, especially women living alone.

Jack Randell in protective mode was going to be tougher than most to placate. He wasn't budging until he'd been fully informed of her role in his aunt's objectives. Cassie's heart warmed at the unmistakable love and concern driving his determination.

'Every situation is different, depending on the needs of my clients. I never try to influence their choices. Satisfied referrals are my main source of employment.'

His body eased and his furrowed brow cleared.

She continued. 'All items are listed on a tablet which stays at the client's home. On completion, they receive a printout and backup on USB then my files are cleared.'

'Completely?' His shirt tightened across his chest as he breathed in and squared his shoulders. It was a very *I'm-the-male-here* action that ought to rankle yet didn't.

She steeled her resolve. Macho didn't impress her but… her practical mind appreciated a man this fit would be handy on many of the assignments she accepted. At least his muscles would; the effect his proximity seemed to have on her might not be so welcome.

'Jackson.' Mel's tone was sharp and every sign of intimidation evaporated.

CHAPTER TWO

JACK SMILED AT his aunt, let out a huff of breath and picked up his coffee, relishing the strong rich flavour. He'd hold his tongue for now and do his own private investigation of Ms Cassie Clarkson later.

He refocused on the alluring stranger with the steady gaze who unsettled his heartbeat and had him speculating how dark her eyes would grow in desire. How many other men had she swayed with her pacifying manner? Not his affair. *Bad choice of word.*

He gave her his full attention as she continued, noting liquid had no effect on her unique voice. Did passion?

Focus, Randell.

'Family contribution and involvement can be emotive, which often leads to controversy. I always recommend nothing is given to charity or thrown away without consultation.'

'We decided the best plan was to bring everything downstairs for me to check,' Mel interjected, and he swung towards her.

'The clothes I want for use will go in the room I'm sleeping in now, and others for keeping can go back to my bedroom. The family will be invited to help themselves from the rest. Now, are you going to play nice or do I ban you until we've finished?'

She wouldn't.

One glance at her beloved, resolute face and he capitulated. Being forbidden to come here was unthinkable, even for a short time. He held both hands up in defeat, his empty mug hanging on one finger.

'Okay, I surrender. Need help with anything? I'm free for the rest of the day.' Though his expertise in women's clothes was more in the line of removing them, not shifting them around.

'I do have a list of minor repairs you can look at. Would you like to stay for dinner?'

'Do you need to ask?' He stood up just as a new symphony came through the speakers set high in two corners. 'It's good to hear Strauss again. I feel a definite urge to waltz you round the furniture right now.'

Mel laughed. 'Give my leg a little longer, and I'll accept.' She rose gracefully to her feet, pride in her voice as she told Cassie, 'I taught all his generation proper ballroom dancing.'

Jack's heart swelled at her lithe movements, belying her age and the trauma she'd been through. He prayed she'd stay as bright and feisty for many years. Seeing Cassie sneak an extra chocolate biscuit as she got to her feet, he raised his eyebrows. She noticed and her eyes sparkled, daring him to comment as she took a bite.

He let his gaze flick over her slender figure then grinned. Dipping his head, he gestured for her to precede him to the door, admiring the delectable view as she did.

He prided himself on his judgement of character, improved through the years of buying and renting properties, and honed by the few instances of being conned. It failed him where Cassie Clarkson was concerned, and he didn't want to dwell too much on the reason. He'd treat her with respect and ignore his attraction, though keeping an eye on her wouldn't be hard to take at all.

Having strangers think he wasn't as affluent as Mel or others suited him fine. He relished the hands-on work he did equally with the intellectual stimulation of the stock market. He enjoyed the easy relationship with the people he did maintenance jobs for, and disliked the fact it would lose its informality if they found out he was also their landlord.

Flaunting his initial successes, even to his family, had seemed conceited so he played it down, not worried if others believed he wasted his potential. He understood how money influenced people's attitude, having let it rule him in his teens. Personal ambition had driven him to seek after-school employment and invest in shares.

He'd soon discovered that for some girls his name and the prospect of money took priority over the person behind them. Now wiser, and matured by experience, he wanted people to admire him because of who he was, and how he acted, not for the numbers on his tax return.

After discussing the precise, neatly written task list with Mel, he went to fetch appropriate tools from his vehicle. On his return, he heard voices from the family room and glanced in. One of the racks was now almost full, there were evening gowns on the second, and more clothes lay on the covered billiard table against the side wall.

He couldn't hear what they said but their mingled laughter tipped the scales in Cassie's favour. Mel was happier than she'd been since the car accident. He backed away and went to tighten the hinges on the kitchen cupboard doors, wishing it were a complicated task to keep his mind from straying to bold walnut-brown eyes and kissable lips.

Cassie made four trips to one of the spare bedrooms for classical evening wear that sparked a slight twinge of envy. She loved the textures, colours and styling of brand names she recognised from magazines. Her yearly spending on new clothing was probably less than some of these dresses or outfits had cost on their own.

During her long meeting with Mel over lunch in the city, and in less than a day here, she'd gained an impression of an ever-expanding well-educated, affluent family with skilled professions and good standing in the community.

It was also obvious they were close-knit and devoted. She'd seen the same in many families, though had no idea how it really felt to have multiple relatives. There had always been friends to play and share birthdays with but over time many had changed school or moved away.

Narelle had been a constant friend since her family had moved into the neighbourhood when they were both eleven. Within the first week at high school, they'd formed a group with two boys and another girl, the bonds strong to this day. Their families had always welcomed her in their homes, encouraging her to be part of their everyday lives and never giving her reason to feel like an outsider.

Yet much of the time she'd felt as if she had an internal barrier preventing her from allowing herself to completely become part of it all. It was as if she were an audience member who had wandered up onto the stage and didn't know her lines but enjoyed watching from up close.

At odd moments in her youth, usually late at night, she'd sometimes fantasise about having a real sibling. She had never, before or now, had any interest or curiosity about her birth parents. Not even when she'd lost Mum and felt completely alone for a while—still did on occasion, no matter how much support her friends gave her.

This was the main reason she'd rented out the home she'd inherited and moved in with Brad and Phil three years ago. They were as close to brothers as she'd ever have, and would probably tease her mercilessly if she mentioned that spark when she and Jack shook hands.

He was an enigma, born into the elite class of Adelaide yet he'd chosen a trade for his profession. As she went through the foyer, she could hear him humming in the kitchen. It reminded her of Mel's excitement after he'd phoned earlier to say he'd arrived home late yesterday and would call in today.

'He's been my mainstay since Bob died. Could have joined the family law firm but studied business management instead and passed with honours. I don't know why he chose to work in property repair and maintenance, though he is buying houses that he rents out.'

She'd said the latter as if it were the epitome of success.

'He can be very reticent at times, and I'm not sure how many he has, three, maybe more by now, plus his home at Port Noarlunga. I just wish he'd find someone special and settle down. Casual short-term affairs, even if they end without acrimony, are no substitute for a long, happy marriage. I'm sure that mishap… No, that's in the past.'

As far as Cassie was concerned, any attractive male his age who'd never come near to being engaged or married had to have serious commitment issues. Her own situation didn't count. Being illegitimate, alone and knowing nothing of her paternal heritage made her wary of close relationships.

How could she offer any man all he'd desire in a wife and partner when there was no paternal name on her birth certificate? When she had no family history to offer?

'Sorry I've been so long. A friend wanted my recipe for jam drop biscuits.'

Cassie started, though she was getting used to Mel's voice preceding her into a room. Adjusting the straps of a dress on the rack gave her a moment to refocus. The red silk under her fingers was so fine, she could imagine the luxurious texture against her skin as she swayed or danced. It was every woman's dream, a spectacular gown for a romantic waltz in a special man's arms.

Mel came closer. 'Oh, my goodness, I don't even remember some of these clothes. How did I collect so many?'

'You could hold a garage sale and finance a Pacific

cruise.' Jack's amused voice made Cassie spin round. She'd assumed Mel was alone.

'Don't be flippant, Jack.' His aunt's tone softened her words. 'We donate unwanted goods, not sell them.'

'There are outlets for high quality second-hand fashions,' Cassie told them. 'They'd fetch a higher price than a charity could charge, and you could donate the money. We still have to empty the second wardrobe.'

'Hmm, what do you think, Jack?'

'It's worth checking into. Now, if Cassie will show me which hinges need tightening upstairs, I'll get them done now.'

His smile didn't reach his green eyes and her instinct was to decline. He could easily tell which ones were loose so why ask for her help? She answered with a curt nod.

Knowing he was following did funny things to her usual composed bearing, and she found herself taking the stairs with slow careful steps. Heat from his eyes skittled up and down her spine and the ripple in her belly was like a soft breeze stirring waves on the sea. Long steady breaths didn't quell her escalating heartbeat.

She twisted round at the top, grasping the rarity of being almost eye to eye. He caught her elbow without giving her a chance to speak, and gently propelled her to the bedroom at the far end of the passage.

Shaking free from his tingling hold, she stepped back a few paces and kept her voice low. 'As if you need help. This is like a second home for you.' Even huskier than normal when she'd meant to sound forceful.

He leant on the doorjamb, the rigidity of his muscles negating his casual stance, and gazed at her silently, features composed. This was a man adept at verbal negotiations. His lips curled confidently, and *her* body quivered as if he'd stroked warm fingers across her skin. She instinctively re-ran her mantra in her head.

Stay strong. Keep distance.

'Sounds like you've heard a lot in one day, Cassie Clarkson.'

'It comes with the job. People, especially if they live alone, often open up to someone who's temporary and won't have a lasting connection in their life.'

'You remember what they tell you.'

'I've learnt not to retain the sensitive personal stuff. But I'll never forget your aunt's courage and determination to rebuild her life for the second time. She's inspiring.'

He straightened up and took a pace forward. She sucked in air and held her ground.

'She's vulnerable since she lost Bob, even more so now.'

'How long since…?'

'Three years. Two months after their forty-fifth anniversary.' His Adam's apple bobbed as he swallowed. 'Imagine losing someone after forty-five years, how suddenly the one you care about is no longer there.'

She heard deep pain in the last few words, empathised as hers had hardly eased. Was it Bob or someone else he grieved for?

'She has all of you. That's more than some people have.'

His head jerked up and she averted her eyes.

He's smart, Cassie. Guard what you say. Keep strong and quiet.

'I assume you have references that can be verified.' Blunt, as if he regretted showing emotion.

'Of course.' She held his gaze. She had nothing to hide except her inexplicable responses to him.

His low grunt showed he wasn't quite convinced. 'Do you have them with you? May I see them?' Calmly stated with an *I-won't-be-dissuaded* manner.

'Not unless Mel requests it.' She mimicked his attitude, prepared to be polite, refusing to be bullied.

He frowned and came closer, into her personal space.

'She can be too trusting. I'm betting she hasn't asked for them.'

She smelt clean male sweat with a hint of sandalwood each time she inhaled, fought the instinct to run from the room. Yet not from fear; quite the opposite. She had an irrational urge to edge forward, minimise the gap.

Jack could sense a women's attraction for him, but it didn't mean he'd follow through. Cassie was giving out mixed messages. Her body implied *yes*, her eyes were wary and her voice said *no*. She boldly locked eyes with him— he now discerned a fine gold rim round her dark brown irises, yet at times there were shutters, like a misty blind she lowered at will.

She had spunk, hadn't backed off even though he came near enough to detect the faint aroma of peaches. Sweet. Enticing. He was aware of her in a new, unnerving way and his body responded to her, male to female.

His gut feeling said she had secrets hidden behind solid barriers no one was permitted to breach. She could keep them unless they caused trouble for Mel. His life ran smoothly and his long-term strategy for success was on track. As alluring as she was, he'd never let his guard down, never again let a woman believe she could manipulate him.

Tara had swayed him so many times, with her pouting lips and soft caresses, had been convinced she'd succeed again on the trip to the snowfields nine years ago. With blue eyes misting, she'd denied flirting with the ski instructor, only he'd seen her and anger had flared at her lies. Bitter accusations had ended with him telling her to find some other patsy and flinging himself onto the bed they'd shared, telling her not to wake him if she came back.

She hadn't returned. An impulsive decision to ski alone on an unfamiliar track had ended her life. He couldn't change the past but by keeping rigid control of his temper he had command of his future.

Challenge flared in Cassie's eyes, her lips curled and she tilted her head like a beguiling child. 'Why don't you check with her when you come down?'

The emotive tone in her voice didn't quite match the softer personal one in her eyes. And he wasn't sure which one he'd like to pursue, despite his recent vow. He gestured for her to pass and she did.

Too quick. Too close. Her fingers brushed his arm and a bolt of energy shot through him, like nothing he'd felt in his life. She'd been affected too, though she hid her reaction well. Had she picked up static from moving around a large carpeted house all day? Had to be that.

So touch her again and prove it.

Not a chance he was game to take at the moment.

Cassie wasn't sure how she made it out of the room without buckling to the floor. She huffed out the air captured in her lungs when the electrical charge from his touch short-circuited coherent thought and action. Fleeing to the safety of the family room, she was thankful to be alone.

Once she could dismiss as an anomaly, twice was… Did he pick up static electricity in his work? Didn't tradies' boots counteract that? Logic told her they did, as there'd been no reaction when he'd hugged his aunt.

She didn't want to be logical. She wanted to be safe from any involvement with Jack Randell or any other man of his social status. Conceived during an illicit one-night stand, she knew exactly what she was, and how she'd be regarded by elite society. And how easily a man's declared devotion could evaporate when tested.

Jack's appearance and actions gave the impression of a man working his way up the financial ladder, but he had wealthy connections and he'd probably inherit. Whatever the incentive for his current lifestyle, it would be an easy switch to his family's world of fancy cars and fine dining.

She'd never have the luxury of such a choice—her world was compact sedans and home cooking.

Letting out a light self-deprecating laugh, she walked over to the desk where she'd left her laptop next to Mel's computer and printer. Any spark of attraction he'd felt would dissipate at her lack of encouragement.

He'd have jobs waiting to be done during the day and friends to catch up with at night so he probably wouldn't be around much. On Thursday afternoon she'd give Mel her printouts plus a list of exclusive second-hand fashion boutiques, and drive away. That just left tonight to resist his innate charm.

Her body relaxed as she slow breathed, doing her steadying count to fourteen and repeating her mantra. *Stay strong. Keep distance.* She resumed checking labels and sizes, mystified by a world where haute couture and fashion changes were all-important. Why should someone be judged by the brand or style of the clothes they wore?

Neat comfortable jeans and muted tops or jumpers were her standard uniform. Her casual sneakers, boots or safety footwear were a far cry from the large array of high-heeled shoes she'd seen upstairs. They and others with sturdy low heels would be brought down and sorted for the female family members to view.

CHAPTER THREE

JACK WAS MULLING over his conversation with Cassie when he found Mel setting the table in the dining room. His heart lifted at the sight of the flower centrepiece and the crystal glasses beside each place setting, as they'd always been at dinner before her accident. A few stupid seconds of driving inattention to check a text and a teenager's car had veered towards the kerb. Overcorrecting had sent it slamming into Mel's daughter's passenger door. And Mel.

The weeks in hospital and drawn-out rehabilitation, with a broken leg and lacerations on her arm and across the top of her chest, had taken a toll. Table decorations didn't sound like much but he thanked whatever gods there were that she seemed to be embracing the life she'd loved again.

Not being able to drive, stand for long to cook and having to convert the small lounge into a downstairs bedroom had been hard enough. Being reliant on others for everything when she'd struggled so hard to be independent after Bob's fatal heart attack had almost broken her spirit.

If having the distraction of Cassie Clarkson here for a few days was the price to pay for getting his beloved Aunt Mel back to her old self, so be it.

'Going classy, huh? Do I need to race home and change?'

Mel's smile lit up her face, and her eyes shone. 'I thought Cassie deserved it. She's a sweet girl, and I like her. What we're doing is good for me, Jack.'

He walked over and hugged her. 'I wholeheartedly approve of anything that makes you happy, Mel.'

'Even if I take it further?'

He pulled back to see her expression. 'As in?'

'As in asking Cassie for a quote for a full downsize. Not all at once—over a few months, in between her other contracts. That way it won't be so tiring and easier to accept.'

A full house sorting? The first step to moving, selling her home. Life-changing for her, and she wanted his approval. This was a chance to make a small repayment for her and Bob's unconditional support.

'If it's what you want and feel you're ready for, I'm with you one hundred percent. You know you can rely on me, Mel.'

He kissed her cheek and stepped back. 'Do I have time to take Sam for a run before we eat?'

'Twenty minutes.' She patted his cheek as if he were a schoolboy again. 'Go.'

He went.

As he pounded along the footpath his mind churned with Mel's revelation. He'd fallen into the trap of believing that Mel's continuing recovery meant life would one day be as it always had been. Though he'd hoped she'd relent and have someone move in with her for company and safety.

She, Bob and their home had been his lifeline when home trauma threatened to derail his carefully planned objectives. He'd managed to get through the usual rebellious stage of drinking and partying without irreparable damage to his reputation.

He'd refused to study for the degree his father had wanted him to take, or to join one of the Randell established businesses, which had caused deep-seated angst. His dream to build a property empire had only been shared with Bob. During their discussions in the garden workshop, his great-uncle had taught him how to repair and maintain a home and its contents. He'd also instilled Jack with respect for his tools and the knowledge of their care and maintenance.

He and Mel had encouraged him when he'd got his first

after-school job, shelf-stacking at a local supermarket, and celebrated with him after he signed the contract to buy his first rental property. His one small consolation when Bob died was that he'd shared in every success, and had been thrilled when Jack had become a millionaire. Even if it was only on paper or consisting of bricks and mortar.

Thinking of that gentle man caused his heart to ache as if he'd run a marathon. He pushed through the pain. They'd always put his needs first; now it was time for him to man up and do the same for Mel.

Even she didn't know the true extent of his current finances. Having everyone believe he was buying a few properties and earning his daily living in maintenance kept him grounded and his demons at bay. Even then he could never be sure if it was him or the knowledge of his family's assets that attracted women. Tara had made it clear that she'd never date anyone she considered below her social status.

Mel's experiences had further proved that wealth drew frauds and con artists. So many people wanted easy money rather than work for it. Did Cassie? Was she wary of him as Mel's protector or as a man? Would her attitude change if she found out about his new business venture?

Sometime soon, when he took the next—this time gigantic—corporate step, he'd tell his family, prior to an official announcement. If the current bank negotiations were successful, he'd be purchasing a small suburban shopping centre and have the capital to extend and improve it.

Cassie stood in the shower, combing conditioner through her hair, trying to make sense of the intensity of her responses to Jack. Her normally guarded nature had abandoned her and she had no idea why.

There'd been interest in his captivating eyes despite his reservations about her presence here. For a second or two she wished she'd packed at least one dress and some make-up to wear in the evenings. A mild flirtation with a handsome eligible man to give her self-esteem a boost was tempting.

What was she thinking?

An hour or so ago, she'd been grateful their association would be short-lived. The man scrambled her brain. Clients' family members were taboo. Even those with alluring grass-green eyes, football hero muscles and unmanageable hair.

She was blown away by the table décor when she helped Mel carry the steaming dishes into the dining room. There was even a bottle of wine in an ice bucket near the place settings at one end. This all proved the gulf between her life and theirs. Most evenings at home, she ate from a lap tray while watching television.

Her stomach rumbled as she breathed in the mouth-watering aroma of grilled steak and onion sauce. Until that moment, she hadn't felt hungry at all.

'I'm having rosé to drink,' Mel said as she filled the water glasses. 'How about you? Jack will probably get a beer from the fridge after his run with Sam.'

'A run? In his work boots?'

'He always keeps running shoes in his ute, and it's a regular outing for Sam. He sulks if any of the younger visitors don't have time for at least a short walk.' Mel settled at the head of the table.

'Rosé sounds nice.' Cassie poured the two drinks, sat on her hostess's right and took a slow look around the room. She hadn't seen it, apart from a quick glance in on her arrival.

The antique mantelpiece, the polished sideboard and two of the papered walls held photographs of family. In here they were casual or celebratory. In the family room, school and sporting pictures covered all four walls. Jack was easily recognisable in many of them.

'Does Jack call in often?' She oughtn't to ask, but couldn't hold back.

'It depends on his work. Though he lives twenty minutes from here, most of his regular clients are in the northern and eastern suburbs. *You* understand the drawbacks of driving that distance.'

Cassie sipped her drink and pondered. Travelling time plus fuel-inflated costs influenced choices, especially for pensioners. Word-of-mouth referrals meant the majority of her clients lived north of Adelaide, as she did. Mel's insistence she stayed the Tuesday to Thursday nights in her Woodcroft home meant her quote had been favourable.

'He wasn't too pleased at your sleeping here. He tends to be cautious where I'm concerned. I told him he should be pleased I wasn't alone.'

'It's good he isn't sensitive about showing how much he cares.'

'True, I love that the family are so considerate, just don't like to be reminded I'm getting older. I've warned Jack but he can be tenacious, Cassie. He'll try to sneak subtle questions into general conversation.'

He already had, and wasn't subtle at all.

'He can ask anything he likes.' She didn't have to answer.

Sam's bark echoed from the hall. A moment later he trotted in and curled onto a rug. Jack followed shortly behind, wearing a clean green T-shirt, his boots replaced by black and red runners. Uncapped bottle in hand, he stooped to kiss Mel's forehead.

'Sam was pretty keen today; didn't stop once.'

He sat opposite Cassie, took a deep swig of beer and surveyed her with penetrating interest, causing her to stretch her shoulders. Neither he nor Mel seemed to find it incongruous for him to drink from the bottle at a formally set dinner.

As if reading her thoughts, he carefully poured the remaining liquid into the glass by his cutlery. His sudden grin tripped her heartbeat and sent her pulse racing. She so had to find a way to combat his charm.

'Maybe you should come with us next time. The way your skin glows, I figure you run on a regular basis.'

He thought she glowed? How could one sentence in a casual tone send tiny quivers of pleasure dancing down her spine? Her fingers trembled as she sipped her wine, hoping she didn't choke from the sudden tightness in her throat.

Unless all three housemates were home she ate simple meals and salad. This setting was perfect, the grilled steak delicious and the vegetables slightly crunchy, the way she preferred them. This was how she imagined dining in a fancy restaurant would feel, except Jack would be dressed in appropriate attire.

She tried to picture him in a tailored suit and tie and failed. Yet that niggling thought that he projected only what he wanted people to see persisted. His upbringing almost guaranteed black tie in the wardrobe.

'Cassie, are you with us?' Mel's question startled her.

'Sorry, I was daydreaming, trying to remember when I've had a tastier meal.' She avoided looking across the table, hoping the blush spreading up her neck and cheeks wouldn't be noticeable under the soft lights of the overhead chandelier.

'Thank you. We were discussing my granddaughter Janette in Melbourne, whose baby is due in five weeks. I'm going to be a great-grandmother.'

Cassie was acutely aware of Jack's keen interest, but didn't understand how that concerned her.

'That's so exciting.' An ideal event to strengthen Mel's mental recovery.

'Another sign that life moves on. Deciding to cull my clothes has been freeing for me. I think I'm ready to let go of some items I keep simply because of the past. Would you consider working out a plan to help me downsize in short stages between other commitments?'

Wow, that came out of the blue. She liked Mel and her positive attitude to life, and would happily take on the assignment under normal conditions. Yet Jack's presence added an emotive element; one she'd have to conquer if she accepted.

He'd be occupied elsewhere during the day and hopefully there wouldn't be too many evening visits when she stayed over on weeknights. She'd have to be polite and aloof in his company, professional to a T, and avoid any physical contact.

'I'm sure I can.' As she finished speaking, she turned as if pulled by an invisible thread to Jack's enigmatic green eyes.

Jack hoped his features didn't reveal his conflicting thoughts. Mel living alone in this big house had worried the family since Bob's death. Any attempt to discuss sharing or buying a smaller residence had been firmly rejected so the subject had been dropped. If Cassie's references were as good as Mel claimed, he'd normally have no reservations about her employment.

The problem was him and his instant attraction to her. Hell, he was a mature man and the solution was obvious. Avoid visiting when she was here, and act like the mature man he was supposed to be whenever they met.

'Won't that be inconvenient for you?' He kept his tone as impassive as possible, not easy when her eyes glinted as if she'd read his indecisive mind.

'Many of my clients are retired, often with health problems. Every contract allows for unforeseen contingencies, and I've become extremely adept at rescheduling. There have been times when I've juggled multiple jobs successfully.'

She faced Mel. 'Tomorrow we'll sit down with diaries and discuss what and when.'

'Good, that's settled.' Mel lifted her wineglass in salute and Cassie clinked it with hers as a signal of agreement. Jack followed suit with his near-empty glass of beer, trying to fathom why he felt as if he'd somehow scored a win.

They debated their favourite television shows over a dessert of fresh fruit and whipped cream. Jack teased Mel about her favourite soap operas, claiming she'd converted many of his generation into avid fans. And wondered why Cassie's smile at the interaction wasn't mirrored in her eyes.

He professed not to watch much at all. 'Sport, documentaries or investigative programmes—whatever's on at the time. I'd pick you for a movie girl, Cassie, romance or high adventure.'

'Wrong. Comedies or space sagas, as long as they're well written and acted. If not, I switch channels. I also enjoy home improvement shows.'

'How long do you give them before you click?' He intensified his gaze as he spoke and waited for her answer. Her viewing habits were irrelevant; her character intrigued him.

'That depends on how bad it is, what else is on and how tired I am.'

Clever, evasive answer.

The heat coursing through Cassie's veins had nothing to do with the fake wood fire warming the room, and everything to do with the fact that Jack had turned his attention towards her. His smile and slight raise of one eyebrow hinted he read her true thoughts. He was wrong, couldn't possibly know Mum's favourite programme, always set to tape so never missed, was an enduring Aussie soapy.

Stretching her back, she rose and reached for his bowl. 'I'll stack the dishwasher if you make the hot drinks?'

'None for me,' Mel said. 'I'll watch the news with you then I'm off to bed. I feel tired in the nicest possible way. Tomorrow I might have a baking session.'

Which would leave Cassie alone with Jack unless he called it a night too. She'd had a long day, exacerbated by her body's inexplicable reaction to him, new and unnerving. Could she feign plausible fatigue? How did she somehow know her excuse would be met with scepticism and that eyebrow quirk?

The moment his aunt pushed back her seat to stand, he was there to ease it away and hold her arm. She spoke quietly to him with her back turned to Cassie, and his answering grin stirred a feather-light fluttering in her stomach.

'Always, Mel.' He picked up the empty glasses and large bowl. 'You get settled in the lounge and rest. And I'll expect cherry and ginger cake next visit.'

He headed for the door, his husky chuckle flooding Cassie with a longing for the easy banter that came with deep affection.

'Confident boy, isn't he? Do you think he'd accept something fresh from the bakery?' Mel's tongue-in-cheek remark was accompanied with a gentle laugh.

Cassie took a moment to answer, her mind still processing 'boy'. She doubted there was a single immature cell in Jack Randell's body.

'From what I've seen, he'd settle for home brand plain biscuits to spend time with you, Mel.'

'I admit to resorting to packaged cakes and biscuits since the accident, and he's never even hinted the standard was lower.'

CHAPTER FOUR

JACK WAS FILLING the dishwasher when Cassie brought the remaining china into the kitchen. She kept a good space between them, admiring the way his muscles flexed as he reached up to the bench then bent forward to place each item.

No, you don't. You mustn't.

He pivoted round, as if sensing her appraisal. She wasn't aware of having made a sound, and the gurgle of the coffee machine should have covered any if she had.

'Coffee, tea or hot chocolate?' His sombre eyes and polite tone put her on alert.

'White tea, thank you. I'll finish here.'

Instead of moving away as she expected, he stepped sideways, resting his hands and butt against the bench and crossing one foot over the other. A very masculine stance which should not affect her. Renewed flutters in her stomach proved otherwise.

'I'm not totally convinced about this extra sorting. It might prove too much for her.' Corporate tone. And she knew there was no uncertainty in his mind at all.

'Because you care for her.'

His brow furrowed, his chest expanded and he crossed his arms as if preparing to challenge her reasoning. She forestalled him.

'She's been through a prolonged, trying time. Getting rid of clothes that no longer fit is cathartic and means she's looking forward. I can schedule a few days at a time, and if she finds it tiring or too traumatic we can stop.'

'Your contract will…'

'Have an out clause which allows for either of those as well as unforeseen circumstances.'

Jack wished he could explain why he wanted a longer break before Mel disposed of anything else. His treasured aunt was on a high at the moment, and he feared she might regret the impulse later. Any delaying tactic would be welcome. Unfortunately, his normally active mind was blank.

Well, not really. It was a jumbled mass of thoughts and images of the dark-haired beauty who was regarding him with stunning, empathetic eyes. She had no conception of the perceptive and compassionate woman who'd been the mainstay of the family as long as he could remember. Mel had been the one they'd all turned to for guidance until Bob's death had shaken her belief in life and herself.

'She lost confidence in her own judgement. People she trusted as friends tried to scam her while she was grieving for Bob. Two years ago, an acquaintance claiming to have been a business colleague almost coerced her into signing a contract to put this house on the market.'

He'd been in Queensland that time too. He pushed to his feet, needing action. The exasperated breath he took filled his nostrils with her delicate scent, distracting him. He shook his head, fisted his hands.

'She had the sense to tell my cousin, and he warned the guy off. She wasn't ready then—why now?'

'She may not be.'

What the hell? He glared at her, irked at her composed and conciliatory demeanour.

'Then why the charade?'

Her lips curled and his exasperation dissolved, his taut muscles slumping like Sam after a run. The combination of her beguiling eyes, enticing smile and husky voice was irresistible.

'It's not. She needs to know she's in control after months of relying on you and your family for so much. I'll ensure she doesn't do anything irrational without consultation. *You* have to ensure no one else puts pressure on her in any way.'

Easily done. Whatever was best for his aunt—*his great-aunt*. Accepting she was ageing cut deeper than he'd imagined. The thought that this home might no longer be his family's focal meeting place was mind-numbing. The likelihood had been mentioned occasionally; now it was looming as a reality.

Verbally committed to the new business purchase, he'd be unable to buy the property himself in the foreseeable future. He rubbed the back of his neck in frustration as he turned towards the bench to make the tea and coffee.

On the positive side, staggering the downsizing over months pushed any definite decision into next year. There would be time to find out what Mel really wanted, time for family discussions about the future ownership of the house they all loved. Time to work out an optimum solution for everyone.

For now, strong coffee and reliving today's encounters with Cassie Clarkson would probably keeping him awake tonight, surprisingly not an unpleasant prospect.

He heard the dishwasher start up and glanced sideways to see Cassie pulling on rubber gloves to rinse the wine-glasses. Picking up the two drinks, he left her alone, unable to think of a suitable parting remark.

Cassie let the hot water cascade over her hands, allowing treasured memories of her and Mum to flow back. If they were both home, they'd share the cooking and cleaning up, then often settle in front of the television with drinks and home-baked biscuits.

The pain of losing her had barely diminished. The love and laughter they'd shared was as vivid and powerful as ever. She'd been the one who'd taught Cassie to believe in herself and never let anyone demean her, either as a woman or a person.

Jack's bond with his aunt was reminiscent of hers with Mum, as close as that of natural mother and child. She'd give up everything she owned to share life with an ageing Julie Clarkson. Death had denied her the gift she hoped Mel's family appreciated.

She drained the water, flipped the gloves off and squared her shoulders. Jack Randell had been told to play nice and he better had. No more disturbing tingles, and hopefully he'd be busy doing repairs and maintenance a good distance away any time she was here.

Cassie's tea was just right, the after-dinner mints melt-in-the-mouth and Jack's presence in her peripheral vision distracting. Even the TV interview with the hunky action movie star hadn't grabbed her attention. Yesterday it might have. She shifted position, curling her legs up, angling her body away from the big armchair.

A distinct *humph* made her swing round and catch him frowning at the weather pattern on the screen. The presenter was forecasting steady rain for two days.

'That cans tomorrow's lawn mowing. Looks like I'll be working through that list of yours, Mel. And any other chores you think of.'

'Are you sure, Jack? There must be…'

'The inside jobs booked for next week can't be brought forward. I'm all yours.'

Those three little words created unfamiliar and unwarranted sensations in Cassie's abdomen. Like a ferry ride in rough weather, exhilarating and heart-stopping. They spread warmth to her toes and up to her cheeks, and she quickly looked away. Bending her head, she sipped her drink, hoping he'd think any colour came from its heat.

Mel muted the sound and left the remote on the coffee table.

'Do you want to stay tonight, Jack?'

Her innocent question almost had Cassie choking as she swallowed. Jack sleeping in the room across the hall from hers. Jack showering in the bathroom one wall away. Jack…

What was the matter with her?

She shared a house with two men, and didn't turn a hair if they wandered around draped in a towel.

'I'll go home, thanks. How about I pick up breakfast in the morning? Special treat.'

'Ooh, yes, delicious egg and bacon rolls, full of calories and cholesterol. Delightfully wicked at my age,' Mel enthused. 'Just don't tell my doctor.'

'It's a deal.'

'With that pleasant thought to send me to sleep, I'll say goodnight. Thank you both for a lovely day, the best I've had for ages.' After turning the sound up again, she left the room.

Persuasive advertisements urged them to buy, buy, buy, backed up by jarring music. Cassie finished her drink, held on to her mug and tried to formulate an intelligent topic opener. Nothing came to mind.

'Yawning might help.'

Startled, she almost dropped her mug. His smooth-as-silk deep timbre coiled around her heart, enthralling her. His wide smile and the provocative gleam in his eyes activated warning signals in her brain.

She set her mug down, clenched her stomach and mentally strengthened her resolve. If he thought she'd be easy to charm, he was in for a disappointment. The foolish romantic side of her hoped he'd try.

'Help what?'

His grin widened. 'Convince me you're tired and want to go to bed.'

Her sucked-in gasp wasn't nearly as incriminating as the heatwave that swept over her skin. The surge of desire at his unintended suggestion stunned her, left her speechless and fighting for breath.

He caught the double meaning, chuckled, and that darn Outback scene flashed into her head. She blinked it away. Too late—he'd noticed.

In a rapid switch, he leant forward, hands clasped between his knees. His now sombre expression matched the thoughtful contemplation in his eyes. She drew in a steadying lungful of air and waited.

'Your choice, Cassie. I can leave now or we can a while. We're going to see quite a lot of each other in the next few months. The more at ease we are together, the happier Mel will be.'

Easy for you to say, Jack Randell. Your hormones aren't going crazy whenever you're near me.

She wriggled back into the corner.

As if that little bit of distance will diminish his potency. Her brain scrabbled for an intelligent question.

'How long have your parents lived in Queensland?' Background stuff, not *too* personal. If he followed suit, her disclosures could be of similar ilk.

All Jack had gained was a few minutes' grace so why the crazy, unwarranted *zing* of success? He felt muscles he hadn't noticed become taut, loosen, and wished he were on the settee beside her. Close enough to inhale her alluring aroma. Not tonight, perhaps—*would there ever be a good time?* And what had happened to his *stay away when she's here* decision?

'Nine years. My mother hated Adelaide winters, always spent part of them up north with *her* family. She met Dad on a spring cruise to the Pacific Islands and married him six months later.'

He relaxed into his chair, legs outstretched, arms loose on the side arms. When Sam walked over and plopped beside him, head over Jack's ankles, he bent to scratch the dog's ears.

'She put up with the cold because she loved him and he was an integral part of the family law firm, handling the accounting department. Once my brother, sister and I were self-sufficient, Dad resigned, sold up and they relocated to Queensland. He works for himself with an assistant. Less pressure, more time together.'

An abridged version, omitting his mother's depression in his teens, and his struggle to avoid becoming ensnared in the Randell legal world.

'Mel said most of the family find a reason to visit them during the year.'

Jack's gut tightened at the faint tremor in Cassie's voice and the wistful expression in her eyes. Quickly blinked away.

'Especially during our winter. Your family aren't within easy contact?'

She stilled, broke eye contact and her shoulders pressed back. Away from him or the question?

'No.' Steady. Resolute. 'Mum died four years ago. There are no other relatives.'

Her stark sentences left him dumbfounded, mouth open, back stiffening as he jerked forward.

'No one?'

No way could he envisage a world without his parents, aunts and uncles, his siblings and numerous cousins. Noisy, sometimes boisterous get-togethers had always been an integral part of his life.

He'd rebelled at the pressure from his father and mother to conform, to gain entry to law school and follow the path they'd chosen for him. There'd been loud, occasionally acrimonious arguments about his partying and seeming lack of study even though his grades were always high. Even at those times, there'd always been someone there for him, often a choice of many. They might not have agreed with his decisions but they'd given him moral support.

Watching the obvious change in his expression, he saw chagrin flood her face as she gave a choking laugh.

'That came out as if I'm alone and abandoned. I never felt deprived because there was only the two of us, and I have a very supportive group of friends.'

'You live alone?' Spoken instinctively. He hadn't meant to ask; it went beyond the bounds he'd set himself.

'I share a house with two school friends. And you?'

'Just me in my place near the beach at Port Noarlunga South.'

'Do you surf?'

'Best way to get the adrenaline going in the morning, though work takes precedence these days.' Actually, it was the second best, and the sudden thought of sharing the first with her sent his pulse racing.

'I tried years ago. Couldn't see the attraction of getting dumped every time I tried to stand up.'

The sudden sparkle in her eyes belied her words; she'd enjoyed the experience. He imagined her in a sleek wetsuit and his body responded, causing him to shift in his chair.

'Maybe you need an expert to teach you.' Had he meant that to sound like an offer? Yes, if she was still around when the weather warmed up.

'Or better balance.'

A strident voice in increased decibels made both heads swing towards the television.

'That certainly won't entice me into their store.' Jack reached for the remote, pressed off, and said with reluctance, 'Time I went home.'

He ensured Sam was settled on his bed in the family room while Cassie took the mugs to the kitchen. She seemed reluctant to approach him as he waited, hand on the back doorknob, to say goodbye. Was she regretting the disclosure of personal aspects of her life?

'Lock up behind me, Cassie. I'll see you in the morning.'

'Goodnight, Jack.'

He closed the door, waited in the cold air until he heard the key turn, then walked to his ute.

Cassie blew out a huff of air, ashamed for the awkwardness that had stopped her from going too near as he'd left. Little as it was, she'd revealed more to him than she ever had to anyone she didn't know well.

She waited until he'd driven off then went to her room, turning off lights on the way. After mulling over their conversation, she drifted in and out of restless sleep, trying to make sense of her uncontrollable responses.

Early next morning Jack parked at the side of the house and sat contemplating the vegetable patch where he and his contemporaries had spent so many happy hours. Whatever happened, he'd always have those cherished memories.

Hearing Sam's bark alongside, he hopped out and ruffled the dog's fur. He was rewarded with a frantic wagging of the tail and avid attempts to jump up and lick any flesh Sam's wet tongue could reach.

'Easy, boy. I've already had my shower.'

Sam dropped and raced to the rear of the vehicle. Following, Jack found Cassie, fingers clenched, staring wide-eyed at his ute as if she'd never seen one before.

He walked to her side, checking her line of vision. Couldn't see anything wrong.

'Good morning, Cassie. Am I missing something?'

'Mel said you had a ute.' It sounded like an accusation. 'That's…'

'A silver twin cab, multipurpose utility with accessories. I got a great deal in an end-of-year sale last June. Good for work, family and camping.'

'It's so big. And clean.'

His instant roar of laughter made her blink and her eyes became dreamy, as if recalling a treasured scene.

'I'll take that in the spirit I believe you meant. It handles the biggest and heaviest loads I carry, fits five people and goes off-road like a dune buggy.' He put his hand on the polished tailgate and captured her gaze with his. 'And I take good care of what's mine.'

She didn't stir, didn't react. Thankfully, she didn't break eye contact, allowing him to see the flickering of awareness, along with the soft blush on her cheeks. He'd noticed the faint colouring last night, but failed to detect the reason. Undeserved macho pride flared, triggering an impulse to puff out his chest, a desire to caress her silken skin.

Sam's nudge to his leg broke the spell. *For now.* Sooner rather than later they'd touch again. He wouldn't deliberately engineer it but if a chance arose he'd take it without hesitation.

'Better get inside while the rolls are still hot.'

'Mel was setting out the coffee mugs when I left. She's looking forward to your arrival.'

'And you?'

He'd bring breakfast every day to earn a sweet smile like the one she gave him now.

'What do you think? Walking Sam's given me an appetite, so I hope you brought enough.' She shivered as a few raindrops fell on her head. 'Come on, Sam.'

She moved towards the house. The dog hesitated, looked up at him then took off.

He grabbed the bags from the front seat, and caught up in time to open the door for Cassie. A hint of peaches hung in the air as she passed him, sweet as the ones from the tree at the bottom of the garden. Mentally telling himself to get a grip, he followed her, nearly tripping on the eager dog who'd stopped to shake off the rain.

CHAPTER FIVE

CASSIE WASHED HER hands before following Jack into the lounge, where Mel was waiting with a pot of freshly brewed coffee. She heard him tease her for insisting they ate from the wrappers.

'Fast food always tastes better this way. I have great memories of sitting on the beach, eating fish and chips from butcher's paper and fighting off the seagulls.'

'It was always fun, wasn't it? We'll do it again when the weather clears. Today it's indoor chores.'

The tenderness in his voice, and the way his features softened with affection as he spoke to his great-aunt, caused a lump in her throat. Moments like the ones they referred to were a major part of her treasured memories.

She stared through the window, remembering the unconditional love she and Mum had shared, so much joy and few regrets. The past couldn't be changed. Today was the time that mattered, and she had a task for Jack if he was willing.

'I noticed some of the light fittings are dusty, Jack. Do you have the time to clean them?'

'Checking lights comes under downsizing?' A sceptical look accompanied his gentle dig.

'Under due diligence and caring, a courtesy for clients. In your line of work, you should know most people don't notice the grime until they have to replace the bulbs or tubes.'

'True. Consider all the house fittings on my list.'

The three of them chatted about the house and garden as they ate, and Cassie learned how Bob had relished teaching the younger generation the tool and gardening crafts that Jack had turned into a profession. That his father had wanted him to study law and become his uncle's partner didn't surprise her; his telling her did.

Mel's mobile rang, and she answered. 'Well, you know I'd love to normally but at the moment…'

Cassie tapped her arm.

'Hang on, Dot.' Mel held the phone to her chest. 'The Mortons have invited me to go with them and visit a friend in Murray Bridge for her birthday.'

'Say yes.'

'I can't. It's overnight and you're here. We've got…'

'Other days for sorting. Say yes.'

She was aware of Jack's shoulders straightening and his head snapping back, let it slide. No chance for even a moment of happiness should ever be missed. Mum was proof the future was unpredictable.

'Are you sure?' Mel glanced from her to Jack, who nodded. For Cassie, her grateful smile was worth rearranging her schedule.

After accepting the invitation, Mel switched off her phone and sank back in her seat looking a little dazed.

'They'll be here at nine-thirty.'

Jack lifted the coffeepot to refill her cup. 'Packing for one night won't take long, so you've got plenty of time to finish your meal.'

She stopped his action and laughed. 'Not advisable before a long car trip.'

'Cassie?' He held up the pot and smiled, making her pulse blip. As soon as she'd finished labelling the outfits Mel had selected, and listed everything, she'd leave. On Friday there'd be her and her employer and no heart-melting distraction.

The Mortons were punctual, and the rain had eased to a drizzle as they settled Mel into the back seat of the car and waved goodbye. Cassie shook off the drops from her hair before re-entering the house, trying not to dwell on being alone with Jack. This morning his cologne was fresher, more enticing, and hard to ignore from right behind her.

'Thank you, Cassie. She'll have a great time, hasn't been out much, apart from with family, for a while.'

His voice was deeper, as if emotional. Giving her hair a final flick with her fingers, she let her hands fall to her sides as she looked up into speculative green eyes. Did he still harbour suspicion of her after their talk last night? Better for them both if he did and kept distance between them.

'It's no big deal. Would you like me to prepare something for lunch later?'

'That'll be great. I'll get my tools and start upstairs; you can select the music.' He paused as if to add something, dropped his gaze to her lips for a moment then walked out.

There were few modern CDs in Mel's collection of film soundtracks, classical and compilations. She chose one with familiar songs, a favourite old movie of Mum's.

Although she couldn't see Jack, soft sounds filtered down from the second floor, disturbing her concentration. She chastised her heart for beating faster at the thought of him standing on his steps in the bathroom to clean the fluorescent lights. She knew how easily the tubes shattered and how sharp the shards could be. There was no logical reason to worry. He was a competent tradesman and could take care of himself.

Taking extra care had nothing to do with Jack's competency. He was alone in the house with the most distracting woman he had ever met. She'd kept him awake last night and invaded his dreams when he'd finally fallen asleep.

Cassie was a mystery the pragmatic part of his temperament was determined to solve. How, he hadn't figured out yet. Getting too close might be painful for them both. On the surface, she was bright and open, but behind her incredible dark brown eyes lay painful secrets.

As long as they didn't affect her employment with Mel he shouldn't give a damn. Yet he did. He wanted to know why sorrow veiled them from view, why she turned away when he and his aunt shared fun moments. To know why an attractive, intelligent twenty-seven-year-old woman had chosen a profession that basically limited her clientele to the older generation.

He focused on reattaching the light fitting in the back bedroom, checked all bulbs lit up, and grinned as a song he hadn't heard for a long time drifted up the stairway. He made a mental note to show Cassie where the switches were for the speakers he'd installed on the second floor so she could listen while working up there.

She obviously shared the same taste in music as Mel and Bob. This house had rarely been silent and he'd subliminally learnt the lyrics of so many musicals, sometimes causing him embarrassment in front of his teenage friends.

Now he was secure in who and what he was, and didn't care who heard him. Mel was well on the way to being fully fit and socially active. The investment he was negotiating was on track. On the negative side were the possible sale of the house and his Cassie-activated libido. Somehow, he'd come to terms with both problems.

He picked up his folded steps and toolkit and headed for the next room, singing along with the rousing action hero.

Something was different. It took Cassie a minute or so to realise it was Jack, singing along with the CD in an assured pleasant tone as he moved from room to room upstairs. She couldn't prevent her imagination picturing him taking the lead, and gliding across the screen with the beautiful heroine.

She moved along the clothes racks, lightly brushing the

garments, loving the different fabrics, the smooth silks and satins, the elaborate brocades and the delicate lace designs. None showed signs of wear, all hung beautifully as if new; such a difference to some of her chain store brand purchases. It was time she added a few quality items that would never date her wardrobe.

She appreciated these were not just clothes. This was a timeline spanning many years of happy marriage. When originally bought, each outfit represented a birthday, an engagement or wedding, a business celebration. Every piece held memories; now they'd create new ones for delighted buyers who'd dreamt of owning designer quality.

The romantic love songs playing in the background suited her mood. In her mind, she could see the colourful costumes twirling from enthusiastic dancing, and Jack swinging the heroine off her feet and spinning her round.

Believing he wouldn't hear, she felt confident enough to sing softly, letting herself be drawn into the magic. Keeping time, she almost skipped into the kitchen for a glass of water prior to settling to input her handwritten notes into the computer.

She drank slowly, watching the rain fall on the well-tended garden. This was a peaceful home, a haven of love and sharing. The current song ended in a crescendo then silence, and she recalled the hero dipping his head to kiss the heroine in that quiet moment.

Without warning, the hairs on her nape stood up, tingles skittled down her spine. She pivoted to confront Jack in the doorway with a wide grin on his handsome face. He'd heard her singing. Warmth flooded her cheeks, and the urge to run was stymied by an overwhelming desire to see what he'd do next.

Pinning her with riveting green eyes, he walked forward as the introduction to the next song started. Cassie froze. This was a hero's serenade. A half step back and she was pinned between his mesmerising gaze and the sink behind her.

Captivated, she allowed him to take her hand and draw her closer, caught her breath as he placed his free hand on her waist and led her into a dance. He guided her with gentle expertise, and she followed as if they'd been partners for ever. His eyes gleamed like the rain-kissed leaves outside, and his work-rough palm gently grazed hers, evoking tiny quivers that radiated and grew.

Like a prince and princess in a fairy tale they glided around the floor, her heart beating time with the music. The heady mixture of male and sandalwood heightened her senses. The soft pressure of his thigh against hers as they spun and twirled stirred new and thrilling sensations.

Even beautiful dreams had to end and theirs came too soon. They stilled, eyes locked and bodies swaying to unheard music. His lips parted, his head bent towards hers.

A new song, rough and loud, by the whole male cast, ruptured the silence and severed the spell that bound them.

Jack moved away from Cassie, his hands reluctant to break the connection, his body craving closer contact. Her quiet singing had drawn him from the second floor, with no concept of his intent.

He'd known the second she'd become aware of him, and couldn't stop the smile from forming as she'd turned. Her beautiful, sparkling brown eyes had widened with uncertainty, a sweet blush coloured her cheeks and her mouth formed an O as she sucked in an unsteady breath.

His heart had hammered on the short journey across the room and his stomach tightened in anticipation of an energy zap like last time they'd touched. Today he fully intended to hold on, discover where it led.

The opening chords had sounded as he'd reached for her hand, and he'd relished the *zing* that sizzled along his veins.

With his free hand on her waist, he'd begun to waltz her around the kitchen, keeping steady eye contact. Mentally he'd harmonised with the love-struck singer.

His heartbeat had surged as Cassie synchronised with his steps. They and his guidance were automatic; his mind and body were totally focused on the woman in his arms. Soft and pliant, she'd moulded to his form, her peach scent beguiling.

The music ended, and he couldn't let go. Her eyes had invited and he'd accepted, bending his head towards her.

A loud, raucous drum roll filled the air, followed by grating unintelligible words. Cassie blinked as if startled, and arched away. He shuffled back, delayed letting go as long as possible. Once he did, this magical moment would be over.

She seemed as dazed as he felt, her arms limp at her sides and her chest rising and falling in agitation. She swallowed, had difficulty speaking.

'It's… I… You want coffee?'

Way down on his list. Why the hell couldn't he form coherent words? He'd had no trouble singing someone else's.

'Give me five minutes. See you in the lounge.' He walked out, trying to remember where he'd been heading, and why, when he'd heard her singing.

The seven minutes he took allowed Cassie to regain composure and perspective, at least on the outside where it showed. She'd been caught up in a fantasy, beguiled by his charisma, lost in the moment. In future, she'd be prepared and resist him with dignity and grace.

Who are you kidding? Your resolve will crumble at his slightest touch.

So she'd avoid contact while she finished the tasks agreed with Mel earlier. Hopefully he'd have prearranged activities elsewhere on Friday, and that would be her last day until the next session here.

Mum had always stressed the importance of decorum. An achievable state until he walked in with sombre eyes and a rueful smile, and her pulse dumped composure for roller coaster speed. He picked up his steaming mug and settled into the armchair as if it were made for him. Sam curled at his feet, making a perfect picture of master and faithful hound.

English was a vast language so why was her mind blank of a conversation opener?

What would you like for lunch? Thank you for the dance. It was heaven in your arms.

'I'm sorry.'

His words hit like a soccer punch to her stomach and she recoiled, pressing into the cushions. She squeezed her eyes shut and dug her nails into her palms. He regretted the moment she'd always treasure.

'No.' *Clunk.* The two sounds were simultaneous.

Her eyes flew open. Jack thrust forward, hands spread in appeal. His mug was on the table surrounded by splashes of coffee.

'Not for the memorable dance. I'm sorry if I've made you feel uncomfortable, Cassie. That was never the intention, though I have to admit I'm not sure what was.'

Her pain dissolved in the warm glow that soothed as it radiated from her abdomen. He'd enjoyed what they'd shared. It had been one of life's inexplicable happenings which must never recur.

She tried to justify her own response. 'Getting caught up in the music. Having all that open space. But you're related to my employer so I should have refused.'

His fingers gripped the chair arms, his lips thinned and his eyes narrowed. 'Are *you* sorry, Cassie?'

'No, it was…' How could she describe her feelings without revealing her vulnerability?

She sprang to her feet. 'As you said, memorable. A spur

of the moment, one-off event. I'll get a cloth to wipe the table.'

It was as if her muscles gave a sigh of relief as she quickened her pace to the kitchen. On the slower return trip, she ran task-related topics through her head.

Jack's mind ran a similar course in a methodical manner, at odds with his erratic emotions. He adored Mel, and would never do anything that might embarrass or hurt her. Coming on to the woman she'd hired to help her move on in her life definitely came under that banner.

Cassie's words indicated a strict code of work ethics, so she'd be as spooked by the attraction that flared between them as he was, and seemed as powerless as he to resist.

His desire to learn more about her was undeniable. His gut feeling said whatever she hid didn't necessarily relate to her profession. That was really none of his business; he had secrets of his own he'd never shared with anyone.

It didn't stop him avidly waiting for her to reappear, for his muscles tensing and his heart skipping beats when she did. Remorse shamed him as she knelt by the table to mop up. She'd raced from the room before he had the chance to say he'd go.

'My mess; I should be cleaning it. Thank you, Cassie.'

'You're welcome. Do you want a refill?' She smiled, and his breath caught in his throat. He'd almost kissed those delectable lips today, couldn't guarantee not to if the chance arose again.

'No, this will do.' He drank almost half in one swallow. 'What's your next task?'

'Bring down Mel's footwear, list, label and double-check everything. Then I'll go home.'

Rapid control prevented another coffee spill, this time on himself. 'Why?'

'Because it'll be easier if everything's in one room. There's stickers and she can—'

'I get that. Why are you going home?'

'I'll have done all I can without her being here. She can make decisions at leisure tomorrow, and when I come back on Friday I'll finalise her lists and print out copies.'

His breath caught in his throat, trapped by the lump that clogged his air passage. There'd be no telling when he'd see her again. For someone who'd rarely had a problem swaying opponents to his point of view, he was confounded by his inability to reply.

A fruitless search for her on social media before retiring last night had irked but not discouraged him. Offering to recommend her services would provide him with her number, and save him having to explain why if he asked Mel.

'So I'd better get started. Does lunch at one suit you?'

Lunch? It didn't help that she was so eager to leave. How had life become so complicated in less than twenty-four hours?

'Yeah, one's fine.' He watched her walk out, glared at his coffee mug as if it were responsible then drained it. Couldn't figure why he was annoyed at himself.

He stooped to ruffle Sam's fur. 'Come on, Sam.' Pushing himself to his feet, he headed back upstairs, the dog close behind him.

CHAPTER SIX

CLEANING LIGHT FITTINGS and replacing globes was routine for Jack, needing care without much concentration. If he encouraged Cassie to talk about her work over lunch, she might inadvertently divulge more about herself. Personal questions needed a different atmosphere. The spark of an idea grew into a full plan.

He'd never felt such a spontaneous desire for a woman before. The doubts he still harboured stemmed from previous attempts to con Mel and, if he were honest, his own experiences with women seeking a rich husband.

When she walked in, he instinctively smiled, his chest tightened and his pulse raced. It was as if she brought sunshine, even though it was raining outside.

'Ham sandwiches ready when you are.' Brown eyes shining, she gazed around the sunroom. 'Every home should have a room like this, bright and sunny most mornings and snug and intimate in the evenings.'

To Jack it had always been the small room at the front of the house, containing a sewing machine, long table, odd chairs and a large lockable cupboard where Christmas and birthday presents were hidden. A woman's room as opposed to Bob's workshop, where he'd spent so many happy, productive hours learning handyman skills.

'Good timing. Can you pass me that bulb from the table, and stay to switch on when I say?'

He grinned when it lit up, and stepped down. 'Never can tell with these old fittings. What are you thinking?'

Her head was at a slight tilt as she studied the now sparkling chandelier, her expression reflective. He followed her gaze.

'How hard it must be to face the prospect of leaving a house you decorated, where many of the fittings and furniture were chosen as a couple. All of them would have been selected with the aim of providing a loving family home.'

Her voice grew softer and emotional towards the end, as if she were describing a personal memory. Their eyes met and he glimpsed a fleeting sadness that proved him right.

'She and Bob moved in two years after their wedding, and renovated every room together. She never wanted to live anywhere else and always said she'd be here till...'

He faltered. When Mel made the statement it sounded right. He couldn't bring himself to say the final words.

'I've been helping with repairs for years and never considered any of their belongings in quite that way before. It makes a difference. Thank you, Cassie.'

A new concept flared like a beacon, breaking through the gloom of Mel's health-related intention to move. Too new and undefined to share. They could install brighter lights, rails, new, easier to manage taps and other safety measures. Redesign the downstairs bathroom if need be. Mel was sure to agree. The changes would enable her to stay as long as she really wanted. For many, many years if he had his way.

If that was what she really wanted—that was the pivotal point. And there was no denying she did need someone living with her. He'd make notes and talk to her tomorrow.

'Let's have lunch.'

He ushered Cassie from the room, eager for food and talk. Sinking into his usual spot, plate of sandwiches on his lap and cold beer within reach, he relished the comfort he felt from being in Bob's favourite chair. If Mel ever decided to let it go, he'd take it home, make it his. For now, he'd settle for the contentment it evoked right here.

He liked that Cassie had chosen a favourite spot too. She looked good, snug against the corner of the settee, outwardly at ease though her breathing was slow and controlled and the fingers on her right hand were curled but not clenched.

Lifting his drink, he took a long swallow and dived in.

'Where do you live? Mel mentioned north of the city.' He watched for signs of hesitation or evasion. There were none.

'Oakden—twenty minutes from the city in good traffic.'

'So why take a job involving possibly two hours' driving daily?'

'I wouldn't normally.' She matched his gaze, letting him know she wasn't fooled by his seemingly casual questions.

'Mel called me and we met for coffee in the city. I advised her to find someone local to make it affordable and she offered accommodation Tuesday to Thursday.'

'You accepted the job without coming here?'

Her laugh was unexpected and accompanied by a tantalising sparkle in her eyes. The inevitable ripple through him was accompanied by a stomach clench and an instant acceleration of his pulse.

'Would you estimate on a job unseen? I came for lunch, toured the house at her insistence and visited a couple of wineries on the way. My quote included an allowance for food and board.'

Jack bit into his sandwich and chewed slowly as he considered her answers, which were open and plausible. The same could apply to the woman who'd conned his mother into investing in a dodgy jewellery business. And the man who'd plagued Mel for weeks after Bob's death about a special memorial site until she'd told Jack and he'd informed the police.

'Have dinner with me tonight.' He realised he'd voiced his thoughts when he heard the words and saw her startled reaction.

'What?' She'd jerked forward, her sandwich held in the

air, her brown eyes darkening, widening with astonishment. Big and beautiful, drawing him in.

'You were supposed to stay here, so you can't have anything planned.'

'Why? You don't trust me.' Defensive. Wary.

'I never said that. Let me get to know you. And you, me. I'll pick you up at seven and we'll go somewhere local.'

Cassie stared at the nonchalant figure watching her with a resolute expression. This didn't have the feel of an *I-like-you* invitation, more a *come-into-my-web* trap.

She'd be crazy to accept. Probably regret saying yes, definitely would if she declined. If she agreed, and gave him limited information, maybe he'd be satisfied and let her do her job unhindered.

That's it, Cassie. Logical, reasonable thoughts to help you make a rational decision.

'Strictly platonic.'

And that tells him you've been thinking the opposite.

Her mind registered the sudden tension in his shoulders and neck, her eyes only saw the quick flare in his green eyes that sparked a heated response in her abdomen.

'Absolutely. I'll need your address and phone number.' He reached for his mobile on the shelf beside him.

She hesitated. 'It's a long way to come. Couldn't we meet somewhere between?'

'No way. I invite a girl to dinner, I pick her up and ensure she gets home safely.' He scrolled to his contacts list, thumbed in her name and silently waited for her reply.

After entering the information, he thanked her then added, 'You'll need my number. In case.'

There was a hint of caution in his voice, as if to say it should not be used for a change of mind. Once she'd closed her phone, he relaxed. Not in an arrogant way, more like quiet satisfaction.

That was exactly how Jack felt, as if he'd negotiated a truce. Keeping it was up to him.

Thirty-six minutes past two. Cassie shut everything down, leant her elbows on the table and pressed her face between joined thumbs and fingers. Closing her eyes didn't make her problem vanish. Instead, it conjured up images of Jack, and the widely diverse expressions in his compelling green eyes. How many women had found themselves succumbing to their spell?

She straightened her back, shook her head and exhaled loudly. Taking the new lists from the printer, she turned to look at the neat rows of footwear. Cassie's collection fitted in the bottom of her wardrobe; Mel's began next to the first leg of the billiard table and ended over halfway along the opposite wall. A reminder of the social chasm between this family and her, no matter how friendly they were.

Why was she sitting here daydreaming instead of packing up and heading home? Because, even allowing for traffic, showering or a leisurely bubble bath and getting ready for—not a date—there'd still be time to kill.

Had she made the right decision? Conversation wouldn't allay Jack's fears about the effect more sorting and decision-making might have on his great-aunt. Physically seeing her happy at being organised and prepared for the future would. So why had she succumbed to his invitation? Because she'd been spellbound by his tingling touch, his deep alluring voice that hijacked her pulse and his mesmerising green eyes.

Arching her spine, she brushed away those disconcerting images. Perhaps taking a detour to her local shopping centre to browse for a while would settle her. Better than being dressed to go early and pacing the floor. Drat the man and his innate appeal.

* * *

He was in the downstairs bathroom, taking measurements and writing them in a thick red diary, when she went to say goodbye. As far as she could tell, there was nothing in the room that needed adjusting or repairing.

Jack didn't enlighten her, merely placed the book on the washstand and leant against it, arms folded, body at ease.

'All done?'

'Until Friday. I've left printed sheets and highlighters by her computer.'

And I'm not sure about tonight.

Thankfully, he didn't pick up on her reservations. 'I heard you make quite a few trips up and down. How many pairs are there?'

'More than I'll ever wear out. High quality and in good condition.'

His crackly laugh shimmied up and down her spine. An Outback trip to authenticate her fantasy was now on her bucket list, earmarked for this summer.

'What is it with women and shoes? You seem to need a pair for every outfit.'

'Hey, no stereotyping. It's a personal trait. And what about men and their gadgets?'

His hands came up in surrender. Without warning, she imagined them caressing her into submission, and felt her skin burn at the thought. His smile and sparkling eyes did nothing to ease the heat or embarrassment, especially when buffalo grass-green darkened to near black.

'I'd better go. I'll see you tonight.' She swung away, eager to put distance between them.

'Seven o'clock, Cassie. I'm looking forward to the evening.'

Less than a minute later Jack heard the back door close. That was the quickest exit he'd seen anywhere for a while. And what the hell had caused that beautiful deep red blush? He recalled their discussion without finding a reason.

There'd been gentle teasing, nothing awkward. He let it go, not wanting to upset her for Mel's sake. His aunt's happiness was paramount, not that it meant he wouldn't try to find out more about Cassie Clarkson.

Opening his diary and picking up his tape measure, he tried to concentrate on his renovation plan. His head refused to cooperate, persistently flicking up images of Cassie. After he'd wrongly read a figure twice, he took Sam for a run, followed by a strong black coffee.

Cassie was ready at quarter to seven. She turned the television on then off, not wanting it to drown out his arrival. Believing he'd come early so she'd invite him in, *her* plan was to meet him outside.

Repeated brushing of her hair hadn't changed its style, and peeking through the blinds didn't make him miraculously appear.

Checking the hall clock against her wristwatch proved both were aligned. Going to the kitchen for a glass of water to ease her dry throat took one minute. Checking her reflection in the mirror above the lounge mantelpiece simply gave her cause to chastise herself for being so uptight.

Although there was no denying the chemistry between them, she sensed his resolve to avoid any form of close relationship. This wasn't a date; he'd stated the objective was to become more at ease with each other for his aunt's sake. And she could hardly complain when having a shining knight's protection was most women's fantasy come true. It was even on her own *some-day-in-the future* list.

Was Jack prepared to talk about his relatives, as in one-for-one questions? The snippets she'd learned from Mel had stirred her interest in the close-knit, yet diverse family.

She slipped on her jacket and went to the window overlooking the street. Three minutes later—it seemed so much longer—the ute drove past, slowing down to park by the kerb. Feeling an almost childish eagerness, she picked up her handbag, walked out and was halfway down the drive-way when he strode into view.

If this *wasn't* a date, heaven help the women he dressed to impress. The combination of royal blue shirt, navy tie, dark denim jeans and brown suede jacket could feature in any classy magazine. His shiny black boots looked new, and his hair… She didn't think there was a woman alive who wouldn't be tempted to finger comb his unruly brown hair into place. Again and again.

His sensual wide mouth curved into a stunning smile that triggered warning flashes in her brain.

'Hi, Cassie, I'm glad to see you too.'

Had she smiled first? It was an automatic female re-sponse to an attractive male coming to greet her.

Taking her arm, he led her to the vehicle, clicking the locks on the way. Leaning past to open the door, he stayed close enough to assist her if needed. His sandalwood co-logne teased her nostrils, inviting her to sway towards him and inhale deeper.

She resisted, tossed her bag onto the seat and reached for the handle high on the inside of the cab. With the other hand on the back of the seat, she stepped up and swung in, his light guiding touch arousing quivers she had no way of hiding.

Her 'Thank you' sounded breathy and choked. His 'You're welcome' resonated with an undertone she couldn't identify.

Jack walked around the bonnet, chest tight and pulse rac-ing. He'd thought parking in the next street until seven minutes before his due arrival was a good idea. Manners would dictate he be invited in while she put on her coat, and introduce him to her housemates if they were there.

Instead he'd been thwarted in the driveway by a capti-vating beauty in a fitted red woollen dress that covered her knees, black tights and heeled red ankle boots. Her unbuttoned thick navy jacket fell to her hips.

He'd fought for air as his gaze met enticing brown eyes, enhanced with make-up for the first time since they'd met. She'd also added an unneeded—as far as he was concerned—slight touch of gloss to her red lips. Her sudden smile had sent a surge of heat zapping from head to foot, and all points east to west.

Standing behind her as she boosted herself into his ute had allowed him a closer view of her curvaceous hips and shapely legs, with predictable results. So much for keeping calm and in control. He'd become aware of his gritted teeth and set jaw, and with effort managed a stilted reply to her thanks. Necessity ensured he take a moment to refill his lungs before opening his door and climbing in beside her.

He flicked her a glance, checked his mirror and pulled away. 'You look nice, Cassie.'

Idiot. That was an understatement and a half. She was delightful, exquisite. The line between knowledge for Mel's protection and discovering the woman behind the professional persona became more blurred with every breath, every look. Every touch.

'Thank you. Where are we going?'

Her voice captivated him, pleasurable to hear with its unique edge. And he had all evening to enjoy the sweet sound.

'North Adelaide. Australian menu. Do you have any preferences or absolute dislikes?'

'Apart from very hot or spicy, I'll eat almost anything. Mum and I enjoyed finding new venues and sampling different foods.'

He caught the tense. Before her mother died, leaving her alone. That might be a subject best left for another occasion.

Traffic was light and they drove in comfortable silence towards the city. She hadn't mentioned her father so he wouldn't. He'd blow any chance of her opening up to him if the man had treated them badly.

Cassie had been to many of the diverse cultural restaurants in O'Connell Street and the surrounding area. She regretted not having been for a while. Her memories from here were all happy, comforting her when she became nostalgic.

She caught her breath when Jack slowed and activated his left indicator as they approached a two-storey colonial-style building. The wide steps with their Roman-style columns, peaked eaves and romantic balconies were reminiscent of a classic Hollywood movie. Was that their destination or was he looking for somewhere to park?

Jack made another left turn into the low brick-walled enclosure. It *was* here. A magnificent hotel she'd always admired yet thought too grand for the casual nights out she'd shared with Mum and friends.

There were plenty of spaces yet Jack drove to the one by the far wall and deftly reversed in. His consideration earned him Brownie points as she remembered numerous frustrating times trying to see beyond a vehicle this size at shopping centres.

'Hang on.' His soft tone negated the order in his words.

She unfastened her seatbelt and waited for him to open her door. The touch of his warm fingers clasping hers sent a tremble way down past her knees. She held tight as she alighted, praying they wouldn't buckle and send her sprawling or into his arms. Which wouldn't be a bad thing. Would it?

As if he sensed her apprehension, he placed his free arm around her, holding her steady as he closed the door and activated the lock. She didn't demur when he kept it there to guide her to the entrance and up the steps.

CHAPTER SEVEN

IT WAS COSY and warm inside, and they were ushered to a table next to a decorative brick wall and under a glass awning. Cassie loved the padded plush black seats, and the way the softened lighting gave the whole room a subdued ambience. It was ideal for private conversations.

Both declined pre-dinner drinks and enjoyed a lively discussion of the menu, eventually agreeing on entrée and main course. Dessert would depend on the size of the first two courses.

'You'd easily manage all three, wouldn't you?' Cassie bantered after they'd given their order. 'Your job must build up an appetite.'

'Most days the work's steady rather than strenuous. I try not to overindulge, with an exemption where Mel's desserts are involved.'

She laughed, saw his eyes flash, and her heart flipped at the message they conveyed, causing her to blurt out the first words that came to mind.

'You look fit and toned. Do you exercise regularly?'

His lips curled into a knowing smile and heat flooded her cheeks. She'd admitted to noticing his physique. His light chuckle sent tingles down her spine and ignited heat coils in her belly. If she closed her eyes she'd be able to count the Outback stars in the image the sound generated. She fought the impulse, keeping them locked with his amused gaze.

'I have a few weights at home and I swim and surf most of the year. Plus our frequent family picnic or barbecue get-togethers always include team games resulting in friendly riots. Never missed unless I'm interstate.'

That pang hit again. Family gatherings involved genuine hugs, kisses and lots of fun and laughter. She'd had those with Mum and although her friends' families had been sincere in their affections, it just wasn't quite the same as actually being related.

'Cassie?'

She blinked, looked across the table into caring green eyes and came back to the moment.

'I'm trying to picture a gathering of all the close relations Mel says you have. How do you keep track of birthdays and anniversaries?'

He shrugged and the sticky moment passed. 'Computer calendar, and a great-aunt who never forgets and keeps everyone up to date.'

The waitress returned with a bottle of Chardonnay, and he nodded his approval.

'That's fine, thank you, no need for tasting.'

Once the bottle was in the ice bucket stand and they were alone, he raised his glass and quirked an eyebrow.

'Any special toast you'd like to drink to?'

'To Mel, enjoying the fun of discovering forgotten treasured mementoes, and staying in the home where she's been so happy for many more years.'

Jack froze. He couldn't think of anything better, though having Cassie in his arms again came close. This time ending with a kiss he wouldn't be pulling back from as he had this morning.

He was surprised to see the liquid in his glass rippling from the trembling of his hand. Cassie's was steady as a rock as she completed the ritual then sipped her wine. Watching the slight movement in her throat, he imagined her pulse accelerating under his lips as he pressed them to her delicate skin. The tip of her tongue licked a stray drop of wine from her lower lip and *his* pulse shot to the sky.

Get to know her, huh.

Forget life and history. He wanted to taste the sweetness of a fervent kiss, feel her yield to his caressing hands. Memorise her uninhibited sounds as they made love.

He gulped a mouthful of wine, silently sending an apology to the maker for the insult. By focusing on the crisp cool flavour as it slid down his throat, he regained some inner semblance of restraint.

'Would you rather have a beer?' Cassie's concerned tone deepened his guilt.

'No, forgive my lapse in manners. Wine is my preferred choice when dining with a beautiful woman.'

Her burst of natural laughter undid the calming effort in one second flat. Every cell in his body responded to her musical delight.

'That, Jackson Randell, is an old cliché unworthy of a modern gentleman.'

Her imitation of his aunt left him both flabbergasted and elated. His airway seized up, immobilised by a clear view of her slender neck as she proudly lifted her chin, the sparkle in her eyes and the unintended invitation of her parted lips.

This teasing aspect of her nature was a revelation, one he'd like to explore at leisure. And encourage every chance he got. When he finally managed to draw breath, he pointed his finger at her and feigned a sombre expression.

'The reason they are clichés is because they are so often true.'

For a split second he saw the sparkle dim. Before he could confirm it, she broke eye contact as the waitress appeared with bread rolls.

Jack could see the slight furrow of her brow. It seemed she didn't agree with or hadn't liked his last remark. He'd meant it as light-hearted banter. Had she taken it as flirting?

Her face lit up as she selected a roll for her side plate. 'Ooh, they're warm and smell fresh baked. And thank you for the compliment.'

'Your expression disagreed.'

'A flashback from the past. I once dated someone who frequently quoted for effect without feeling the sentiment. For me sincerity is as important as honesty.'

'If I say it, I mean it.' His eyes were drawn to her neat white teeth as she bit into her roll, and he felt a surge of desire as the tip of her tongue licked away a few stray crumbs from her tempting lips.

'Mmm, a small touch yet it makes the meal special.'

Struggling for normality, he leant back in his seat. 'Have you always lived in Adelaide?' He immediately regretted his brusque tone.

Cassie stopped chewing, forced herself to swallow. *The start of the get-to-know-you quiz.*

Was she ready? Would she ever be with this charismatic man who could charm secrets from a clam? She met his steady gaze, surprised to see a shade of remorse in the usually clear green eyes.

'Yes. I enjoyed school and have friendships that date back to my first year in secondary. They, and Mum's friends, were my lifeline when her cancer was diagnosed. Without them, I'd have been lost.'

His brow creased and his eyes narrowed as if he found difficulty in visualising life without all his relatives. 'And there's really no other family?'

'Mum's sister lived overseas and we lost contact years ago.' Not the full answer. Not a lie.

'Wanna share mine? There's a few I'll willingly farm off at times.'

The mood lightened with his teasing remark. Their laughter mingled and it was the nicest sound she'd heard in a long time, sparking a warm glow in her abdomen that radiated to her fingertips and toes.

'Do I get to choose?'

'Only from the ones *I* select.' The inflection in his tone and the gleam in his eyes suggested none would be young, handsome males.

The arrival of their entrées, chicken wings with small side salad for her and ravioli for him, deferred talk for the moment. When the waitress reached for the wine to top their glasses up, Jack drank the remainder in his before nodding and allowing her to proceed.

Cassie's perplexity must have shown because Jack explained his action.

'If it's refilled from empty I can keep track of how much I drink. I don't claim to have always been that smart but I've never driven if there's the slightest chance I might be over the limit. Learnt an early lesson.'

'You had an accident?'

'A close call when a car shot out at speed in front of my cousin on our way home after pizza dinner out with friends. He'd had two beers spaced through the evening. Even one more might have slowed his reactions and it could have been a lot worse.'

Her fingers stilled on her cutlery. She froze, wanting to cover her ears and not hear the rest.

'John swung left and the guy veered enough to sideswipe the bonnet and spin us round. Apart from almost writing off both cars, the other driver spent a week in hospital, and lost his licence for a year. We four ended up with minor injuries and bruises. It was… Cassie?'

When she didn't react, he reached over to cover her hand with his. She started, blinked and gave a quick shake of her head.

'You've gone pale. Have I stirred up a bad memory? You should have stopped me.'

She stared at his worried expression for a moment then down at their joined hands and took a shuddering breath.

'No, I imagined you… A silly notion. I'm fine, really.'

He trailed his fingers along hers as he withdrew his hand, as if reluctant to break the physical connection. She regretted the loss of his comforting touch, almost twisted her hand to keep it there. Almost.

Picking up her knife and fork, she concentrated on her food. She hadn't expected the answer to her casual question to have such a profound effect on her. As he'd spoken, images sprang into her mind—Jack helpless as the car bore down on them. Jack hurt and bleeding, in pain, waiting for help.

Why had her imagination suddenly burst into full force? Why not when she'd struggled to write essays for her English classes? And why had she ordered chicken wings, which were so awkward and messy to eat with cutlery?

'Use your fingers, Cassie. It's allowed.'

Her head jerked up and her heart skipped more than a beat at the playful look in his eyes and his warm smile. She stole a furtive glance around the room. No one was looking their way except the waitress returning with a finger bowl of warm water.

Reassured, she chose a wing and took a bite. It was delicious and spicy, tingling her tastebuds. If the main was as flavoursome, and they avoided controversial subjects, she'd have no regrets at the end of the evening.

Jack watched Cassie's colour return, wished she'd finished her sentence. It didn't take much nous to work it out, though. He wavered between liking the rush of satisfaction that she'd cared about him being injured, and concern at the knowledge she might.

'Have you travelled much, Cassie?'

Her smile proved he'd chosen an acceptable topic. You

couldn't get more uncontroversial than holidays, and people's choices revealed a lot more than they realised.

'The eastern states during school or work breaks. One trip to New Zealand with Mum and another with two friends for a wedding. We hired a car and stayed for two weeks. I'd love to travel through Greece and Italy.'

'Not the bright lights and night life of London or New York?'

She had his total concentration; his elbows were on the table, fingers locked and his chin resting on his thumbs. Everyone else in the room faded, their voices becoming a muted background hum.

'To me they're pretty much like any capital city in Australia, apart from iconic features. It won't happen often, so I want to experience something new and completely different to what I'd find here.'

'True, you…' He straightened up as a group of new arrivals were ushered past their table.

Cassie spoke before he could continue. 'This place is a good example, another reason for avoiding popular western cities. Why fly hundreds of miles to eat familiar meals in similar establishments to those in your own suburbs? If I'm going to spend big money on air fares and accommodation I want to try true local cuisine.'

'I agree. When you do, remember that in many places abroad local cuisine is tailored to suit western palates.'

He'd bet the value of his treasured ute she didn't realise how much her body language and expressive eyes revealed.

The sharp wrench to his gut earlier when he'd called her out of her daydream added to his growing certainty that she still mourned the loss of her mother. In the seconds she'd taken to blink and refocus, he'd seen deep-seated sorrow in her lovely brown eyes.

Don't go soft. His main objective was to protect Mel.

Involvement with the beguiling woman facing him across the table could mean pain for any one of the three.

She dipped her fingers in the bowl, wiped them on her serviette then pushed her plate to the side. Leaning forward, arms on the table, she gave him a smile that generated a heatwave in his stomach. It was like hot coffee on a cold morning, hitting the spot then spreading throughout the body. A perfect awakening any morning.

'I take it the wings and salad were as tasty as they looked.'

'The best I've had for ages.' After sipping her wine, she tilted her head, just a tad, a very beguiling action.

'Do you enjoy gardening or is it a labour of love for Mel? The lawns and vegetable plots are large for a city dwelling.'

Shoot, she was good. If he didn't get his act together, she'd be the one going home with all the knowledge and he'd have learnt little about her.

'It's part of the maintenance side of my business, which I admit I find therapeutic. There's also the added bonus of fresh harvested fruit and veggies—beats store bought any day. As kids we grew up picking and eating whatever was ripe at the time, and I'm especially partial to peaches, oranges and apricots.' And since yesterday their scent on soft pink-tinged skin.

'You don't grow your own?'

'No, out back I have a small lawn and border; the front's landscaped with shrubs and stones. How about you?'

'We have miniature lemon, apricot and mandarin trees, plus whatever anyone gets the whim to plant in the cleared area.' She looked behind him. 'Here come our mains. Let's see if their vegetables taste as good as our home grown.'

They chatted about movies, favourite Australian tourist spots they'd visited and Jack's parents' home about twenty kilometres from Brisbane's city centre. He made her laugh with tales of trekking to the top end of Queensland.

* * *

Cassie didn't want the meal to end. Jack had sampled her barramundi and given her a taste of his steak. Sumptuous setting, scrumptious meal. Charming and attentive company.

After a meticulous perusal of the dessert menu, she laid it on the table with a heartfelt sigh. 'They all sound scrumptious, and if I wasn't so full I'd be tempted to try one.'

'Maybe next time. Would you like to go for a walk and have coffee?'

Her heartbeat fluttered and she tingled all over. He wanted to extend the evening, *and* repeat their shared experience some time. Keeping her voice normal and level took effort.

'Hot chocolate would be a great way to round off the evening.'

Cassie more than liked the way Jack helped her into her jacket. The protective arm he put around her as they crossed the street somehow became a handhold that felt warm and protective. They strolled along, checking every open venue. Finally selected a quiet café near the hill leading down to the city.

She hid a grin when he asked for extra marshmallows in her hot chocolate and ordered black tea for himself, claiming her choice was too sweet for him. They took a table for two by the window and watched the passing parade of people enjoying a night out.

Hers was coming to an end and she'd have to face the crucial decision. If he tried to kiss her when he took her home, did she let him? Did she want him to? What if he made no attempt, just said a polite goodnight? That last thought was surprisingly depressing.

'They must be freezing.' Jack's voice held a hint of amusement as he stared through the glass at three girls in form-fitting tops, short skirts and ultra high-heeled shoes. Stunningly made-up, they drew the attention of every male they passed as they headed for one of the popular night spots in the area.

Cassie laughed. 'At that age you're immune to the weather, especially when you're about to enter a room full of eager, available young men.'

She envied them their confidence and poise, and wished them success in their search for their special man. Hers was still out there somewhere, hopefully looking for her.

CHAPTER EIGHT

JACK SEEMED LOST in thought on the drive home, or perhaps he'd run out of conversation. Her gaze kept straying to his hands on the wheel, noting their firm competent control. Her stomach clenched as she recalled his long, strong fingers when he'd assisted her into and out of this vehicle, and on her waist as they'd danced. Her palm tingled at the recollection of his workman's palm on her lotion-smoothed soft skin as he'd clasped their joined hands to his chest.

As the familiar music and lyrics played in her mind, she closed her eyes and leant back onto the headrest. The quiet rhythm of the ute's engine seemed to be part of the orchestral sound.

'Tired, Cassie?' Jack's resonant voice penetrated her dreamy haze.

By the time she languidly opened her eyes, his head was facing forward. She caught back the sigh that rose in her throat at his striking profile.

'A little. Thank you for inviting me out tonight, Jack. I'm glad I accepted.'

'My pleasure. I guess you'll be sleeping in tomorrow.' She heard a hitch in his voice, a growing edginess as he spoke, and couldn't think of a reason.

'Maybe. I'll have to do the chores I'd planned for Friday.'

'Leave them. Treat it as a bonus day and relax. Do something for yourself that you've been putting off. When's your next job?'

'Monday, all next week over near the plaza. A ten-minute drive from home.'

* * *

Jack's fingers involuntarily tightened on the wheel. Growling internally, he forced them to relax. They'd met about thirty hours ago; no way should he be affected by the prospect of not seeing her for a week.

'You'll be at Mel's on Friday?' They were a few blocks from her home, not much time left to talk.

'Yes, to finalise what we've done and arrange another session if she still wants to proceed. Having two days to think it over might have made her reconsider. Even staggered full clean-outs can be daunting.'

'Much as I hate any reminder that she's getting older, I have to concede it will ease her mind. Won't stop the idea of her not being in that house tearing me apart.'

'She'll be around for a long time yet, Jack.'

In his peripheral vision he saw her hand lift towards him, and his heartbeat rose then fell when it dropped back into her lap. She'd reached out in comfort, changed her mind, and the depth of his disappointment shook him.

He drove into her driveway, ignoring the empty space in the street. Parking there meant walking her to her door and, seeing she'd come out to meet him earlier, he figured she'd prefer he didn't.

'Hang on, I'll come round.'

He couldn't resist lifting her from the cab, allowing his hands to linger on her waist, and pulling her a little closer before setting her on the ground. He basked in the warmth of her sweet grateful smile before releasing her and stepping back.

She looked tired and there'd be no goodnight kiss, not even quick and gentle, much as he wanted to feel the softness of her lips under his.

'Thank you, Jack. I had a…memorable evening.'

'Me too. Sleep well and enjoy tomorrow. If the timing's right, I'll see you Friday afternoon.'

Was it hope that flared in her stunning brown eyes? And what word had she bitten back?

He closed the door and kept his arm around her until they were at the driver's side of the bonnet. Fighting the desire storming through him, he caressed a gentle path down her cheek and cupped her chin with his fingers. Wasn't sure how he kept his voice steady. Or stopped himself from pressing a gentle kiss on her lips, which were slightly parted and so inviting.

'Sweet dreams, Cassie. I'll wait until you're inside.'

She hesitated for a second before uttering a husky, 'Goodnight, Jack,' and turning towards the house. He watched every graceful step, curling his left hand's fingers on his thigh as she unlocked the door and disappeared inside. Was she describing her evening as memorable to whoever was waiting in the front room?

The tautness in Jack's muscles began to ease while he was waiting at a red traffic light two blocks away. He'd been a hair's-breadth from wrapping her in his arms and finding out if she tasted as sweet as he imagined. Might have, if he hadn't seen the glow from the television.

He'd proved once that his lack of control could lead to tragedy. Letting someone get close meant letting your guard down, revealing your emotions, allowing theirs to sway you against your better judgement.

He hadn't lost his temper since Tara had died, never allowed any situation to get out of hand. And he avoided women who used cold shoulder treatment or flirting to get their own way. Keeping his true assets secret discouraged attention from those who favoured wealthy men.

Cassie was different. He sensed she'd compromise and placate rather than inflame. Knowing he came from an affluent family seemed to discourage her from closer contact. He slid a USB into the port, hoping the Guns N' Roses soundtrack would distract him. Didn't work.

Sunlight creeping around the edges of her blinds woke Cassie without help from her alarm. So much for predicted rain. She felt loose and relaxed as she did a slow leisurely stretch plus a few neck circles.

Had she dreamt of Jack? Couldn't remember. She'd slept deep and sound, from the moment she'd snuggled under her quilt and closed her eyes. His suggestion popped into her head, making her smile. A bonus day, for special treats. Infinitely better than washing clothes and cleaning the bathroom.

Grabbing her phone, she scrolled to Narelle. Her best friend's young son spent Thursday with his grandma so with luck she'd be free. No answer so she left a message suggesting they meet for lunch and window-shopping therapy. Rolling onto her side to return the mobile to her bedside cabinet, she gazed at the framed picture there and smiled.

'You'd have liked him, Mum. Open and direct. Doesn't hide his disapproval but is ready to hear another opinion and admit he might be wrong. Not the man for me, though. But then I'm not sure there is one I could completely trust and confide in.'

She threw back the covers, and shivered when her bare feet landed on the cold lino. Perhaps carpeting her bedroom should be shifted from third on her to-do list to top. Unless spring warmth arrived early this year.

A short hot shower brightened her up, and the heady aroma from the coffee percolator drew her to the kitchen and Phil, a cheerful early riser.

'Hi, stranger.' Phil put her special mug next to the one already on the bench. 'You're not due back till tonight.'

Taking two slices of bread from the packet, she set them

to toast. 'Sorry, I forgot to change the chart last night when I came home to change. I'm going back to Woodcroft tomorrow for one day, not sure when I'll be back.'

The chart the three housemates had devised kept track of when they'd be home and the division of chores. Even allowing for the occasional lapse, it had worked well for them for over three years.

'Hitch in the job? It's a long drive for a day's work.'

'Unavoidable, and the lady might have more for me to do in the next few weeks. Brad home?'

'He left before sun-up.' He placed her steaming drink on the table and sat down with his. 'What's your plan for the weekend?'

Narelle's call came as they talked and, after arranging their meeting, she passed the phone to Phil while she cleared the table.

'Barbecue with the gang on Sunday,' he told her as he put her mobile down and took his mug and plate to the sink. 'See you later.'

Her mobile rang again as she walked back to her bedroom. *Jack.*

'Hi, Cassie, sleep well?'

'Very. Thank you for calling, and again for last night.'

'Just checking. You have a relaxing day.'

'I will. I'm having lunch with a friend.'

'Good. I'll see you tomorrow, Cassie.'

'Mmm, tomorrow.'

She disconnected and cradled her phone in her palm, staring at his ID. Why had he called, and why had her brain gone missing? Because it had been occupied with drying her throat, ranking up her heartbeat and prickling all her nerve endings.

Narelle's blonde hair with green highlights and her flair for colourful fashions made her easy to spot in the spacious food court of the shopping centre. Salad wraps and milk-shakes were on the table.

They chatted about friends, Narelle's progressing second pregnancy and the challenges of rearing an active three-year-old boy. Laughing off his latest escapade, her astute friend pushed her plate away and studied Cassie with questioning eyes.

'So, give. I can't quite pick it but something's happened. You have an aura about you.'

Her emotions showed? How the heck could Cassie say she was attracted to a charismatic man who was very protective of her employer, his great-aunt? And that the desire, even if merely physical on his part, was reciprocated. Hey, wasn't that what it was for her?

'Cassie Clarkson, you're blushing.'

'I'm not. I was thinking.'

'About who?'

About how to describe the last two days with drastic editing.

'The house is similar to the historic one you considered buying when you got married, beautifully maintained and furnished. Mel is friendly, down-to-earth and well on the way to full recovery after a car accident.'

She drank through her straw, gaining time to formulate the right words.

'And she has this great-nephew who—get that match-making look off your face, Narelle—is handsome, charming and so out of my league I'm surprised we speak the same language.'

'Handsome as in to-die-for?'

Mesmerising dark green eyes, finger-itching unruly brown hair and a tempting full mouth. Add to the mix that haunting crackle of a laugh...

'With a smile on your lips.' Removing the straw, Cassie emptied her glass. 'Let's go and challenge my bank card.'

Yet even as she placed the food wrappers in the bin she was thinking of Jack rather than the clothes she was about to try on. Was he having lunch with Mel right now or mowing the lawns he'd postponed yesterday?

At roughly the same time as Cassie used her credit card for the third time, Jack drove into Mel's driveway. He'd barely hit the bed before he'd fallen asleep last night, and had spent today recalling Cassie's revelations. He'd learned a lot about how she responded to words and actions, yet little of her life or history.

He wasn't sure why he'd called her this morning. To hear her voice and find out how she'd slept? To ask what she had planned because the sunshine meant he'd be working not far from her most of the day? Whatever he'd intended, her response meant he'd spent the day pondering whether her friend was male or female.

Sam greeted him as he walked in the back door, and Mel was in the family room rearranging footwear. He hugged and kissed her, held on a little longer than usual. Hated having to accept the realities that ageing brought.

'You look tired, Jack. Another late night?'

'No, a very pleasant one, actually.' He kept the details to himself because she might ask why, and he had no plausible answer. 'Did you really wear every one of these shoes?'

'I must have. Coffee and scones?'

'Tea, and I'll get it. I've had a few ideas I want to discuss with you about the house.'

Her face clouded for a moment. 'So have I. It's all so confusing but better to have everything worked out now rather than the family having to deal with it.'

He drew her back into his arms. 'We'll all do whatever you feel most comfortable with, Mel. Your peace of mind is top priority.'

She tapped his cheek, as she'd done hundreds of times over the years, smiled and pulled away.

'I'm reasonably healthy, my leg is much better and I can still cook up a feast. Go pop the scones in the oven for a few minutes. The jam and cream are in the fridge.'

'Do you want any of those shoes taken upstairs?'

'No, Cassie will check them off on her list first.'

Cassie. Tomorrow. And soon for a week at a time.

By then he'd better have worked out how he was going to handle this magnetism between them.

The electric jug was boiling and Mel's homemade biscuits were fresh from the oven when Cassie arrived on Friday morning. They sat in the lounge and, after she'd heard about the trip to Murray Bridge, discussed the day's agenda.

'The clothes and shoes are sorted and ready for the final tick-off. Jack and I phoned everyone and the women are coming Sunday afternoon to take their pick. The men and children will be here for a barbecue later.'

Cassie thought of the wide veranda along the back of the house packed full of people enjoying each other's company, laughing, joking and telling stories. For a moment the injustice of fate twisted her heart and her fingers curled into her palms. She was grateful Mum's suffering had been short, but sometimes couldn't help but be angry she'd lost her too soon.

Blinking away threatening tears, she turned her head and found herself staring at Mel and Bob's wedding photo. What were Jack's words? *'Imagine losing someone after forty-five years.'* More if you counted the courtship.

Yet the woman opposite her had overcome her despair, and was winning the battle against physical pain and loss of independence, buoyed by family support. Cassie accepted that growing up with no other relatives but Mum had influenced her view on life. Her friends and their families had proved she need never feel alone, yet sometimes she couldn't escape the void.

She knew she had so much to be thankful for. Shaking away the blue feeling, she helped herself to another honey and almond biscuit.

'Better hope for sunshine. Will they all fit on the veranda?'

'Out there, in here and in the family room, depending on whether you want to talk sport, gossip or play hide and seek.'

'You have a wonderful house and garden for children to play in.'

'My home is what I need to think about.'

It was the kind of mixed feelings day that left Cassie drained by the time she got home around four after being held up three times by roadworks. Knowing she was partly to blame, well, mostly to be truthful, for her high expectations of seeing Jack didn't help. Neither did telling herself she'd lived twenty-seven years without his presence so what was the big deal about not seeing him for ten days.

He'd made a quick call mid-afternoon to tell his aunt he'd been held up and would pop in tomorrow. Hadn't asked about her or to speak to her, which hurt a little though the conversation barely lasted two minutes so he must have been in a hurry. She could also understand he might want to keep last night's dinner a secret from his family.

She took a long hot shower, something she rarely did, trying to lather away her blues. Dressed in warm trousers, a thick bright green patterned jumper and her favourite mood-picking-up red boots, she studied the contents of the larder and refrigerator. Nothing there tempted her appetite.

Two phone calls, a 'Fancy eating at the pub tonight?' greeting to Phil when he arrived home, and the evening had been arranged. Just what she needed. A packed room,

Aussie rules football on the wall-mounted televisions and enough chatter to stop her thinking. The food might not be as fancy as Wednesday night but it was always fresh and tasty.

CHAPTER NINE

THEY ENDED UP in the overflow dining area next to the poker machine room. Sipping her Malibu and lemonade, she joined in a spirited debate on the current football finals. If someone hadn't tapped her on the shoulder and pointed to her handbag under the table, she'd have missed her ringtone.

It had stopped by the time she'd pulled her mobile out. Sliding it open, she saw Jack's caller ID and went into the quieter entrance. There was no reason for the uplift in her spirits, or for her pulse to race. Probably just a query on next week's agenda.

'Cassie.' She heard the smile in his voice, which rekindled heat in her abdomen, scary yet exciting. Seeking more privacy, she stepped outside, sheltering under a canopy.

'Hi, I'm sorry I missed your call. It's kinda noisy here.'

'I can hear it. Quite a crowd you've got there.' Did she imagine the slight bite of disapproval in his tone?

'I had a rotten drive home, and didn't feel like cooking. Called some friends and we met at the pub for dinner. Didn't realise it would be so busy, but it's fun.' She knew she was babbling, tried a different topic.

'Have you seen Mel today?' There were traffic sounds in the background so he wasn't at home.

'No, I spoke to her earlier. The quick repair job I'd planned turned into an all-dayer.'

'You're not driving now?' *Idiot.* She heard the concern in her voice, hoped it didn't transmit down the line.

'No. But it's nice to know you care, Cassie.' It must have. 'I prefer to pull over and talk, keep hands-free for necessities. I've stopped to pick up Chinese takeaway.' It sounded as if he was clearing his throat. 'I thought about you today.'

Their talk was a continuation of her day, emotions shooting up and down, uncertainty fogging her normal comprehension. Answering with the truth wasn't an option. She dredged her mind for a light, harmless answer. *Ditto* came to mind, discarded as too clichéd.

'The correct reply is I thought of you too.'

Now he was laughing at her. Or with her? Either way, she liked the intimacy he managed to instil into his resonant voice. She could play the flirting game too, over the line, where she was safe from his compelling green eyes, intoxicating touch and seductive lips.

'Are you fishing for compliments, Jack Randell?'

Even across the expanse of a major city and using a mobile phone didn't diminish the power of his crackling laugh. She could almost feel the heat from the campfire and hear the rustle of spinifex being blown across the sand.

'Not until I can see you and tell if you mean it. Wanna do FaceTime?'

'No.'

'Are you blushing, Cassie?'

How the heck could he tell? 'Why would I be? We're just talking?'

'I can hear it in your voice.'

It was her turn to chuckle. 'You're full of it, Jack Randell. You should be selling stuff, not repairing it.'

'Pity *you're* not buying.' His voice deepened as he emphasised the second word, sending quivers shooting up and down her spine. What effect would he have on her if they were together? The very thought robbed her of breath and coherent reasoning.

Thankfully, she heard his name called in the background, saving her from replying, giving her seconds to regroup.

'My order's ready.'

'You'd better go. Enjoy your exotic meal, Jack.'

'Don't have too much fun, Cassie. Sweet dreams.'

'Goodnight.' She stayed outside, inhaling and exhaling slowly and steadily. How could she stay immune to the charisma of a man who could turn her inside out over the phone?

Jack accepted his carry bag of hot foil containers and strode out of his favourite Chinese restaurant. He'd ordered two mains and a special fried rice—wished it were more, and that Cassie was joining him to eat.

Who was 'we'? Did it involve the same person she'd met for lunch yesterday? Tossing his dinner onto the passenger seat, he slid into his ute and was buckling in when he became aware he was grinning.

Cassie had been flirting. Bet she wouldn't next time they met. There'd be no safety of distance between them. The idea of provoking her, and seeing her creamy cheeks blush rosy red, was appealing. Tracing a slow fingertip path across her skin to her chin even more so. Especially if it led to him tilting her head and covering her irresistible lips with his.

His libido was driving his imagination again, a problem he'd been having since mid-afternoon Tuesday. Only three days ago, but it seemed like a lifetime.

He ate in his dimmed lounge, feet on the coffee table as he watched a documentary on distant solar systems. For the first time since he'd moved in, he was conscious of the space around him and the absence of any other person's presence apart from numerous family photos in the downstairs rooms.

That was the way he wanted it, right? No permanent housemate disturbing his peace, no one else's belongings lying around or cluttering his bathroom, and no annoying habits to trigger his temper. No fights, no repercussions. No more regrets.

He'd had family and friends for short visits but, since moving in two years ago, he'd never had a woman stay overnight. Had rarely taken anyone upstairs to his bedroom, preferring to keep any intimacy in their homes. His stormy relationship with Tara had far-reaching consequences.

Her statement that she intended to marry a rich man had amused him when they'd met at nineteen. As they'd dated, her craving for attention from him and other men, and her sense of entitlement for anything she took a fancy to, had become tedious. The fights had grown more bitter until that last tragic time when he'd turned his back and let her walk out.

At her funeral, guilt and pain had strengthened his vow to avoid that type of woman, no matter how beautiful, and never, ever lose his temper, no matter what the provocation.

Why did the strict control he maintained on his mind and body slip away whenever he saw, spoke to, even thought about Cassie Clarkson? He had no idea when he would next see her. From Monday, she'd be with her next client.

She and Mel had pencilled in the following week for her to come to Woodcroft. For him, it suddenly seemed like the long wait for Christmas morning.

Gathering up the leftovers and his empty beer bottle, he headed for the kitchen. Once the trash was in the bin, bottle in recycle and the coffee table wiped over, he sprawled on the settee with a finance report. Had to read it twice to take anything in.

After less than two and a half days with her new employers Cassie found herself wishing for an early end to the project, a very unusual occurrence for her. She couldn't help comparing the semi-retired couple with most of her other clients.

While they were friendly enough towards *her*, the air of discord between husband and wife affected her normal relaxed manner. There'd been no warning signs when she'd come to quote on the assignment. It was becoming clear that very little from their overcrowded home would be sold or given away, and she'd bet they'd still be here years from now, each blaming the other for the lack of space.

The *ding* alerting her to an incoming text was a welcome diversion. Her pulse tripped at the call sign. *Jack.*

Call me when you are free. Only need a few minutes.

She called immediately, realising the second his phone began to ring that this might seem too eager. Too late to hang up now.

'I caught you on a break, huh?'

Not from her body's reaction to the sound of him, or from his image flashing into her mind. It had been four days and seventeen hours since she'd heard his voice.

But who's counting?

'A quick one. Is there something you need?' Was it her imagination or did he groan? His reply was definitely gravel-rough.

'Are you free to have dinner with Mel and me in the city tonight? She'd like to talk to you.'

'I'm free but…'

'Good. Take a taxi and I'll reimburse you. We'll drive you home.'

'I'll catch an O-Bahn bus, much quicker from home than in traffic.'

'I'd rather you—'

'Gotta go. Where have you booked?' Taxis were an indulgence for special occasions or emergencies, though his protective attitude was endearing. It wouldn't have surprised her if he'd offered to pick her up.

There was a pained silence for a moment. His disgruntled throaty rumble was followed by the name and address of the restaurant. 'I'm looking forward to seeing you, Cassie,' he replied to her thanks in his gravelly voice, leaving her with a racing heartbeat and trembling knees.

She spent the rest of the day pondering the purpose of the meeting while automatically typing lists for her clients. What had changed and why couldn't it wait until she arrived in Woodcroft on Monday? And why the two of them?

Selecting what to wear to the classy city hotel that evening was another worry. Her new red dress was out, already worn. She finally settled on mid-grey trousers and a new matching sleeveless buttoned top over a dark blue blouse. Her long black boots would keep her legs warm and weren't too high for the two short walks ahead.

Spinning away from the image in the mirror, she slipped on her winter coat, picked up her handbag, and huffed. She'd never been concerned what people thought of her clothes or status in life, was proud of the woman she was because of Mum's guidance. But then she'd never been wined and dined by the upper echelon of Adelaide until last week.

Cassie arrived at the venue two minutes early, and was told her hosts were already seated. She was escorted to their round table adjacent to the balcony, and Mel's open arms drew her into a hug. She instinctively answered with a soft kiss on her hostess's cheek then moved round to where the maître d' waited, holding her chair.

As she sat, her foot touched Jack's stretched out leg under the table. He made no acknowledgement so, thankfully, he mustn't have felt anything. The glow of his welcoming smile sparked a fire in her belly, spreading heat along her veins, and she couldn't control the delicious vibration that followed. He and Mel already had pre-dinner drinks. She declined, thanked the waiter who filled her water glass and took a soothing mouthful.

'You look beautiful, Cassie. Thank you for coming.' Jack raised his glass in salute, and any cooling effects from the icy liquid were instantly negated by the burning admiration in his dark green eyes.

She looked the same as last Wednesday, so how had she evolved from nice to beautiful?

'I concur,' Mel chipped in. 'I'd love to have worn some of the fashions around today when I was young.'

'From what I've been told, you were right at the forefront of whatever was trendy, Mel.' Jack tipped his glass towards her. 'And photos I've seen show you carried it with flair.'

'Flatterer.' Mel tapped his hand, and they grinned at each other. 'Now, I hope you don't mind, Cassie, we've already ordered a bottle of Semillon. It's my favourite with fish and I fancy the grilled whiting tonight.'

The menu choices were comprehensible so why didn't Cassie's brain process them? Could it be the tantalising aroma of an exotic cologne teasing her nostrils, and the brush of an ankle against hers, stirring her blood? She daren't meet Jack's gaze, found it hard to breathe, and gave a husky response to the waiter's offer of wine.

She sipped the pleasantly crisp-tasting Semillon as they discussed starters, wishing she had a better knowledge of South Australian grown wines. The consensus was for a shared dip plate entrée; Jack ordered salmon, and Cassie veal scaloppine.

She handed her menu to the waiter, reassembled her jumbled thoughts and spoke to Mel. Sensing Jack's intensity, she forced a light, casual tone. 'I appreciate being invited to dinner, and I'm sure I'll enjoy every course, but *why* am I here?'

Mel answered. 'My granddaughter's husband phoned

this morning. The specialist is concerned about the baby's growth so she's admitted Janette for monitoring, and mentioned the possibility of being induced. Janette's asked if I'll go over, though I'm not sure how much help I'll be.'

'Immeasurable, just by being there,' Cassie said. Her indomitable presence and optimistic outlook on life made her the heart and spirit of every generation of the family. Cassie knew because she'd lost the one who'd provided that essence for her.

Jack made a silent vow to thank Cassie for her insight when they were alone. As he covered his aunt's hand with his and squeezed, endorsing those few accurate words, he smiled at Cassie, letting her see his gratitude.

'Cassie's right, Mel. We don't acknowledge it enough but we all depend on your help and advice.'

Mel's eyes glistened with emotion and he swore never to take her being there for granted again.

'And my baking.'

They all laughed, though he noticed Cassie's lips didn't quite make a full smile. The sparkle in her eyes had dimmed.

'So you'd like to postpone our arrangement. Not a problem. We can reschedule once you're home.' Matter-of-fact tone. Business mode.

He couldn't fathom the reason for her sudden mood change. She'd told them postponements weren't unusual so why…? Without warning, his heartbeat revved up and anticipation surged. Could it be because any delay meant not seeing him? That sounded egotistical but there was no denying the attraction between them.

He concentrated on Cassie's face for her reaction as Mel explained.

'Not exactly, dear. I'd just like to alter the conditions. Would you consider house-sitting for me, and doing an inventory of each room while you're there?'

It was like watching a flame flicker into life as Cassie's eyes widened in surprise then glowed. She made no sound. Her lips opened, forming a perfect O, and her fingers slipped down the stem of her wineglass and fanned out on the white tablecloth. He imagined them splaying across his chest as he covered her tempting lips with his mouth.

'Are you sure? There must be a family member who'd be happy to move in while you're away. I'd never even stayed overnight on a job until you invited me.'

She was so delightfully bemused, he ached to take her in his arms and reassure her. His own instant elated response had surprised him, made him re-examine his attitude. Cassie's appeal was different to any woman he'd known but his vow to never form a lasting relationship was absolute. She might not judge a man by his financial standing but proximity could reveal faults and weaknesses.

His aunt's proposal included him calling in regularly to give her support, day-to-day domestic contact when true character couldn't be suppressed for long. But he'd kept his quick temper under control for nine years, wouldn't risk losing it ever again.

'No one's available at such short notice,' Mel replied. 'You've already allocated me next week, and I won't be a distraction while you work. If you have to leave for your next contract, Jack will arrange something.'

Cassie turned towards him and he gave her an encouraging smile.

'It'll be similar to your normal life, except listing and living will be in the same building, and you'll be dog-minding as well. Plus there's the added attraction of me being available any time you need help.'

He arched his eyebrows in an attempt to make her laugh and succeeded. That was when he realised how much he'd missed the rippling effect her musical sound created in his body.

Their dips and assorted breads arrived and, as they sampled and compared tastes, they discussed Cassie's moving in and the order of rooms to be inventoried. Jack sensed Cassie's enthusiasm overrode her apprehension. She really loved the career she'd chosen.

His career was about to veer onto the new path he'd planned from the beginning. The downside was that suits and corporate meetings would inevitably replace hands-on repairs and maintenance. But he'd willingly keep doing handyman jobs for Mel and his family.

'My sister Val is travelling with Mel tomorrow; she's happy for any excuse to catch up with relatives, and shop in Melbourne. Sam can come with me until you move in.'

'I'll finish my current job late Friday morning.' Her eyes met his, now bright and shiny, open and honest. 'Should be able to leave home mid-afternoon.'

'I'll arrange my work so I can meet you at the house with the keys. Call me when you're ready to head off.'

He topped up the women's wine, the residue making up his limit for driving. Now the main objective of the evening had been accomplished, he could devote his time to entertaining them.

He cajoled both of them into ordering rich calorie-laden desserts, claiming he couldn't resist and he'd feel guilty eating alone in front of them. And emphatically dismissed Cassie's suggestion she take a taxi home.

'I'd be scolded all the way home if I allowed it. Apart from being ingrained behaviour—' he grinned at Mel '—it'll be my pleasure.' Arching an eyebrow, he reminded Cassie of his statement when he'd invited her out before.

Cassie conceded to his request, or rather insistence, with a smile. When he went to fetch his ute, she complimented his good manners.

'I'll admit to enjoying being spoilt and cosseted occasionally. Especially so smoothly.'

Especially by Jack.

Mel laughed. 'Doesn't every woman? I've always tried to instil respect for others in the younger generation. Some of the boys were more challenging than others, but thankfully they finally matured.' She gave a beaming smile. 'I'm proud of each and every one of them.'

She didn't need to state the obvious but it was what she hadn't said that interested Cassie. How *bad boy* had Jack been, and what had caused him to re-evaluate his life?

CHAPTER TEN

CASSIE CLIMBED INTO the driver's side of the rear bench seat as Jack helped his aunt up into the front of his ute. Her fingertips twitched with longing to smooth his unruly brown hair, within her reach. Closing her eyes, she pictured his suntanned, work-rough hands, so competent on the wheel, so heart-stopping when he touched her.

She slipped into a dream world of physical contact, those first *zings* over her skin, his lean fingers linked with hers as they'd strolled after dinner, and their oh-so-magical dance that she relived every night as she fell asleep. Even the mere memory sent a tingling glow from her toes to her scalp. Her eyelids dropped and her head sank forward.

A blast of rap music from a passing car startled her awake, wrenching her head up. Blinking to clear her blurry sight, she looked into the rear-vision mirror, into piercing green eyes. One quick glance from him was all it took to have her feeling vulnerable, as if all her secrets were open for him to read.

How could one look make her tremble? Had there been time to shutter her thoughts? Maybe house-sitting with him living nearby and popping in any time wasn't such a good idea. Scrap that, no *maybe* about it. She could only hope his work, family and friends kept him occupied, and that she had the strength to politely keep him at arm's length.

The house lights were on when he stopped in her driveway; he placed a finger on his lips, nodding towards a sleeping Mel. He left the engine running as he alighted, pushed his door almost shut and opened Cassie's as she reached for the handle. She had no choice but to accept his proffered hand, and didn't resist when he edged her towards the rear of the vehicle, closing her door.

Her unbuttoned coat fell open as he leaned in, placing his hand on the roof of his ute. Even without contact, the heat from his body seared her skin through their clothing. She tried to draw in air, tried to swallow. Tried to remember Mel was nearby.

'Thank you for agreeing to house-sit. It'll be one less worry, and she can relax and enjoy her stay in Melbourne.'

He spoke quietly, his breath tickling her earlobe and his lips brushing her hair. Her heart pounded and her lips tingled. A slight turn of her head would put them within kissing range. Exactly what her illogical side wished for while sensible reasoning feared the consequences.

'It's…not…a problem.' She didn't seem able to talk and think rationally at the same time, forced herself to focus. 'I'd better go in so you can take her home.'

'Mmm. You're right.' He inhaled through his nostrils, but made no attempt to move away. 'Cassie…' Deep and rich, resonating through her.

A motorbike roared past and his head jerked up. Passion and rational thought warred in his dark green eyes, thrilling her even as it triggered alarm bells. She squeezed her eyes shut and curled her fingers. Getting involved would surely end in pain.

So why did she feel cold and alone when he stepped away, craning his neck to check on his aunt. Cassie wrapped her coat tight, skirting past him to the driver's window, from where she could see Mel stirring.

When she opened her eyes and smiled, Cassie went round to say goodnight, and thank her for the evening. Mel let the window down so she could hear.

'You enjoy your time with Janette and the baby when he or she arrives. And don't worry about Sam. I'll walk him every day and take care of your home as if it were mine.'

'I'm sure you will.' Mel kissed her cheek. 'Take care of Jack too. Like all men, he thinks he's immune to human frailties.'

His attitude implied that she was correct as he leant casually on the bonnet waiting. The fluttering in her abdomen, and the ache to have him wrap his arms around her and kiss her senseless, proved she certainly wasn't.

As if there was the slightest chance he would with Mel watching.

'Goodnight, Jack. Thank you for bringing me home. I'll see you on Friday.'

'Goodnight, Cassie. Sweet dreams.'

She kept her back straight as she walked away from him, the warm prickling on the back of her neck proof he watched every step. Fighting the temptation to look towards him before closing the door, she pushed it shut, listening until the engine noise died away.

Cleansing off her make-up, she weighed up the pros and cons of her acceptance. And resolved to cope with the way he affected her because it was never going to be a happy ever after. Their worlds were too different. They were too different.

She slipped into bed, fully aware that, no matter how hard she tried to think of something—anything—else, her sweet dreams would be of him.

Jack watched until the door closed behind her, wondering if she'd dream of him. And who had been peeking through the curtains.

Her light fragrance hung in the air, teasing him. The chilly air had cooled his skin; the fire in his gut still blazed. The aroused male wanted to hear her say she was free, there was no one in her life. The flawed man whose decisions were even now sometimes governed by the consequences of that snowfield trip had an aching feeling it might be better for both of them if she wasn't.

* * *

On Friday Jack pulled into the driveway of Mel's house well in advance of Cassie's four o'clock estimated time of arrival. He unhitched Sam from his harness and let him out, allowing him to race around, glad to be home. Jack followed, strolling through the vegetable garden to the peach tree by the back fence.

Since he'd been old enough to hold a child's trowel, he'd earned blisters digging every patch in this yard. Many of the full-grown productive fruit trees had been planted with his help, and the adults had let the eager young gardener believe they'd survived due to his attentive watering.

No childhood hours could have been better than the ones spent in that way, or assisting Bob in the shed workshop and Mel in the kitchen. What was disguised as fun for his generation had been a solid grounding in self-reliance.

Hunkering down, he scooped up a handful of dirt and let it run through his fingers. He breathed in the pungent aroma and felt his muscles clench. Life went on, evolved and changed. Pain was the price of accepting you couldn't fight fate.

Sometime in the future, nearer than he could bear to contemplate, there'd be a heated swimming pool surrounded by fake lawn in place of the garden. Bob's home-built shed would be demolished in favour of a fashionable man cave, complete with television, bar and pool table.

Though more suited to modern life, none of it could create better memories than those he, his siblings and cousins treasured and often reminisced about. Stealthily harvested fruit, fresh from its source, always tasted better than any served at a table. He plucked a Pink Lady apple from its tree and savoured the tart, ripe taste as he toed his boot into the ground underneath.

Sam's bark alerted him to Cassie's arrival and his melancholy mood evaporated in an instant. Tossing his core onto

the compost heap, he strode over to greet her, beaten by the
dog, who jumped up as she alighted from the car. He couldn't
blame him, felt the urge to get as close as possible too.

'Down, Sam.' Even with its slight edginess, her tone was
more encouraging than commanding. Sam sat. Jack wasn't
so sure he'd have been so prompt to obey.

'Hi, Jack.' Addressing *him*, her voice was more guarded,
indicating she'd decided on a strict courtesy line. His head
might agree it was best; every other part of him craved contact, close and physical. Like in his erotic dreams last night.

'Hi, Cassie. Need a hand with your luggage?' He kept the
same tone, went to the rear of her car and lifted the boot.

'Thank you. If you take the suitcase and computer
satchel, I'll bring my overnight bag and groceries.'

He lifted her luggage without effort, frustration grind-
ing in his gut. If they got any more civil and mundane, he'd
be standing to attention.

'Cassie?'

She froze, body bent as she reached for the remaining
items. He saw the movement of her shoulders, swore he
heard the deep slow intake of air before she reversed into an
upright position. Took an age to face him, brown eyes wary.

'Forget it. Let's go inside.' He wasn't sure which displeased him more, her original wariness, her relief at his
statement to ignore his tacit plea, or his inconstancy in how
he wanted her to act towards him.

Cassie accepted Jack's offer to take her two cases up to the
bedroom she'd occupied last week, thankful for the chance
to regroup her defences. Telling herself to stay strong and
keep her distance had little influence against Jack's smile—
heart-stopping yet pulse-stirring—his eyes—irresistible
rain-glistened green magnets—and his crackling laugh—
an Outback-adventure-transporting melody.

He'd only have to make an entrance at any venue to

have women sending him subtle invitations or blatantly flirting with him. Whatever he said or his glances implied, she was way beneath his social status, and probably just a playful diversion.

She filled the kettle, switched it on and began to unpack the food she'd bought on the way then frowned. Jack hadn't mentioned tonight's meal. Did he intend to have it here, and was she supposed to cook?

If he expected home-baked dessert, he'd be disappointed. Though, as she gaped at the array of appliances on the walk-in larder shelf, she realised staying here gave her a great opportunity to hone her basic skills. The devil in her claimed if he intended to flirt with her he ought to be prepared to act as her guinea pig. Common sense countered she'd be playing with fire and could end up scorched beyond healing.

Why couldn't her head and emotions agree on a common-sense attitude whenever she was with him? Or thought about him. Or dreamt of him.

The hum of the open refrigerator and the bubbling kettle drew Jack to the kitchen door and the tantalising view of Cassie from behind. A few paces forward and her delicate peach scent would stir up more than a hunger for food.

Her thigh-length brown and gold top tightened over her hips as she bent to place something on the bottom shelf. His mouth dried and his chest tightened as his brain flashed back to his first sighting of her under a table. The thud of his heartbeat outraced the tapping of his fingers on his leg.

He had to leave. Now. To prevent him from doing something profoundly stupid, like hauling her into his arms and proving her lips were as sweet and delectable as he fantasised. One kiss would never be enough. Kissing, however deep and numerous, might not be enough.

As silent as he thought he was, she raised her head and paused. Incapable of even breathing, he stood immobile as she straightened up and pivoted. Flanked by the cold interior and the open door, she stood and met his gaze. Whatever she saw in his eyes caused hers to grow bigger, darker. The steady rise and fall of her breasts proved her agitation.

The click as the water reached boiling point seemed too loud, the temperature in the room too high. The distance separating them too great.

'I should go.' The commonplace, sensible words scoured his throat as he forced them out. They weren't the ones jostling in his head. His feet felt leaden, reluctant to walk away from her. His fingers itched to caress her skin.

She gave the slightest of nods and a forced smile. Knowing his attraction was reciprocated made it harder to leave.

'I'll need the keys and security code.' The unique raspy edge in her tone was delightful. He ached to hear it thick with passion.

'Yeah, the box is by the back door.' He led the way, digging into his pocket for the spare set of keys he'd collected from the drawer in the lounge. She brought a notebook and pen from her handbag, and hid the numbers he gave her in a reminder notice about a friend's upcoming birthday.

'Just in case I have a memory lapse.'

She brushed her hand over her hair as she turned to go back to the kitchen, and he recalled that same unconscious action on Tuesday when he'd upset her. Remorse slammed into his gut. He was a self-centred idiot, acting like a coward prepared to run. She had been kind and gentle with Mel and deserved more consideration.

Admit it, you fool. You want to stay.

Hoping he appeared more casual than he felt, he tried for a conciliatory tone. 'Fancy home-delivered pizza for dinner?'

She swung round, features composed, eyes a mixture of caution and hope. 'You're...'

'...Not sure what's happening between us. But running won't change it.'

Since the day the loss of his temper had resulted in tragedy, he'd kept control in any situation, faced the problem and tried for a solution, or at least compromise. His emotions were strictly compartmentalised between family and friends, and others. They were never involved during business transactions and restrained when he dated.

With Cassie, the walls were hazy and he swung from mentally needing to solidify them and physically wanting to breach them. Moments ago, he'd prepared to walk out, now staying and talking, even for a short while, was his optimum choice.

Keeping eye contact, he walked towards her, stopping within touching distance, his arms loose at his sides.

'I'd like to stay for a while.' His breath caught in his throat and his fingers curled into his palms as he waited for her reply.

She studied him with an intensity that kickstarted heat-waves in his stomach. Talking slid a long way down on his list of activities he'd like to share with her.

'Australian topping with a side of garlic bread. You can choose dessert.' A sudden, mind-boggling smile, a half spin and she'd gone. A surge of tangible pleasure, a huff of exhaled air and he followed, catching up with her as she set two mugs on the kitchen bench.

It was her radiant smile that had crashed his caution and drove him into her personal space, less than his arm's length behind her. A heartbeat away. The set of her shoulders showed she was aware of his close proximity.

'Cassie?' With his fingertip, he traced a circle on her neck, over the pulse below her ear, and saw the resulting tremor rack her body. Desire swept away all reservations. With a gentle hold, he turned her to face him, and found himself even closer.

Near enough to feel the warmth of her body, see the golden sparkle in her eyes and smell the essence that was pure Cassie. His lips were a breath away from hers.

'Conversation won't answer the questions keeping me awake at night.' He slid his hand around her neck. 'Like… how will it feel to have you crushed against me?' He tilted her chin up with his thumb. 'And are your lips as delectable and sweet as I imagine?'

He lowered his head and covered her mouth with his in a tender exploratory kiss. Her body stilled then melted into his, causing an instant physical reaction. His heart blipped, then soared when she didn't pull away. His fingers caressed and firmed as his free arm encircled her waist, binding her to him. His chest expanded and fire flared in his stomach, rapidly spreading to every extremity.

Cassie's arms snaked up and around his neck, her fingers tangled into his hair and he trembled. There was no awareness of time. It was an instant or a lifetime until necessity for air forced his lips from hers barely long enough to gasp and let a possessive male growl escape before settling again. He heard her contented sigh mingle with his low rumble.

The tip of his tongue traced an appeal for entry along her lip line, slipping inside as her lips parted. She tasted even sweeter than he'd imagined, with a hint of something spicy. He stroked and teased the soft flesh, tangled with her tongue and fought the craving for more intimate contact, fought the urge to lift her and…

Flump. A deep doggy sigh shattered the enchantment. Cassie wrenched free, slamming onto the work bench and sending him stumbling away, almost falling over Sam, lying close by.

What the heck? He recovered, glaring at the dog before swinging back to Cassie. His demand for an explanation dried in his throat at the sight of her bright red face. The remorse in her eyes hit him square in the gut, searing him with guilt as she clasped her hands over her mouth and rocked forward and back.

He took a step forward, hands held out in appeal.

'Cassie, what's wrong? Tell me what I did.'

'It's wrong. We can't…we mustn't.' Her hesitant words were muttered against her palms as she dropped her head.

'It felt more than right to me.' Frustration governed his gruff statement; she'd been as willing as him until Sam interrupted them. Her head came up and he locked eyes with her, challenging her to refute his claim. She glared back.

'It's Mel's house. She employs me. Trusts me.'

His spontaneous short bark of laughter startled her. Before she had a chance to recover, he moved in and caught her chin, tilting her head up.

'*Here* is wrong?' Hoarse, as if being forced from his throat. He trailed his knuckles down the side of her face, his lips curling in satisfaction when she quivered.

'Not *me*? Not the *kiss*?'

She blinked under his scrutiny, her brown eyes moist and wary. As if lost for words, she shook her head and he instantly gathered her into a one-armed embrace. His free hand caressed her hair, and her hand landed on his denim shirt over his pounding heart.

She wasn't rejecting him. It was the location. He brushed his lips on her forehead.

'I'd suggest we forgive ourselves that transgression but that would be admitting we're sorry. I'm not. Are you, Cassie?'

'No.' An instant, whispered yet distinct answer. Satisfied that she didn't blame him, he eased away. They both needed recovery time.

'How about you find the cake Mel told me she left in the larder? I'll make coffee. And we'll talk in the lounge.'

CHAPTER ELEVEN

CASSIE CARRIED THE plate of sliced carrot cake, and Jack followed with the steaming mugs. He asked her to hold them, enabling him to move the low table within easy reach of where she liked to sit. Instead of taking Bob's chair, he settled in the centre of the settee, bending his leg on the upholstery, and hooking the other over his ankle.

Her brow furrowed as she swung her head from his usual spot to where he was now, holding out his hand for his coffee. He grinned and quirked an eyebrow, making her smile as she relinquished the mug.

Her pulse blipped at the accidental brush of their fingers. Still keyed up from his kiss, she tried to hide her reaction, selected a piece of cake, sat and wriggled into the end corner of the settee. He faced her, his shoulder pressed against the back, seeming content to just watch her. Didn't drink.

'I meant every word, Cassie. I'm not sorry I kissed you, and I want to again. Even more now I know how... Incredible doesn't come close to describing how good.'

She felt the same; her body still hummed from the rapture of being moulded to his. Her pulse was almost normal yet she knew one special look or even the slightest curl of his full lips would send it rocketing. Every breath she took was imbued with his essence and sandalwood aroma.

'It's not about want.'

She saw his fingers tighten on his mug at her words, saw it shake as he balanced it on his knee. Regretted the loss of tenderness in his eyes.

'There's a lot of places outside Mel's home and you won't be working twenty-four-seven.'

She straightened her spine at his blunt statement. 'No, and...'

'Is there anyone who might have a grievance because I kissed you?'

If it hadn't been for the slight judder in his normally smooth voice, she'd have thought he'd reverted to his suspicions of her the day they'd met. He was as shaken as she was, merely better at concealing it.

'No, there's no one.'

'So we're both free, and we like each other. We can take it easy and see what happens.'

'We can be friends?'

His eyes widened, his eyebrows shot up and he huffed. 'You kiss your *friends* like that, Cassie Clarkson?'

'No! I meant...' She surged forward in distress, shaking her head, and spilling her drink. 'How could you think I'd...?'

Sam was on his feet in an instant, trotting over to her, nudging her hand. Jack scooted along at the same time, dumping his full mug on the table as he went. He took hers from her trembling fingers and placed it alongside. His face contorted with guilt as he cradled hers with his hands.

'I was joking, Cassie. Stupidly trying to cover how mind-blowing it was for me. An immature male reaction to you pulling away first. Forgive me?'

The genuine remorse in his eyes tugged at Cassie's heart. He'd questioned her credentials, and tried gentle pressure when they'd first met; he'd never been cruel. And the oh-so-light feel of his work-roughened hands was turning shaking from dismay into quivers of delight.

There was no way she could voice her certainty of the chasm, cultural and familial, between them. From the day he'd been born, he'd never been alone unless he'd wished it, always had similar age relatives to bounce off and confide in. He'd never had to live within the bounds of a limited budget. And never would.

'I didn't handle it well. It was… I… I've never been kissed like that before.'

Sam nudged again and Jack released her with reluctance, allowing her to stroke the dog.

'I'm okay, Sam.' She ruffled his ears. 'He's very perceptive. It must be comforting to know he's here when Mel's alone.'

'He is, more than most people, including me. Val says my tendency to make jokes about anything emotional is an attempt to hide my insecurities. She knows me better than anyone so she might be right.'

Cassie was stunned at his revelation. She couldn't imagine him sharing this personal information with many people, certainly not a comparative stranger. She felt shy and yet elated.

'I'll try to remember that in future.'

'And I'll try to curb my childish outbursts.'

His lips curled into a stunning smile that rebooted her senses into overdrive. The realisation they were forging a new understanding which needed slow and steady pacing warred with an inexplicable longing for fast and furious.

To hide the blush rising on her cheeks, she bent her head to check her watch. 'Sam must be wondering when his walk's coming.'

'As soon as we settle boundaries.'

Looking up, she encountered glittering eyes and familiar determined features, though without the stern resolve from the past. He wrapped his hands around hers, creating a bond that twined its way to her core.

'While we're here, we'll keep everything light and friendly. Anywhere out in the big wide world, we'll let life unfold and see where it takes us. Agreed?'

They'd be working miles apart. They both had friends

and social lives, and he'd have family commitments. Their time in that big wide world would be limited so it was reasonably safe to comply. But then reason didn't come into how being near him shook her mantra: *Stay strong. Keep distance.*

'Agreed.'

He raised her hands and kissed her knuckles.

'Coffee's cold. Do you want to walk Sam now and order pizza on the way so it's delivered soon after we're home?'

The air cooled as soon as the sun began to set, even on the warmer days they'd been having lately. Clad in thick zippered parkas, they let Sam lead the way, Jack's fingers linking with Cassie's the moment they stepped off the back veranda. A guy had to ensure a lady didn't slip on the damp path, didn't he? And it gave him the added pleasure of her distinctive perfume with every breath.

'Did you have pets as a child?'

Did you learn a musical instrument? Did you like school?

He'd have to limit his questions to general topics at first. And was he prepared to answer any questions she had with the same honesty he expected from her?

'Goldfish for years, and a succession of cats and dogs, always from Animal Welfare. Mum chose older ones who had little chance of being adopted otherwise, and they returned her affection unconditionally.'

She smiled as if recalling a treasured memory. 'The cats and smaller dogs would curl up on her lap as she watched television.'

'Did you have a preference?'

'I loved playing with the dogs, teaching them tricks and trying, not very successfully, to train them. I admired all our cats, who tended to be self-reliant, solitary and often standoffish. And I learned that trust takes time and patience to build.' She laughed teasingly. 'I can't imagine you with cats, more a romp with the pedigree dog type.'

She'd painted a picture of mutts and strays, boisterous fun and limited or no formal training. The complete opposite of the Randell domestic animals. And, without realising, she'd given him an insight into her view of her place in the world when she'd spoken of the cats.

'We always had pedigree dogs, two at all times. The one cat in my lifetime was a present Val bought herself for her fifteenth birthday, still her favourite pet. The dogs were professionally trained but we boys did our best to un-teach them and get them to join in our rough and tumble games.'

'And now?'

'I won't own a dog and leave it alone all day. My cousin had Sam when Mel was in hospital, and he's well behaved so I've taken him with me the last two days.'

He flicked a glance at her, saw her lips part and guessed what was coming. He got in first.

'And no, I'm too old for goldfish and have no interest in an aquarium.'

'Mind-reader.' Their mingled laughter caused a warm glow in his stomach. It sounded natural, nice, something he could get used to. Something he'd miss when she was no longer around.

'Val's threatening to give me a cat for my birthday, says I need the company and something living to take care of. I'm terrified she actually means it.'

'It might do you good to have a flatmate you can't dominate.'

'That's my worry. Can you hold Sam while I make the call?' The alternative was to let go of her hand. Not an option.

Cassie complied, urging the dog to her side. Twilight walking hand in hand with Jack was comforting. She was convinced it could be habit-forming and probably addictive.

Pizza ordered, they walked to the next corner and turned back, Sam remaining under her control.

'When do you intend to start Mel's listing?' Jack asked.

'Tomorrow morning. I have charts in my computer, and I'll do one room at a time.'

She sensed the turn of his head and felt his penetrating gaze. He halted and swung to face her, pivoting her body with his hold. The overhead streetlight reflected in his green eyes reminded her of the lush foliage of a Queensland rainforest. Her body responded in the same way it had trudging up a hill on that hot, steamy day.

'It's the weekend. No days off between contracts?'

'That's what I'm here for. I'll fit in odd hours or days off as I go.'

She wasn't surprised by her heart racing and the fluttering in her stomach, or by the tingles leaping from cell to cell. But how was it possible to feel breathless when her lungs were working overtime pumping air in and out? Especially when his cool fingers caressed her cold cheek and ignited heat.

How was it possible for his eyes to darken any further or to intensify beyond soul-searching? Seconds, minutes— who knew how long the spell lasted?

A raking shudder, a harsh huff of air, and it was broken. He'd wanted to kiss her, and her logical brain silently thanked him for resisting. Her heart regretted his self-control.

'Make sure you do.' Grating, as if from a dry throat, the way hers felt. 'Keep a lookout for the Batman car I lost twenty years ago.'

His hand dropped to his side and they resumed their walk.

'I'm committed for the weekend so if there's anything that needs to be moved or lifted, let it wait. Text me, and I'll get there when I can.'

She had mixed feelings about not seeing him for days. Heck, she had mixed feelings about every aspect of their relationship.

She certainly didn't expect him to be beholden to her because of a kiss. A kiss like no other. A kiss she'd remember for ever.

Cassie was torn when Jack sat in the armchair instead of alongside her. It was more aligned to the television, it did mean they could set the pizza at the end of the table, and it lessened the temptation to shift closer. It also meant he was always either in her peripheral vision or leaning in front of her for food.

They ate all bar two slices of the pizza while watching the news, followed by hot drinks, cheesecake and a multitimes rerun of an American sitcom.

'I'll bet I'll still be laughing at the same gags when I'm old and too deaf to hear the words,' Jack said as the credits rolled up. 'Are you tired or ready for another show?'

She scrolled through the selection.

'Renovations, repeats or reality shows. Unless…there's a sci-fi action film starting in six minutes. Enough time to clear the table, and brew another coffee if you want.'

'What, no popcorn?' His exaggerated aggrieved tone made her laugh, and suddenly it was almost like the evenings at home with Brad and Phil. Almost, because they were like brothers to her, and she'd never ever be able to think of Jack that way.

After the movie finished, they let Sam out for a run before bed. Jack took her hand, walked across the veranda and down a step before twisting to face her.

'It's cold and dark so we'll count this as neutral territory.'

He brushed his lips over hers in a kiss as soft and gentle as the other had been passionate. A swarm of butterflies fluttered in her stomach, generating feather-light sensations

from head to toes. Their only physical contact was their
lips and linked hands, yet his heat enveloped her, cocoon-
ing her from the chilly air.

She swayed forward. He lifted his head. And Sam
barked.

Jack's forced smile told her he didn't want to go, the
gleam in his eyes said he believed she was beautiful, and
his hard kiss on her knuckles confirmed he'd return.

'Sam, inside.'

Keeping his eyes on Cassie's face, he stooped to pat the
dog trotting past him.

'Go lock up then I can leave. Sweet dreams, Cassie.'

'Goodnight, Jack.' She turned to smile at him as she
closed the door.

A little later, she smiled again as she switched off her
bedside lamp and burrowed under the quilt. How could she
not have sweet dreams when during her waking hours, he
invaded her thoughts with images of slow dancing, moonlight strolls and campfires under the stars?

Cassie wasn't sure what woke her in the night; it might have
been a dog barking or a car. There was enough light from
the streetlights for her to see the dim shapes of the furniture
in the room. She rolled over and the quilt slipped, exposing
her shoulders to the chilly air that snapped her to full alert.

She pulled it back but knew there was no point in trying
to force sleep. Thinking about the morning ahead might
have worked if a vision of Jack hadn't driven every other
thought from her mind. Jack, his expression resolute, walking across the foyer towards her after suggesting they order
pizza. His eyes had held hers spellbound as he'd narrowed
the space between them.

Trying to steady her breathing had meant inhaling sandalwood and Jack's essence, a mixture that scrambled her
logic and jellied her insides. She'd ached for him to touch

her, then he'd stunned her with his admission of wanting to stay, his eyes soft and pleading.

A surge of pleasure had whooshed through her, making her grin like a child on Christmas morning. Words had shot from her mouth, bypassing her brain and surprising them both. She'd spun on her heel and fled to the kitchen.

She'd been reaching for a mug when she'd felt his heat behind her. Every cell in her body had stilled then quivered at his feather-light caress on her neck. Butterfly tremors had stirred her stomach and she'd had no resistance as he'd eased her round, drawn her into his arms and...

He kissed her.

There'd been nothing and no one else in her world. She'd been conscious of only his touch on her skin, the smouldering fire in his eyes and his firm lips settling over hers.

Unexpectedly soft and cautious, his kiss had provoked liquid warmth low in her belly, exhilarating prickles that raced across her skin and an overwhelming desire to nestle tight into his body, eliminating even the air between them.

Time had stood still. His lips had lifted and she'd sighed, heard and felt his grunt of pleasure rumble up his chest, and sighed again when they resettled on hers.

His arms had tightened, moulding her to his frame. She'd woven her fingers into his hair, rejoiced at his trembling. Her lips parted, allowing him entry, and the outside world had evaporated in a burst of sensations she could never have imagined.

Kissing had never been this sensual, so astonishingly thought-draining, so breathtakingly thrilling. He'd tasted of strong coffee with tart apple, and a craving for more of both enveloped her. More tang, more flavour. More Jack. She was weightless, soaring...

Flump.

Sam. Mel. Mel's house...

Remorse had shaken her, as hot and soul-searing as

Jack's kisses. How had she so easily forgotten where she was, who she was?

Pushing him away, slamming her spine on the work bench as she'd stepped back, and then dithering over an explanation hadn't helped. Only when his irritated retort had sparked a clear response from her had he understood she wasn't upset because he'd kissed her. And he'd made it quite clear he'd like to repeat the incredible experience, away from Mel's home.

In the clear light of day, she'd argue the wisdom of complying. Alone in the blanket of night, she snuggled deeper, closed her eyes and let herself drift back into sweet dreams of that moment to come.

CHAPTER TWELVE

HER RESERVATIONS KICKED back in when her alarm woke her at seven o'clock. Being friends with Jack would be nigh on impossible given the magnetism that drew them to each other whenever they met. That original spark threatened to flare into bushfire heat with each encounter.

Now that they'd kissed, *twice*, once hot and heady, and later so tender and sweet, she feared her heart was already defenceless.

Standing under the hot shower, she resolved to be stronger, certain she could be when he wasn't around, not so sure if he smiled at her, touched her or gave that special crackling laugh.

A folding card table from the family room served as a desk upstairs for the laptop, printouts and her mobile. After the third call on Mel's landline, she took the cordless phone wherever she went. There had also been two women who'd opened the back door and called out.

On Monday evening Val popped in, chatted over coffee about her weekend in Melbourne and promised to visit regularly. Cassie liked her, hoped she would. During her last stay, she'd heard Mel receive numerous calls and deduced she had a wide circle of friends as well as her large family. She'd met a few while Mel had been there but Cassie hadn't realised how many of them phoned or visited on a regular basis.

To her disappointment, just two calls had been from Jack, the first late on Saturday night as she'd prepared for bed. He'd sounded tired, asked about her day and said his had been gruelling but productive. Without elaborating, he'd wished her sweet dreams.

On Sunday afternoon, she'd heard childish squeals, voices and a chainsaw in the background, almost drowning out his voice. Again, he'd kept it short, almost business-like, until the end when one of those children had demanded Uncle Jack's attention. His 'Gotta go' had dampened her already low mood further. His whispered 'Miss you, Cassie' had sent her heart soaring. So much for keeping distance, even when they were.

Whenever she took a break, she wandered round the house studying the photographs that adorned every room. Being able to pick out Jack as a toddler gave her a warm glow of satisfaction, and from that she followed his life through school and into maturity.

She found one she presumed was taken at a high school formal. He had his arm around a very attractive blue-eyed brunette who wore her red figure-hugging ballgown with the confidence and grace of a model. The way they posed, bodies close and relaxed, their smiles natural, proved they were dating.

The girl's image stayed with her all day. Where was *she* now? Had the teenage romance failed the test of moving into the working world? Who had ended the relationship?

Jack hadn't rung by the time she fell asleep. She had no right to expect a daily call, text or visit. She'd had no reason to call or text him.

So he'd kissed her, turning her muscles into jelly. So he'd said he wanted to kiss her again, and then given her an almost-not-there brush of his lips. *To be fair, it was still the second most thrilling kiss of her life.* So he'd told her he wanted to get to know her, and had said little more than hello and goodbye over the phone in three days.

Hadn't she been telling herself not to let his charm override her caution since the moment they'd met?

* * *

Her ringtone woke her from a deep sleep. She blinked, noted faint light around the curtains and groped for her phone. Didn't check the caller ID as she held it to her ear, and began to drift back to sleep.

'Cassie?'

'Jack?' Caution evaporated with one word. Every sense sprang to alert as she struggled up onto one elbow. 'What's wrong? What time is it?'

'Early, darling. It was too late to call last night. The forecast is for sunshine and I'm free until eleven.' His voice was animated and alive, in contrast to their last two short conversations.

'Do you and Sam want to come for breakfast and a walk on the beach? There's a café ten minutes' walk from here, and they'll be opening soon.'

She sank back and stared at the ceiling. He'd barely spoken to her since that last spine-tingling brush of lips, and now he expected her to drop everything she had planned and race to his side.

'Cassie? You've worked for eight days straight—time for a break. I'll come and pick you up.'

'No. I'll drive.' How could she refuse? 'And, before you say anything, I've had a GPS for years, and now I've got a car harness for Sam. All I need is where you live.'

'Smart as well as beautiful.' His laughter crackled along the line.

As she stepped into the shower a delicious flood of adrenaline swamped her. Jack had called her 'darling'.

Jack leant on the railing of his bedroom balcony, watching the waves through the gap between the houses across the road. He knew he was grinning, and didn't want to stop. Between meetings regarding his shopping centre enterprise, scheduled work at his rental properties and a commitment to attend his nephew's birthday, he'd hardly had time to eat or sleep since Friday night.

Through it all, Cassie and those two kisses had hovered at the back of his mind, surging into prominence whenever he took a break, or settled in bed at night. How come there were times he could be so logical and reinforce all the reasons they shouldn't get involved, and yet when she was near, or he recalled the way her eyes shone or her sweet smile, logic and reason dissipated? Leaving only yearning and the anticipation of something new and extraordinary.

His determination to never get too involved with another woman was based on logic and his acute awareness of his flaws and weaknesses. He knew little about Cassie's personal life and friends, and almost nothing of her family background.

He did know he'd missed her. She'd agreed to come for breakfast with him. He'd have a chance to claim a third kiss, maybe more.

Cassie didn't need the disembodied voice of the satnav to tell her they were nearing Jack's home. Sam strained towards the rear right window, head up, body quivering with excitement. *Her* body reacted in the same way at the sight of the familiar figure waiting by the brick and iron fence of a modern two-storey glass and tan house with twin balconies on the top floor.

As she slowed down, he walked to the kerb, waiting until she'd stopped before opening the passenger door. His smile was warm and inviting, the dark shadows under his eyes indicating a lack of sleep. He lifted her bag from the seat, slid in and held it on his lap.

'Hi, Cassie.' Leaning across the central column, he kissed her lips. A brief touch that blew away her vexation for his lack of communication since Friday, replacing it with heartfelt longing. So not the cool, calm mindset she'd sworn to have.

'Drive straight into the garage.' He glanced between the seats. 'Hi, Sam, ready for a walk?' The answering *woof* echoed in the enclosed space.

Their entrance automatically activated overhead lights in the spacious garage running the length of the house. Cassie parked behind Jack's ute and stepped out, staring in amazement. This was the cleanest, tidiest workshop area she'd ever seen, and she'd been in quite a few.

A wide bench cupboard stretched about two-thirds of the way along the right-hand wall, ending at the rear, where there was a matching roller door to the back garden. On top of the bench—absolutely clear except for a chainsaw in pieces—were a mixture of cupboards and shelves for the length of his ute. Shadow boards displaying tools and equipment covered the remaining wall space.

Everything was packed neatly away, nothing out of place, no oil spills on the floor. The one incongruity was the large framed painting hanging on the wall next to the door leading into the house. It depicted a mountain in winter, reminiscent of holiday brochure photos for the ski season in the Snowy Mountains. Its snow-covered peaks led the eyes down to increasing expanses of trees on the lower slopes.

Why had he deliberately placed it so it was in his direct eyeline whenever he came home?

'Cassie?'

She turned to find Jack, with an amused expression, and Sam, head tilted and tail wagging, waiting for her by the boot of her car.

'Sam and I are hungry.'

So was she, and not just for food. She drank in the sheer masculinity of him, from his colourful runners to his natural mussed light brown hair. In his tan chinos, brown polo neck sweater and zip-up green jacket he epitomised an outdoor man. The idea of him spending his life wearing a suit and sitting in front of a computer in an air-conditioned office was absurd.

And so was the soft bright red patterned zip-up bag hanging on his shoulder. She burst out laughing, startling man and dog, who exchanged puzzled looks. Lifting it off, she slipped it over her head then gave him a once-over.

'Much better for your image. Let's go.'

'Ladies first.'

He glanced back at the painting as she passed him, deepening her intrigue. Once he'd closed the roller door, he pocketed his keys and took her hand, enclosing it in his. The air was cooler than she'd expected, justifying her choice of jeans and roll-neck jumper beneath her wool-blend jacket. Winter socks and sneakers kept her feet warm. She rarely wore gloves or anything on her head.

'I like the garden. Your work?' In truth, she loved the setting of pebble stones and three large rocks, interspersed with ground cover and plants of varying heights, different shades of green and some with bright coloured leaves.

'My plan, plus a barbecue for family and friends who helped. I'll show you the back yard later.'

'It's an impressive home. Not very old, from the style.' She daren't imagine the size of the mortgage, if he even had one. Family connections might have helped out there.

'It was a lucky break for me as I knew the couple who were building. He was offered a promotion entailing a five-year stint in the States a few days after the foundation had been poured. I took over their contract, negotiated a few changes, and moved in mid-December two years ago.'

Jack was well aware of how lucky he'd been. A short time earlier, the couple would have cancelled the contract and sold the empty block. A month later and he'd have already invested his equity in another property. He was also convinced that luck followed those who planned ahead, and were able to take advantage of it.

A gust of wind caught them at the corner leading down to the esplanade. Two women power-walked along the sand, a large black Labrador bounding beside them. Seagulls circled above them, squawking loudly before dipping towards the sea. He turned to Cassie and her radiant smile dried his throat, preventing speech.

'Mum used to call this brisk. Cool morning air with a nip in the breeze. I love it.'

It showed. That breeze stirred strands of her hair, blowing them over her chilled red cheeks. Her eyes sparkled as if this were a big adventure, and her smile gave him the credit for arranging it. His chest swelled as he sucked in cold air, and his heartbeat raced, faster than when he ran. He'd happily accept any acclaim, especially if it furthered their friendship.

'You're not too cold? I ought to have told you to bring gloves and a beanie. Or lent you one of mine.'

'And mess up my hair? You're not wearing one.' She laughed, the sweet sound wrapping around him, enticing him to pull her closer to his side.

'I'm used to it. Uh-huh, not chauvinistic.' He pre-empted her next words. 'I run in the mornings as often as I can. It definitely gets the adrenaline going during the cold months.'

They stopped to cross the road, Sam straining to get to the sand.

'Heel, Sam. Breakfast first.'

The café was a short walk along the esplanade, with outside seating under large umbrellas. Sam settled next to a large ceramic bowl filled with clean water in the corner. Jack dropped the leash on the ground, held the canvas seat with an ocean view for Cassie then sat by her side.

'I'm having the big breakfast and coffee, and I guarantee whatever you fancy will be fresh and tasty,' Jack said, not bothering to check the menu. 'A solid run, a hot meal and I'm ready for the day. Hi, Sue.'

He introduced Cassie to the waitress, who owned and ran the business with her husband. They shared a joke as she wrote down his order plus two grilled meat patties for Sam, though he was aware of Cassie's gaze flicking up and down the menu as if rereading the items would help her select one.

'Too many choices? Pick one and have another next time.' He loved the way her brows arched, as if questioning his mind-reading ability.

Loved? Figure of speech.

She finally placed the menu down with a soft *huff* and smiled at Sue.

'I'll have a ham omelette, please, and an apple and ginger tea. I've never tried that flavour.'

'It's delicious and refreshing. Won't be long.'

Jack arched his back, gave Cassie a rueful grin when she noticed and her expression became thoughtful.

'It's been a hectic three long days. Didn't get home till near eleven last night, too late to call.' Because he'd missed her and her unique voice, and wouldn't have been able to keep it short.

'You look tired. It might have been better if you'd slept in.'

He gave her his best horrified stare. 'And miss breakfast with you two.'

Her laughter was worth any number of hours sleep.

'This week it's back to normal. Can I come to dinner tonight?'

His abrupt question startled Cassie. A picture of old-fashioned domestic bliss flashed into her head; a cosy dinner for two, hot and ready for the man of the house the moment he arrived home from work. Candles and music and...

'*Awk.*' A seagull swooped to the ground right by their table to scoop up a discarded scrap of food. Sam barked and the vision dissolved in a pang of regret. Jack's arrogant smirk didn't help.

'See, I even provide tableside entertainment.'

She tilted her head, and pursed her lips.

'You? Hmm. Okay, give us an encore.'

'Well, um. Ah, saved by the lady bearing drinks.'

Cassie sipped the hot, invigorating tea, enjoying its tart flavour, and trying to recall what they'd been talking about before. Oh, yes. Jack's request. She looked up into appealing green eyes and wondered if anyone ever refused him. Her normally coherent brain certainly couldn't come up with a single reason.

'I'm a basic cook, nothing fancy like you're probably used to.'

His face darkened for a second then cleared, so fast she might have imagined it. The fingers of his hand flattened out on the table, his chest rose and fell and his penetrating eyes held hers captive.

'Is that how you see me, Cassie? Part of the elite who dine rather than eat, are served rather than cook, and expect to have their wineglasses refilled throughout the meal?'

'No!' Her cup clinked as she abruptly set it down. Her stomach churned and her cheeks burned with shame. 'How could you think that? I know your family is well off, and you often have meals with Mel, who has great culinary skills, but you bought hamburgers that morning and...'

'I'm an idiot who just overreacted.' He reached out and lifted her hand, cradling it in his, and stroking her knuckles with his thumb in a slow, mesmerising motion. 'A throwback to teenage years defending my family status from contemporaries who thought I believed I was superior.'

'*I don't.*'

He threw back his head and laughed. She realised her

ambiguity, and pulled her hand away in remorse. Closing her eyes made it worse as her mind conjured up chops and onions grilling over a crackling campfire. Complete with tantalising smells.

'Here we are.'

Her eyes flew open to a view of a fluffy omelette garnished with parsley being lowered in front of her. The stronger aromas making her mouth water were from Jack's meal in Sue's other hand.

Big breakfast? It was *huge*, more than she normally ate in a whole day—bacon, two fried eggs, two sausages, tomato, mushrooms and a hash brown. She was still staring when Sue returned with a rack of toast, a dish of scrolled butter and the two patties on a disposable plate for Sam.

'You're going to eat all that?'

'A working man needs sustenance. This, and a sandwich for lunch, will keep me going until dinner when I'm active.' Jack picked up his cutlery and began to eat. 'Other less physical days, I cut back. Aren't you going to eat? Tastes better hot.'

'So you're working this afternoon.' She began to eat her omelette. It was delicious, lighter and tastier than she'd ever been able to achieve.

'Yeah, and it's this side of town so I can be with you before seven. If I'm still welcome?'

He phrased the remark as a question, putting the burden of veto on her. She didn't answer, ate and thought, weighing up the risks. More contact meant more chance—no, certainty—of closer involvement. He'd already proved how easily he could obliterate any resistance to his touch. If—when—he kissed her again, would she be able to fortify her defences enough to say no, should he try to take it further?

She raised her head and found him watching her with such a hopeful expression her heart flipped and the sudden sharp wrench to her stomach left her breathless.

Dropping her gaze was an instinctive action to hide the answer he'd have no trouble reading. She wouldn't refuse him but appearing too eager would give him the advantage.

Yeah, as if he doesn't already know he has it. You can't keep distance. Try to stay strong.

CHAPTER THIRTEEN

JACK REACHED FOR his coffee mug and drank the strong brew. At the time of suggesting they spend time together, he'd told himself finding out more about her would protect his aunt. Now he knew he'd been deceiving himself.

His resolve to treat Cassie with detached respect in consideration to Mel, and to Cassie herself, was being undermined by his attraction for her, the desire to see her, touch her, and hear her edgy voice which always sent his pulse racing.

Sitting across the table from her was pure pleasure. He'd be happy to stay here all day, and drink in the soft sheen of her dark hair, the delicate curve of her silk-smooth cheeks and her red lips with their tiny quirk.

She'd looked down so quickly he hadn't been able to gauge her response. A controlled man, unlike the easily provoked teenager he'd been, he'd learnt anything worth having was worth waiting for. He finished his meal and was draining his coffee mug when she pushed her plate away and made eye contact. In an unusual occurrence for him, he couldn't read the message in her sombre contemplation.

'I'm pushing too hard, aren't I? It's as if… Hell, I can't explain. Let's eat and walk. I'll abide by whatever decision you make before you go home.'

If he'd told her the truth, she'd think he was crazy. Since he'd kissed her, he'd had a sense of being on restricted time, and he had no idea why or what for. He didn't believe in hunches or premonitions, basing his life on solid facts and experience.

He'd never lacked confidence with women, found it easy

to approach someone he fancied. Cassie was like no one he'd ever met, independent yet vulnerable, prepared to stand up to him yet mindful of her employed position. With her, he wasn't sure of the rules of play but her enchanting smile and simple nod of acceptance satisfied him.

He went inside to pay, leaving Cassie to finish her tea and stir up Sam who, happy and fed, was curled up, dozing. They waited for him on the footpath, Cassie hunkering down to scratch Sam's ears. He was shuddering with delight, his tail sweeping the ground as she talked to him, and Jack knew exactly how he felt.

Two heads turned and two pairs of solemn eyes regarded him for a second then Sam barked a greeting and Cassie's lips curled into an encouraging smile before she spoke.

'Chicken stir-fry with rice? No critiquing allowed.'

'Not even if it's positive?' He made a mental *Yes!* gesture in his head, tempering the urge to say it out loud and punch the air.

'I'll take that in writing.' She laughed and relinquished control of the dog.

He took the leash, relishing the now familiar ripple that flowed through him at her musical sound, and linked their fingers. They crossed the road towards the beach.

Although the sun shone, the breeze had picked up during their meal on the sheltered veranda. Maybe this wasn't such a great idea? Would it be better to go back to his house, and invite her another day when it was warmer?

Cassie noticed a few hardy swimmers keeping a good pace through the water, arms and legs pumping them along. She admired the resilience of the surfers sitting out there on their boards, legs dangling in the surf, waiting for a perfect wave. Not understanding why their muscles didn't cramp from limited motion in this cold weather, she shivered, hugging her jacket tighter.

'Too cold?' Jack let go of her hand and slipped his arm around her, drawing her closer to his side.

She shook her head. He'd invited her for a walk and she'd hold him to it.

'No, I'm fine. Wouldn't be out *there* for anything, though.'

'Wetsuits and adrenaline nullify the cold when you catch a good wave. Sure you don't want to try?'

She picked up on the challenge in his voice.

'Not until summer.' Slipping from his hold, she stepped onto the sand and headed for the sea.

'It's a date.' He came after her, almost knocking her over when she suddenly swung around. He caught her by the waist to steady her, dark green eyes gleaming.

'That's not…'

'No chickening out. And—' he pressed a quick kiss on her lips to stifle her protest '—we can hire or borrow a wetsuit your size.' Arms outstretched, he scanned her body, and wriggled his eyebrows. 'Slender perfection.'

She tapped his chest in mock displeasure. 'Idiot.'

He unclipped Sam's lead, ordering him to stay close before letting him go.

'Isn't he supposed to be kept on a leash?' There were signs clearly stating council regulations.

'Kept *under control*. He won't go more than a few metres from us even if another dog comes near. Unless it threatens you or me, and then a firm "Stay, Sam" will have him sitting, but ready, between us and the danger.'

'He's a credit to whoever trained him.'

'Bob and Mel, with help, and I use the term loosely, from any child who visited. Let's go.'

He retook her hand and they strolled along the shoreline, passing morning joggers and dog walkers, many giving their pets a free romp in the sea. Jack hadn't been kidding;

Sam ran ahead then either splashed in the foam until they reached him or loped back.

Jack described the different moves and stances the surfers made on their journey to the shore, and claimed tongue-in-cheek he could have been a champion. She admitted to giving up after not being able to stand up in motion.

'Wait till you try with an expert coach.' His attempt to look humble made her laugh.

'Humility's not your style, Jack Randell.'

He joined in. 'You wouldn't want me to lie, would you?'

This was nice, friendly. Comfortable. She'd be content to stroll all day, talking casually about the world around them or in companionable silence.

They were within sight of the café on the return trip when they stopped to laugh at a black and white terrier challenging the might of the ocean. Focused on his antics, they were oblivious to undulation behind them until the water swirled around their shoes.

Cassie skittled up the sand, looked back, and stilled. She held her breath and clasped a hand to her chest as a lump formed in her throat. This was one of those special moments to be stored away and brought out when her spirits needed a boost.

She turned her head from left to right, noting every sight and sound. The sun's radiance, tempered by banks of clouds being blown across the sky, a cruise ship on the horizon, inciting holiday dreams, and the surfers weaving their way to shore. This backdrop, the people and their pets, were essential images of the whole. And in centre foreground stood Jack, now on firm sand, arms folded, head slightly tilted, regarding her with a quizzical expression.

Closing her eyes, she seared the panorama into her mind for the future. Not enough—the urge for something more tangible gripped her. Her phone was out in an instant and she snapped him before he had the chance to protest or alter that look. Took two more for insurance.

She would now be able to see Jack, wind-blown hair, tanned skin and athletic body, any time, wherever she was, wherever he was. She gasped as reality struck and her arm dropped to her side. Hard bands of steel bound her lungs and an iron fist squeezed her heart. He was everything her dream man should be—except she didn't fit in his world and, with her lack of proven family, never would.

He noticed the change. Brow furrowed, he strode over, catching her by the shoulders. The intensity of his gaze seared and she couldn't control her trembling.

'What is it, Cassie? The cold? We'd better go back.'

'No, I…'

It's you who makes me tremble and stirs emotion I can't control.

Not to be uttered out loud. And she had no chance anyway, as he lowered his head and covered her mouth with his, so gentle at first then deeper as she responded. His arms stroked her back before settling into a firm hold, and hers slid around his waist to complete the embrace.

The sounds around them muted into the background. His sandalwood cologne mingled with her peach fragrance, creating a unique blend with every inhalation. And the rich coffee taste of him invigorated and enthralled her.

Jack had no sense of place or time. He was lost in the ecstasy of having this woman in his arms, her lips returning his kiss with an ardour that threatened to undermine his control. She roused a stronger desire than he'd ever felt in his life.

With supreme effort, he raised his head and eased his body away before he embarrassed them both. How would she react if he voiced his preferred way to warm them both?

Her wistful eyes told him he hadn't been alone in his

fantasy. Prior to his kiss, they'd been clouded with despair, and for some reason he'd felt himself the cause.

He'd watched her gazing seaward, slowly turning her head to take it all in, an enchanting smile on her face. She'd been fine until she'd snapped a photo of him. He'd seen her chest rise, her lips purse and her arm drop slowly to her side, and instantly moved to find out why. She'd quivered at his touch, and he couldn't explain why the motion spread up his fingers and throughout his body.

Kissing her had been an instinctive action and, despite his physical response in a public place, he'd never regret the impulse. He touched her cheek, gently stroked two fingertips on the soft underside of her chin, silky soft, cool to his touch.

'Hold that thought, darling. Hot chocolate and dunking biscuits await us at home.'

One blink, a tiny *huff*, and her face cleared. She looked at Sam, lying patiently nearby, his head on his front paws.

'I'll need Sam's leash.' Hearing Jack say his name, the dog trotted over and sat beside them to be harnessed. Cassie unzipped her shoulder bag and held it out. The brush of their fingers proved the heat of their kiss hadn't waned.

The journey home was quicker, due to the enticement of warmth and hot drinks. They entered through the garage then Jack unlocked the door leading into the house. Cassie was immediately aware of the warmth inside but not so distracted that she didn't notice his quick glance at the painting. She wondered if he was aware of the tension and release of his fingers on hers.

He waved her into a laundry with a bathroom at the far end. The equipment was top brand as expected, the lack of any normal clutter astonishing. No cleaning products in sight, no clothes in a basket or piled on the washing machine. As neat and tidy as his garage. Okay, so he had an excellent cleaning service.

And gets his work ute detailed?

Without a word, she followed him into a hallway wide enough to allow for the wooden staircase with cupboard space beneath. The walls were painted light tan, and all other surfaces varnished to showcase the natural detail.

Jack released Sam who, obviously a regular visitor, shot off towards the back of the house.

'I keep bowls and a bed handy for when he stays over,' Jack explained. 'Turn around and I'll take your jacket to hang up.' Did he deliberately let his fingers glide over her neck, knowing how her body would respond?

He shrugged his off, and hung both in the closet by the front door. His eyes shone with pride as he gestured to the rooms on either side.

'Welcome to my home, Cassie. Lounge on my left and spare room right; open kitchen and dining, plus family room down the hall. My study, two bedrooms and main bathroom upstairs. Would you like to explore while I make the hot chocolate?'

Yes, of course she did, very much. Admitting it was a different matter; it would be like invading his privacy. His lips curved and his eyes twinkled brighter at her hesitancy.

'You want to. Remember I've got two sisters and numerous female cousins. They all love sticky-beaking in other people's houses. Enjoy.' He kissed her cheek and followed Sam.

Cassie took a step the same way, stopped, and swung towards the stairs. She did like seeing the different ways people furnished and decorated their homes, the personal touches that told of their lives. And this exclusively designed house would reveal his true character.

She peeked into the bedrooms, unsure which was his. Both were showroom neat with double beds, one blue

themed and the other green. The study contained all the
fittings of a city office, not even a paperclip out of place.
They were all well-furnished and stylish, a tribute to the
decorator. However, it was the bathroom that had the wow
factor for her.

The shower was big enough for two, and the deep free-
standing bath had a view out of the window, presumably
one way only. The marble wall tiles and double basin vanity
complemented each other with limited patterning streaks
of light grey and red. Everything shone with cleanliness,
even the chrome fittings, and there were no toiletries, no
toothbrush or holder in sight. She was fascinated by the
pristine mirror the length of the vanity.

The niggling doubt that had begun in his workshop grew
with each room she visited. It had nothing to do with the
furniture and fittings, which were manly and tasteful. The
colours were neutral, and wall decorations consisted of a
few bold paintings and family photographs in matching
frames. A similar, smaller alpine painting to the one in
the garage hung, a deliberate distance from the large wall-
mounted television, in direct eyeline of anyone walking
into the lounge room.

Domestic help had to be the answer. Apart from proving
he was minimalist in taste with few adornments, nothing
seemed out of place. Even the television remote sat neatly in
a holder on the coffee table. She felt an irrational desire to
pick up and casually toss down the large bright blue cushions on the extra-long burgundy leather sofa.

This was too organised for a bachelor's home. She'd
lived with two men for nearly three years now, dividing
cooking and chores, and had other male friends, single and
married. For most of them, housework was something to be
avoided if possible, or done with minimum exertion when
it could not be put off any longer.

Moving to the back of the house, she was impressed with

the open-plan across its breadth. Glass doors led out onto a covered, paved patio and lawn. Garden beds of colourful shrubs and occasional small ornamental trees ran along the three fence lines. An ideal setting for summer barbecues.

She ran her fingers over the smooth top of the round dining table, part of a rich reddish-brown wood grain suite. Beautiful. And yet…for a moment, she was lost in a daydream of a cosy home with comfy furniture and normal scattered family possessions.

Shaking it away, she turned towards the kitchen area. The sight of Jack watching her as he waited by the marbled stone bench top, near two steaming mugs and a plate of biscuits, threw her for a moment. In the silence, as she'd wandered, it had felt as if there could not be a living soul in this immaculate house with no personal stuff lying around.

CHAPTER FOURTEEN

HER BREATH CAUGHT in her throat and tiny flares of heat swamped her body as her eyes feasted on his muscular torso and arms, firmly shaped by his polo neck top. Recalling their first meeting and her full scan of his body, the inevitable blush spread up her face, heating her skin.

'Do you actually live here?' Her hand flew to her mouth to stifle her gasp. What she'd been thinking had slipped out without censorship.

Jack's spontaneous laughter made her feel worse.

'I'm sorry—that was rude and…'

'No, you're right. It is very show-homey, isn't it? It is, however, practical for the life I lead.' He grinned. 'Except for the guys' pizza and sports watching nights.'

'Men only? That's sexist,' she teased, glad he wasn't offended.

'It would be if it wasn't the women who declared we should be segregated. They're welcome to join us any time. So are you.'

She hadn't realised she'd moved forward until he reached out and caught her hand, bringing her closer with little effort. His arms enfolded her, giving her little choice but to lay her hands on his chest. There was no doubting the strength and firmness of his muscles under the material. Or the steely intention in his green eyes and her own willingness to comply.

Her pulse stuttered as he lowered his head. He crushed her against him and she felt his heart pounding. Her own erratic beat throbbed at every pulse point. His mouth settled over hers, and she heard her own sigh of contentment.

His lips caressed and teased, claimed and possessed. Hers complied and tempted, provoked and soothed. And parted at his request. She heard his sharp intake of air, took one of her own and inhaled his unique aroma and the salty smell of the sea.

His tongue tangled with hers, stroked the soft flesh and aroused a longing for unknown pleasures that could be hers if she surrendered. Digging her fingernails into his shoulders, she raised up onto her toes and arched her back. The warning bells ringing in her head were ignored.

Suddenly his lips broke free, his forehead rested on hers and his chest heaved. She couldn't breathe, her knees were buckling, and his strong embrace was the only reason she hadn't sunk to the floor.

'Cassie—' rough as if he'd swallowed sandpaper '—I want you. More than I've ever wanted anyone before.'

He traced trembling fingers down her cheek, and she sucked in a shaky breath. Her touch on his jaw evoked a convulsion of his Adam's apple.

'I swore I wouldn't let kissing you get out of hand this morning. Not when I have to leave in an hour.'

She jerked back, her stomach clenching. He'd driven her to the brink of surrender, and now he wanted to stop? She tried to push him away but he stood solid, arms firm around her, dark green eyes locked with hers.

'Having you near makes me forget everything else. I wanted to spend time with you, meant to keep it friendly. The way you looked at me made it impossible not to kiss you. I swear I didn't mean to lose control.'

His eyes pleaded for her to understand. How could she not when she'd been as uninhibited as him?

'You weren't alone,' she replied, struggling to keep her voice from breaking.

'Oh, darling, I know that.' He pressed a quick kiss on her brow. 'When we make love, I want time to hold and caress you, make every moment pleasurable with no time restraints.'

His hands slid over her hips then stilled. She felt his shoulders lift as he inhaled, felt his warm breath on her skin as they fell.

He *wanted* her. No promises of undying devotion, or happy ever after. Yet not in the quick-romp-under-the-sheets way either. She wanted him, more than she'd ever known it was possible to desire a man. She so wished he'd carried her to his bedroom and taken her now, while she was consumed with heat and longing.

By tonight common sense and logic would have resurfaced, and they'd be meeting in Mel's home. She'd be governed by her rules of propriety. He'd respect her wishes and might have realised staying platonic was best for them both.

With deliberate care, she steadied her breathing and stepped back, hoping her eyes didn't betray her regret. His arms fell to his sides, letting her go, the remorse in his eyes blatant and unrepentant.

'Our drinks are getting cold.' Her rasping voice gave her away but he quirked a smile and reached for the mugs.

'Let's go into the lounge. You bring the biscuits?'

Cassie led the way, pummelling one of those big bold cushions before settling into it. Jack sat an arm's length away and held out her drink.

'Try a dunker, and tell me what you think.'

'Dunker?' She'd thought they were shortbread, now realised they were firmer, less crumbly. Her still-raised pulse blipped as he flashed his playful smile.

'Have to be dunked into a hot drink. Minimum five seconds. It's the rule.'

She did as he said and the biscuit melted in her mouth with a burst of unique flavour. A drink of the hot chocolate straight after had her smiling with delight.

'No way these came in a packet,' she stated. 'Have to be Mel's.'

His eyebrows shot up and he feigned an insulted expression. 'Really?'

'I can tell the diff... Oh.'

Jack loved her confusion, loved the gentle blush that coloured her skin, and fought the urge to reach out to touch and reassure.

'You made them? You cook?'

'Can you imagine any child who spent time with Mel not becoming proficient in the kitchen? Come back tonight and I'll prove it.'

His offer surprised him, as did the warm glow of anticipation in his stomach. Followed by a twinge of apprehension. Going to her would be safer, more prudent. His rules of no involvement were changing. He was changing and, inexplicably, he wasn't sorry.

She looked down at the biscuit and mug she held, her top lip covered the bottom lip then drew back. He dunked, bit, drank and waited.

She finally raised her head. 'Yes. What's your favourite colour?'

What the heck? He watched her lips curve and her eyes sparkle. And understood.

'Don't have one. Yours?'

'Blue or red for clothes, neutral and red for décor, silver for cars.'

'Yours is blue?'

'I got a good deal. Favourite male singer?'

By the time she left, they'd joked, laughed and learnt a lot of random facts about each other. As he watched her drive away, he was acutely aware that it was all surface detail. Deeper feelings and emotions had been avoided.

* * *

Cassie picked at the sleeves of the V-neck jumper she wore, uncertain if it was suitable for…for what? Seduction on a winter's evening? This was dinner at his house, and he'd be bringing her home after.

She stood up and paced, ran her hands down her thighs and huffed out a breath. Sucked in a deeper one at the sound of his ute.

It was dinner at his house. Nothing more, unless she wanted it to be. The sensible side of her brain advised caution. Her body and heart clamoured *yes, yes*. Yes. Regret for things not done could be more powerful than for bad decisions taken.

Common sense flew off with the wind when she met Jack at the corner of the house. She ran into his open arms, and was lifted onto his chest. Tangling her fingers into his hair, she gave herself up to the magic his lips wove as they covered her mouth in a tender kiss.

She pressed closer, melting inside, and exulted in the animal growl rising in his throat. It was no longer *if* but *when* they'd make love. Preferably sooner, as the time limit of their relationship was unknown.

The shudder he gave as he broke the kiss and set her on her feet excited her. She'd been the cause, a delicious fact to remember in the future.

'Temptress. Let's go before I…'

He left the rest of the sentence unsaid and she tingled at the images her imagination created.

'You'd better say hello to Sam before we lock up.'

His eyes darkened and he spoke slower and softer than normal, betraying stress she hadn't expected.

'You're leaving him here?'

'I'll be coming home.'

Please accept my decision without question.

For a moment, she thought he'd argue but he let it go with a curt nod.

Studying him as he drove, she became aware of a vague sense that something didn't gel. He wore the same clothes as this morning, but that wasn't it.

'Problem, Cassie? You look perplexed.' He flicked her a quick glance.

'I'm not sure.'

He was heart-stoppingly cowboy handsome—macho features, hypnotic green eyes and strong jaw. *His jaw?*

'Did you go home before picking me up?'

'No, why?'

That first day at Mel's he'd been stubbled. She wasn't sure about other occasions but he definitely hadn't been any time they'd kissed.

'You've shaved.'

'Glad you noticed. Check the glovebox.'

Would she ever be immune from his special chuckle? She checked, and pulled out a rechargeable shaver.

'I've used it more in the last two weeks than the previous few months. Wanna guess why or who for?'

Warmed by the inner glow his words evoked, she broke road rules and laid her hand on his thigh. Felt him tense and his muscle contract. For a fleeting moment, his hand covered hers then returned to the wheel.

Jack gritted his teeth, kept his mind on the road and tried not to think about the heat spreading from Cassie's hand. His chest felt tight and his pulse was faster than the ute's speedo. Legally, he ought to ask her to remove her hold but the words stuck in his throat. Wouldn't make a difference; its mark would last longer than the trip home.

He knew she was nervous. Her tension filled the cabin but this wasn't the time or place to tell her she had only committed to dinner with him. When they were face to face, he'd convince her that *when* they made love wasn't as important as her not having a skerrick of doubt it was right for them.

Her features appeared calm every time he glanced her way, though he never caught her looking at him. Her breathing was regular, and her fingers lay still on his leg. No way did he want to disturb her when he couldn't hold her in his arms.

He'd slowed down, activating the roller door as he turned into his driveway. Before the engine had fully died, he turned to her and cupped her face in his hands. Her skin was warm, her eyes were soft and inviting, and he was human flesh and blood.

'Cassie, the evening's yours. The table's set, and the meal's ready to be cooked. We can eat, talk and watch TV and I'll take you home whenever you say. I'm happy just to be with you, see you smile and hear you laugh.'

'Thank you, Jack.' Polite and mundane when he wanted breathless and passionate.

With every kilometre, Cassie's insecurities had grown and she'd become a ball of taut muscles and cold, churning insides. Unable to face him, she'd had no choice when he'd turned her head towards him. His hands were warm and protective on her skin, and the desire burning in his bright green eyes wrapped around her like a cocoon.

She heard her bland reply, and cringed inside as the flame dimmed.

Forget the meal. I want to taste you on my lips much more than I want to taste your cooking. Coward—say it out loud. Tell him.

'Hmm. Let's go inside.' He brushed a feather kiss on her mouth, backed away and opened his door. Jerked back, and burst out laughing.

'Taking off my seatbelt might help.'

In a heartbeat, her mind cleared. All reservations and

fears for the future were swamped by a wave of longing so powerful it stole the breath from her body. As long as he wanted her, she was his.

She laughed with him and slid from her seat to meet him as he came round the bonnet. He held her hand as he ushered her through the door and laundry into the hall. She stopped him there, rose up on her toes and kissed him.

'Take me to bed now, Jack. Please.'

Startled eyes stared into hers for the few seconds it took for her words to sink in. Then he swung her up into his arms and strode towards the stairs.

'Any time you want, my darling Cassie.'

A week later, Cassie stood in Mel's dining room staring at the empty plate in her hand, unsure what had happened to the sandwich she'd made for her lunch. She walked back to the kitchen, berating herself for the umpteenth time for daydreaming.

It was all due to Jack. A week ago, she'd returned from their walk on the beach, facing the enticing probability of becoming his lover. Since then they'd been together every evening, except Saturday when she'd been at home catching up with her friends and personal stuff.

The mere act of closing her eyes transported her in her mind to his bed or that wide, extra-long sofa where she'd experienced pleasure beyond anything she'd believed existed. He'd made love to her with a tenderness and devotion that quelled any remaining qualms the first time and deepened her adoration for him with unbelievable passion every time after.

She quivered at the memory of his eyes hot with desire, his gentle hands arousing her, and his kisses urging her higher until she touched the stars. She'd never be the same again, never be able to look at any other man without comparing him to Jack. This might mean she'd be alone for the rest of her life but she'd never regret a moment.

Her phone rang, ending her reverie. She ran to the family room where she'd left it, felt her stomach dip as she sighted Val's ID instead of Jack's.

'Hi, Cassie! Mel called to say Janette had a healthy little boy. Ten days early and both are well so they might go home in a couple of days. I'll organise a party to celebrate when Mel comes home and you're invited.'

Neither she nor Jack had told anyone of their affair. For her it was too special, too intimate to share, even with Narelle. Now, with the prospect of Mel being home soon, she wondered how much longer it would last.

They chatted for a while and Val promised to pop in for coffee on Friday before saying goodbye.

What did a party mean to them? Adults only or children included? At someone's home or an upmarket restaurant? Casual or formal dress?

Too many questions she had no answer for. She'd ask Jack tonight.

Her warm glow returned. She found her sandwich, poured a glass of water and went to the sunroom to daydream about this evening while she ate.

CHAPTER FIFTEEN

THE FOLLOWING MORNING, Cassie worked in the dining room accompanied by continuous rain on the roof. She walked Sam during a clear break before lunch, then continued.

Mid-afternoon, she took her coffee and the paperback she'd bought on impulse into the sunroom, her favourite in the house. This was a place for solitude or shared confidences, not like the other areas which resonated with echoes of family get-togethers and boisterous laughter.

Curling up in the comfy old chair by the window was like being back in the house she'd grown up in, warm and inviting. She could reminisce about happy times with only a gentle twinge of regret.

She wriggled back, sipped her stimulating drink and lost herself in the story of two brothers and a sister fighting the elements for the survival of their family's cattle ranch in southern Queensland.

Totally engrossed, it took a moment or two for it to register that the soothing classical music had stopped. She went to the lounge to check the sound system. No red light, no response to turning it on and off. A job for Jack.

Walking into the hall, she became aware of the silence. Where was the hum of the fridge and freezer from the kitchen? She clicked the nearest wall switch. Nothing, which probably meant a short power outage. Not surprising considering the torrential rain.

First thing: check the switchboard on the side wall of the house. Coat on and umbrella out, she walked out into the downpour, Sam at her heels. All the circuit breakers were in the on position, so she went down the driveway and looked both ways. She couldn't see any lights but that didn't help as few people would be home at this time.

She ran back inside, followed by a reluctant Sam who wanted to play in the rain. Because Mel's landline was out, she called the utility company on her mobile, and got bleeps. If their helpline had been inundated, it might mean the problem wasn't limited to the immediate area.

She'd just have to wait and trust it was easily fixed. To be on the safe side, she unplugged the rechargeable torch in the laundry, found the smaller one and spare batteries in the kitchen drawer, and took them to the sunroom. Settling into the chair, she finished her coffee and resumed reading.

It wasn't the same. Going over the same half page twice without taking any of it in was wasting time. She couldn't dismiss the world around her or force her concentration to block it out. She sat thinking, acutely aware of every vehicle that passed the house, the closed book on her lap.

Jack had mentioned his two customers for today lived on opposite sides of the city, and hopefully neither had been affected. Calling him would seem like she was panicking, while he was always cool and level-headed. It hadn't been long and the emergency crews would be stretched today.

She jumped and scrambled for her mobile when it rang, holding her breath. It whooshed out at the sight of his ID on her screen.

'Jack, I was thinking…'

'Are you home? Are you okay?' Rasped out as if *he* were alarmed.

'Yes, to both. We've lost power but…'

His sigh of relief was audible. 'Everyone has, darling. The whole damn state is out, including all traffic lights. Might not be back on until tomorrow. I'm stuck out north, and driving home's going to be a nightmare.'

'Oh.' Her first thoughts of no lights or heating became

instantly insignificant. 'Perhaps you should stay somewhere and come home tomorrow.'

'No way.' Ground out into her ear, its message warmed her better than any domestic heater.

'I have to tidy up this job then I'll come for you and Sam. Conserve your mobile battery, use it only if you have to, and pack an overnight bag. Take care, and wrap up warm, darling. I'll call you when I'm on my way.'

'You too, Jack.'

She switched off, and let her hand holding the phone fall into her lap. The whole state? Until tomorrow? Her mind struggled to grasp the enormity of the situation.

Everyone was reliant on constant electricity, and tended to get annoyed at any loss. They'd be unprepared and frustrated, especially as their mobiles ran out of battery, even more exasperated as they tried to get home in peak traffic.

Jack would be caught up in the turmoil. She didn't want to think of it, needed to keep busy. Her shivering might be from the cold creeping into the now unheated house or from worry about him. Or both. Collecting her notebook and pen from the family room, she went upstairs, taking one torch and her mobile with her.

When she began to pack her airline carry-on bag, she realised what she'd tacitly agreed to. She was going to spend the night with him. In his bed or one of the guestrooms? If he asked, was she ready to literally sleep with him? She selected her favourite pale green and lace nightie. In case she decided she was.

That task finished, she went from room to room, checking power points and switches, making a note of the appliances she unplugged or left as they were. The house was now dim and shadowy, eerie without the usual streetlights shining in.

She huddled in Bob's big armchair where Jack usually sat, wearing her warmest coat and wrapped in a quilt,

Sam curled up nearby. Holding her mobile in her hand, she willed Jack to call.

Even though he'd told her to save the battery, she accessed her photo file on her mobile. She needed a diversion to prevent herself from thinking about him out there in the chaos, and Mum's smiling face raised her spirits. She'd handled everything life had thrown her way with faith and patience. Cassie smiled as memories came flooding back with each picture.

Her ringtone was startlingly loud in the totally silent house, and Jack didn't give her a chance to speak.

'Cassie? I'm less than twenty minutes away. Are you ready?'

'Yes, but…'

'Tell me when I get there.'

Jack hung up, not giving her a chance to voice whatever doubts she might have conceived sitting alone in the dark. He'd been on edge since he'd accessed the power company's website and read their prediction.

The unit he was doing repairs at was his second furthest property from home and, for the first time ever, he regretted the distance. Normally he preferred distance between his working and his personal life.

He had made sure everything was safe before he'd left, knowing he'd have to return and have it ready for the young couple due to move in on the weekend. At least Cassie was safe at home, and had sounded confident and composed.

Keeping calm as he negotiated his way home was easier than he'd expected because most drivers understood the situation, were patient and applied good road rules. And once people got home, they'd stay there. Shops, restaurants and other venues were all closed, unless they had back-up generators.

Even so, the journey took twice as long, the rain didn't

stop, and the churning in his stomach morphed into fear. He wanted, needed to see Cassie, hold and kiss her. Feel her warm and safe in his embrace.

His anxiety eased as he pulled up in Mel's driveway and jumped from the ute. Sprinting round to the back door and up the steps, he was in time to have a bright beam shine in his eyes. He skidded to a halt, blood pumping, chest heaving and heart pounding.

Sam pushed past the dim figure holding the torch, and Jack brushed his ears as he strode forward. No words were needed. He drew Cassie as close as humanly possible and buried his head into her silken hair. She felt soft and warm, smelt sweet and enticing, and was where she belonged.

She clung to him and he murmured words of comfort, ignoring the torch pressing into his spine, macho pride surging as her trembling subsided.

'I'm here, darling. You're safe. Everything's okay.' He'd have been content to stay this way longer but the need to have her warm was his first priority.

Then she raised her head and everything was forgotten except the desire to kiss her now. He trailed light touches from her forehead to her mouth and settled, tightening his grip at the sound of her sigh. The rain, the storms, the blackout—nothing intruded into the magic world of her lips responding to his.

Woof. Sam broke the spell, letting them know he was there.

Cassie pulled away and shone the torch towards the dog.

'I think he wants to get warm. Me too.' In truth, she was burning inside from his kiss, couldn't wait for more.

'Well, let's go. Where's your bag?'

'Just inside. I've checked…'

'Tell me on the way.' He was already pushing open the

screen door. His being brusque shouldn't thrill her, yet it proved how anxious he'd been.

Sam followed as she guided their path to his ute then put the torch on the floor at her feet. It felt surreal, driving in the rain through suburban streets at night with the only illumination coming from their headlights. Occasionally there'd be another vehicle, keeping a moderate speed as they were.

No power meant leaving the ute in the driveway while they entered through the front door. Jack sent her to the lounge, and ran upstairs for blankets. She stayed there for a few minutes then went to find him, setting up on the canopy-protected patio. Wherever he was, she wanted to be.

'Stubborn creature.' His frown and gruff tone when she walked out was negated by his short, firm kiss.

Settling into a folding chair, she admired his expertise that had the barbecue fired up and the patio heater glowing within minutes. When Sam joined them, Jack brought out his bed.

'To him, a barbecue means food,' he said as he set it next to Cassie. 'And kids, and games, and stealing scraps from under chairs.'

The rain eased as the steak and sausages sizzled. Water boiled on a small camping stove, providing hot chocolate for her and coffee for him. Cassie sighed wistfully, thinking of her Outback fantasy. As quiet as she was, Jack heard, stopped turning the food and looked up.

'Cassie?'

She had to give a reason and, to her, fudging wasn't lying.

'I have this image in my head of camping far from any town where the lighting effects the sky. There's a big, bright moon and millions of stars, and no other people around.'

Except you.

He chuckled. And there it was, startlingly real in her mind.

'Sounds a bit solitary to me. Apart from having company, I like it. We don't get away as much as we used to. Work, marriage and kids take precedence, as they should.'

And she'd bet there'd been plenty of girls willing to go along.

Once they'd eaten, he refused help cleaning up and shooed her inside. She curled up in the corner of his long lounge, flicking through phrases in her mind. She'd never been forward with men, didn't know how to be.

She was still undecided when he knelt in front of her.

'It's twenty past eight. Feels much later because it's so dark. You want…?'

'To sleep in your arms, Jack.'

He didn't need to be told twice. He scooped her up, blanket and all, and was heading up the stairs before she'd taken a breath.

Sam's cold nose on Jack's bare shoulder made him shiver. He stirred, waved a hand and told Sam to go settle. He went with reluctance.

Waking a little more, Jack became aware of the soft form nestled into his, and his lips curved. Cassie was here. Their lovemaking had been incredible and she'd stayed. A gigantic positive in the blackout.

He caressed her silken skin, relishing the way she wriggled in response, and opened his eyes. His own sleeping beauty, and he could see her clearly in the light from the hall.

The power was back. He checked his alarm clock on the bedside cabinet. Nine twenty-seven. The repair crews had worked wonders, considering the extent of the failure.

He brushed a finger across Cassie's lips. She blinked, her smile reigniting the heat that had barely died down.

'Hi.' Sleep-husky and sexy as hell.

'Hi, yourself. Anyone ever tell you how sweet you look when you're asleep?'

'No.' She blinked again. 'I can see you.'

'Mmm, and it's only nine-thirty.'

She snuggled closer. 'Better go back to sleep then.'

His heart pounded, sending his pulse into overdrive. She didn't want to be taken home. Hot prickles shot through his body, bringing it fully awake.

He cupped the back of her neck and kissed her with all the passion flooding through him.

'I've got a better idea. We can sleep later.'

Her slow, sleepy-eyed sensual smile told him it would be much later.

Late Saturday evening, Jack drove her home after a day spent at his house. He unbuckled his seatbelt, and pulled Cassie into his arms. She returned his kiss with ardour, knowing they'd have to behave with more discretion from tomorrow when Mel arrived home.

She'd told no one they were lovers because she was convinced it was never meant to last. They hadn't discussed it, and there'd been no hint from his relatives so she assumed he hadn't told anyone either.

'Do you have any idea what you do to me?' His rough words and breathy tone were a pretty good indication. She could arouse him with a smile, a touch or a kiss. And that was all it could ever be.

He ran the back of his fingers across her cheek, kissed the tip of her nose when she trembled. 'When are we going to be together again?'

Tomorrow, but he meant in his bed.

'We can't while I'm here with Mel. I… I couldn't.'

'I'll wait, but not willingly. I want you, Cassie, more than anything else in my life.'

He kissed her again, showing her how much, before forcing himself away with a throaty growl. His farewell at the back door was gentle, reverent. Its effect just as shattering. Every day she cared a little more; every moment with him was going to make the parting more painful.

She had coffee and scones ready when Jack brought Mel home from the airport the next morning. She hoped she'd be forgiven for using a packet mix by serving them warm from the oven with fresh cream and raspberry jam.

Sam was panting with excitement, his tail whipping up a wind storm behind him when he saw Mel. After greeting him with enthusiasm, she hugged Cassie, kissed her cheek and handed her a small gift bag.

'Just a little something from Melbourne as a thank you.'

The *little something* was a sheer white scarf exquisitely decorated with blue roses and pale green petals.

'It's beautiful, Mel.' She blinked back the tears threatening to form and hugged her employer back. 'Thank you. I love it.'

'I'm the one who owes *you* gratitude. Because you were here, I got to hold my first great-grandchild when he was less than an hour old. He's gorgeous, so tiny and so perfect. Let's sit in the lounge. I've got lots of photos on my phone to show you.'

Cassie carried the tray with the drinks, and Jack took Mel's suitcases to her room before joining them. Mel sat in the middle, eagerly scrolling from photo to photo and giving a commentary of each one.

Cassie made appropriate noises and kept her gaze on the screen to hide the envy she knew would show in her eyes. She'd been shocked by the leaden grip that had formed in her stomach at the first sight of the baby. Had never been jealous of motherhood before.

'He's adorable. I'm happy for them. My best friend's

second baby is due in early December and they can't wait. I'm excited too.'

She spoke the truth, and she hadn't felt the slightest bit jealous of them having her godson or his soon-to-be sibling. Until now.

'Do you want some of those snaps printed out for Val's cocktail party tonight, Mel?' Jack asked, and Cassie's answer exploded in her head.

He was the difference. She'd never pictured any of the men she'd previously met as daddy figures, hadn't thought of Jack that way either. Until now. Her heart obviously wasn't in sync with her head.

'Yes, please, Jack. I'm looking forward to it. You're coming with us, aren't you, Cassie?'

A frantic refocus, and she was able to answer calmly. 'Yes, Val kindly invited me.'

'I'd be taking you anyway. I'll rest this afternoon, don't want to fall asleep during the fun.' She turned off her phone, put it on the table and lifted her cup.

'I'll get the scones.' Cassie stood and left the room, waiting until she reached the kitchen before huffing the breath from her lungs.

Jack watched her walk out, attuned to her mood, noting her quick pace and the set of her shoulders. Why had the photos upset her? One of the secrets in her past? Someday soon he'd take her somewhere quiet where they wouldn't be disturbed and find out. It was time he came clean with his own secret, time he changed his vision of the future.

CHAPTER SIXTEEN

MEL WAS RESTED and waiting in the lounge when Jack arrived to pick them up, intending to find time tonight to speak to Cassie alone. The phone call he'd received this afternoon meant he'd be catching an early flight in the morning.

The final meeting. Minor details sorted and the documents would be signed. Time away to sort out why and how his future plans had changed, and how much he wanted Cassie to be a part of them. Time away where her touch, her smile, her very essence couldn't addle his mind and confound his logic.

'You look fabulous, Mel.' He hugged her and kissed her cheek. 'We might even get to have that dance tonight.'

'Flatterer. You don't look too bad yourself. I haven't seen you in a suit for a while.'

'It's likely to become my day-to-day wear all too soon. I…'

Words failed him. His throat was dry as a sandstorm, and he'd swear his heart stopped before slamming into his rib cage then racing as if turbocharged.

Cassie as he'd never seen her, stealing his breath and fuelling his libido, stood in the doorway. He'd seen a 'little black dress' on so many women but it had never had such an effect, had never looked so incredible. It enhanced every sweet curve he knew intimately, and the deceptively simple set of matching silver jewellery suited her to perfection.

From her shining black hair, all the way down her enticing body and shapely legs, to black high-heeled shoes, she was deliciously, delightfully exquisite. A burning desire to whisk her away to his home and rekindle the heat that sparked with every kiss or touch flared in every cell in his body.

Moving towards her, he became aware of hesitation in her usually bright eyes, and in her stance. Others might not notice her slight body quiver, or the tight grip on her small black clutch bag. For him, every nuance was part of the make-up of a special woman who'd slipped through his defences, causing him to re-evaluate his life expectations.

He inhaled her fragrance of peach and sensual woman, took her hands in his and kissed each one, surprised by how cold they were. His pulse hitched as her eyes softened, and her lips parted.

'You are absolutely stunning, Cassie. Forget your nerves. Everyone's looking forward to seeing you.'

Mel backed him up. 'He's right, dear. You look beautiful and it's a small, adults-only family night. Relax and you'll have a good time. I'll get my wrap.'

She walked out and Jack took the opportunity to tip Cassie's chin up and press a quick kiss on her delectable mouth. Found himself fighting the urge to wrap his arms around her and deepen the kiss, have her melt into him. Felt empty as she held up her hand and stepped away.

'Do any of them know about us?' She spoke quietly, her head held high, and he flicked a glance towards the door.

'No.' He bent his head, not wanting Mel to hear, cupped Cassie's cheek and brushed his thumb over her lips. 'I'd like to keep it that way a little longer. Trust me, Cassie.'

Trust him? Cassie was drowning in a sea of contradictions. Starting with the man in front of her, so different to the everyday guy who'd charmed her with breakfast, walks on the beach and laughter.

She'd formed pictures in her mind of how he'd look in formal wear. They'd come nowhere near this debonair macho male, muscles defined in a dark tailored suit, white shirt with silver sheen and green tie matching his hypnotic eyes. Even his unruly brown hair fitted the image.

It seemed as if he couldn't keep his hands off her if they were alone, but hardly touched her in the presence of people he knew. He showered her with compliments every day and passionate erotic phrases as they made love but never spoke of the future, didn't want their relationship known to anyone. She'd heard his comment about the suit. It could only mean he was planning a corporate career.

Being with him made her feel so alive, as if the world was hers for the taking. When they were apart, the reality of the chasm between them slammed home. This cocktail party was a new scene altogether, a chance to show his family he was attracted to her. He'd decided not to take it.

Cassie's trepidation shot skyward as they entered the picture-perfect gardens of a designer-built, exclusive family home overlooking the city. Ultra-modern with the central area two storeys high, everything inside and out had been selected with taste, and no expense spared. It appeared that Val's favourite colours were muted greens and blues with bold splashes of red.

Entering the long reception room, complete with built-in bar and grand piano, overlooking a paved patio and swimming pool, was like walking onto the set of a movie. She'd been introduced to and hugged by so many people she'd lost count. *Small family night, huh.*

The trays of food set out on scattered tables were replenished frequently during the evening. Seats and armchairs had been placed in groups, allowing guests to sit and chat in private.

Confident as far as her appearance went, she was acutely conscious of the gulf between her standing in life and his family's natural acceptance of their wealth and position.

Yet they gave no indication at all that she was in any way not their social equal.

Four of Jack's female first and second cousins invited her to sit with them, their initial conversation about the upcoming finale of a top-rating reality series. Then somehow they moved on to opinions of other guests' apparel, never nasty, mostly complimentary. She listened without comment.

'Jack's looking particularly elegant tonight,' Silvia—or was it Silvana?—observed. 'Is that a new suit? He'll need it if he ends up being the CEO of a chain of shopping centres.'

'Shh, we're not supposed to know.' The girl next to her tapped her hand. 'It's very hush-hush until the initial deal's signed off.'

'I can't picture him behind a desk every day. I thought he'd dropped the idea.'

Cassie's stomach sank lower with every word. He'd talked with such enthusiasm about gardening and his repair and maintenance work—how he enjoyed being outside. Had it all been a sham?

She took a mouthful of her ice-cold drink, and glanced across the room to where he stood with Val, her husband and another couple. One second was all it needed to raise her pulse and stir an aching need in her core.

Tall, handsome and self-assured, seemingly without a care in the world, his personality dominated the group. Dominated the room. Dominated her life.

He turned his head towards her and she dropped hers, raising her glass to her lips. She concentrated on the woman beside her as she talked of her son's escapades.

A waitress offered them a choice from a tray of hors d'oeuvres and she selected blindly. For her it was tasteless. Another brought wine. She emptied her glass and asked for water.

'How's Mel's sorting going, Cassie? Becoming a great-grandmother and offloading unwanted stuff has really boosted her spirits. We're all grateful for your help.'

It was easy to return the compliment with a genuine smile. They were nice people; she just wasn't in their league.

She mixed with other groups, ensuring she was not in eyeline with Jack if he was included. Later Val turned up the music and her husband claimed Cassie for a dance as Jack whirled Mel around the floor as promised. After a second one with a cousin, she sat watching, claiming truthfully she had a slight headache whenever asked. Jack never offered.

They were the first to leave due to Mel feeling tired, and more hugs and kisses made for a drawn-out goodbye. Cassie climbed into the back of the cabin and slumped against the seat.

'Tired, Cassie? It's been a long day for both of you.'

She was weary, apprehensive and her nerves were frayed. Her head throbbed and her heart hurt, the pain deepening at the apparent genuine concern in his eyes as they met hers in the rear-vision mirror. He'd shown none while they'd been with his family.

'Yes, I think I'll go straight to bed.'

He frowned, glanced towards Mel and firmed his lips.

'Sleep's a good idea for you both. Did you enjoy the evening?' Why the hard edge to his voice?

'It was very memorable. You are lucky to have such a close family.'

'Something I don't take for granted, never will.'

'Me neither,' Mel chipped in. 'Every single one of them is precious to me.'

Jack swung out of the parking space, his main focus on the driving, his peripheral thoughts on Cassie, and his gut churning. He knew she was upset, and wasn't sure if it was because she'd heard something or because of his behaviour. He'd fought with himself all night about keeping distance from her.

There was no way he could have been close or danced with her without the attraction being obvious to everyone there. He cared—more than cared—but still had lingering doubts about his past, and his ability to sustain such an intense relationship without reverting to temper outbursts.

Cassie had hidden issues too. He'd sensed her reluctance to become involved from the day they'd met. Now she'd skittled his plan to talk to her alone after Mel went to bed. Not that he'd have told her much, couldn't until everything was signed and sealed.

'I received a call this afternoon. I'll be flying to Sydney first thing tomorrow, not sure for how long.'

His gaze flicked to Cassie in the mirror. She swung towards the window—not fast enough for him to miss the pain sweeping across her face and the quick intake of air.

Hell, he wished he had more time. This was the culmination of a plan dreamt of in his teens, and worked towards since. He knew exactly what he was doing, just wasn't certain about explaining the life changes to others.

'I have no idea when or if I'll have time to call.'

'We understand,' Mel said then closed her eyes and let her head fall back.

The smooth purr of the engine evoked the memory of driving home the first night he and Cassie made love. She'd been sweet and loving, shy, and yet sexier than any woman he'd ever known. His own beautiful enigma.

He glanced at the mirror again. *His. His Cassie.* The phrase echoed in his head for the rest of the drive.

At the house, he told Mel to wait, stepped out by Cassie's already opening door and strode round it to catch her arm as she slid out. She didn't look up until he growled in frustration, and bent his head to her ear.

'Trust me, Cassie. Please.'

She trembled and he pulled her tight against him, brushed his lips on her forehead then released her.

'Please.' Her wide sad eyes tore at his heart.

She nodded and slipped past him to go to Mel. He followed and helped his aunt down, hugging and kissing her. Once they were safe inside, he headed home for a restless night.

Mel persuaded Cassie to go home on Tuesday afternoon, claiming she hadn't seemed well the last two days. Hugging her before she left, Mel urged her to see a doctor if she didn't feel better in a day or so.

Cassie doubted she ever would. Jack hadn't phoned her, and his calls to Mel had been rushed, with excuses of long meetings and no mention of when he'd be home.

Keeping their involvement a secret from his aunt and family was proof it was purely physical on his part. That had been her initial desire too, only now she found she wanted more than he was able to give.

She drove slowly, her thoughts intruding into her concentration on the road, and she almost missed the amber light turning red.

She realised she'd been mentally preparing herself for an *I'm sorry but* speech since their very first kiss. His upbringing and innate honour ensured he'd do it in person, and she'd accept his excuses with as much grace as she could muster and let him walk away. The affair had been of her choosing and she'd never regret a moment in his arms.

Her mindset had subtly changed as her initial attraction deepened and blossomed into love. Now she…

She started as a horn sounded behind her. Giving a wave of apology, she drove off and determinedly blocked Jack out until she reached home. Leaving her luggage unpacked in her room, she went for a walk to think.

'Trust me,' he'd said. Trust him to let her down gently so he could devote his time to his new corporate venture? She loved him. Hearing him mouth platitudes and wish her the best was going to shatter her. Losing control and crying would be embarrassing for him and mortifying for her.

What if she ended it first? Let him walk away with no guilt? His pride might be dented a little but he'd bounce back. For him there was no emotional tie, only, as he'd said, an incredible physical experience.

She meandered aimlessly, her mind searching for and rehearsing the words that would tear her heart in two. Not wanting the stomach-churning anticipation to last any longer than necessary, and definitely not being brave enough for a personal confrontation, she texted him.

Please phone me as soon as possible.

It was not how Mum had taught her to behave, but if he was there his sandalwood aroma would stir her senses, his intoxicating green eyes would cloud her judgement. She'd stumble over her words, stop and start, and completely mess up. If he asked why in his deep smooth voice that tingled her spine, she'd have no answer that she was willing to give.

He rang sooner than she expected but then she'd never have been ready. She picked up her mobile, sat on her bed, stood up and sat again. Her finger trembled as she swiped to receive.

'Cassie, is there something wrong? I've got ten minutes. Can it wait until I get home?'

He sounded hassled, making her feel guilty. Then she hardened her heart. Being hassled was par for the course for an executive of an expanding business; he'd better get used to it.

'No. I can't see you then.'

'What? Are you going somewhere?'

'I don't want to see you again.'

The line went silent. She pictured his face, brow furrowed over darkening eyes, lips parted and hand rubbing his neck as he stretched from sitting too long. There was the sound of a long exhalation of breath.

'You picked a hell of a time to tell me. Do you want to explain?' Harsh and barely contained.

'I can't. It's the right course…the right thing for everyone.' *Please, please hang up before I break down.*

'And I don't get a say in the decision?'

'There's no other option. Please respect my decision. Goodbye, Jack.'

She hung up, put her mobile on silent and hid it in her wardrobe. Collapsing onto her bed, she could no longer hold back the tears. She loved him, and she'd set him free to find someone who'd fit the image of a perfect executive's wife. They'd have a fabulous house and adorable children, and she'd…she'd never stop loving him. She sobbed until her pillow was soaked and her throat raw.

Fourteen hundred kilometres away, in a high-rise office block on Sydney's North Shore, Jack stared at his phone in disbelief. She'd dumped him. Refused to explain.

Anger simmered below the amazement. But he'd be damned if he'd accept it without her telling him why to his face. They were incredible together, perfectly tuned to each other's desires. She was his, had been from the moment she'd asked him to take her to bed. Hell, he'd screwed up. He should have told her how he felt.

'Jack?'

He swung round, pocketing his phone. To heck with dotting every 'i'. They'd work late tonight, and tomorrow they'd sign off on the main points. The peripheral stuff could be agreed by email or at a future meeting.

He had business at home to deal with.

* * *

Jack's flight landed in Adelaide a few minutes early on Wednesday evening. By six-thirty he'd picked up his ute from long-term parking, and made a quick call to Mel, felt relieved when *she* mentioned Cassie first.

'Cassie hasn't been feeling well since Sunday so I sent her home yesterday. Hopefully a few days' rest is all she needs.'

'I'm sure she'll be fine. She's resilient. You take care, Mel. I'll see you tomorrow.'

He parked in the last street space available, half a block from Cassie's home. His throat felt dry and raw, his gut churned and his brain felt overloaded from trying to work out *why?* What if she wouldn't listen to him, wouldn't see him…? No, not to be contemplated.

He swiped his hand across his mouth, jumped from the ute and strode to her front door. There was no sound inside, no sign of life. He didn't have a plan B so he'd wait on the porch until someone came.

Sending up a silent prayer, he rang the doorbell. A door slammed, a male voice called out 'Coming', and something heavy thumped on the floor inside.

He sucked in air and waited. Whatever he'd expected, it wasn't the blond, well-built athlete who, hand on the half-open door, studied him with guarded interest.

'Yeah?'

Jack pulled the flyscreen door open. 'Is Cassie home?'

'Who wants to know?' Was his blunt demand a friend's protection for her or something more?

'Jack Randell.' He hoped it sounded more confident to the man confronting him than it felt, and automatically straightened his shoulders as he was subjected to the most intense scrutiny he could ever remember enduring. Determinedly keeping steady eye contact, he refused to buckle, wouldn't leave until he'd seen her.

With a slight nod of the head, the guardian of the door pushed it wide open and held out his hand.

'Brad Collins. *Cassie's friend and housemate.*' Jack heard the message, wasn't sure it meant he was confirming that was all they were or sending him a warning.

His surprise must have been evident as he returned the firm handshake because Brad's eyebrows rose for a second and he grinned.

'She didn't tell you she shared with two guys? Interesting. Come on in.'

Two guys? Jack was still trying to process that fact as he entered a spacious lounge area and nearly tripped over a large gym bag. His mishap amused Brad even more, though there was no malice in the short laugh.

A toot from outside turned both heads. Brad caught the flyscreen, preventing it from closing, and waved at the blue car pulling into the driveway. 'Be right there.' He walked across the lounge and disappeared into the hallway.

Jack heard a loud double knock on wood then, 'Cassie, you got a minute?'

Not waiting for an answer, Brad returned, swung his bag over his shoulder and picked up a set of keys from the coffee table. His eyes locked with Jack's and the tacit message was strong and unmistakable.

Hurt her anymore and you'll answer to me.

He nodded, still stunned that Cassie had omitted to mention that her housemates were male, yet thankful that she had such a champion, and that the man trusted him enough to leave them alone.

After a short pause, Brad gave a quick echoing gesture and left, closing both doors behind him. Leaving Jack alone to face the challenge of his life.

CHAPTER SEVENTEEN

JACK STOOD, EYES focused on that doorway, every muscle tensed, every cell in his body attuned to the soft footsteps coming nearer. He drew breath and held it, his mouth dried and his hands splayed on his thighs.

Suddenly she was there, framed in the doorway, his gorgeous, sunny, beloved Cassie... Except...?

He felt his heart rupture, painfully ripping apart, and he'd swear it would leave a permanent scar.

Her usually beautiful, sparkling brown eyes were dulled, rimmed with shadows, and her sweet, quirky lips gave no welcome. She looked tired and broken and he couldn't fathom what the hell he'd done to cause such anguish.

'Cassie?' Raspy. Fractured. Like he felt.

She gasped, startled by his presence. Her eyes grew larger, darker, a bright red flush appeared on her cheeks, emphasising her pallor, and her hands flew to clamp round her waist. Her head swung towards the dining area past the front door, as if seeking support.

'Brad left.'

No way would he be following her friend until he'd found out why she'd dumped him. On the damn phone. He tried to suppress the niggling irritation and had to admit defeat. It simmered in his gut, more so now he'd seen its effect on her.

She swallowed, drawing his eyes to the slight movement of her throat.

'I said I didn't want to see you.' He hadn't believed her then, didn't now. There was a yearning in her tone that tugged at his heartstrings, gave him the tiniest glimmer of hope.

'I heard. I want to know why. After what we shared, I deserve that much consideration.'

She held his gaze for so long he was on the point of marching over, taking her into his arms and kissing her. He was positive deep down to his soul that she cared for him, so why the charade? Even now he could see desire—for him—ignite, bringing a faint glow to her lacklustre eyes. One gentle kiss and he wouldn't be able to stop until she melted into him as she always did, alleviating his anguish.

Her sudden blink and quick headshake broke the spell. She took careful steps to an old round-armed chair and sank into its well-worn cushions. He frowned as she drew her legs up and wrapped her arms around her body, as if needing protection. From him?

Scouring his mind for a reason for her apprehension, he sat in the chair on the other side of the fireplace, giving her space. Clasping his hands between his legs and leaning forward, he waited.

The tip of her tongue appeared, and ran across her lip line, nearly tipping him over the edge. Did she have any idea how provocative her action was?

Staying calm was the best way of getting an answer so he dug deep for the self-discipline he'd been so proud of. He wasn't completely successful. Watching her breasts rise and fall in agitation had him fisting his hands, shifting in his seat and digging even deeper.

Cassie hugged her stomach tighter. Jack was here. In her home, asking—no, demanding—an explanation. His male ego must have brought him; limited truth would send him away.

'You. Your family. Your social position and lifestyle.

I don't fit.' Even to her ears it sounded lame. She flicked her hand, encompassing the room. 'I can't live that way.'

Her words made no impression. If anything, he seemed to find them irrelevant. He ground out an oath, one she'd never have expected him to use in any situation.

Her jaw dropped, her head jerked, and a gleam appeared in his green eyes. His sharp bark of laughter cut through the air and its irony had no magic to conjure up her Outback daydream.

'If I believed that for one second, Cassie Clarkson, I'd never have kissed you, no matter how attractive I found you.'

She fought back. 'Your whole family socialise with the elite of Adelaide—Australia, even. You're invited to gala events people like me would need a police check to attend as a waitress.'

Seeing his brow furrow and his eyes narrow, she realised she'd hit a nerve, and her stomach clenched. She wanted, desperately needed, to be alone. Before she broke down and admitted she ached to be in his arms, held close and cherished, his lips kissing away all thoughts of separation. Her head ached, her brain was a foggy mess and she spoke without thinking.

'You're so much more than you divulge to the world.'

He took a deep breath and squared his shoulders. She continued, not giving him a chance to butt in.

'And your new enterprise will take you a giant step further up the corporate ladder.'

His eyebrow shot upwards then his features froze. 'Enterprise? Whose gossip have you been listening to, Cassie?'

He pronounced the words with care, voice flat and devoid of its richness, his eyes as hard as granite. His scornful *huff* hung in the air as he continued. 'Of course, you hear things. I seem to remember you saying you don't retain them.'

'You're not denying it. You kept your corporate ambitions well hidden; now they'll make you super rich and...'

He cut in, restraint abandoned, anger rising. 'And you're not prepared to talk this out, try to find out where what we have might lead? That's not the impression I got from our time together.'

She stared in disbelief at the agitated stranger in front of her, so different to the disciplined Jack she knew. It was as if he were keeping a mere semblance of control by the barest of threads.

She wouldn't cave in. She mustn't. For his sake. Because she loved him more than life itself. Focusing on what was best for him, she ignored the throbbing in her head.

'That's not for me. It's better we split now. Move on with no regrets.'

He lunged to his feet, sending her shrinking into the cushions. A second later a surge of adrenaline sent her upright, facing him with her head held high, determined to negate any argument. Without conscious thought, she narrowed the gap between them a little.

'Move on?' He flung his arms out wide as if to encompass the world. The vein in his forehead pulsed, the corner of his mouth twitched, and his eyes pinned her with scorn. His resentment hung in the air, almost tangible. Surrounding her.

This was a side to him she'd never have imagined, so far removed from the restraint he'd always exercised. Because she'd made the decision, not him?

'That's your future plan? To discard everything we shared—the walks, the kisses?' His Adam's apple jerked in his throat. 'Making love?'

She began to quiver inside as his voice rose with every word, the last two rough and raspy as if painful to get out. Yet she didn't retreat, strangely felt no sense of danger.

He stepped towards her. 'You're suggesting we move on

to someone else, Cassie? Date *them*? Kiss *them*? Make love to *them*?' Each emphasis cut deep, as he intended.

Another step and he loomed over her, green eyes blazing. 'Tell me how the hell I'm supposed to do that when I'm so totally crazily in love with *you*.'

No. No, he couldn't be—mustn't be. Obviously didn't want to be. Her world spun into orbit, leaving her disorientated and gasping for air. Holding up her hand in denial, she backed away until her legs hit the armchair.

'No. No, Jack, I… Please. It…it's…'

Words failed her as the colour drained from Jack's face and his features contorted. His head shook from side to side in slow motion, his fingers clenched then splayed and his eyes glazed over as if he were seeing another time, another place.

'Don't…don't go. I'm sorry. Please. Don't go.' His faltering voice, and the ragged pain in his voice stunned her.

Go? Go where?

A violent shudder ran through him; he staggered back and sank into the chair he'd vacated minutes earlier. Bending forward, he dropped his head into his hands and groaned like a wounded animal.

Cassie's heart ripped at the tormented sound, and she sped across the room to kneel beside him and place her hand on his arm. Everything about him stilled.

A moment later, he was beside her on the carpet, his arms around her, cradling her head to his chest.

'Cassie, forgive me.' Rocking her gently, he repeated his plea, giving her no chance to answer. Last night she'd vowed to keep distance between them, learn to live without his touch. Her resolve hadn't lessened, but oh, it felt so good in his embrace.

His anger shattered by her reaction, Jack was left drained and racked with guilt. The one thing holding him together was having Cassie nestled to his heart, her soft fingers touching his arm and her unique aroma calming him with every intake of breath.

He'd broken his sworn oath and lost his temper, after nine years of rigid constraint. The thought of losing her, of not knowing why, had smashed the restraint on his emotions. Letting *his* fear out as a tirade had frightened *her*.

He steeled himself and stood, lifting her with him. Grateful that she didn't pull away, he cupped and raised her chin, relishing the softness of her skin. Her face was still pale and he didn't deserve the compassion in her tender eyes. He ran trembling fingers over her cheek, stroked her tempting lips with his thumb. Ached to crush her to his heart and never let go.

'I had—obviously still have—a temper. I believed I'd conquered it. Instead, as we've both found out, it was just lying dormant.'

Her eyes widened, so big, so beautiful, and he struggled to contain the riotous emotions raging through his mind and body. Taking her hand, he led her to a brightly patterned couch and, without letting go, sat and drew her down an arm's length away.

Huffed all the air from his lungs, refilled them then made eye contact with her and held it.

'There was a girl. We were both nineteen, both proud and obstinate. She flirted and I liked the attention I got from other women.'

The accusations they'd traded had been childish, worded for maximum insult. The making-up had always been hot and heavy, the best part of their relationship.

'It was my fault she died. I walked out of the room in the middle of a volatile slanging match, and slammed the bathroom door behind me. She stormed off and went skiing alone on a run for experts only. One of the instructors found her crumpled against a tree later in the day.'

Cassie reached out and laid her free hand over his, her sympathetic gesture deepening the guilt for his churlish treatment of her. He'd never revealed the full truth of that day to anyone; now he felt cold and drained.

'That day I swore I'd never lose my temper again. Haven't until now.'

He'd ignored Cassie's request for privacy, and shown her his baser side. Accepting her right not to see him would have been the honourable course of action, however distressing for him. Taking hold of both her hands, he raised them to his lips and kissed each one.

'I'm sorry, Cassie. I shouldn't have come.'

He forced himself to bring both of them to their feet, wanting to beg her to let him stay. To tell him the truth about why they couldn't be together.

Stepping away, he kept touch, sliding his fingers down her arms and over her hands to her fingertips, keeping the connection as long as possible.

'I'd better leave.'

She nodded, a forlorn figure, arms loose at her sides, shoulders slumped, and...hell, he'd swear he'd seen tears forming in her eyes before she dropped her gaze. Nausea struck and bile rose in his throat, rendering him speechless.

Shame drove him, almost running to the door to prevent himself from reaching for her. If he held her again he'd kiss her. If he kissed her again he might never stop.

Standing between the two doors, he flung his head back, jaw clenched, body taut. Daren't turn around for fear he'd crack.

'I love you, Cassie. Nothing in heaven or earth will change how I feel. I'll never stop loving you.'

Closing each door with exaggerated care, he strode down the driveway, fighting tears that threatened for the first time since Bob's funeral. He'd let them fall then, a tribute to the mentor whose love and guidance he would always cherish.

Keys in hand, he stopped by his ute, leant his forehead against the door and thumped the roof with his fist. He'd never felt so low, so impotent. Cassie had stolen his heart, now it lay crushed in his rib cage, its beating sluggish, purely corporeal. If she didn't want him, he might, with effort and tenacity, accept what she said. But he couldn't because her eyes, her touch and her body belied her words.

He couldn't think straight, and his hands were shaking. Leaving the ute where it was, he strode towards the main road that led to the local shopping centre. If the fresh air didn't clear his head, strong coffee would.

He recalled every word she'd said, didn't buy it. She'd spouted clichés and used his background and business venture to hide the truth. Damned if he could figure what that might be.

Cassie heard the doors shut and pictured Jack striding away, spine rigid, features impassive and brain racing. Her own kept repeating his departing vow.

'I love you, Cassie. Nothing in heaven or earth will change how I feel.'

Heart-stopping words declared with deep conviction from an abraded throat. Jack Randell, property owner, and soon to be even richer, loved her. Desirable, connected and eligible, with a choice of any of the beautiful, privileged women in Australian society, his heart had chosen her.

With a jolt, she realised she'd wandered into the kitchen, where the kettle sat ready on the bench. A light ironic laugh escaped her. A nice cup of tea, the age-old standby for any upset or trauma. It was going to take more than a caddy full of teabags to ease her pain tonight. Or for a long, long time.

Hot mug in hand, she returned to her room and surveyed the jumbled bedclothes, where she'd been lying, her mind in turmoil. Tomorrow she'd explain why she'd been upset to the guys and Narelle. They'd hug her, say they were sorry, and promise their support.

She closed her eyes. For now, she'd…

Tremble? She was shaking from head to foot, the liquid in her mug slopping to the floor. With effort, she managed to set it on her bedside table before collapsing onto the crumpled sheets and curling into a ball.

Her heart throbbed with every hot tear that ran down her cheek, and she made no attempt to check them. She sobbed until her tear ducts were dry, her throat was raw and croaky and her ribs hurt from her shuddering breaths. Until, despite her conviction she'd be awake all night, the trauma of her encounter with Jack and insomnia from the night before took their toll and she fell into dreamless sleep.

She woke with a pounding headache, a damp pillow under her cheek and shivering from lying on top of her quilt. Her ceiling light stung her eyes and she covered them with her hands as she rolled off the bed.

Drinking the cold tea eased her dry throat. Her alarm clock read eleven forty-six, meaning she'd slept for over three hours. Her skin was cold and clammy, breathing was painful, and a bleak future loomed ahead. She swallowed two analgesic tablets, grabbed her towel from the rail on her door and headed for the bathroom.

The hot water was refreshing and helped clear the fog in her brain, leaving a troubling vision. Jack, his hands alternating between clenching and splaying, his chest heaving with agitation, and his eyes hauntingly shell-shocked.

Those were the fascinating green eyes that had shone with laughter, playfully enticed her out of her comfort zone and flared with passion as he'd made love to her. Now, in her mind's view, pain and disbelief dominated in their depths.

She'd convinced herself she'd only be a pleasant interlude in his life. Had she been devastatingly wrong?

Wrapped in her winter dressing gown, she accessed the photo she'd taken at the beach for the umpteenth time since that day. She loved his macho stance and, as she'd believed, his indulgent expression. This time, as she lightly traced his smiling image with her fingertip, she really looked with an open mind and heart.

A lump formed in her throat and tears fell unchecked as she saw the truth she'd never dared to dream. His eyes glowed with adoration. And they were focused directly at her.

He'd said he loved her. Jack didn't lie. Waves of longing rippled through her, tingles of warmth drove the chill from her skin, and her heart soared with hope.

Oh, Jack, I've been so stupid. You really do care for me and I rejected you without a valid explanation because of my childish fears. Will you...can you forgive me?

CHAPTER EIGHTEEN

JACK POUNDED ALONG the beach, his feet kicking up a spray as the tide's ripples washed around his runners. A full day after fleeing from Cassie's home, the pain was still unbearable. He avoided looking seawards, knowing the sun was beginning to sink behind the clouds, sending a wash of colours across the horizon. A picturesque backdrop that Cassie would adore. She'd smile, her eyes would light up, and he'd be unable to resist kissing her.

Hell, he'd found it nigh on impossible to resist her from the moment she'd wriggled out from under his aunt's coffee table. He'd been a fool not to realise it was more than physical attraction when a mere brush of flesh could jolt him like a high-voltage terminal.

He loved her and refused to believe the passion she'd shown in his bed was anything else than the ardour that had consumed him. Her responses to his kisses and caresses had made him feel more of a man than he ever had in his life.

Would she still be working for Mel? If so, maybe his aunt's sympathetic nature would draw her into revealing why she'd suddenly rejected him. Maybe...

He faced the truth. Whatever had spooked Cassie was very real to her. The dogged tenacity people labelled him with, tempered with patience, was his best chance of proving his love. When, *please fate make it soon*, she accepted they were meant for each other, he'd be waiting.

Two long, hard runs on sand in twenty-one hours were taking their toll as he turned off the beach. Last night he'd changed into a tracksuit and runners in the garage as soon as he'd arrived home at about ten. He'd turned his concentration inward, blocking out everything but the swinging of his arms, the pounding of his legs and the *thump-squish* of his runners on wet sand.

Tonight, as he powered around the corner, sharp tingles skittled down his spine. He glanced left and right. Nothing. Trying to shake off the feeling, he slowed for the last few metres and activated his roller door.

On the way through the laundry, he dropped his T-shirt and tracksuit top onto the washing machine. Whether Cassie ever knew or not, she'd subtly changed him. He'd always keep his home neat and tidy; now it was also beginning to look lived in.

He went to the kitchen sink and swallowed two tall glasses of water. Shower first, nuke something from the freezer later.

His doorbell rang as he took the first stair, and his first instinct was to ignore it. Not a good idea if it was one of his cousins, come to check why he'd been abrupt on the phone to Val this afternoon.

Bracing for a cheer-up encounter, he opened the door. His breath whooshed from his lungs, his heart somersaulted, then took off like a speedboat, and he knew, absolutely knew for certain, he was wearing the soppiest smile ever.

Cassie, gorgeous, light of his life and possessor of his heart, stood on his doorstep, hands tightly gripping her handbag, white teeth biting the corner of her mouth and an anxious, pensive look in her beautiful walnut-brown eyes, big as saucers.

He couldn't fathom why she'd come, thanked every star in the sky that she had, and stood aside to let her in. It took effort not to touch her to ensure it wasn't a dream. Couldn't be. If it were, she'd be wrapped tight to his body, her eyes would be sparkling and her musical laugh would be zinging through him.

* * *

Cassie's feet were reluctant to obey his tacit invitation. Her brain commanded she stay and drink in the sight of Jack, dressed in track pants, sweat glistening from his naked muscled torso, until she was satiated.

She was breathless. His chest expanded easily. She was trembling. He appeared to be solid as a rock. Her frayed nerves were stretched to breaking point, and he was smiling as if…as if she were bringing his complete Christmas wish list.

'Cassie?' He only had to say her name and she was molten to the core. She'd spent the day imagining his every possible reaction to her appearance after her adamant statements last night. Most had been cordial at best; she'd even prepared for total rejection. Not once had she visualised his sharp intake of air, the fire flash in his green eyes, and his brilliant, welcoming smile.

Hugging her bag to her chest, she sidled past him, catching the tang of sandalwood, male sweat, and him. The slightest touch and she'd throw herself into his arms.

Every cell in her body was tuned to him as he followed at a socially respectable distance along the hall. The lounge looked as neat as always, except…the alpine painting was missing from the wall. Now she understood its significance.

Heart palpitating, she pivoted to face him, and found half a room distance between them. Framed in the doorway, he gazed at her as if he couldn't quite believe she was here.

'Cassie, I…' He cleared his throat and gestured at himself. 'I've been running. Give me five minutes to shower and change.'

She nodded, not sure where her voice had gone. She regretted his intention to cover up his magnificently honed torso, though it would definitely prove a distraction from serious discussion.

'Take a seat or you can make coffee if you like.' He gave

her a wry smile. 'Just don't disappear. I love you, Cassie Clarkson.'

His leaving coincided with her legs buckling at the repetition of his earlier declaration. Collapsing onto the sofa, she hugged herself, torn between joy and trepidation. She loved him, would forgive anything in his past. With eyes shut, she prayed he felt the same and could overlook the insecurities that had governed her actions.

She discarded her coat, paced the lounge while the coffee brewed, and rearranged the blue cushions. Put the steaming mugs on the coffee table and sat. Her stomach rumbled; she hadn't eaten since lunch, couldn't have kept anything, however light, down. Footsteps on the stairs shot her to her feet, spinning round.

Jack walked in and her world shrank to the space between them. He was the epitome of a Hollywood hero, dressed in navy chinos and a matching polo neck jumper. Everything she wanted, and more, from his damp dark hair to his bare toes.

Their eyes locked, and the desire his radiated sent hot tingles dancing over her skin. His lips curled in a captivating smile, and the yearning to have him close, body-hugging close, overrode reason as she willed him nearer.

Her heart blipped when he gestured to the settee and sat, leaving space between them. His slow caress of her cheek with tender fingertips sent her pulse soaring like a rocket launch.

'If I kiss you, I can't promise I'll be able to stop.' Rough, raw with emotion. 'I can't…don't want to fight the aching need to have you here with me every day, to hold you in my arms while I sleep, and wake to your sweet smile every morning.'

Butterflies beat frantically in her stomach, and her brain turned into liquid mush. He was echoing her greatest wish.

She was aware of her heart racing and her lips curling in an effort to emulate his smile.

His thumb brushed over her mouth, her lips parted and the tip of her tongue slipped out to taste his skin. He shuddered, sending a wave of satisfaction through her, followed by a warning signal in her head.

Reason clamoured for her to tell him now, hold nothing back before he kissed her. Before they both lost control. She took his hand in both of hers and lowered them to the cushion. He immediately covered them with his other.

Looking into his buffalo grass-green eyes that had captured her heart at first sight, she prayed he saw the love in hers. She squared her shoulders, took a quivering breath, and jumped right in.

'I'm illegitimate. Mum was my birth mother's sister.'

For Jack this moment instantly become one of his treasured memories—the moment she gave him her complete and utter trust, even if she didn't realise. It was an honour he would never endanger as long as he lived.

The blush on her cheeks accentuated the pallor of her skin. Her beautiful walnut-brown eyes held an enthralling mixture of uncertainty and hope. For him, her silent plea was as clear as if she'd spoken out loud.

Please believe in me.

His heart twisted. She'd been suffering the same pangs of despair he had. Lifting their joined hands, he closed the offending gap then laid them on his thigh.

He'd been prepared to beg, on his knees if he had to; he'd been prepared to accept friendship if that was all she'd offered. Then he'd have determined to resolve her perceived objection to their being together.

'I don't know who my father is and I have no idea if my birth mother is dead or alive. Her last short phone call was from Los Angeles fifteen years ago.'

Her husky whisper triggered the release of tension in

his muscles, replaced by elation that she was keeping nothing back. Drawing her close, he cradled her head on his shoulder, and grunted with satisfaction as she slid her arms around him. Bending his head to catch every word, he leant his cheek against her hair, relishing its silkiness on his skin.

'Tell me.' He kept his voice gentle and persuasive, and made soothing motions with his hands.

'She left me with her sister when I was two days old, and I only have a vague recollection of a lady who visited once or twice when I was young. My only feeling towards her is eternal gratitude that she gave me to Mum to raise.'

She paused, lost in a world Jack couldn't even imagine, then resumed, her voice more assured, strengthened with love.

'Mum was, and always will be, my mother, and I'll never regret a moment of my life—except for losing her too soon. All my memories are happy and of being loved unconditionally.'

A deep tremor racked her body, and his arms tightened. It hurt having no way to help except to be there. In future, he'd encourage her to tell him more about this special lady who had instilled so many redeeming qualities in the woman he loved.

She raised her head, her resolute expression telling him she had more to say. It came out in a rush.

'My parentage will impact on your family. I'm public school educated, don't know how to make small talk to strangers at parties or dress for elaborate occasions. I'll never have the social graces Mel, Val and the others are ingrained with; it can't be learnt. I'd be an embarrassment to you and your family. You should…'

Jack's jaw had dropped as she spoke, adrenaline stormed through him and he grabbed her by the shoulders, holding her at arm's length.

'You sent me away, were prepared never to see me again

because of a misguided belief you aren't good enough for us? Dammit, Cassie, that's crazy.'

She quivered under his fingers, her lips trembled and she blinked to hold back tears. And he, normally so macho and undaunted by danger, broke.

'Oh, Cassie, my love.'

He hauled her close and kissed her with all the pent-up hunger from four days and nights of not being able or allowed the pleasure. His hands stroked and caressed her back, her hips, her shoulders—anywhere they could reach. He couldn't get enough of her softness and warmth under his palms.

Her hands skimmed over his shoulders where they'd landed, over his collar and onto his skin, sending prickles of fire speeding down his spine. Her fingers teased into his hair, anchoring his head right where he wanted to stay. Her lips parted, his parted, and he…pulled away, chest heaving and every cell screaming rebellion.

He framed her beautiful stunned face, and dropped a brief kiss on the tip of her nose. Shaking his head from side to side, he searched for the right words, and felt them rasp his throat as he tried to explain why all she'd said made no difference to their future together.

Their future together.

It sounded good. It felt right.

'My precious, adorable Cassie. You captured my heart from the second I saw you, though I wasn't aware of how powerful an emotion you'd evoked. Now I love you even more for your courage, and your trust in me.'

Her eyes softened and she lifted her hands that had fallen to her sides and laid them, fingers splayed, on his chest, one over his rapidly beating heart.

'Temptress.' He groaned with need, had to resist long enough to make his final confession.

'When I carry you up those stairs, I want nothing hidden between us, my darling. Let me explain why I am who I am, then there'll be no more secrets.'

Cassie gazed into earnest green eyes shining with love and saw her future, bright and full of joy. She raised one of his hands from her cheek, twisted her head and kissed his palm. The tremors that racked his body echoed in hers.

'I feel like I've been released from shackles that bound me since Tara died. I'd rebelled against my parents and the career they chose for me. I'm ashamed of some of the things I did, the drinking and smoking. And there were always girls willing to date me and my friends because we had money and fast cars.

'Mel's home was my refuge, and Bob my confidant who kept me grounded with calm advice and no judgement. Away from them, it was as if I had no safety catch on my temper, and I would just let fly.'

He fell silent, and the bleak expression in his eyes confirmed he was remembering that fateful day. Cassie felt his heart hammering, and loved him even more for his vulnerable side, that he'd allowed her to see it. She hugged him harder, letting him know she understood.

'Tara was as selfish and hot-headed as me. Our fights grew more bitter and accusing. I was a jerk, she was a spoilt brat. There was no way we should have been together, and I'd intended to break up before the trip but she'd been looking forward to it.'

He stopped talking, shook his head as if to clear it then suddenly pushed upright and set her onto her feet.

'Let's go for a walk. Find some of that fresh brisk air you like so much.'

'Yes, please.' They'd share more details another day. Revealing long-held, deep-set feelings was emotionally draining. Cool, crisp spring air would be welcome and refreshing.

He helped her into her coat, picked up his keys and ushered her into the hall. Watching him shrug into his jacket, she felt a bubble of amusement rise in her throat and couldn't stop it from escaping.

'What?'

His endearing puzzled expression gave her a heart-warming vision of the future with a challenging child. Hopefully two or three. Or more. Pointing down, she managed to choke out a few words amid her glee.

'Intending to paddle?'

He stared at his bare feet as if he wasn't sure where his shoes and socks were, grinned and, in one smooth movement, swept her up into a long, deep, pulse-shattering kiss. She swayed when he let her go, bracing her hand on the wall for support.

'See what you do to me. Don't move.'

He took the stairs two at a time and came down almost as fast wearing sneakers but no socks. He stole a quick kiss, linked their fingers and opened the front door.

Stepping down to ground level, he turned to face her, features sombre, eyes twinkling in the porch light. He leaned in, close enough to kiss her, yet didn't. He was teasing. She swayed forward, frowned when he moved his head away.

'There seems to be a disparity in this relationship, Cassie Clarkson.' He tried to sound stern; she heard the underlying joy. 'I've declared my love for you a number of times. Don't recall hearing you say it.'

'Of course I have. I…' She hadn't. She'd thought the words so many times, told him in her mind and in her dreams. Been so stunned and then elated when he'd voiced them, she hadn't replied.

'I love you, Jack Randell. I'll love you with all my heart and soul for as long as I live.'

Flinging her arms around his neck, she pressed her lips

to his for as long as her breath allowed. Laughed with delight as he lifted her feet from the step.

'Hey, I want longer than that.' He swung her around and onto the ground. 'Until the next big bang won't be enough.'

Cassie wriggled in Jack's arms, smelt scented air and gum trees, and felt a light breeze. There was also a crackling sound she couldn't place, especially with a cover over her eyes. It was three days since their confessions and declarations of love, and they'd spent every possible moment together. Family and friends now knew they were together, and she'd been lovingly welcomed by everyone.

Yesterday Jack had been secretive, making phone calls in other rooms and kissing her senseless when she queried his motives. He'd kept her up late last night, and woken her early for a run on the beach. They'd hardly stopped for breath all morning then he'd told her they were going for a drive in the afternoon.

Soon after they'd stopped at Port Pirie for a snack, she'd fallen asleep wearing the eyeshade he'd thoughtfully brought along. The sun through the window and the soporific low drone of the engine had ensured she didn't wake.

Jack had flicked occasional glances across the cabin, and couldn't help smiling every time. His Cassie, his angel, features soft in repose. He loved her, his family loved her, and incredibly she loved him.

Pity she'd missed the beauty of the Flinders Ranges as they'd driven along the road parallel to the iconic hills with their unique bluish tinges. She'd see them on the return journey. This was a special trip to make her dream come true, and the cases and Esky he'd secretly packed were in the boot.

He'd detoured onto a track he'd travelled countless times, finally parking near a stream edged by native trees. He left the engine running, hoping it would prevent Cassie from waking too soon. The camp was set up, and the last rays of sun had disappeared before he gently roused her and lifted her from the now silent ute.

Placing her gently onto her feet, he drew her close and told her to keep her eyes closed as he covered her lips with his in a long, loving kiss. As he raised his head, he removed the eyeshade and stepped away.

'For you, my love.'

Her reaction was all he'd hoped for and more. Her hands clasped together at her throat, her lips parted in a joyful smile and her eyes grew wide, sparking with delight. His pulse soared and his heart pulsated with elation.

Cassie looked up at the bright yellow moon surrounded by a million stars in a satin-black sky. To the left where a light brown tent, big enough for two, had been set up. To the right where a shallow stream flowed between shrubs and eucalyptus trees. And to the front where two folding chairs stood beside a portable barbecue and a crackling wood fire surrounded by rocks.

'This is…' She was lost for words. 'Oh, Jack.' She threw herself into his arms and kissed him passionately. 'It's just like the image I see when you laugh, only better. It's magical.'

'I love you, Cassie. Love you and need you more than I can ever express in words.' His kiss was tender, reverent. 'Marry me, my darling. Have babies with me. Live, love and grow old with me.'

Joy exploded inside her like a New Year's Eve firework show.

'Yes. There's nothing I want more.'

With a whoop of delight, he swung her up and round then cradled her into his arms, tight against his chest. Wrapping her arms around his neck, she pressed hot kisses on his neck and chin.

'Nothing, my darling? I think barbecue dinner can wait. First I'll show you the pleasures of sleeping in the Outback.'

She laughed softly as he strode towards the tent, knowing that sleeping was the last activity they'd be sharing tonight.

* * * * *

If you enjoyed this story, don't miss
A BRIDE FOR THE BROODING BOSS
by Bella Bucannon, part of the 9 TO 5 series.
Available now!

If you can't wait to read about another
gorgeous and wealthy hero,
then make sure to treat yourself to
HER NEW YORK BILLIONAIRE by Andrea Bolter.

"Can you raise your legs? One at a time?"

She did that, feeling satin around them. The wedding dress. From the wedding that hadn't been. Because she'd run away from it...

"Okay, very carefully, I want you to try to move your head—can you do that?"

She could do that, too.

"Any pain with that? Any tingling in your shoulders, arms or legs?"

"No."

"Nothing? No pain—shooting or otherwise?" the man asked.

"No," she said softly as she went on assessing his face and finding more and more to it that made him seem like the boy she'd known. And loved.

And learned to wish she hadn't...

Those full lips.

Those eyebrows that were a little thick and as dark a brown as his hair.

Then her neck was free and he raised his eyes to her face.

And that was when she knew for sure.

No one except the Madison brothers and their sister, Kinsey, had eyes like that. Cobalt blue that was bluer than blue.

"Oh, my God!" she said in alarm.

"What? Pain? Numbness?" he asked with more urgency.

"You're Conor Madison," she accused scornfully.

He relaxed and nodded. "Hi, Maicy," he said calmly.

"I get it—I've died and gone to hell," she muttered.

* * *

Camden Family Secrets:
Finding family and love in Colorado!

AWOL BRIDE

BY
VICTORIA PADE

MILLS &
BOON

First Published in Great Britain 2017
By Mills & Boon, an imprint of HarperCollins*Publishers*
1 London Bridge Street, London, SE1 9GF

© 2017 Victoria Pade

ISBN: 978-0-263-92322-3

23-0817

Our policy is to use papers that are natural, renewable and recyclable products and made from wood grown in sustainable forests. The logging and manufacturing processes conform to the legal environmental regulations of the country of origin.

Printed and bound in Spain
by CPI, Barcelona

Victoria Pade is a *USA TODAY* bestselling author of numerous romance novels. She has two beautiful and talented daughters—Cori and Erin—and is a native of Colorado, where she lives and writes. A devoted chocolate lover, she's in search of the perfect chocolate-chip-cookie recipe.

For information about her latest and upcoming releases, visit Victoria Pade on Facebook—she would love to hear from you.

Chapter One

"This is not turning into a good time."

There was no one else in the rented SUV to hear Conor Madison's observation as he drove through a Montana snowstorm that was getting worse by the minute.

When his plane had landed in Billings on that mid-January Sunday, snow had been falling. As promised, he'd called his sister Kinsey to tell her he'd arrived safely. But when he did, he'd discovered that Kinsey wasn't in their small hometown of Northbridge, where she and Conor were slated to meet. Instead, she was snowed in inside her Denver home.

And by now, the snow was in his path, piling up fast. Conor could barely see two feet in front of him on this mountain road.

And on top of that, he was worried about his brother and thinking this whole idea might have been a mistake.

When he'd left the veterans' hospital in Maryland, his younger brother Declan's condition had been stable. In fact, Declan—who had been severely wounded in Afghanistan—had been doing so well he'd pushed Conor to make this trip. But when Conor had talked to Declan from the Billings airport, Declan hadn't sounded very well, though he'd insisted that Conor stay.

But an hour and a half into the drive, when he'd called to check in with Declan again, Declan had been even more sluggish and lethargic, and had informed Conor that he'd spiked a fever—which could herald a dangerous complication that Conor wouldn't be there to monitor.

As a doctor Conor couldn't treat family, but he could follow what was being done closely. Monitoring his brother's condition was the reason he was on leave from his own duties from the navy. Now he wasn't where he felt he should be—by his brother's side. If he hadn't learned that all flights in and out had been canceled due to the storm, he might have headed back.

But there was no going back either to Billings or to Maryland, so all Conor could do was get somewhere safe—and get back to worrying about his brother once he arrived.

He'd grown up around here so he recognized where he was—about fifteen miles outside of Northbridge. But visibility was getting worse by the minute, and he was having more and more trouble plowing through the deepest of the drifts. There was no way he was going to make those last fifteen miles.

Luckily he wasn't far from a cabin owned by the family of an old friend. When he noticed his patchy cell service was working for the moment, he'd called

Rickie Dale to find out if the cabin was still standing and if he could use it.

Thankfully, the answer to both of those questions had been yes.

Just before he reached the turnoff, he saw the first car he'd seen in the last hour—nose-first in a ditch.

The sedan's horn was blaring and the driver's side door was ajar so the dome light was on. In the dim glow he could see that the driver was still in the car, slumped over the steering wheel.

As a doctor, his duty was clear. He came to a slippery stop and ran against the wind to the other vehicle.

The driver was a woman. In a sleeveless wedding dress without so much as a coat on over it. There was an abundance of blood from a head wound, likely the result of hitting the windshield since—for some unknown reason—the airbag hadn't activated.

She didn't react to him opening her door. He couldn't even tell if she was breathing. So the first thing he did was check for a pulse, grateful to note that it was strong. She might be unconscious, but she was alive.

"Miss!" he shouted to be heard over the howling wind. "Can you hear me?"

She didn't so much as moan.

But Conor was a doctor of emergency and trauma medicine and a commander in the United States Navy, trained to work in the field. He knew what to do.

He took off his jacket and wrapped it firmly around her neck to stabilize it. Then, keeping her head and neck aligned, he eased her back against the seat.

She had a massive amount of hair and much of it had fallen forward into her face, heavily coated in blood.

Still, something about her struck him as familiar. But nothing concrete clicked for him, with his focus on her condition. Right now, all that mattered was getting her out of this cold.

He dashed back to his SUV and opened the passenger door, lowering that seat so it was as flat as it would go. Then he ran back to the sedan. With special care to keep her head and neck supported, he eased her from behind the steering wheel into his arms, took her to the SUV and laid her on the passenger seat.

Conor reached across her to crank up the heat, closed that door, ran back to the sedan to turn it off, lock it and pocket the keys before he rushed back behind the wheel of his own vehicle and put it into gear again.

It was a little less than a mile to the cabin. But already the dirt drive was covered in snow and drifts. The only thing Conor could do was go slow enough to feel that his tires were in the wheel ruts, letting them guide him. And hoping like hell that he'd opted for the right road and was headed toward shelter.

Just as he was beginning to doubt it, he caught sight of the small log cabin in the clearing of trees.

Breathing a sigh of relief, he drove the SUV up to the cabin's front porch and stopped. Leaving the engine—and the heat—running for his passenger, he made his way onto the porch and found the key in Rickie's hiding spot. He unlocked the door and entered with a mental thank-you to whoever had used the cabin last and left wood and tinder in the fireplace, ready to be lit.

If only he could find matches.

Matches. Matches. Matches...

After a moment of searching, he finally found a

box of stick matches near a bucket of wood to the side of the hearth.

With a fire going, he returned to the SUV and carefully removed his passenger.

Inside with her, he laid her on the floor in front of the fire, letting the hard wooden surface act as the backboard he would have used had he had one.

She was breathing without any problems—that was good.

As he covered her with a blanket from the worn sofa nearby, the woman groaned.

"Good girl," he praised. "Come on, come to…"

But when she didn't stir again, he ran outside to turn off the SUV and then returned to survey the territory.

With the exception of shelter, the cabin didn't likely offer much in terms of medical tools or supplies. Rickie had assured him that there was plenty of bottled water so Conor went in search of that, a cloth of some sort to clean the wound as best he could and a first-aid kit.

Returning to his patient—who was moaning again—he saw that bleeding from her head wound was increasing as she warmed up.

Working fast, he dampened the cloth with the bottled water and cleaned the wound.

"Can you wake up for me?" he urged. "Come on, open your eyes…"

More moaning but her eyes remained closed.

The wound was a clean cut free of debris. It could have used a couple of stitches but he had to settle for three butterfly bandages covered with a compression wrap.

Then he wet the cloth again to clean her face and

get the hair away from it. The more he saw of her, the more he was struck by that sense of familiarity.

Her hair was thick and lush and the color of a new penny—he hadn't registered that before but now he did.

Red hair.

Maicy had had hair like that…

Just as that thought struck him, the woman opened her emerald green eyes.

Conor reared back and froze.

It couldn't be.

Could it?

No, it couldn't be. It just wasn't possible for the woman coming to on the floor in front of him to be the girl he'd left behind.

And yet the more closely he looked at her, the more he knew it was…

Everything was hazy. Maicy's mind, her senses, were slowly fading in from darkness. She could hear a voice but she couldn't quite make out words. And she felt too heavy to move.

Her head hurt. And she was lying on something hard.

Why would that be?

She remembered that she'd been in her car…

And it had been cold. So cold.

And then, too, there was that voice. A man.

She faded in a little more and blinked open her eyes. Her vision was blurry, and the light seemed dim. There *was* a man there…

"Good girl! Come on, wake up."

This time she heard the words.

But she still couldn't quite focus her eyes. And she

was so disoriented that for a minute the sound of the man's voice actually made her think of Conor Madison. As if *that* made any sense...

"Can you tell me your name?" the man asked.

Definitely not Conor Madison, then—he would know her.

"Maicy," she managed.

"How about your last name, Maicy?"

"Clark," she muttered.

She heard him say, "Holy..." under his breath before shifting back into a calm, professional tone to ask, "Can you tell me what year it is?"

"A new year. January..." The date rolled off her tongue.

But maybe that wasn't the right date. Maybe she only said it out of habit. She'd given that particular date a million times in the last few months while planning the wedding.

The wedding...

"How old are you?" the man asked.

These questions were dumb. "Old enough," she said peevishly.

She pinched her eyes closed against the pain in her head and reached up to feel the source. She discovered that her hair was damp and that there were bandages of some sort on her forehead, just below her hairline.

"Good, you can move your right arm. How about this side?" the man asked, taking her other hand. "Can you squeeze my hand?"

She did that. He had a big hand.

"Strength is good," he decreed. "How about your feet? Can you flex those for me?"

She did as he asked and felt that her feet were bare.

Bare feet? She didn't leave home in her bare feet. Her wedding shoes…

"Where are my shoes—I love those shoes!"

He didn't answer her question. Instead he asked, "Can you tell me what happened to you?"

She opened her eyes again. Her vision was a bit clearer this time, and the fuzzy image of the man on his knees beside her looked even more like her old boyfriend.

This really was bizarre.

"There was a deer. I swerved to miss hitting him," she said, remembering. She also recalled that it was her wedding she'd come from.

And Gary…

"What's around my neck?" she asked when she also became aware that there was something there.

"My coat," the man answered. "Are you experiencing pain anywhere?"

"My head."

"Anywhere else?"

"No."

"Any pain in your neck? Your shoulders? Your back or arms?"

"No."

"I'm going to pinch you a little bit—tell me if you can feel it."

He did, pinching different spots on her arms and legs. She could feel it so she told him so.

Then he said, "Can you raise your legs? One at a time?"

She did that, feeling satin around them. The wedding dress. From the wedding that hadn't been. Because she'd run away from it…

"Okay, very carefully, I want you to try to move your head—can you do that?"

She could do that, too.

"Any pain with that? Any tingling in your shoulders, arms or legs?"

"No."

"Good. I'm going to unwrap your neck but I'm going to do it slowly, if you feel *anything* out of the ordinary, you tell me right away, okay?"

He came closer to unwrap his coat and her vision cleared more so she could take a better look at him.

He had dark hair the color of a double espresso—short on the sides, longer on top—and a handsome face even at that odd angle.

In spite of it she could still tell that his nose was slightly long and flat across the bridge but worked well with the sharp lines of a great bone structure—high cheekbones and a strong jawline and chin.

All refined and tougher versions of what she remembered of the young Conor...

Why did he keep coming to mind?

"Nothing? No pain—shooting or otherwise?" the man asked.

"No," she said softly as she went on assessing his face and finding more and more that reminded her of the boy she'd loved.

And learned to wish she hadn't...

Those full lips.

Those thick eyebrows, the same dark brown as his hair.

Even his ears...

Conor had had really nice ears...

Then her neck was free and he raised his eyes to her face.

And that was when she knew for sure.

No one she'd ever met except the Madison siblings had eyes like that. Bluer than blue, with silver streaks in them.

"Oh my God!" she said in alarm.

"What? Pain? Numbness?" he asked with more urgency.

"You're Conor Madison," she accused.

He relaxed and nodded. "Hi, Maicy," he said calmly.

"I get it—I've died and gone to hell," she muttered.

As much as she'd wanted to escape her own wedding today, she wanted to get away from Conor even more. So she started to sit up.

"Whoa! Whoa! Whoa!" He held her down by the shoulders. "I don't want you moving at all yet, let alone like that!"

"And we know that what you want is all that counts."

He didn't address that. He only said, "It's important that I make sure you don't aggravate any injuries. So please, just let me check you out?"

"I guess that means you *did* become a doctor?" she said, curious but trying to hide it.

"I did. So let me do my job," he reiterated.

Begrudgingly, she conceded to that, doing some checking out of her own as he continued his examination.

Conor Madison. How, on this day of all days, could she open her eyes and find herself with him?

Maybe she was hallucinating. That would be so much better...

But if she was hallucinating, wouldn't she see him as

the boy he'd been when they were last together rather than this solid, muscular, all-grown-up version of him?

The man who was fully developed—broad of chest and shoulders, with biceps that filled and tested the sleeves of the gray sweatshirt he had on.

He'd aged from youthful good looks into a striking handsomeness.

That aggravated Maicy all the more...

"Shouldn't you be wearing a uniform?" she asked with some impudence.

"I'm on leave," he answered curtly as he took her pulse.

His voice was the same. It had been deep then and it was deep now. But now it held more confidence, more certainty, more authority, as he told her what to do.

"I'm fine," she insisted when his examination seemed finished.

"You aren't *completely* fine," he said. "You were in a car accident, you have a gash in your head and were unconscious for some amount of time. If I had you in a hospital I'd send you for X-rays and a CT scan. But since we aren't in a hospital—"

"Where *are* we?" she said.

"The Dale family's hunting cabin."

"Rickie Dale?" She hadn't thought of him in years.

"Right—glad to see that you seem to be firing on all burners. That's a good sign when there's the potential for a brain injury."

"And how is it that I'm here with you?" she asked derisively, thinking that she'd answered enough of his questions and followed enough of his instructions to have earned some reciprocity.

"I was headed for Northbridge when the storm hit,

and I knew I wouldn't make it. I called Rickie and asked if I could use the place now, to wait out this weather. I came across your car on my way here."

"My car…" Maicy said. "Did I wreck it?"

"You were nose-first in a ditch."

Maicy closed her eyes again, overwhelmed for a moment by all this day had brought with it.

"Hey! You aren't passing out on me again, are you?" Conor said in a louder voice.

She opened her eyes. "No," she said, hating that there was gloom in her own tone for him to hear. "It's just been a bad day," she added, hoping he'd leave it at that.

No such luck.

"Yeah, I'd say so… Were you on your way *to* your wedding or coming from it?"

"Neither." She just wasn't sure how to qualify it. "I got to the church but left before the wedding happened."

"Without a coat?"

"I took my coat—it's in the back seat with my suitcase. I just didn't put it on. I was in a hurry."

He didn't push it. Instead he said, "Do you feel like you can sit up?"

"Sure," she answered, not revealing that she felt unsteady and drained because she didn't want him to know there was any weakness in her at all. Not now or ever again.

"I want you to take it slow," he told her. "Let me help you, and tell me immediately if you feel any hint of pain or tingling or numbness."

"Yeah, yeah, yeah," she clipped out.

He helped her sit up, and she made it there without

saying anything, containing the groan that almost escaped when her head throbbed with the movement. Her expression must have shown her pain, though, because he said, "There's some pain reliever in the first-aid kit but I don't want to give you that until I know that the bleeding is under control. Can you stand to wait?"

"Yes." And even if she hadn't been able to, she wouldn't have told him. "Now can I get off this floor?"

"Give it a minute. Let's see what sitting here does first."

Maicy sighed, feeling impatient. Methodical and cautious. That was Conor Madison. To a fault.

And she *had* faulted him for it. With good reason.

Glancing down, Maicy noticed her dress.

"Oh, I'm a mess…" she lamented. And it had been such a beautiful dress—white satin, scooped neck with cowl-like draping to the hem that ended at her ankles in front and gracefully expanded into a short train in back. Now it was wrinkled, soiled and stained with blood.

"Actually, you look pretty damn good…" Conor said. She might have been flattered if she'd been willing to accept a compliment from the likes of him.

But as it was she ignored the remark and announced once more, "I feel fine. Now can I get up?"

"How's the dizziness?"

"Good. Gone," she lied. "I'm sure I can drive. All I have to do is get to my car and back it out of the ditch and—"

He looked at her as if she was crazy. "In the first place," he said, "you're *not* fine—you're doing well, but you are not *unscathed.* You're nowhere near ready to go outside into the snow without shoes or a coat, much less to hike a mile to your car—because that's where it is, at the end of the drive up to this cabin. It's not drivable even if you could get to it—it's going to need a tow truck. Then there's the fact that if you were in an emergency room where you belong, they'd admit you to keep an eye on you overnight, and there is no way in hell I'd let you drive even if this was a balmy summer day. So no matter how you want to cut it, you, Maicy Clark, are stuck here. With me."

Oh…it was worse than she thought. Not only had she encountered the one person she'd hoped never to see again in her life, she was stranded with him?

"You look sick—what's going on?" he said.

"What's going on is that I don't want to be here." *With you!* she added in her head.

But what she said was, "I don't see mine, but surely you have a cell phone—call for help! Maybe somebody could come and get me—an ambulance, or the fire department." She refused to believe that things were as impossible as he claimed.

"If I couldn't get *in* to town, no one can get out," he reasoned.

"I don't want to be here with you!" she blurted, unable to stop herself this time.

"I get that," he said. "But right now we have to do what we have to do. And arguing about it will only waste time we don't have to spare. This place is *not* a four-star hotel and we're going to have to work to stay warm and fed. So if you think you're doing okay enough for me to get you onto the couch, there are some things I need to do to get this place up and running—as much as it runs—in order to get us through tonight."

Tonight? They'd be spending the whole night together in this cabin?

Could this day possibly get any worse?

First her wedding had become a disaster.

And now here she was, isolated and alone with the guy who had broken her heart and abandoned her in her most desperate time of need.

Oh yeah, it definitely would have been better if she were just hallucinating.

Maicy took a deep breath, rallied the strength she'd had to find in herself years before and said, "I can get to the couch myself."

He ignored that.

Which was good because once he'd helped her to her feet her knees buckled and she nearly collapsed.

He caught her in strong, powerful arms that—if she'd had even an iota of strength herself—she would have slapped away.

As it was she had no choice but to let him help her to the sofa.

Once she was there, she shrugged out of his grip and swore to herself that if she couldn't get back up again without his help, she would stay rooted to that spot.

Because the last thing she would ever do again was lean on Conor Madison.

Chapter Two

"Dammit!" Conor shouted into the wind.

After trying several different locations outside, he'd found a spot where he had cell phone reception... temporarily. It lasted long enough to reach his brother's doctor and learn that Declan's fever was rising. Then he'd lost service again. And no matter where he went now, the phone showed no signal.

Meanwhile, the storm was worsening. Now that it was dark the temperature had plummeted, and the wind was howling and making the snow a whirling dervish that was even more impossible to see through.

So Conor turned his attention to the other reason he'd bundled up to come outside—firewood.

He circled to the back of the cabin where the wood-pile was, staying close to the log structure so as not to risk losing his bearings. But he was far less worried for himself than he was for his brother.

He'd heard the stories about the shoddy, outdated conditions of some stateside veterans' hospitals, constantly understaffed and undersupplied. And since he'd been back with Declan, he'd seen it for himself. Doctors and nurses were stretched thinner than Conor knew they should be, and he had to put pressure on them to make sure his brother had what he needed.

Was Declan's care suffering now that he wasn't there to keep an eye on things?

Why the hell had he thought it was a good idea to leave Declan's side in the first place?

But Declan had been doing so well and they'd both known that one of them had to get to Kinsey to talk some sense into her before she shook up their lives with her quest to build a relationship with the family they hadn't known they had.

For cripes sake, Kinsey, why couldn't you just leave well enough alone? Who cares if Mitchum Camden was our biological father? We were just his dirty secret, hidden away from his high-society wife and family while he carried on with Mom behind their backs all those years.

They'd barely even seen the man while he was still alive. And after he died—in a plane crash with various other members of his family—their mom had eventually moved on. She'd married their stepdad, the man who truly raised them. And she'd never told any of her children about their father...until her deathbed confession to Kinsey.

Now Kinsey was determined to build a relationship with Mitchum Camden's other children. And neither Conor, Declan nor Declan's twin, Liam, were on board with that. She was determined to build a relationship the Camdens didn't seem to want, either.

With Declan laid up and Liam on special assignment overseas with his own marine unit, the job of dissuading their sister had fallen to Conor. But since the weather was keeping him from meeting Kinsey, this trip was a complete waste.

Well, maybe not a complete waste since it did put him here to save Maicy.

But still, thinking about what he *should* be doing for his brother made frustration hit him all over again. Frustration that piled on top of the uneasiness that had been dogging him for a while.

Initially in his career he'd liked the excitement, the speed, the exhilaration of emergency and trauma medicine, of being the first person to treat injured military men and women, to safeguard their lives just as they safeguarded the world with their service. But the longer it went on, the more it had begun to eat at him that it wasn't up to him to give extended care, to see his patients through and make sure their ongoing treatment was successful. Declan was the first patient he'd been able to stay with—and now he was letting his brother down.

Conor reached the woodpile and, with a vengeance born out of those frustrations, threw back the tarp covering it.

There's nothing you can do about it! he told himself firmly. Nothing he could do about Declan or about any of the hundreds of military men and women whose treatment it was his job only to begin.

Nothing he could do other than continuing to look

for a phone signal at any rate, so he could stay on top of Declan's care from here, no matter what it took.

It didn't ease his anxiousness a lot, but at least having a plan, setting a course of any kind, helped a little.

And in the meantime he had to deal with the situation he was currently in.

Which was also one hell of a situation.

The cabin was stocked for the winter with plenty of already-cut wood, bottled water and nonperishable food. Nothing luxurious, but enough to keep them safe.

Maicy was more of a problem.

So far it appeared that she didn't have a serious brain injury, that she had a minor concussion that a little rest would cure. But if she took a turn for the worse like Declan and the storm, they were going to have bigger problems.

Bigger even than the fact that it *was* Maicy Clark he was stranded with—the one person in the world who had every reason to hate his guts. And apparently did.

Sometimes it just sucked to do what he thought was right, what he thought was best for everyone involved.

And when it came to Maicy it had left him with guilt he could never dislodge.

Not even now, when it didn't seem as if she had done too badly for herself.

After all, the car she'd crashed into the ditch had been a high-end sedan, and looking at her...

Despite her injury, she *looked* great—certainly not world-weary or worn or as if life had gotten the better of her.

She'd always had that amazing head of hair—thick and wavy and shiny. It used to feel like heavy silk whenever he'd gotten his hands into it, and it was no less lush now.

And that face? Time had *not* taken a toll on that, either. Instead it had only improved on perfection, removing the girlish immaturity and leaving her an incredibly beautiful woman.

Her skin was like porcelain and her features were delicate and refined, with elegant, high cheekbones, a thin, graceful nose, and soft ruby lips that he'd never been able to get his fill of.

And if that wasn't enough—along with the lush way her compact little body had blossomed—there were those eyes.

Sparkling, vibrant, emerald green.

One look from those eyes in days gone by and he would have moved mountains for her...

Though he had managed to stand his ground that one time. And from what she said, it was clear she had not forgiven or forgotten. Never mind that the choice he'd made all those years ago had been every bit as much about what he'd thought was best for her as what he'd known he had to do himself. He'd still hurt her.

And now he had to contend with the fallout.

All these years later.

Alone in a small space with her and all of her anger.

The young Maicy had been a sweetheart. Uncomplicated and good-natured, agreeable and soft-hearted. But now? Somewhere along the way some spunk and feistiness had been added. And a touch of temper to go with that red hair. Cut and bloodied and reeling and barely conscious again, she'd still shot barbs at him and had seemed very prepared to make his life miserable until they could get out of here.

But like having unreliable cell phone service, when it came to Maicy he was just going to have to do what he could and cope, he told himself as he picked up the canvas sling that he'd filled with as much wood as it would hold.

And maybe he needed to use this strange opportunity to see if he could finally explain why he had denied her request—an explanation she hadn't listened to eighteen years ago.

It might not make any difference, he thought as he inched along the rear of the cabin to get to the back door again, but he'd like to try.

Because along with the other things that were eating at him lately there had also come some wondering, some questioning, about his own course, his own choices. And if he'd made the right ones.

First and foremost, about Maicy.

Maicy had dozed off, and when she woke up daylight was gone, darkness had fallen, and the only sounds were of the raging storm outside and the fire crackling inside.

"Conor?" she called out. There was no answer.

She sat up on the worn plaid sofa where she'd fallen asleep, keeping the blanket around her and wondering if Conor had deserted her. After all, it wouldn't be the first time.

The couch was under the cabin's front window. Peering through it, beyond the snow blowing like a white sheet in the wind, she thought she could see flashes of his silver SUV. So he had to be around somewhere.

Her head hurt and she reached up to feel the bandaging. The blood had begun to dry. She assumed that meant the gash must have stopped bleeding. But her whole body was more stiff and sore than it had been before. And she felt weak. Drained.

Hard to tell whether that was from her physical condition or her mental state, she thought.

She slumped back against the soft cushions, studying her surroundings in the dim firelight.

She'd never been to this cabin before. Rickie had brought friends out for camping or hunting, but never for parties—and now she could see why. Built by Rickie's great-great-grandfather, the place provided shelter but it was hardly a showpiece.

The living room she was in featured rough-hewn log walls and a wood-planked floor, the old couch she was on and a scarred coffee table. Off to one side, the kitchen section was made up of a small utility table acting as an island counter and a few cupboards. There was also an old black-and-silver wood-burning stove in the corner, but that was it—no refrigerator, no other appliances at all.

A doorway off the kitchen led somewhere she couldn't see into, and another to Maicy's left appeared to be a bedroom with a four-poster bed that looked old enough to have arrived by covered wagon.

If there was a bathroom, she couldn't see it from the sofa and she worried that the only facilities might be an outhouse.

All in all, it was nothing like the cozy, quaint bridal suite at the Northbridge Bed-and-Breakfast, where she'd planned to spend tonight.

Instead she was here. A runaway bride.

What a mess this had all become...

Rather than being at her wedding reception tonight,

dancing and celebrating as Mrs. Gary Stern, she and Gary were over. And as if that wasn't bad enough, she was stranded in a log cabin with yet another, earlier example of her lousy taste in men.

"I keep thinking I'm making better choices than you did, Mom, but maybe I inherited some kind of faulty man-reader from you," she muttered.

There was no question that her mother had chosen poorly in Maicy's father. At the first sign of any problem—big or small—John Clark had taken off. Disappeared, sometimes for a year or two at a time.

Her mother had excused him, saying their shotgun marriage after her mother had discovered she was pregnant with Maicy had not been easy for him. Maicy hadn't had much sympathy.

To her, her father had been a drop-in houseguest whom her mother waited—and waited and waited—for. A man who never stayed long before he was gone again.

And every time he left, her mother had sunk into dark depressions that lasted for months.

Once, Maicy had asked why her mother didn't divorce him and find someone who would be there for her. For them both.

Her mother's only answer had been that she loved the man.

That had seemed silly to twelve-year-old Maicy.

Until she'd fallen in love herself.

With Conor.

Sitting sideways on the sofa, she pulled her knees to her chest and huddled under the blanket, staring into the fire now, wondering where he'd gone.

Conor was as unreliable as her father, she reminded herself. As untrustworthy.

But Gary? She'd thought there was no risk with him.

Steady, conservative, hometown Gary.

Gary, who had been hurt as badly by love as she had.

Gary, who she'd been convinced was predictable and safe...

Oh yeah, she definitely had a faulty man-reader.

She wasn't sure if it made things better or worse that she hadn't been wholeheartedly in love with Gary, the way she'd been with Conor. When she'd caught him today, she'd still been angry. Hurt. Embarrassed.

But she was also secretly relieved.

And now, sitting alone in the aftermath, she couldn't help wondering why that was—because relieved was still how she felt.

"I really need to talk to you, Rach," she muttered, wishing she had her cell phone to call her friend.

Everything was just such a mess...

Pain shot through her gashed forehead just then, forcing her eyes closed until it passed.

If the bleeding had stopped or at least slowed down, maybe she could finally take something for the pain.

"Conor?" she called, hoping maybe he'd hear her from wherever he was—maybe there was a basement or a cellar or something...

But still there was no answer.

Where *was* he?

It occurred to her suddenly that if he was outside in this storm, maybe something had happened to him.

That sent a strong wave of alarm through her and she got up.

Too fast.

Her head went into such a spin that she fell back onto the sofa.

"Okay, that wasn't great," she said out loud.

She waited, took some deep breaths, tried to relax. The dizziness began to pass.

But the worry that something might have happened to Conor didn't. She had to see if he was okay.

She got up again, this time much more carefully. She was definitely weak. Her knees felt as if they might give out.

But she wasn't going to let that happen. She did what she'd been doing since the day Conor had left her on her own—she willed herself to push through. Pain, weakness, fear, depression, whatever—she stood on her own two feet regardless!

And now that she was on those two feet all she needed to do was go to the other side of the room. That was nothing, she told herself.

She wrapped the blanket around her shoulders like a cape and clutched it in front with one hand. Keeping her other hand against the wall for support, she took careful steps, aiming for the other side of the room and the window over the kitchen sink. Hoping as she did that she wouldn't discover Conor outside, hurt or incapacitated in some way. Because she was in no shape to rescue him.

Along the way she reached the doorway off the kitchen and found that there was another small room with a door leading outside.

The room appeared to be a catchall—a pantry stocked with food and a supply room where she saw snowshoes and a shovel and an ax among other things.

Other things that didn't include Conor.

So she bypassed the room and finished the trip to the kitchen sink.

When she got there she maintained her grip on the blanket with one hand and held on to the edge of the sink with the other.

"Wow," she said as she peered out the window at the storm. She'd seen some bad ones, but this topped the list.

Just then the snow swirled away from the cabin and she caught sight of something moving to the left.

She craned forward, looking hard through the window. There was definitely someone out there. Someone big. It had to be him. Maybe at a woodpile? Getting firewood made sense.

Feeling relieved, she turned and slowly retraced her steps back to the couch as a slight shiver shook her. Even with her blanket cape, the blood-soaked wedding dress was *not* the warmest of attires.

The sofa was a welcome respite when she got there again. Sitting at one end she pulled her knees up to her chest, tightened the blanket around herself so every inch was covered and returned to staring into the fire that was the only source of heat.

Her short venture had used up the little oomph she'd had and she rested her head to the back of the sofa cushion, thinking that it was a good thing Conor *didn't* need her help.

And what kind of a weird practical joke was fate playing on her today, anyway? First Gary's old flame dropped into his lap and now hers?

She closed her eyes at that thought and made a face.

She did *not* like the way things had gone with Conor so far. Most of all, she didn't like that she'd lost control over her emotions. She hadn't even realized she was still that angry with him. What had happened with him was ancient history. She'd come to grips with it long ago, chalking it up to experience. It had taken her some time—well into adulthood, actually—but she'd even come to think that he'd probably made the right decision. How many teenage marriages actually worked out?

So, if it was all water under the bridge—which it was—why hadn't she just been indifferent, detached, completely unemotional toward him?

She should have been. Instead, she'd been anything *but*. The only explanation she had for it was that today had just thrown too much at her. Seeing Conor again had been the straw that broke the camel's back...even if he happened to be the person who had kept her from dying today.

The person she should have been grateful to.

She chafed at that thought.

Grateful to Conor Madison?

This really was a practical joke on fate's part—now she had to be *grateful* to the guy who had dumped her?

Fabulous, she thought facetiously.

But she also wasn't happy to have behaved so poorly toward Conor.

Not that he didn't deserve her scorn and contempt. But showing it put her in a position she didn't want to be in. She didn't want to be the smaller person. The grudge-bearer.

And she didn't want him thinking she cared.

So that lashing-out thing wasn't going to happen from here on, she vowed. Not when it might make him think she hadn't gotten over him. That their childhood

romance had been so important to her that she was still
hurt or mad or something. Anything.

Because she wasn't.

It wasn't as if she would ever choose to be stuck in
a snowstorm, in a small space with him, but since she
apparently couldn't alter that, she wasn't going to let
it be a big deal. She was just going to make the best of
it until this all passed.

Then they would part ways again.

But in the meantime he was not going to get to her.
He was basically a stranger to her now. A stranger
whose company she would have to endure for a little
while whether she liked it or not.

A stranger who had grown into one of the best-
looking men she'd ever seen…

That didn't matter, either.

Even if it *was* the truth.

He'd always been handsome, only somehow time
and a few years had done wonders for him. It had taken
chiseled features and added some hardcore masculinity and a ruggedness that screamed raw sensuality. It
had built even more muscle mass onto his body and
turned him into a hunk-and-a-half.

But it really didn't matter. Not to her. It didn't have
any effect on her. *He* didn't have any effect on her.

So move on, storm, she commanded.

Because as soon as it did, she could get out of this
place and put Conor Madison back in the past, where
he belonged.

When the back door opened she knew it. The sound
of the screeching wind wasn't muffled and a frigid
blast of air whipped through the cabin.

Maicy didn't budge. She just went from looking at the fire to watching for Conor to appear through that door.

Finally, he came into view. Snow and droplets of water dotted dark hair that was in unfairly attractive disarray. The collar of his navy blue peacoat was turned up to frame his sexy jawline, and the coat accentuated shoulders a mile wide now.

But none of it was going to have an impact on her, she told herself.

"You're awake," he said when his eyes met hers.

"I am," she confirmed, forcing her tone to be completely dispassionate and neutral. "What time is it?"

"Almost ten. How do you feel?"

"I'm okay," she insisted, unwilling to confide more in him.

"I need to know, Maicy," he reprimanded, so she told him the details, still assuring him she was fine, but adding that she wouldn't mind a little pain reliever for her headache.

"And I don't suppose you brought my suitcase from my car when you got me out, did you?" she asked, huddling in the blanket.

"I didn't," he said, leaving his coat in place as he brought firewood around the utility table. "I was only paying attention to you—I didn't even notice anything else in the car. I have my duffel, though. You can wear something of mine when you're up to changing—something warm."

"I'd appreciate that," she said even though she wasn't thrilled with the prospect of wearing his clothes. And while she was at it, she said, "And I also appreciate what you did getting me here. You saved me. Thank you for that."

"Any time—" he said before cutting himself off as if he only just remembered that their past made that promise into a lie.

He turned from her to arrange the firewood, and Maicy's gaze went to his thighs stretching the denim of his jeans to capacity—thick and solid.

"If you're up to it," he said as he loaded the bucket, "there are some logistics we should discuss."

"Okay," Maicy agreed.

"We're pretty socked in by this storm," he began. "Cell service is spotty—at best. I get service one minute, lose it the next. And until this storm quits, I don't know when we'll be able to get out of here."

"Tomorrow—"

"I think that may be optimistic and we have to plan for a little longer than that."

"How long?" she asked, trying to keep her distaste for that idea out of her tone.

"I don't know. I just know that we have to conserve supplies, just in case. It's impossible to tell at this point how long we'll be here, but better safe than sorry."

Maicy clenched her teeth to keep from making a snide comment about that being his guiding rule.

"Here's how it is up here," he continued. "We're off the grid. That means no electricity, limited water. The water in the storage tank downstairs is the only non-drinking water, and the only power we have comes from a solar-powered generator. Both of those are at about half capacity. I can get us by for a while with what we have, but only if we're careful. The water in the tank isn't for eating or drinking but there's plenty of bottled water for that. We have a pretty good stock of dried and canned food. The woodpile is high—

that's good. But, for instance, something like taking a shower—"

"No showers?" Maicy said in horror, thinking of how sticky she felt with the blood in her hair and down her neck.

"Yes, showers, but here's how they happen—there's a propane tank hooked to the water heater in the basement. I can turn on the gas and heat the water but every time I do that, we're using up propane and water. So to shower it'll take half an hour to heat the water. Then, in the shower, there's a chain to pull to turn the pump on and off. You pull the chain, get wet, stop the water. Lather up. Pull the chain to rinse off. All as quick as possible so you use as little water as you can."

"Okay…" she said, already missing the long, steamy showers she ordinarily took. But trying to look on the bright side, she said, "So this must mean that there *is* a bathroom?"

"There's a room," he hedged. "Off the bedroom. That's where the shower is, along with a composting toilet."

"I don't know what that is."

"It's a john that'll take some explanation, too. But it *looks* like a regular one, if that helps," he joked, giving her that familiar one-sided smile that had made her feel better about most anything when she'd liked him.

It still worked, damn him.

"I also stocked the bathroom with candles and some kerosene lanterns, so you'll have light in there, anyway," he said.

He was so confident, so sure of himself. No wonder she'd believed in him when she'd been at her most distressed…

"I've been in worse," he concluded. "We'll be fine, we just need to conserve what resources we have." He'd finished with the firewood and he stood up, unbuttoning his coat and taking it off. "Let me get a lantern and check your head," he said next. "Any nausea or are you getting hungry?"

Food was the last thing on her mind. But she said, "I'm not nauseous."

"Good. For tonight I just want to get some food and water in you, and get you to bed."

There wasn't any insinuation in that but still it set off a tiny titillation in her that she tried to tell herself was just the chill.

"Where are you sleeping?" she heard herself ask.

He laughed.

No, no, no, no, not his laugh. She'd always had a weakness for his laugh, too…

"I'll take the couch," he assured her. "But we're playing hospital tonight so I'll be in every couple of hours to check on you."

And crawl into bed with her and hold her and keep her warm with those massively muscled arms wrapped around her?

Ohhh, that was some weird flashback to the teenage Maicy's fantasies…

A blow to the head… I've suffered a severe blow to the head. It must have knocked something loose…

Something she would make sure was tightened up again.

"We'll deal with everything else tomorrow," she heard him say into the chaos of her thoughts.

"So I can't shower tonight?" she said when that sank in.

"Nope. I'll heat enough on the stove for you to clean

up a little better, but I want you down until tomorrow. We'll see then if you can shower," he decreed, before heading to get the lantern.

And as much as she didn't want to, Maicy couldn't help checking out his walk-away.

That had gotten better, too.

But it's what's inside that counts, she lectured herself.

And she didn't mean what was inside those jeans.

It was what was inside the man that counted.

The man whom she had—once upon a time—asked to marry her.

Only to have him turn her down.

Chapter Three

Maicy would have slept much better on Sunday night had Conor not come in every two hours to check on her—the way he'd warned her he would.

The four-poster bed was the most comfortable thing she'd ever slept on. Conor had given her a brand new T-shirt and sweatpants straight out of the packages to use as pajamas, the sheets were clean, and with two downy quilts covering her and the slowly burning fire in the shared fireplace—that Conor also kept watch over all night—it would have been heavenly if not for her headache, and the interruptions.

She awoke Monday morning to the sound of wood being split outside. Using the blanket that had covered her on the sofa the night before as a robe, she tested her strength and balance rather than bounding out of the bed.

She was still weak and sore in spots, but much better than the night before. So she left the bedroom and went into the kitchen.

Looking out the window over the sink she could see that the wind had calmed slightly, but snow was still falling heavily on top of what looked to be more than two feet already on the ground.

Conor had shoveled a path to the woodpile and was there, splitting logs with the swing of an ax.

That was a sight to wake up to!

One she was leery of standing there to watch.

She was not going to be sucked into admiring the fine specimen of a man he'd become. There was nothing personal between them at all anymore, and that was the way it would stay. Their former connection had died an ugly death. And even before it had, it clearly hadn't been as meaningful to him as it was to her. So what he was doing for her now was merely being a good Samaritan, there wasn't anything else to it.

She just had to stop cataloging—and yeah, okay, admiring—his physical improvements, and make certain that she didn't read anything into his behavior. He was a doctor—taking care of injured women who fell in his path was just part of his job. It didn't mean anything. She didn't *want* it to mean anything. She was indifferent to him now. So she didn't let herself stay at the sink and watch him splitting logs. Instead, she moved across the room to the front window to survey that side of the cabin.

He'd shoveled off the front porch and cleared the snow from his SUV but she wasn't sure why he'd bothered. There was no driving on the road with all that snow.

"Come on, snow, just stop," she beseeched the weather to no avail, plopping down onto the couch dejectedly.

Conor came in not long after and made powdered eggs that weren't too unpalatable, and then removed the dressing from her head.

As he did she said, "So you *did* become a doctor, but what about career military?"

"Yes, that too—so far," he answered as if there was some question to that. But she didn't explore it. Something seemed to be on his mind today, troubling him. He was checking for cell service obsessively and with every failed attempt the frown lines between his eyebrows dug in a little deeper.

But the days of feeling free to just ask him anything, the days of confiding in each other, were long gone.

Once he'd checked her wound and judged that it was healing properly, he cleaned around it, redressed it and sealed it in a makeshift wrapping that allowed her to take a shower and very carefully wash her hair.

It wasn't the best shower or shampoo she'd ever had but it still made her feel worlds better.

Then she put on another pair of Conor's gray sweatpants and a matching gray sweatshirt that were many sizes too big for her but were warm and soft inside.

The trouble was—despite the fact that they were clean—the sweats smelled like Conor.

Not that it was a bad scent. The opposite of that, actually. They carried a scent she remembered vividly, a scent that was somehow clean and soapy yet still all him. A scent she hadn't been able to get enough of when she had feelings for him. A scent that brought back memories that she had to fight like mad to escape.

But fight them she did. And mostly failed.

After a lunch of potato soup made from dried potatoes—and making sure that Maicy was well enough to be left alone for a while—Conor decided to snow-shoe down the road that led to the cabin in hopes of finding a cell signal.

He left her with orders to rest but because Maicy felt well enough to look around a bit, she spent the afternoon getting the lay of the land, for her own peace of mind.

It wasn't as if she thought Conor wouldn't come back this time. It was just that her past had taught her to always make sure she could take care of herself in any eventuality.

So she explored the supplies in the mudroom, counting bottles of water and calculating how long they would last, and learning what types and quantities of foodstuff were available.

She located flashlights, lanterns and kerosene, an abundance of candles, boxes of matches, more snow-shoes, heavy gloves she hoped she never had to put her hands into because they were pretty gross-looking, and a second ax.

She even opened the back door and stuck her head out so she could get an idea of how to reach the wood-pile from there.

Then she found the stairs that went from the mud-room to the basement and she made her way down.

She checked everything out, read the instructions attached to the generator so she could feel as if she had a working knowledge of its operation. She located the two extra propane tanks and studied how the one that was currently attached to the water heater could be replaced if necessary. She also discovered where Conor had come up with the additional blankets and pillows that he'd used to sleep on the couch.

Then she returned upstairs and opened every cupboard door to see what was inside, figured out how to work the wood-burning stove, and decided she was going to make the evening meal—canned chili and cornbread from a mix.

The only thing she didn't go through was Conor's duffel bag. But as daylight was waning and he still hadn't come back, she began to plan what she would do if he didn't return. How she could use a pair of the snowshoes that were in the mudroom and layer on more of the clothes he must have in his duffel, if she needed to go in search of him.

But then she heard stomping on the porch just before the front door opened and in came Conor.

He was so covered in snow that he barely looked human, bringing with him her suitcase, purse and the pink cake box she'd snatched from her wedding when she'd run out of the church basement.

"You went to my car?" she exclaimed, thrilled to have access to her own things—especially to clothes that didn't smell like him.

"I was almost there before I got cell reception, figured I might as well go the rest of the way to get your stuff." He set everything down, took off his gloves and coat and opened the front door again to shake the snow from them before laying them near the fire to dry.

"You kept the fire going—that's good. I didn't think I'd be out this long. And what are you doing over there? You're supposed to be resting," he said, surveying things.

"I'm fine," she insisted. "I'm cooking. And you brought dessert."

"I did?"

"That pink box. It's the top tier to the wedding cake. My friend Rachel Walsh made it. We met in college."

"I wondered what that was. I just figured I'd bring everything I found. I have to make a confession and ask a favor, though," he added.

"What?"

"I, uh… I got into your purse to find your cell phone."

Maicy did not like the idea that he'd gone through her purse. But there was something grim in his attitude as he removed his boots and put those by the fire, too, so she curbed her own reaction to that and gave him an excuse. "Were you thinking that mine might work better up here than yours?"

"I already tried that on the way back. It doesn't. But the favor I need is for your phone to be a backup so when my battery is drained, I can use yours while I recharge in the car—which we shouldn't do often because we don't want the car battery and the gas depleted, either."

"Bottom line," Maicy said, "is that even if I can get service on mine at some point, you don't want me to use it."

He bent over so his head was toward the fire and ran his hands through his hair to rub the water out of it with a punishing force.

Maicy couldn't help the glance at his rear end—until she realized that was what she was doing. Then she put a stop to it by putting the cornbread in the oven.

When she turned back to the utility table Conor was standing with his back to the fire, apparently to get warm.

"I'm sort of sitting on a powder keg," he told her.

"And the phones—for what little good they're doing—are my only hope."

A single explanation occurred to Maicy and it hit her hard enough to make her blurt out, "You have a pregnant wife somewhere who could deliver any minute."

And why had there been a note of horror in her voice?

Or, for that matter, horror at the thought. *She'd* been about to get married. She *would* be married right now had things gone differently. Why was it unthinkable that he might be?

But it didn't matter. She still hated the idea.

"No. I'm not married and nobody is pregnant," he said as if he didn't know why she would even suggest such a thing.

"Do you *have* kids?" Another burst she couldn't stop.

"No," he repeated, adding a challenging, "Do you?"

"No."

"This is about Declan," he said then, getting back to the issue.

"Your brother," Maicy said, trying to follow what he was saying while gathering her scattered thoughts.

"Declan was hurt in Afghanistan a few months back. In an IED explosion," Conor explained.

"That's a bomb, right? An IED?"

"Right. It stands for improvised explosive device."

"And he lived?"

"He did, thank God. But he's been critical for a long time—"

"I'm so sorry. Is he going to be all right?"

"I thought so. I took leave time to follow him from hospital to hospital to make sure everything was done right—he was so messed up that I worried something minor might be overlooked while his major injuries were being dealt with."

Some things about Conor clearly hadn't changed—like his need to control any potential problems.

"I wasn't going to let that happen," he added.

She'd heard that from him before.

"I can't treat family," he was saying, "but I could damn sure be with him through it all and get *everything* that needed to be done, done."

The *right* way—it wasn't what he said but for Maicy it was an echo from the past.

The right way according to Conor.

He definitely hadn't changed, which left Maicy with no doubt that he'd been vigilant on his brother's behalf.

"We've been stateside for two weeks and he was doing well enough that he wanted me to make this trip to meet Kinsey in Northbridge. Yesterday I checked with him the minute the plane landed. He sounded a little off to me, but he said he was okay. On the way up here—before I lost service—I called again and discovered that he'd developed a fever."

"Not good," Maicy said, interpreting his dire tone.

"*Really* not good," he confirmed. "A fever that comes on that fast is a red flag on its own. But then I couldn't get through again until today and when I did, the news was what I was afraid of—he has sepsis."

"I don't know what that is."

"You've heard of blood poisoning?"

"Sure."

"Well, that's sepsis. An infection has gotten into his blood stream, and depending on how his body fights it and how it's treated, it could kill him. He hasn't gone into septic shock but he's back in intensive care, and he could go into shock in the blink of an eye and—"

"You're trying to keep tabs on what's going on with him."

He nodded. "I have to stay on top of it. VA hospitals here are overcrowded—the staff doesn't have enough time for sufficient individual care. I can't let Declan go down because something gets missed or mishandled. Plus he's allergic to a lot of the antibiotics it would be best to use and I need to make sure he gets the combination he can tolerate that's still strong enough to give him a chance."

"I'm so sorry," Maicy repeated because she didn't know what else to say.

"I should have gone with my gut and stayed with him," Conor said, more to himself than to her. "But there's been stuff with Kinsey and..." He sighed disgustedly. "And then I was up here, stuck in this damn storm."

Ooo. Maicy had never heard him curse the way he did following that statement. He was really upset.

Collecting himself, he shook his head, drawing back those broad shoulders and stiffening up as if it helped contain some of his stress. "I also got through to Rickie while I had service to see if he could get up here, if he could get me to somewhere I could fly out of."

"Could he?" Maicy asked hopefully.

"Not any chance in hell," he said with disgust. "The Billings airport is still closed—along with most of Billings—and now so is the highway between here and there. And there's been an avalanche and rockslide just outside of Northbridge, on the only road in or out. That'll keep everybody stuck there until the storm passes. Then they'll have to bulldoze through the slide before anybody will be able to get to us from that direction. That's why I went the rest of the way for your things—we're looking at being here longer than I thought."

And he was irritated and more shaken up than she'd ever seen him. More like she'd been yesterday when she'd realized what was going on and with whom she was stranded.

Maybe it was her turn to have the cooler head that prevailed, Maicy thought, because Conor looked like he could put a fist through a wall at any moment. And it didn't seem like he'd be deterred by the fact that these weren't just walls, they were tree trunks.

"I'm not a medical person," she said calmly. "I don't know anything about that kind of thing, so help me understand… Do you feel like Declan's doctors are incompetent?"

"No, they're good. They're just overworked. His primary is actually a guy I was with for a while on a tour on an aircraft carrier—Vince Collier. I'd let him treat me."

"So his doctor is competent and conscientious," she said, then, "I know I'm always asked if I'm allergic to anything when I see a doctor, so you must have told everyone about Declan's allergies, right?"

"I made sure it was noted in big letters everywhere, and yeah, I've said it to everyone who's come near him."

"Plus Declan knows his allergies and he hasn't gone into shock, so double-checking his antibiotics is something he can make sure of himself."

"I don't know about that—a fever like he has could leave him confused."

"Okay, but you've been there with Declan, so everyone knows you, too—that you're a navy doctor, that you're keeping an eye on them and everything they do, yes?"

"Yes, but I'm not there to do that now," he said impatiently, as if he didn't see the point of any of what she was asking.

"But the groundwork is laid," she said. "And you've got two brotherhoods working for you—the brotherhood of doctors, and the whole military brotherhood. It seems to me that whether you're there or not, everyone is going to try that much harder not to drop the ball with Declan."

That gave him pause for just a moment before he conceded. "I don't know…maybe… This is just really serious…"

"But you said Declan was doing pretty well before this—it would be worse if this had hit him when he was even weaker, wouldn't it? Now he's in good enough shape for you to feel like you *could* leave him, so he must have a little bit to fight this with."

"Sepsis is dangerous no matter what," he insisted.

"And if you were there with him, what would you be doing?"

"Keeping watch!" he said, again as if she was clueless.

"And you'd see a lot of people doing their jobs—which is what's still happening. Sitting in a chair in his room would make you feel better, but it wouldn't necessarily change anything," she reasoned. "So yes, we'll keep my phone as backup and you'll still keep trying to get through so you can put your two cents' worth in, but maybe you can trust—at least a little— that you've gotten Declan this far and put him in the best position, and whatever he needs will be done now with or without you being there?"

Conor drew his hands through his hair again, pulling so hard on his scalp that he yanked his head back and glared at the ceiling.

From her vantage point Maicy saw his upturned jaw clench and she wondered if she'd pushed too far, if reason wasn't what he'd wanted to hear.

Then he took a deep breath and sighed hard as he dropped his hands and brought his head down again to look at her.

"Yeah, you're right," he admitted. "About all of that. And I did talk to Collier for a few minutes before the phone cut out again. I think—*think*—he's doing what he should. It's just that this is really bad," he said in a tone that was thick with fear and worry. "And I should be there…" His voice dwindled off, letting Maicy see just how much this bothered him.

But before she could think of anything more to say he let out a mirthless chuckle. "I guess this must be what Kinsey feels like with us all in active service— afraid for us and helpless as all hell."

Knowing nothing about what that might be like, Maicy agreed with that observation only with a raise of her eyebrows.

That inspired a shock of pain that reminded her that she was injured. She thought that they were quite a pair stuck here snowbound—her with a head injury and him climbing out of his skin with worry about his brother.

Then Conor drew himself up as if coming to grips

with some of his demons and said, "I'm gonna heat the water and take a quick shower."

"Sure. Good idea," Maicy said.

Conor disappeared downstairs. In the meantime Maicy retrieved her suitcase and purse, feeling as joyful as a kid at Christmas to have them with her again, and took them into the bedroom.

Then she relocated the pink cake box to the kitchen, setting it aside for later.

By the time Conor's shower was finished the cornbread was cooked, the can of chili she'd opened was simmering on the stovetop, she had plates, bowls and bottles of water waiting, and she'd lit some of the candles she'd found in the mudroom to add a little light.

Not in any romantic way, she made sure to tell herself. Just so they could see what they were eating.

What she *wasn't* prepared for was the impact of looking up from her tasks to find the freshly showered and shaved Conor rejoining her in that candlelight.

He was wearing navy blue sweatpants and a matching hoodie with NAVY emblazoned across his expansive chest.

His dark hair was shower-damp. His face was bare of whiskers and even more handsome with all the sculpted lines and planes revealed. And that soapy scent that had tormented her from his clothes wafted out from him and went right to her head.

But only for a minute before she got a hold of herself. She focused on stirring the chili so she didn't have to look at him, thinking that this was a dirty trick on fate's part. If Conor had aged into a troll of a man it would have been bad enough to be in this situation with him. But as it was, his appeal had doubled from what it had been when he was eighteen and this was turning into a constant test of her resistance that she didn't appreciate.

"I'll shut off the propane on the water heater but we should still have enough warm water in the tank to do the dishes," he said as he headed for the basement again.

Maicy didn't respond to that, working to remind herself not to let the way he looked have any effect on her.

She thought she had it under control until he came back. But one glimpse of him rattled her all over again.

It doesn't matter how hot he is, she lectured herself, *think about who he is and what he did.*

Holding fast to memories of old injuries, she ladled out the chili and cut the cornbread, then he took his plate and she took hers to the coffee table to eat, sitting side by side on the sofa, facing the kitchen rather than each other.

After a few bites, Conor said, "Now that you've talked me off the ledge—thanks for that by the way—tell me about this wedding of yours so I can think about something else and stop obsessing over Declan and things I can't do."

Maicy wondered if it had rocked him at all to think of her with someone else—the way it had rocked her earlier when she'd thought he might want cell service to keep up with a pregnant wife. But there were no indications of it.

Before she'd said anything he said, "I know you didn't stay in Northbridge—my mom said you left a year after I did and never came back—but you were getting married there?"

"I got a scholarship to the University of Colorado

in Boulder, I went there for undergrad. Then I got my masters at CU Denver campus and stayed," she explained.

"What did you get your degrees in?"

"Career counseling and development. I own my own career counseling service in Denver."

"So you went to Colorado, live in Denver, but went back to Northbridge to get married?" he said, returning to the original subject.

"A little over a year ago I ran into Gary Stern on the street—"

"That little dorky guy from your graduating class?"

"He evolved out of the dorkiness," she defended even though she didn't feel particularly inclined to support her cheating former fiancé. Granted, she couldn't argue that he wasn't little—only two inches taller than Maicy's own five feet four inches and slight enough that if she'd been wearing Gary's sweatsuit now it would have fit her perfectly.

Then she went on. "He'd just moved away from Northbridge after Candace Jackson turned down *his* proposal."

Okay, there might have been a touch of snideness to that last part, but if Conor had heard it he didn't say anything. He only said, "Candace Jackson… She started out my year, got thrown from a horse and had to be held back into your class because she missed so much school."

"Right. But she's perfectly healthy now…" Maicy said sardonically.

"And she turned down Stern's proposal and he moved to Denver, where you met up with him again and…what? Hit it off?"

Commiserated as two people dumped by high school sweethearts, was more like it.

But that wasn't how Maicy framed it. "At first we were only old friends meeting again after a long time. But then yes, we hit it off, started to date—"

"You and Stern..." he mused, glancing at her in disbelief. "I can't see it."

"We were good together," she said, defensively again. "At least I thought we were. Gary's transition from small town to big city was a little rough, though. He worked as an account manager at a brokerage house but six months in, the company let him go."

"That's not good. How come?"

"They said he just didn't fit in—it was kind of a high-profile firm and it seemed like Gary just didn't have the... I don't know...the panache for their big clients. Anyway, about that time his apartment lease expired and his rent almost doubled from the move-in rate—"

"And being newly unemployed, he couldn't afford it," Conor said for her.

"Right. I was giving him career counseling and trying to help him find work. But Denver's population is booming and there's a lot of competition for every opening—"

"And he wasn't the cream of the crop even with you in his corner."

There *was* a hint of Conor not liking the thought of her with Gary—it was in his tone and that comment.

Maicy found some satisfaction in that.

"Gary was down on his luck," was all she would admit to. "And things between us were going well, so I didn't want to see him move back to Northbridge. I have a two-level house that I bought so that I could live in the lower level and rent out the upper level. Gary had been wanting us to move in together even before he lost his apartment—"

"But you hadn't said yes to it."

"Not quite," Maicy hedged, though the truth was she had not been sure she was ready for that. "But between not wanting him to move back to Montana and the need for him to find another place—"

"You caved and let him move in."

"It wasn't caving, really…" Although it actually had been. "Gary has worked construction, too, so he offered to do the upstairs remodel for me—which saved me a lot of money. And he did a nice job."

She was torn—she had cause to be bitter and angry at her almost-husband and that made her disinclined to say anything good about him. But she also didn't want Conor to think she'd been about to marry someone who was a lesser man.

"And then you just decided to get married?" Conor asked.

"He proposed about three months ago."

"Without a job, living off you in your place?"

"He was at a low point," she said with some impatience of her own because she could hardly deny what was the truth. "But he said he loved me and that even though he didn't have much to offer, he was hopeful that he'd rebound and he wanted to take the first positive step by asking me to marry him. *He* asked *me*," she finished pointedly.

"And it would have been kicking him when he was down to say no."

Yes.

Instead of saying that, Maicy said, "And I knew how awful it was to propose and be rejected. Especially how awful it was to be in the middle of a really bad time and—"

"Okay, I have that coming," Conor said to stop her.

"And I loved Gary," she went on anyway. "Maybe not with all that teenage obsession—"

Something she hadn't felt since she *was* a teenager. Something she'd only ever felt for Conor...

"—but I loved him in a comfortable way that can make for a good, content, companionable, life-long marriage," she continued. "I want a family and so did he, and he was a good candidate for that, too. I didn't think there would be any *surprises*—" She said that word as if it were a curse. "Better a rational, mature, thinking-person's choice than teenage heat of passion that lets you down!"

So much for being the cooler head...

But all Conor said was, "So you said yes."

Maicy took a deep breath, wishing again that she hadn't shown so much emotion.

"So I said yes," she confirmed more calmly. "We were going to get married in Northbridge because that's where Gary's family is. The only person I really cared about being there was my friend Rachel—"

"Who made the cake."

"But after she'd said she'd be my matron of honor and do the cake—she's a pastry chef—she got pregnant and couldn't travel. So she just made the cake and arranged for a bakery in Northbridge to assemble it when I got it there."

"I only found that one little box," Conor pointed out.

"That's because the rest of the tiers are at the

church, put together by the person the local bakery sent—Candace. But before she got to the top tier, she got to Gary."

And that was when her anger and hurt returned to her voice. To her.

They'd finished eating and Conor sat back and angled in her direction. Maicy slumped back, but stayed facing straight ahead to avoid looking at Conor.

"What do you mean *she got to Gary*?" he asked kindly.

"I was dressed and ready for the photographer to take the pre-wedding pictures in front of the church. On our way outside, we had to go through the room in the church basement where the reception was going to be. And there it all was—three layers of cake looking beautiful and Gary kissing Candace."

"Ohh, Maicy..." Conor said sympathetically.

"The poor photographer froze. She didn't know what to do. But I did. I knew there was no way I was marrying him! So I grabbed that last bakery box—because I wasn't going to leave *all* of Rachel's hard work for those jerks—I grabbed my purse and my suitcase, and I got out of there!"

"And where were you going in this snow?"

A reasonable question that didn't have a reasonable answer.

"All I could think about was getting as far away from Gary and Northbridge as I could. I headed toward Denver, not thinking about the weather or...or really anything but getting away. I didn't even notice that the weather was bad—although now that I look back, I don't think it was quite as bad yet in Northbridge when I left. I just kind of drove into the storm as it was coming. And then the deer appeared out of nowhere and I hit the brakes and… That's it. The next thing I knew I was waking up here."

She could feel his eyes on her and she finally glanced over at him, finding him watching her, his eyebrows arched and an expression a little like the photographer's had been.

"I don't know what to say… I mean, there are a lot of things I *want* to say, but—"

"Go ahead," she dared him, "tell me that's what I get for not being as strong as you were, not being strong enough to say no when he proposed because maybe I didn't really love him, and because he was another guy who probably didn't really love me. Go ahead and tell me that I was his rebound that he ditched when one look at his old girlfriend sent him running to her. Go ahead and tell me that if I'd really loved him I wouldn't have been half-glad to find them that way or feel relieved that I didn't end up having to marry him," she said, once again blurting out more than she probably should have.

"I was *not* going to say any of *that*!" he protested, taking a turn at being defensive.

Then he sighed and said, "I have no right to judge your relationship with Gary. But when it comes to us… nothing you're laying at my door is—"

Right. As if he really *had* loved her but bailed on her anyway.

"All I'll say about Gary," he said, "is that you deserve so much better than that—because you do. I can tell you that I think you *should* be relieved because you dodged a bullet not marrying some guy who should have gotten his act together before he ever proposed.

A guy who should have been out pounding on every door to get a job, not playing Mr. Fix-it while *you* were trying to do that *for* him. A guy who did you a favor by showing his colors *before* the wedding—"

"You'd like Rachel, you think alike," Maicy muttered since she knew those were things her friend would also have said. Rachel had been a little leery of Gary all along and suggested that, if nothing else, maybe the wedding shouldn't happen until after he was employed again.

Conor sighed a second time and Maicy peripherally saw him shake his head. "Sorry," he said. "It isn't easy for me to hear about you with some other guy. I should just be supportive and understanding. You're probably hurt and—"

Maicy made a face and shook her head. "I'm really not, that's the thing... I mean not..." Not the way she'd hurt when Conor had rejected her. But she wasn't going to confess to *that*! "I know it probably says something rotten about me, but I do keep feeling like I dodged a bullet. And then feeling guilty for that."

"What I think is that that's *your* gut talking to you the way mine was yesterday when it sounded to me like Declan was a little off and it crossed my mind to get back to him instead of coming here. *Something* was wrong with you and Gary, and deep down you know it's just better that you didn't get to the altar."

That was putting everything in a nutshell but it helped more than he could know to think that her relief was coming purely from instinct. And not because of the issues Drake—the man she'd been involved with before Gary—had accused her of. She really didn't want to end up dying alone someday—the destiny

Drake had so ominously predicted as the result of her independence…

"I hope you're right," she said, sitting up once more to stack their bowls and plates to take to the kitchen.

Conor stood and followed her. "And now we have cake!" he said, clearly forcing cheerfulness into the mix in an attempt to lighten the mood.

Maicy laughed at his attempt and that helped, too. "Just show me whatever tricks need to be used to wash these dishes," she mock-grumbled.

He took over, using the same tactics for dishwashing that they had to use for showering—water on only as needed—while Maicy dried them, ignoring his orders to sit down and let him do the cleanup.

When the pot, pan and dishes were finished and put away, Maicy opened the cake box.

But cake wasn't the only thing inside. The cake topper was there, too. A groom carrying a bride he was kissing.

And that gave her pangs.

The trouble was, the pangs weren't over Gary. The groom was too tall-seeming, too brawny and broad-shouldered to resemble her former fiancé and instead looked to her like Conor.

Conor who—even though she hadn't been aware of it yesterday—must have carried her over the threshold like that groom was carrying his bride.

Conor who, once upon a time, had kissed her like that groom was kissing his bride.

Conor who had kissed her like no one since…

She swallowed hard and pushed even harder on those memories and the absolutely stupid urges they triggered for him to kiss her like that again…

Absolutely stupid! she silently shouted at herself.

And of course she wouldn't let that happen. Even if he was so inclined. Which she knew he wasn't.

"You know, on second thought, I don't feel like cake. I think I'm just going to go to bed," she said then, feeling defeated by so many things but most of all by her inability to stop thinking about kissing Conor.

"Are you okay? How's your head?" he asked with low-grade alarm.

"I'm just tired," she insisted. "I probably should have done more resting than I did today. Like you told me to. But feel free to have cake if you feel like it."

"I'll wait," he said.

Maicy took the topper out of the box and dropped it unceremoniously into the trash bag before she closed the lid on the cake.

Then she glanced up and caught Conor watching her, taking it all in, a softness and compassion in his blue eyes.

"I think you did the right thing by running out on that wedding before it could happen," he said, that deep voice of his quiet, soothing. "You really do deserve better."

She merely shrugged, appreciating his words but wishing they were being said by anyone else.

Then he said, "I won't wake you the way I did last night, so you don't have to leave your door open. But I will keep the fire burning—somebody was smart to build that thing so it opens into both rooms."

"I can sleep but you aren't going to?" she asked.

"Doctors get pretty used to interrupted sleep so it isn't any big deal. After a lot of years of it, I can wake up instantly and go back to sleep the same way, the minute my head hits the pillow again. I just won't bother you when I do it."

Maicy merely nodded and said good-night, escaping into the bedroom.

But those uninvited thoughts of kissing him went with her.

And she ended up feeling as if she and Conor were still too close for comfort.

Chapter Four

By Tuesday the snow total went up and so did Conor's stress level. He still couldn't get a cell phone signal anywhere near the cabin.

To make matters worse, the roof had begun to groan under the weight of the snow accumulated up there. When he'd gone up the ladder to take a look, he'd discovered dangerously deep drifts.

He knew that put the roof at risk of caving in so rather than heading away from the cabin in search of a signal as he'd intended, he had to stay and deal with that.

At least the hard physical labor of shoveling the snow off the roof helped the tension. And today he needed that on two counts.

With the development of sepsis, a patient like Declan could go into multiple organ failure in the blink of an eye and it had been twenty-four hours since he'd been able to make any contact with his brother's doctor. Twenty-four hours during which anything—the worst—could have happened.

"You better be fighting like hell even without me, D," he said as he shoveled snow off the roof, as if his message would somehow get to Declan through the cosmos.

Then he reminded himself of the things Maicy had emphasized for him the night before—that both he and Declan had made Declan's allergies widely known; that Vince Collier was a good man, a good doctor who covered all the bases; that there was the possibility that everyone treating Declan might be inspired to put a little extra effort into his brother's care because they knew Conor was a navy doctor and that Declan was a decorated marine.

He just had to hang on to hope. But Conor was still so worried it was eating him alive and hard physical labor was the only thing keeping him sane.

Well, not the only thing.

It had, after all, been Maicy who had pointed out the very things he was using to get a grip. That meant she had a hand in his sanity, too.

He was grateful for her injecting some reason into his out-of-control worries.

Now that he thought about it, he was also grateful not to be here alone with those worries. To have someone to vent them to. Someone to distract him from them. He couldn't imagine how much worse this would be if he was alone up here.

On the other hand, Maicy being here was the second reason he needed the hard physical labor to distract him from his frustration and guilt—and other feelings he didn't want to think about…

She hadn't forgiven him—that seemed to be getting clearer and clearer. Not that he deserved it, because he didn't. But over the years he'd hoped—that damn word again—that maybe she had.

Instead, when she'd had that spontaneous out-pouring last night, he'd realized that far from being forgiven, his actions had twisted in her mind into something far worse than they'd truly been.

As if it hadn't been bad enough.

And if that warped version was what she'd taken away and carried around with her since she was seventeen, it only compounded things.

They were going to have to talk about it, he realized.

He didn't want to. It was opening an old wound that he wished would just finish healing already. But the longer they were here, the more clear it became to him that healing wouldn't happen until they resolved things between them.

He'd hoped he might use this time in the cabin to mend fences. But now he saw that he needed to be making corrections, too, and he couldn't go on putting it off. Because if she thought what she seemed to think, she was wrong.

Or was he the one who was wrong?

He'd assumed when she'd made that remark about Gary being *another* guy who hadn't really loved her that she'd been referring to him not loving her eighteen years ago. There wasn't a third guy, was there? Someone other than him—and now Gary—who had hurt her, too?

God, he hoped not.

She really—*really*—didn't deserve that. What he'd done was bad enough. He couldn't stand the thought that anyone else had come along and caused her equal amounts of pain. Let alone that there might have been two to follow in his footsteps.

Of course he didn't want to think there had been anyone who had followed him with her, period, he admitted.

Maicy with another guy? *Any* other guy? Ever? Yeah, he hadn't let his mind go there.

Even the whole wedding dress thing—he'd only been able to handle the idea of her all dressed up to marry someone else by convincing himself that she'd run away from her wedding because the guy she'd been about to marry hadn't lived up to him.

He knew that was self-centered and arrogant. But it was the sole way he *could* think about her on the verge of marrying another guy. And she hadn't seemed too upset about the aborted wedding so that had fed his delusions.

But what topped the strain of thinking about her with someone else, was thinking about someone—or multiple someones—hurting her. It was harder even than knowing he had. Because at least he'd had good intentions.

As if that mattered.

Or had made any of it any easier.

And God, nothing about it had been easy…

That first year he'd been away at college, that first year after he'd left her, it was a miracle that he'd passed his classes and kept up with the training and demands of his ROTC scholarship. His head—his heart—had still been back in Northbridge. With Maicy.

For months he'd called home every day—sometimes two and three times a day—asking anyone who answered the phone how she was doing. Until his family had taken a hard line with him and refused to talk about her.

She's going to school and doing what she's supposed to be doing, and that's what you need to be doing, too. So stop this and get on with it! his stepfather had said sternly before telling him that no one would talk to him about Maicy from then on—he'd made it a house rule.

Only his mother hadn't strictly adhered to it. She'd tossed him a crumb of information about Maicy here and there after that. Not much, but enough to reassure him that Maicy was all right, that she was doing fine without him.

And as much as it had ripped him apart to consider that she might have just forgotten about him, he'd also told himself—and known—that it was for the best if she had.

It was just that he hadn't been able to stand the thought of other guys being included in that moving on.

But the possibility that she might think that he'd rejected her proposal years ago because he hadn't loved her? That was not something that had ever occurred to him. And that did make the situation worse.

They were definitely going to have to talk about it. He couldn't let her go on believing that, especially if the misinterpretation might be still influencing anything in her life.

So they were going to have to talk about the past. While he contended with the present...

He'd been through the navy's toughest training. He'd been through military conflicts. He'd been stationed on an aircraft carrier and a submarine and in some of the harshest conditions the Middle East had to offer.

And nothing had been as hard as facing the fact that he and Maicy were a long—*long*—way from how they'd been years and years ago.

It wasn't as if he hadn't resolved his feelings for her. It was just that sometimes, alone in this cabin, he looked at her and it was like he was a kid again. As if they'd just suffered through a summer apart and now they were together again.

A summer apart, not eighteen years.

And he just wanted to grab her and pull her into his arms and kiss her hello…

It was crazy. And of course he'd never do it. But the inclination was there.

Maybe more than an inclination.

Because last night he'd been watching when she'd opened the box with her wedding cake in it. He'd seen her staring at that wedding topper, seen her throw it away.

And while he didn't know what was going on in her head, he'd had to think that regardless of what she'd said about being relieved not to marry Gary Stern, some not-pleasant emotions had struck her. And he'd had to fight to do nothing to comfort her.

He'd had to fight against the damned biggest urge to hold her and have her face against his chest and her body against his…

He took a particularly large shovelful of snow and threw it from the roof with a vengeance.

No, *that* would not go into the talk they needed to have.

Whatever feelings he might still have for her, he sure as hell wouldn't act on them.

Couldn't act on them.

Because they weren't kids anymore and they hadn't just spent a summer apart. And even if she knew where she was going from here, he wasn't so sure about his own future, and to start anything up with her now wouldn't be any better than what Gary Stern had done.

So he'd just keep shoveling snow, he told himself. He'd just keep trying to get through to the hospital and Declan and Declan's doctor, and using hard physical labor to keep everything contained.

Everything including keeping his hands to himself.

But he and Maicy did need to talk. Like it or not.

And he was going to make sure they did.

After witnessing three dizzy spells that had forced Maicy to grab for the nearest thing to keep herself from falling, Conor had given her even more strict orders to rest.

And so, reluctantly, Maicy had spent Tuesday on the couch, curled up with the magazines and the book she'd packed for her honeymoon, trying not to think about the fact that she was essentially in Conor's bed.

The couch was, after all, where he slept. And even though his bedding was neatly folded, stacked and out of the way, Maicy couldn't stop herself from imagining him lying exactly where she was. Picturing him here, his big body stretched out in all its male glory, set off thoughts and unwelcome memories.

The last Fourth of July that they'd been together they'd gone into a park in Northbridge to watch fireworks. Conor had found them the perfect spot and they'd spread a blanket under a huge oak tree. He'd sat with his back against that tree and become her chair, pulling her to sit between his legs, his arms wrapped around her.

And even though nearly two decades had passed since then, sitting on that sofa where he slept, the L of the sofa's back and side wrapped around her the way he had been that night, she couldn't escape reliving the way that had felt. They'd fit together so impeccably that it had seemed natural and right and the way it would always be.

And she couldn't help wondering how it would feel if he was there on the couch with her, sitting like that again now. Wondering if they would still fit...

Just read! she commanded herself, trying for the umpteenth time to concentrate on her book. But she only made it about two sentences further before her mind wandered back to Conor.

The rhythmic sound of his shoveling, which came from up on the roof, was soothing. A mental picture of him all bundled up, all muscle underneath the snow gear...

She growled at herself when she realized she was doing it again. Thinking about him again.

He was like a song she couldn't get out of her head.

Of course a song playing over and over in her head didn't mean anything, she reasoned. It didn't even mean she liked the song—in fact, more often than not, it was a song she *didn't* like. It was just a weird, glitchy annoyance. Something that happened for no reason, against her will, that she couldn't stop. That meant absolutely nothing.

Thinking about Conor fell into that category, she told herself. And it didn't mean anything, either.

But she really wished it would stop. It served no

purpose at all—except to irritate her. Bad enough that they were stuck here, in these close quarters, alone together. Not having a minute of peace from thoughts of him, from memories of him, from images of him, only made it worse.

She wiggled around to try to shake him out of her brain just as a fast movement of something outside caught her eye.

She glanced through the window over the couch, thinking that it had probably been a clump of snow falling from the porch overhang or a nearby tree.

Instead what she saw caused her to sit up straighter in alarm.

"Uh-oh!"

The movement had been a mountain lion jumping from the elevation of the piled-up snow onto the top of Conor's SUV.

A mountain lion that looked very interested in the activity on the roof.

The roof that the cat could easily reach from the vehicle it was perched on.

"Oh jeez… Are you seeing this, Conor?" she wondered out loud.

The sound of him working didn't stop so she had to assume he wasn't aware that a cougar was eyeing him like he was its evening meal.

She knew that Conor had gone up the ladder from the back side of the cabin, that that was where the ladder still was. If only he'd see the cat, he could climb down and get inside.

But she just kept hearing the sounds of his shovel scraping the shingles, the snow thrown off and hitting the ground over and over again.

And the cat was in hunting mode—statue-still, waiting, gauging, definitely not calling any more attention to itself.

Should she go out the rear door and shout for Conor to come in? Warn him?

Or would any change in what he was doing prompt the animal to strike? With the way the cat was watching him, she didn't think she had much time. She had to do *something* before it pounced!

She'd grown up in Northbridge—a rural town surrounded by open countryside. Wild animal sightings weren't unheard of. She tried to recall what was supposed to be done when faced with one. Play dead? Get away as fast as possible? Make noise and commotion and *not* run because that would prompt the animal to chase?

Which scenario was best for this?

She wasn't sure.

The lion tilted back ever so slightly and raised its head, surveying, just waiting for its moment.

There was no time to warn Conor.

Scaredy-cat...

It was a dumb thing to go through her mind but she decided to take it as a cue for the right choice of response—scare the cat away.

Afraid that pounding on the window might not be enough, she ran to the kitchen, grabbed a metal pot and a wooden spoon and ran back to the cabin's door. She could still keep an eye on the cat from there.

Not wanting to make herself a target, either, she only opened the door a crack, keeping her knee on the back of it so she could slam it closed if the lion's attention turned to her.

Then she started banging with all her might on the bottom of the pan and shouting at the top of her lungs, "Shoo! Shoo! Shoo! Get out of here! Shoo!"

Startled, the cat made a quick pivot, leaped off the SUV and ran into the woods.

"Oh, thank God!" Maicy muttered to herself while her heart went on racing. Dizziness hit her again and as she closed the door she rested her forehead to it, waiting for the spinning to stop.

That was when it occurred to her that the sounds of Conor's rooftop snow shoveling had stopped.

Then she heard him call, "Thanks," before he went back to work.

"I hope the look on your face means that you couldn't get a cell phone signal on the roof," Maicy said when Conor came in an hour later, after dark. One glance at those chiseled features told her he wasn't happy. "Or did you get through and get bad news about Declan?"

"No signal," Conor answered dourly.

"You know the saying—no news is good news…" Maicy offered.

"Not sure that applies here," he grumbled.

"I know. I also know it probably doesn't matter, but for what it's worth, I'm trying to stay positive."

He'd shed his outerwear and was setting it in front of the fire to dry again, so there was a moment before he said, "Declan needs a whole lot more than positive thinking to help him, but it's good for me. It also helps to come in here and see you and get out of my head a little bit and know I'm not in it alone." Then he left the room to take a shower.

Like the night before, though, the shower seemed to

lessen some of his tension. When he returned—again looking better than he should in his sweatsuit—he was in slightly improved spirits.

As he heated canned spaghetti he asked how she felt and how much dizziness she'd had while he was outside.

"Not as much as before," she assured him.

But still he refused to let her get up to help and brought everything to her.

As he settled on the couch, he actually laughed before he said, "*Shoo*? To a *mountain lion*?"

Maicy glanced at him over her shoulder. When they were teenagers and he'd laughed or smiled, lines hadn't been drawn at the corners of his eyes the way they were now. But they somehow accentuated those eyes, and Maicy judged the lines a nice addition.

"Did you see the cat before that—because I could still hear you shoveling and I didn't think you had," she asked.

"No, I hadn't seen it. I heard that racket you were making and looked up just as it turned tail and jumped off the car. That was a close call—one leap and it would have had me."

"That did seem to be what it had in mind."

"But *shoo*?" he repeated, laughing again and making her realize that lighter spirits put parentheses on either side of his sensual mouth, too. "Again—who *shoos* a mountain lion?"

"I didn't know what else to do. Did you want me to just let it get you?" Maicy asked.

He laughed again, this time wryly. "It probably would have given you some satisfaction if it had. So thanks for not giving in to that and saving my ass."

"Now we're even…for you hauling me out of my car so I didn't freeze to death."

That sobered his expression and arched his full eyebrows. "But nothing evens the score for all those years ago when you needed me to save you and I didn't," he said as if filling in the rest. "I wanted to talk about that…"

"There's nothing to talk about. It was what it was." A rejection from the only other person she'd trusted besides her mother. "But just to be clear," she added, "I wasn't asking you to save my life back then. Just to move up the schedule."

After dating for nearly three years and falling in love with him, believing him when he'd told her they'd have a future together, she'd turned to him instinctively when her mother had been in a fatal car accident just before the start of her senior year of high school.

No one had heard from her father in four years, and there hadn't been any other family. Maicy had been left with her mother's small bank account, only the remainder of the month to stay in their apartment and nothing besides the income from her part-time job at the ice cream parlor to live on.

"I was just asking you to marry me *ahead* of the schedule we'd already planned," she reiterated.

"I know. But—"

"You didn't want to," she said flatly.

"It wasn't that, Maicy. You know how it was—I was going to college on an ROTC scholarship *and* an accelerated program that combined college and medical school into six years. That meant a heavy course load along with ROTC training and obligations. We were supposed to do things long-distance until you graduated college and *then* get married—"

"But things had changed, and colleges have housing for married students," she said in a calm, reasonable tone that was nothing like the frantic, desperate, scared way she'd said it to him long ago when she'd begged him to marry her before he left so she could go with him.

"It was so much more complicated than that," he responded. "I was leaving in two weeks, but I wasn't going to turn eighteen for two more months and there was no way my mom or Hugh would sign permission. It was too late to arrange for couples' housing and under the terms of my scholarship, I was required to live on campus. Even if something had opened up at the last minute in married housing, my scholarship wouldn't have covered it—we would have had to come up with rent money. And on top of all that, you still had a year left of high school—I didn't want to risk you not graduating. Even if you'd tried finishing school in Missouri, would you really have been able to pull it off? Married, trying to work to earn our rent money and commuting to a high school without a car? With me needing to study as much as I knew I would have to—as much as I *did* have to? With me not having a minute to spare for you? For us?"

He'd finished his spaghetti and set the bowl on the coffee table before he leveled those piercing blue eyes at her and went on. "You were upset about your mom, in a panic…anyone in that situation would have been. But you weren't thinking clearly and I *had* to. I had to make sure all the bases were covered for us both—"

"Like you did for your own mother. And for your

brothers and sister and the farm when your mom bottomed out when you were a little kid."

"Yeah, it *was* like that! You weren't thinking any straighter than my mom was then. Again, I understood, it was an emotional time for you—"

"But not for you," she accused.

"Yes, for me, too!"

"But not nearly enough for you to actually go through with what we'd talked about and get married."

"Because neither of us was ready to get married, no matter what our feelings were," he said gruffly. "And that's exactly what I wanted to talk about. That remark you made last night that Gary was *another* guy who probably didn't love you. You don't really think that, do you? That I didn't love you? Come on…" he chastised a second time in disbelief.

Disbelief? Really? He was really that surprised that she'd gotten the message that he didn't love her? What else was she supposed to think? She'd believed that he'd put them first—that staying together was as important to him as it was to her. But when she'd proposed, he'd just been full of excuses for why she couldn't come with him.

"Then don't go…"

That's what she'd said to him eighteen years ago when they'd had this argument the first time.

And along with rejecting her proposal, he also hadn't chosen the option of staying.

If he'd loved her the way she'd loved him, he would have done one of the two, no matter what it would have taken. When he hadn't, she'd known that he didn't love her the way she'd loved him.

"It's all water under the bridge," she said rather than answer his question.

"You're wrong if you believe that I didn't care," he said earnestly. "I never intended for us to go our separate ways—I just wanted us to stay the course we'd set. Once I knew that arrangements could be made for you to move in with the minister and his wife to be the nanny to their kids while you finished high school, I just wanted us to get back on track. I wanted you to go on to college and graduate, and *then* we could get married the way we'd planned. It was you who broke up with me."

It *had* been her who had broken up with him. Because his refusal to make any change to the plan, to stand by her when her entire life had fallen apart, his choice to leave, smacked of her childhood.

"Yeah, my father always claimed to have *feelings* for my mom and me but that didn't stop him from bolting at the slightest bump in the road."

"Oh, that's not fair, either! Comparing me to your old man?"

"Actually, as time went on and I got over…things…I gave you points for *not* doing what he did, for not marrying me and *then* running out on the promises that marriage came with. At least you nipped it in the bud before we got married. But it still wasn't what I was counting on from you."

"Ah, Maicy…" he lamented.

"Like I said, water under the bridge."

He took a breath and sighed. "It was a lousy situation at a lousy time."

"For me. It didn't change your life at all. You did what you were set to do—you went to college, became a doctor and joined the navy the way you'd always planned."

"I asked about you… My mom said you were doing okay."

There was some accusation in that that Maicy didn't understand. But it was so ludicrous it made her laugh.

"I was doing okay?" she repeated. "Yeah, I was doing great. That whole year, I did just great," she said sarcastically. "And then I did great the first year of college, too." She refused to confide in him about the days when she hadn't been able to get out of bed, or when she barely went through the motions, overwhelmed by more tears than she'd thought she was capable of producing, feeling as if she was in such a deep, dark hole that she might not ever get out of it.

"My mother was just trying to make me feel better by telling me you were okay," he said as if he'd always feared that might be the case.

Maicy didn't think she needed to confirm it. Instead she said somewhat defiantly. "I did learn not to depend on anyone—that's a good thing. When I imagine the person I might have been had you *not* left me hanging I'd rather be who I am now."

Conor was staring at her, scrutinizing her, and she didn't like that so she stood, took his bowl and hers and went to the kitchen with them.

He followed her with the box of crackers, replacing them in the mudroom.

When he joined her as she washed the dirty dishes, he leaned against the counter beside where she stood at the sink, facing the opposite direction, dishtowel in hand, at the ready for drying-duty.

"What would you have ended up being?" he asked then.

"Weak," she answered with more defiance. "Dependent on you instead of being independent." Though that unyielding self-reliance had been what had irked Drake, and her strength had maybe not been the best thing when it came to Gary...

"I guess I might have just been your tagalong rather than my own person," she added. "Or worse, what my mother was—constantly waiting for a man who was off doing his own thing without any regard for her or his kid."

"So I had no love, no *regard* for you. And your mother's lot in life is how you would have ended up if we *had* gotten married," he concluded as she dried her hands on one end of the dishtowel he was using and then took up a stance with her hips against the utility table across from him.

She only raised a challenging chin to his summary.

Finished with his part of the chore he tossed the dishtowel to the counter with some force before he scowled at her. "I had regard for you then and I still do. I've never *not* had *regard* for you."

Maicy shrugged as if it didn't matter. And she wouldn't let it matter because she couldn't really believe him anyway.

He shook his head as if he was shaking something off. Then, in a less agitated tone, said, "What if, Maicy? What if nothing bad had happened to your mom and once we were apart life had just insidiously taken us on separate paths and what we were to each other had just dwindled off the way first love can? Would everything that came before, everything we did and shared, all we had together, still be canceled out? Because we *were* happy together...really happy..."

She wouldn't concede to that and still didn't answer him.

He went on anyway.

"Take away that shadow, Maicy, and that time before, those *years* before, are still the best memories I have, and I can't tell you how much I hate that that isn't true for you. I have moments when I remember something so sweet or nice or funny or…so you…and I can't stand to think that all that's left of that for you is bad."

She closed her eyes tight, fighting, fighting, fighting so hard against it.

But when she opened her eyes again it came out anyway. In a whisper.

"It isn't," she confessed.

"So the ending didn't poison everything that came before," he said quietly, his deep voice even deeper. Standing there tall and straight and strong and so sexy she just wanted to hit him.

But it didn't change anything—not the fact that he'd made her think about how the first snow every year reminded her of when he'd shown up at her door to take her for a midnight walk in it.

Not the fact that he'd made her think about what it had felt like every single time he'd held her hand.

Not the fact that he'd made her think about picnics and country drives and kisses in front of her school locker and how no one had ever been able to make her laugh like he had.

And not the fact that he was now the most gorgeous man she'd ever been in this close a proximity to.

None of it changed anything, she told herself firmly.

Because the way they'd ended *had* cast a big black

shadow over everything else for her. And she needed not to let that shadow recede.

Especially not when she was locked here in this tiny cabin alone with him, mere days after running out on her wedding to someone else. She needed some serious time and thought put into her future relationships before she ever ventured near another one. Especially with Conor.

So no, she couldn't let anything be changed.

But something else had shifted with that stupid admission that she hadn't forgotten the good because suddenly he took a step that put him in front of her. For a moment, it seemed as if he was going to move the few inches nearer to start kissing her now…

She raised her chin a bit higher in what she convinced herself was more defiance. A dare for him to just try it so she could shoot him down.

But after another minute of whatever it was that was hanging in the air between them, he pulled back, nearly plopped against the counter again, and glanced at the pink box that still held the uncut top of her wedding cake.

"Dessert?" he asked in a voice more jagged than it had been.

Maicy had no idea why she was suddenly struck by a double punch of frustration and disappointment, but it soured her on the idea of cake for a second night.

So she said, "No, saving your ass tired me out—I think I'll just go to bed and read awhile."

He smiled at the *saving his ass* part and nodded. "I do want you to get rest."

"Good night then," she said aloofly, heading for the bedroom.

But after stepping into it, before closing the door behind her, she stole another glance at him.

He was still standing there, still watching her.

With an expression on that handsome face that made her think he was reliving something from their past.

The good or the bad? she wondered.

Knowing as she closed the door that even though it was memories of the bad she wanted to take to bed with her, now that he'd made her think of them, it was more likely memories of the good that were going to haunt her tonight.

Chapter Five

Wednesday brought Conor more worry and frustration along with still more snow from that unrelenting storm.

He spent the morning shoveling the porch and the path to the woodpile, and again clearing snow from the cabin's roof and from his rented SUV before letting the vehicle run for ten minutes to keep the battery from dying and to add a little charge to his cell phone.

When he went in to warm up he also heated water for the shower Maicy said she was desperate for since he'd persuaded her to skip one on Tuesday in order to do nothing but rest.

While she was showering, he ate a lunch of dried salami and crackers and tried not to think about Maicy naked and wet just a room away.

When he couldn't stop himself from fantasizing

about joining her, he decided he'd better get out of there.

So he bundled up again to snowshoe away from the cabin in search of cell service, hoping to God he didn't have to go another day without word of his brother.

When he did find a spot where he could get reception and he reached Declan's doctor the news wasn't good.

His brother had had an allergic reaction to one of the combination of antibiotics he'd been given. His blood pressure was alarmingly low, his lung and kidney functions were compromised. And the results of lab tests to isolate the bacteria causing the infection had been delayed because the lab was shorthanded.

"I'm going to the lab myself right now," Vince told him. "And I'm not leaving until I have an answer. I'm sticking with him, Conor, I haven't left the hospital since I got here yesterday morning. You should know that whichever of the antibiotics he reacted to wasn't one on your allergy list—I'm making sure he isn't getting any of those. But apparently there are others he can't take, either. I'm starting him on a new combination now and I'm administering them myself, one at a time, and monitoring him for a reaction so I can be sure he can tolerate them. We're doing our best for him."

Conor knew the warning tone in the other doctor's voice because he'd used it himself too often—it was the implied *but* that meant that despite doing his best for Declan, Declan was getting worse.

"I need to be there!" Conor said through clenched teeth.

"Believe me, I wish you were—for Declan's sake and because I could use the help," said the other doctor, who sounded as tired and overworked as Conor knew he was. "But I promise you I'm doing everything I can."

"I know, I know. And I'm just keeping you from it," Conor said, trying to be patient when he was anything but. Then he said, "Any chance I can talk to Declan?"

"I have him heavily sedated."

So no.

As much as Conor didn't want to cut off the connection once he had it, he knew Declan needed Vince's attention more than he did so he let the call end. Then, fighting hard against the out-of-control feelings his helplessness sent through him, he forced himself to refocus, sent the text Maicy had asked him to send to her friend Rachel if he found service, and—since he still had reception—called Rickie in Northbridge.

Unfortunately, Rickie still couldn't give him a timetable for when he might be able to escape the small town to plow the road up to the cabin in order for Conor and Maicy to get out.

Rickie also informed him that there were even more road closures and that there wasn't an airport in all of Montana open, dashing any hope at all that Conor could get back to Declan anytime soon.

So with his stress level at the limit, Conor returned to the cabin and took it out in splitting more wood.

And somehow, somewhere along the way, he went from worrying about Declan to thinking about his conversation with Maicy the night before.

She really was holding one hell of a grudge against him. And even after all these years, she still didn't see things the way he had.

But she *was* right that he'd gone into a mode similar to what he'd had to do as a kid when his mother had bottomed out—something he'd told Maicy about when they were dating.

He'd been seven years old when it happened for no reason he'd understood at the time. One afternoon, a few months before Kinsey was born, they'd come home from school and she'd been sobbing at the kitchen table over a newspaper article about a plane crash. The plane crash that he'd learned later had taken the life of his mother's *friend* Mitchum Camden.

After that there was a long period when his mother hadn't gotten out of bed, when she'd just stayed there crying. It had been up to him to get breakfast, fix school lunches, to get himself and the twins dressed and onto the bus that would take them all to the school where he was in the second grade and where the twins went to preschool.

Days and then weeks and then months when his mother had left it up to him to fix dinner, to give his brothers a bath and put them to bed at night. She'd managed to give him instructions on what to tell Smith— the man who ran the farm for them—but she wouldn't leave her bed to see her orders carried out, which left it up to him. Conor had to be *the man of the house*, his mother had told him.

He'd been scared. Confused. Worried, too, because he hadn't known what had happened to change his usually cheery, caring mother. But he'd taken the responsibility she'd placed on him seriously. And he'd begun to map out how to take care of everything that needed to be done.

He'd learned that if he planned ahead and stuck to

his plan, to his schedule, he could make sure Declan, Liam and his mother were taken care of.

He'd learned to be the intermediary between the rest of the world and his mother—who had lost the desire to leave her room even when she did start getting out of bed every day.

He'd learned the importance of organization—even though he didn't know that word—and had made sure lunches were packed the night before for himself and his brothers, made sure they got up on time in the mornings, had breakfast, left the house and never missed the bus that would take them into town.

He'd learned to solve problems that arose—how to stand on a chair brought to the front of the washing machine to do the laundry, how to use that same chair to put away the groceries his mother ordered and had delivered.

He'd become his mother's courier, distributing the checks she wrote for the farmhands on payday, bringing her the mail, putting the checks she wrote to pay the bills out in the box.

He'd kept everything and everyone going until months later when Kinsey had been born and his mother had seemed to come out of her funk.

But even after the burden of looking after his family and the farm were finally taken off his small shoulders, Conor was never the same. He'd been left with a strong sense of responsibility and the need to do everything he could to try to prevent bad things from happening, to take every possible disaster into account and plan accordingly.

He'd become a cautious kid who grew into a cautious teenager, and then a cautious adult, a cautious physician.

So yes, when Maicy's mom had died so unexpectedly and Maicy had been left in a state of panic, both his sense of responsibility and his need for careful restraint had kicked in.

He'd felt responsible for making sure Maicy didn't go off the rails. Responsible for making calm, rational decisions for both of them when she couldn't. Which, to him, meant sticking to their plan in order to make sure that she finished high school and they both got through college before marrying. He'd been convinced that it was his job to keep them both on course the same way he'd kept his family on course when he was seven.

And if he looked at where he and Maicy had gotten in their lives, he thought a case could be made for him having been right. Maicy *had* finished high school, gone on to college and an advanced degree, started her own business. And he'd accomplished what he'd set out to accomplish, too. If he'd given in to her proposal, who knows what might have happened? Even she admitted that she preferred the person she was now to the person she might have become.

But still she resented him for having said no.

Could he use this time together to get her to let go of that grudge?

He really wanted to see that happen.

And the day *was* at an end, he thought, his spirits bouncing back at that prospect.

Without cell service again, he was once more cut off from the outside world, leaving nothing but going inside for an evening with Maicy. And the opportunity to possibly gain a little more ground against that grudge seemed like a worthwhile way to spend that time.

Who are you trying to kid? he asked himself as he finished splitting logs and loaded them into the sling.

Yes, he was again grateful that being with Maicy would offer a distraction from his troubles, and yes, he was glad to have more chance to work on her lingering ill will against him.

But that wasn't the real reason he was eager to go inside. Despite her resentment, he was still looking forward to just being with her. To talking to her. Like in the old days.

He recognized that thinking like that now was a little crazy. These definitely were not the *old days*. And whether or not he broke through the barrier that had risen between them, they'd still walk away from this as two people who shared a past with a bad ending, forced together by circumstances until they were finally able to go their separate ways.

But he'd meant what he'd said when he'd told her that the memories of their past *before* that bad ending were the best he had. And what he hadn't told her was just how often he still revisited those memories. His memories of her.

Memories that had hit him so hard last night that for just a minute he was back with her under the bleachers. Back to when she was his girl and it had been killing him that she was hanging onto her virginity. Back to when he'd at least been able to kiss her.

And he'd wanted to kiss her so much at that moment that it had pushed him to close the distance between them in the kitchen…

Before he'd snapped out of it.

But still it had seemed as if the universe had shifted a little all the way around in that moment. As if it had been okay that he'd gotten that close. As if just maybe, when she'd looked up at him, she hadn't despised him.

And as stupid as it seemed, that split second felt encouraging to him. It had him looking forward to spending the evening with her as more than merely a distraction or a chance to work on her grievance.

There was some danger in that, he told himself.

Because remember there's nowhere for anything to go from here.

But even knowing that was true, he couldn't stop the feeling of urgency to get inside and have this time with her.

And while he'd successfully kept himself busy and away from the cabin all day, now that night was upon them, he could finally give in to it.

Wednesday was the first day that Maicy felt reasonably well again. She only had a slight headache, some periodic dizziness, fewer aches and pains, and less stiffness and weakness. With the exception of the healing cut on her forehead she felt more like herself. And she wanted to look like herself again, too—rather than like a recovering patient.

So even though it used up more water than her first cabin shower had, that afternoon she took a more thorough one with her own bodywash, and she gave herself a far better shampoo, too.

Then, she devoted her afternoon to her appearance. Because the better she looked, the better she felt.

At least that was her reasoning while she tried to

ignore the fact that lurking behind every choice she made were thoughts of Conor.

Conor and what she could do to knock his socks off.

But not to entice him, of course. Only to make him sorry for what he'd passed up. What he'd passed up years ago—and again last night when she'd thought he was going to kiss her. She was tired of being so resistible to him. Especially when it seemed like her own eyes popped out of her head every time she looked at him.

So it was time to get herself back on track.

She was a notorious overpacker and the fact that she'd thought to be spending a few days in wintry Northbridge and returning from her Jamaican honeymoon to also wintry Denver meant that she was equipped for two seasons.

Today she chose a pair of jeans that fit to perfection, and a hunter green, high-neck cashmere sweater that provided the exact amount of accentuation where she wanted it.

Her red hair was thick and naturally wavy, and while she couldn't use her hairdryer, she was careful as she dried it in front of the fire to scrunch it every few minutes. That aided the waves so that it didn't need to be hooked behind her ears or tied up, and could be left loose to fall over her shoulders.

Being a natural redhead, she had the pale porcelain skin to go with it so she never went anywhere without blush and a touch of bronzer to add some color, plus mascara to darken her lashes, so she applied all of that, too.

Standing in front of the mirror in the bedroom, she parted her hair on the side in order for it to camouflage her wound and the two butterfly bandages over it before taking a final assessment.

None-the-worse-for-wear was her verdict.

About how she looked, anyway. But she was reminded that she wasn't at a hundred percent when she realized that her afternoon of beautifying had worn her out.

To deal with that, she rested awhile before turning her attention to dinner.

And to watching, rather impatiently, for Conor to come back.

It was just cabin fever, she told herself. It wasn't that she wanted to see *him*, to spend the evening with *him*. It was just that after hours alone in that quiet, small space with little to do, company—no matter who provided it—became something to break the monotony.

And she decided she was also going to blame thinking about him every minute on cabin fever, boredom and isolation. On not having anyone or anything else *to* think about right now.

And she was going to blame the fact that last night she'd dreamed about him on her head injury.

None of it—not a single minute of any of it—had anything to do with any feelings on her part for the man himself, she assured herself as she kept an eagle eye out the window for him. It didn't matter that he was fantastic-looking or too-sexy-to-believe now. It didn't matter that he had those amazing blue eyes. And it certainly didn't mean that she had any lingering or new attraction to him.

What had been between them was over and done with. And when it became time for her to move on, to date and try to find a new relationship, it would be time to move *on*, not to move backward. To learn from her mistakes—which included him—and use those lessons not to make more mistakes with anyone she let herself get involved with.

The minute she could get out of here Conor would be nothing but history again. Painful, better-forgotten history. And she couldn't wait for that to happen. She couldn't wait to be back in Denver again, to have Rachel to talk to, and to once more put Conor well, well, *well* behind her.

But for the time being, Conor Madison was all she had to counteract the cabin fever, boredom and isolation so he was a necessary evil.

Although even after reassuring herself of all of that, there was just no explanation for why nothing but a necessary evil made her pulse speed up when she heard him return to the cabin.

He didn't come inside right away, though, and she battled disappointment at that. Instead he went around back and began splitting wood behind the house.

But still he was there. And one glimpse of him in all his heavy winter gear just outside gave her a warm rush that she didn't want to acknowledge.

Any more than she wanted to acknowledge the desire to check the mirror to make sure that her hair and makeup were still up to par.

"Look at you!" Conor said when he finally did come inside with the canvas sling filled with wood.

Maicy fought for nonchalance even though it was ridiculously gratifying to hear the admiration in his voice. And even more satisfying to see his gaze go from top to bottom and back again, and to have his eyebrows arch in approval.

"I was tired of convalescent clothes," she said simply.

It must not have fooled him, though, because his eyes went to her hair as if it was the telltale sign of all the effort she'd put into getting ready for tonight.

Or maybe he just liked the way it looked when it was down because he smiled before he went off to heat water and shower while Maicy worked on the evening meal.

Salmon loaf made from canned salmon, cracker crumbs and powdered egg; and mashed potatoes from dried potato flakes.

Maicy thought that this place was the best diet she'd ever been on because she certainly had no desire to overeat.

Conor, on the other hand, ate heartily, assuring her that he'd had worse.

Maicy wondered if it was stress eating when he updated her on how sick Declan was. Conor's even-more-elevated tension and concerns were evident.

Between her inclination to make him feel better and the fact that she was in a stronger frame of mind today, Maicy decided tonight was the night for cake.

Moist, dark chocolate cake with Rachel's delectable buttercream frosting—far superior to what had become common cabin fare.

And it seemed to do the trick for lightening the mood because after taking their slices back to the sofa, where they sat on opposite sides of the couch, each of them angled toward the center, Conor breathed a sigh of satisfaction and said, "Chocolate…if I'd known this wasn't plain old white cake under that frosting this might not still be around. But of course your wedding cake would be chocolate—I should have guessed."

It was an obsession they'd always shared.

"Not just chocolate, *triple* chocolate," Maicy said. "It's a recipe Rachel—who used to own a bakery—makes especially for me so it'll be chocolaty enough."

He tried a bite—savoring it rather than inhaling it the way he had the rest of the meal.

"Now that's good cake," Conor judged. "Too bad you didn't run off with all the tiers."

"I wish I had," Maicy agreed.

"And your friend Rachel couldn't come to the wedding because she's pregnant?"

"After years of fertility treatments and failed attempts to have a baby. Because of her history it's a high-risk pregnancy and her doctor won't let her travel. Otherwise she'd have been my matron of honor."

"And you met Rachel in college?"

"Our first day—we were roommates. Who became more like sisters. She took me home every vacation. Her family sort of adopted me. I spend holidays with them still."

"Nice. I'm glad to hear that," he said sincerely. "And I did send her the text today when I found service, the way you asked. I said I was a friend—I thought that was better than saying I'm your ex. I told her that you're okay but we're snowed in in a cabin near Northbridge. That I have to hike out for cell service and you'll call when you can."

"Oh good! I'm sure she's worrying. That should help. Thanks."

Now that he seemed more relaxed, she felt she

could broach the topic of his worries again. "You told me before that you left Declan because there's been something going on with Kinsey? Is she still in North-bridge?"

"No, she lives in Denver. We were supposed to meet at the farm to start going through Mom and Hugh's things—"

"Your mom and Hugh…" She trailed off with a question in her tone.

"Hugh died not quite two years ago, and then Mom passed in October."

"I'm sorry. I hadn't heard."

"Yeah… Kinsey handled everything—none of us could get home, even for the funerals," he added with regret.

"The navy and the Marines don't let you come back for that?" Maicy said in surprise.

"It depends on where you are, what you're in the middle of. There were different situations for all of us, but both times none of us could swing it. I was on a submarine when Hugh went, and Liam and Declan were in Afghanistan. When it came to Mom…Declan was hurt the day before she died so there was no get-ting back then for Declan or me, and Liam is Special Forces and didn't even get word of it until the funeral was over."

"So poor Kinsey was alone for it all?" Maicy asked.

"Yeah." More guilt was evident in his voice and ex-pression. "It was a lot for her. We all feel rotten about her being stuck with the whole burden, but there was just nothing any of us could do."

"So you came now to make it up to her?"

"No…" he said and there seemed to be some kind

of hedging in the way he said it. "I mean, yeah, we all wish we *could* make it up to her. But I don't think that's possible. And now there's something else to deal with. Something that came out of Mom's death…"

He was clearly reluctant to talk about whatever that something else was, frowning down at his cake, apparently unaware that Maicy was watching him closely, studying him.

Okay, maybe she was drinking in the sight of him.

But he'd come from his shower dressed in jeans and an exceedingly form-fitting heather-gray mock-neck T-shirt rather than a sweat suit tonight, and she was only human. The T-shirt molded to every muscle of his torso and it was difficult for her *not* to ogle him.

After a moment of wrestling with his thoughts, he finally said, "When Mom was dying she told Kinsey something…she needed to explain a huge chunk of money we were about to inherit. And then there was a letter, too…"

He hesitated again before he took a deep breath, exhaled with what sounded like resignation, and said, "Mom claims that Mitchum Camden was our biological father."

Maicy had never told Conor that his mother's past was actually one of her own mother's cautionary tales to scare her into maintaining her virginity—a single woman with four bastard children to raise alone, looked down on by some of the town and forced to make ends meet on her own while the father got off scot-free. What her mother hadn't said was who the scot-free father might have been.

"Mitchum Camden," Maicy repeated in genuine shock.

The Camden Superstores, founded decades ago by Northbridge native H.J. Camden when he'd gone to Denver to seek his fortune, had elevated the family to distinction and wealth. The current Camden generation and their grandmother were well respected, but those who had come before had reputations for a slew of dishonorable deeds that had long been swept under the carpet. Apparently including married Mitchum Camden's long-term affair with Alice Shea when he'd frequented the Northbridge ranch that the Camdens owned.

"Did you have any idea before this?" Maicy asked.

Another pause. Another sigh. Before he scrunched up his face and confessed. "I'm the only one of us who's old enough to remember things like my mom's 'friend' who visited us sometimes. And stayed over... He brought us presents and took us outside to play. I didn't know a Camden from a hole in the ground but I knew his name was Mitchum and later, remembering that, I put two and two together." He shook his head. "I've never said that to a soul," he admitted then.

"Not even to Liam or Declan? Not to Kinsey?"

"Not to anyone. Declan and Liam have never said anything to make me think they remember him—and they were only three the last time he was at the farm. Kinsey wasn't even born yet. She was still a baby when Mom met Hugh. From her perspective, he was around from the start. She never had to deal with any growing up without a father's name to protect her. Mom and Hugh got married when Kinsey was two, and after that people were more careful about what they said and they stopped looking at us like we had scales so..." He shrugged those broad shoulders and sighed yet again.

"I liked *not* being a pariah better than being one and kept quiet."

Maicy flinched at that, not having known there was a time when little Conor had felt that way. "How were you a pariah?"

"There were just things… Birthday parties I didn't get invited to and comments about why. Even kids who were my friends at school weren't allowed to come to my house. I'd be in town with my mom and see the looks she got, watch people turn their heads and whisper, snicker. I was too young to really know what it was about, but I knew it was something bad. That they thought *we* were something bad. And I *didn't* know why we didn't have a dad around like everyone else did—something my mom wouldn't talk about even when I asked. It was just obvious that there was something different about us, something other people considered wrong or bad. Then Hugh came on board and things got different."

Hugh Madison had been a retired marine. A big, strapping, ultra-serious man whom no one wanted to cross.

"I guess he made an honest woman out of Mom," Conor went on. "And I was glad to put everything before that out to pasture, to forget about it and be a family like everyone else's. It was dirt I never wanted stirred up again."

"But now?"

"I feel the same way now," he confirmed without a hint of a waver. "As far as I'm concerned, as far as Declan and Liam are concerned, Hugh was our father—he raised us, he was there for us."

"Even if he'd wanted to, Mitchum Camden couldn't

have been there because he was killed in that plane crash with so many of his family," Maicy pointed out.

"Yeah, I know, I picked up the slack when my mom hit bottom after that. But there's nothing in anything he did before to make me think it would have been different even if he had lived. We were his dirty little secret and I'm sure that's what we would have stayed."

"So finding out the truth doesn't change anything for you?"

"Not really. Left to me, I'd go on the way I always have. I'd ignore that piece of the past and only honor what came after it—that Hugh and my mother were our parents, our family. The ones who did right by us. I don't give a damn about the bloodlines."

"But Kinsey does?" Maicy asked.

There was another pause that put chagrin in his expression. "We haven't been there for Kinsey. She's had to carry all the weight here at home. It's cost her friends, relationships... After Mom died, I guess it got to be a really big deal to her that she didn't have anybody. And she started to look at that whole slew of Camdens out there and got these crazy ideas about reaching out to them. Trying to be part of their family so she could have more than three brothers who haven't been there for her. Who aren't there for her. Who she doesn't really have any hope of ever being there for her if we all stay career military."

"But you still don't think she *should* pursue it?" Maicy asked, finishing her cake and setting her plate on the coffee table.

"No matter what we think, she already did it," he said somewhat under his breath. "She brought the letter from our mom to the Camden grandmother."

"Who would also be *your* grandmother—"

"Yeah, that's what Kinsey keeps reminding me."

"How did that go?"

"Not well—it sure as hell didn't go the way Kinsey was hoping it would."

"It went the way you were afraid it might?"

"Well, apparently the grandmother didn't call us bastards and kick her out, but she didn't say *welcome to the family*, either. Seems like Kinsey dropped the bomb and then just had to retreat when the old lady met the news with stony silence. That's how it's been since, except that Kinsey found out that the Camdens hired someone to investigate. I know Kinsey sent them a Christmas card but they didn't send one back."

Maicy had always liked Kinsey Madison and she hated to think of the Camdens or anyone else hurting her feelings. "Poor Kinsey," she said, looking closely at Conor, thinking about him in comparison to the Camdens.

From the publicity pictures she'd seen, there was a resemblance. He did have similar dark, swarthy good looks, although she thought he was even better-looking. But it was the eyes that sold it—the Camden blue eyes. Only with those silvery streaks added to them to make them even more distinctive.

"Anyway," he said, "that's why I came—so maybe I could talk my sister into letting it lie. Especially now because she's gotten engaged and won't be alone anymore."

The way he said that made her think of something else he'd said earlier. "Before, when you said none of you were there for Kinsey and wouldn't be *if* you all stay in the military—is there a chance that any of you won't? That she might have one of you home, too?"

There was another pause, this one longer, before he finished his cake and set the plate on top of Maicy's on the coffee table.

"I don't know… I guess Kinsey isn't the only one of us going through some stuff. I've been kind of…unsettled lately. And I'm up for promotion and if I need to make a change now's the time—it wouldn't be right to take the promotion and then get out."

"What? You mean one of Hugh's recruits might not stay in the military until retirement?" she goaded mildly. Back in the day, she really had been a little resentful of the way that Hugh had pushed all the boys into the idea that they needed to join the military. Conor always swore it was what he wanted, what they all wanted, but she had her doubts. From what Conor had said about his childhood before his mom got married, it was easy to see why he'd practically hero-worshipped his stepfather. The thought of disappointing him would have been a powerful motivation to fall in line with Hugh's plans.

"Believe me, that's part of what makes it tough. I know he'd turn over in his grave if he knew. He might even haunt me," Conor joked.

Maicy was glad to see the lighter side of him still there tonight even though it was waffling with the more serious subjects.

"It isn't the possibility of a haunting that makes this tough on you," she said then. "It's that you need to stick to your plan and if you're starting to doubt the path you're on that's a *huge* deal for you."

"You know me too well, is what you're saying," he said wryly.

Maicy merely challenged him to deny it, with the arch of her eyebrows.

"Yeah, I'll admit that. It goes against my grain. Big-time. Tell me it serves me right."

Just a little...

But she didn't say that. Instead she said, "You could just make another plan."

He made a sound that was something like a growl. "And you always say that as if it's nothing."

Maicy shrugged. "I counsel a lot of people making job changes. It *is* hard. But it *can* be done."

"It's more complicated for me—and not just because everything in me tells me to stick to the current plan," he insisted.

"Everybody thinks that," Maicy said.

"That doesn't stop it from being true. When I went through rotations in med school I liked being that first guy to help traumatically injured patients—that's why I picked my specialty. Plus I was willing to be stationed overseas, in the thick of any conflict. But as time's gone on I've started not liking that I just patch people up to ship them off, that I don't know if they're getting the care they need afterward. And on top of that I've been hearing about the troubles with the VA hospitals—where my patients need to go when they come home. Now, being with Declan, I've seen for myself the holes in the system those military men and women could easily fall through and that there's cause for concern. But for me to change what I do is—"

"I know, it isn't easy," Maicy sympathized.

"Particularly for people who've had my kind of education and training. In order for me to practice another kind of medicine, it means another residency—that's not going back to square one but almost. The navy has what it paid for in my education. A do-over is not really an option. To make a change, not only would I have to go in reverse, I'd have to leave the navy to do it," he concluded.

"Okay, you're right, your situation is more complicated than most," she allowed. "But what if you separate the two things? If you were a civilian would you stay the course or take the do-over?" she asked.

He frowned. "I guess I never thought about it like that. Separate them, huh? Take the military out of the equation and only focus on the job? *Then* figure out if that's important enough to leave the navy..." he mused.

"Knowing the one might help you make the decision about the other."

"Hmm... I'm gonna have to think about that," he said as if it were a revelation.

Since he seemed to be swimming around in the idea, Maicy opted to leave him to it and took their dessert dishes to the sink to wash. When she'd finished that and turned back to Conor he was in front of the fire, poking at it with the stoker, making room to add wood to the flames.

As so often happened, she was stalled for a moment as her gaze stuck to him. The last couple of hours of being with him and talking as easily as they always had had shaken her determination not to be attracted to him.

But then he took two split logs from the pile he'd brought in earlier and something else caught her eye.

"Mouse!" she cried as it ran out of the stack.

Conor spun around, looking for it, one of the logs in his hand held like a weapon, poised to hit it.

"No, don't kill it!" Maicy said, running around the utility table. "It's just a baby."

A baby frantically looking for cover.

"It can't be a pet, Maicy," Conor countered reasonably.

"I'll open the door and you chase it in that direction."

"Chase it?" he said as if she were out of her mind, but at the same time trying to scare it in the direction of the cabin's front door as Maicy ran to open it.

"This is crazy. One swat and—"

"Catch it if you can, then," Maicy ordered.

"Do you know what kind of diseases mice carry? Maybe you should try to shoo it away," he added facetiously.

Maicy did try that and while it didn't have the same effect as it had had on the lion, stomping her feet sent the mouse in Conor's direction, where he swiped at it to send it to her. Back and forth they volleyed the small gray rodent until Maicy got it close enough to the door to scare it out of the cabin.

"Good! Good! Go find your mom!" she called after it, ahead of the sound of Conor laughing.

"Seriously? You *save* mice now? I seem to recall a time when you were afraid of them."

Maicy couldn't help her sheepish expression because she'd been caught in a long-ago lie.

She closed the cabin door, shivering. And avoided the topic by saying, "It's *still* snowing and it's so cold it's never going to stop."

"And you just let out all our heat to save a damn

mouse. Come by the fire," he advised, going over to stoke the flames and add that log she hadn't let him use as a weapon. "And tell me how it is that you lost your fear of mice."

Just when she'd thought he might have moved on from that...

"Yeah... Hmm... I was never afraid of them," she said, tiptoeing around the subject as she joined him.

She sat on the floor in front of the hearth, her legs curled to one side, bracing her weight on one hand to lean toward their only source of warmth.

Once the fire was roaring, Conor sat on the floor, too, near enough to share the heat, one leg curved in front of him, one bent at the knee to brace his elbow. "You played me?"

"I *let* you play rescuer," she amended.

All the Madison sons had been over six feet tall in high school and with the workouts their stepfather had put them through preparing them for the military they'd been better developed than most boys their age. It had been nothing for Conor to scoop her up into his arms to protect her from the dreaded mouse when she'd pretended to be scared that day in his barn.

Up in his arms where she'd been able to wrap her own arms around his neck. And thank him with a kiss. A lengthy kiss full of teenage fervor...

"And I don't recall any complaints then," she pointed out.

"You played me," he repeated, this time an accusation, not a question, holding his ground.

Maicy couldn't suppress a smile. It *was* funny that she'd put one over on him even though the new Maicy would never, ever act like a damsel in distress for any reason.

Conor was staring at her but suddenly there was something different than challenge and playful accusation in those blue eyes. Something that was softer and warmer than the heat of the fire. "God, I always loved to see you smile like that... I've missed it..." he said in a quiet voice.

He was making it so hard to keep hating him. To keep being mad at him.

The smile went away with those thoughts. With the realization that she didn't feel the animosity she'd felt at the start of this and for so many years before. Feeling unbalanced, she stared into the fire as if he hadn't said anything.

"And now it's gone and that's all I get?" he cajoled.

She glanced back at him, a part of her wanting to skewer him with a cutting remark just to keep her own controls in place.

But for some reason she didn't. For some reason, once she was looking into those remarkable blue eyes of his, seeing that lingering softness and warmth—and maybe something that might have been affection—in them, she couldn't even think of one.

Then he brought his free hand up and under her hair to the back of her neck and kissed her.

There was sweet familiarity and more in that kiss. So much more that he'd apparently learned over time because this was worlds better than any kiss they'd shared in the past. Worlds better than any she'd had since.

With lips that were parted just enough.

With a lazy sway that soothed and drew her in and tantalized her all at once.

With the perfect amount of confidence and command that invited her lips to part, too.

Because yes, she was kissing him back. And while her resolve not to get emotionally entangled hadn't changed, there was also nothing in her now that wanted to stop.

Which, in itself was alarming, so after a few more minutes, she did pull back.

"Yeah…that's not what we're gonna do," she muttered as if she hadn't just given as good as she'd gotten.

Conor's only response was a raise of his chin that left her unsure whether he was agreeing or conceding or maybe just humoring her. But it didn't matter because *she* wasn't going to let it happen again.

She stood up. "It's probably better if we say goodnight."

He nodded.

"Thanks for not killing the mouse when you could have," she said.

Conor chuckled. "Sure. I didn't have to anyway— we make a pretty good team. Still."

Maicy didn't comment on that, either. She merely said, "See you in the morning."

"See you in the morning," he parroted as she went into the bedroom and changed into her pajamas. Afterward, she peeked through the fireplace to see if Conor was still sitting where she'd left him.

He wasn't.

She repositioned to watch him arranging his pillow and blanket on the sofa.

It was only when he'd finished that, stood straight

and tall, and crossed his arms over his middle to take hold of the hem of his shirt to peel it off that she yanked up, refusing to let herself watch that.

But not because she was taking the higher moral ground.

After that kiss she knew that if she did too much peeping she might not be able to keep herself from going back out into that living room and kissing him again.

And that was just not what she was going to let herself do.

Regardless of how much a part of her might want to.

Chapter Six

"Die alone!"

Her own outcry woke Maicy with a jolt.

"Shh, hey, you're okay. You aren't dying. And you aren't alone."

She *had* been alone when she'd fallen asleep on the couch on Thursday afternoon, so Conor's voice startled her almost as much as her nightmare had. Even though his tone was soothing and comforting.

Embarrassed, Maicy sat up and put her feet on the floor before she said, "When did you get back?"

It took her eyes a minute to focus before she spotted him across the cabin. His multiple layers of clothes and outer gear were covered in snow.

"I just came in the door. I need the tote for tonight's stock of wood. Are you okay?"

"Fine," she answered. To prove it she got off the

couch, retrieved the canvas sling and took it to him. "I just dozed off and had a dream." A bad dream.

"Any more dizziness?"

Maicy made a face. Earlier that day, he'd caught her in a dizzy spell when she'd wobbled into a wall. Since she'd had him believing that the dizzy spells were gone and now he'd learned that she was still having them, he was back to insisting that she sit idly and rest.

"Honestly, it happens less and less. I just stood up too fast before. And I really do feel better every day. If I was home I'd have gone back to work yesterday and I'd be at full speed today."

"Not with me as your doctor you wouldn't," he claimed. "A head injury is nothing to fool with, Maicy. Now that I know you're still getting dizzy I better not see your butt off that couch for anything but bathroom breaks."

She rolled her eyes at him.

She hadn't followed that order when he'd given it earlier. Once he'd left again she'd done what she'd done the day before—spruced up.

After showering, dressing in jeans with a chunky snow-white cable-knit sweater on top and putting on makeup, she'd spent an hour doing a hairstyle she rarely had time for, elaborately twisting and weaving her hair in back while still leaving it loose enough for artful, wavy, come-hither wisps to fall around her face.

"And tonight," he went on, "I'm cooking and you're eating—no more of that picking at your food the way you've been doing this whole time. You need a substantial meal. We're having stew—meat, potatoes, vegetables—and you're eating every bit of what I put in front of you."

She was about to say *okay, Dad*, until the word "meat" registered.

"What kind of meat?" she asked suspiciously. "There's only canned ham and dried salami and pepperoni—stew needs real meat. And I'm not eating squirrel or something," she warned.

"It's not squirrel. It's just meat," he hedged, accepting the log tote from her.

"Deer? Elk?" she asked although neither of those seemed likely.

"No rifle, no arrows, so no, no deer or elk—although I did see a beauty today—"

He was trying to change the subject and she wasn't going to let that happen. "I'm not eating it unless I know what's in it," she said with a hint of challenge. But it was still an even-tempered challenge, not belligerent or hostile like she might have been days ago. While neither of them had mentioned that kiss the night before, it had changed the tenor between them. Maicy's antagonism was gone and she was feeling more convivial than she had been. More like years ago. Without the affection, of course.

Even if that kiss *had* been on her mind since the minute it had ended.

"When did you get so stubborn?" he challenged back, also amiably.

"I learned from the best—you," she said, and even that had a friendly tone. "What kind of stew are you forcing me to eat?"

"Rabbit."

"You killed a bunny?"

"It was a mean, vicious snaggletoothed beast that attacked me in the woods. A pure case of him or me—"

"Bull," she said.

"It'll taste like chicken and you're going to eat it. You need the protein. You just pick at the beans when we have them and the only time you've cleaned your plate since this started is last night when you ate cake. And I'm not letting you have the rest of that cake tonight unless you eat my stew. Now go sit down again. I'll be back in a few minutes."

Maicy gave him a flippant salute and stayed where she was. He shook his head at her as he turned and left through the mudroom.

Maicy was in the bedroom when he came in again twenty minutes later because she didn't want to see this particular meal before it was safely in a pan.

"You might want to stay in there a little while," he warned from the kitchen. "I'll let you know when the coast is clear."

"Gross," she called back.

"Pretend it came packaged from the grocery store. It'll be delicious."

Since she was close to the bathroom anyway, she went to the only mirror in the place—the one over the sink in there—to make sure her nap hadn't smudged her makeup or ruined her hair.

But looking at herself now she stopped a little short.

Maybe she'd done too much…

All she would need was a cocktail dress added to the hair and makeup, and she could have gone to a New Year's Eve party.

What had she been thinking, glamming up like this in the middle of nowhere?

Dumb question.

She'd been thinking about Conor. And about another evening alone here with him tonight. And how much she'd liked him taking notice last night.

And about that kiss.

And how much she'd been craving another ever since that one had ended...

Oh, Maicy...

Hoping Conor hadn't taken too close a look at her yet, she retrieved cotton balls from her suitcase and used them to mute some of the eye shadow, blush, bronzer and highlighter until she looked less party-ready. She left her hair, though, because there was enough whimsy to the style to pass for casual. Plus, he might not notice the makeup, but he was sure to realize if she changed her hair and he might even think she'd redone it *for* him. So the hair stayed.

Then she glared at her reflection in the mirror to reprimand herself for primping as if she were preparing for a date with a new man she really, really liked and wanted to really, really like her.

Only this man was Conor Madison. Not someone she really, really liked. Not someone she wanted to really, really like her. Those days were done and gone. But okay, yes, she admitted that it had been satisfying that he hadn't been able to resist her last night. That had been her goal and she'd met it. And returning to being resistible hadn't been her aim today, that was for sure. So maybe she'd gone a little extreme.

What was the point of trying so hard to wow him?

For most of that first year after they'd broken up she'd hoped and prayed and wished for him to change his mind about marrying her, to surprise her and come back, to tell her he didn't know what had gotten into him, that he'd been wrong, that he loved her above all else, couldn't live without her and would give up everything to have her.

But when that hadn't happened she'd toughened up. She'd stopped even the slightest fantasies about them getting together again. Certainly now a relationship with him, of all people, was inconceivable. So why did she want him drooling over the sight of her?

Then something else occurred to her.

Maybe she was looking at this the wrong way. Maybe it didn't have anything to do with Conor or the feelings she'd had for him as a girl.

Maybe this was about walking in on Gary kissing his old flame. Maybe this was about rebounding and finding a way to feel attractive and desirable again.

Now *that* made sense!

Sure, it could be argued that Gary kissing his ex meant that he hadn't gotten over Candace, not that he wasn't attracted to Maicy. But it was still a blow to her self-esteem. It had still left her with some doubts about herself, even if she *had* felt relieved that she hadn't had to go through with the wedding. She'd still been cheated on.

And when a person got cheated on, she rationalized, the first thing they needed was to feel appealing and attractive again.

That was where rebounds came in.

And maybe the universe had given her that in the form of Conor.

Conor, who owed it to her after devastating her himself.

Plus it could be accomplished so tidily when she was already stuck in the wilderness with him with nothing better to do than hair and makeup that made it impossible for him *not* to take notice. Then, by the time she got back to Denver it would be done—rebound wrapped up.

And she could move on.

It was all so efficient and convenient. She liked that.

Looking at it like that she decided that what she was doing was nothing but the logical and necessary step to getting over finding her fiancé kissing someone else on their wedding day. It was understandable. And she didn't have to worry about it. She could just roll with it and let it accomplish what it accomplished.

It wasn't the big deal she had been sort of worried that it might be. It didn't signal that she still had feelings for Conor. It was just an ego thing.

And the fact that he'd rejected her, too—even if not for someone else—was no doubt playing a role, she went on reasoning. It was only natural to want him to see her as someone he'd missed out on, to regret not doing everything he could have done to hang on to her. This was really the universe killing two birds with one stone—she could feel as if Conor was seeing what he'd missed, and she could transition from Gary.

"Just don't overdo it," she whispered to her reflection.

Did kissing Conor qualify as overdoing it? Probably.

But she'd already told him that that was not what they were going to do and she'd meant it. Kissing blurred the very clear line between them. Between then and now. Between control and no control.

And she was never comfortable not being in control.

Plus it was one thing to fill empty hours putting on makeup and doing her hair, another thing entirely to spend them kissing. Kissing could lead to occupying empty hours with more than kissing...

A shiver ran up her spine at just the thought of Conor holding her when he kissed her—something that hadn't happened last night.

At just the thought of Conor kissing her in a way that was more than simple and sweet—the way he'd kissed her last night.

At the thought of feeling his hands on her body and taking him to that downy bed with her where she could satisfy the curiosity about what it would be like to have him make love to her. The curiosity she'd been left with all these years because they hadn't gone that far as kids even though they'd both wanted to something fierce...

No, no, no, no, no! Stop that! she ordered herself, reining in the insane wanderings of her mind.

Whatever was going on was *not* going there! *They* were not going there. It was not even getting as far as a second kiss.

"Remember," she again whispered to her reflection.

Remember how he'd deserted her when she'd needed him eighteen years ago. And remember the realization that had occurred to her earlier, when he'd left on to-day's hunt for cell service.

She needed to remember how crystal clear he was

making it that when he truly cared about someone—
the way he did about his brother—he pulled out all the
stops for them. All the stops he hadn't been willing to
pull out for her when she'd needed him most.

There was no greater indication of how little he'd
felt about her years ago than that. If Conor had truly
loved her, nothing would have mattered but her—the
way the cold and the weather and the hardship of being
out in it every day just to find even a minute of phone
service to check on his brother didn't matter as much
as getting that check on Declan.

And no way was she letting herself be vulnerable
to someone who had already proved the limitations of
his feelings for her.

So thanks to the universe for providing a little balm
to her self-esteem.

But that was as far as anything with Conor was
going.

Having made herself feel better about the hours of
primping, she left the bathroom and went to sit on the
edge of the bed, calling to him from there.

"Did you get through to your brother today?"

"Not to him, he's still heavily sedated and in ICU.
But I talked to his doctor. The lab results came back—
the ones that cultured the bacteria to narrow down the
antibiotics that'll work best against it. That gave them
a better idea of how to treat him. He's not better but
he's not worse."

"That's a little bit of good news."

"Nothing to celebrate but, yeah, at least his condition is stable," Conor repeated as if he was hanging
on to that. "He's not out of the woods by any means,

though. I should still be there where I could watch him, stay by his bedside."

Which Maicy had no doubt he would be doing if he was in Maryland. Pulling out all the stops for someone he truly cared about…

"Did you talk to Rickie in Northbridge?" she asked then, thinking that the sooner people could dig out of the small town and get them out of this cabin, the happier she'd be.

"I couldn't even finish the call with Vince before service cut out. I was just glad I got as much information as I did."

"And it's still snowing…" Maicy lamented to herself more than to him. "We *are* going to get out of here before spring, aren't we?" she asked, feeling some fear that this storm would never end.

Conor chuckled. "We'll get out before spring," he said, not seeming concerned about that. "You know how it is around here—the storm will stop, the sun will shine and a week later it'll be like it never happened except that the ski slopes will be plush."

"And you'll be with Declan in Maryland and I'll be home in Denver," she added to remind herself that when this was over they would likely never see each other again.

For some reason she didn't understand that made her feel a little sad.

But she shoved it aside and said, "Smells like your stew is cooking."

"It is. A little more cleanup and the coast will be clear."

He went on to tell her that he'd had to go as far as the main road today before finding phone service so he'd checked on her car. Unfortunately, it was completely covered, and the road leading to the cabin was also impassable. Even when Rickie could get out to them, he'd probably only be able to pick them up and bring them into town. There'd be no traveling home for either of them anytime soon.

"It's another reason you need something nutritious to eat—we're probably going to have to snowshoe out to meet Rickie when he *can* get around the rockslide."

"What about our cars?"

"Yeah, that'll be another story. I'd say a day more to dig out yours so it can be towed into town, and the road up here will have to be plowed to get mine out."

"So we'll have to stay in Northbridge?" That was a horrible thought given that it was such a small town and Gary, Candace and dozens of almost-wedding guests were there.

Maicy's dread of it must have sounded in her voice because Conor said, "Sorry, but yeah, I'm sure we will. Were you staying with Gary or his family?"

"No, I was in the minister's guesthouse—where I lived that last year of high school."

"That's not too bad then, is it?"

The accommodations weren't the problem.

Maicy didn't respond and after a few minutes of silence Conor said, "Okay, done in here. Stew is cooking. I'm going to shower."

The arrival of that particular time of day didn't thrill Maicy. She couldn't keep her mind off thoughts of him naked during the shower and then he always came out clean-shaven and looking and smelling so good that it weakened her defenses.

But that was her problem to deal with. She could hardly tell him he couldn't shower. Or why.

So she steeled herself, stood up from the bed and went into the main room.

"I could make cornbread again to go with—"

"You can sit on the couch," he said firmly before she'd even finished the suggestion. "I already threw together a mix for focaccia and put it in the oven. I'll tell you what you can do, though—from the couch. You can try to decipher my handwriting and start a more legible list of what we've used. Then when we do get out of here I can give it to Rickie so he knows what to replenish."

"You've been keeping track?" It was something Maicy hadn't thought to do. But of course the man-with-the-plan had.

"I have been."

Now that she thought about it, though, she realized it was the right thing to do. "Sure. And then we'll split the cost to reimburse him."

Conor didn't comment on that as he slid a piece of scribblings-laden paper across the utility table to her. Then he opened the cupboard drawer and took out a tablet and a pencil.

"Now take it over to the couch and sit!" he ordered as he handed her the writing equipment.

Grateful for something to occupy her mind while he showered, she immediately tackled the task.

And it did help because his handwriting was so bad she had to put all of her attention on figuring out each item on the list.

But unfortunately she was finished when he returned and at a loss for a distraction. And there he was again, smelling clean and looking all the more rugged and sexy because he hadn't shaved tonight.

An anti-kissing measure of his own maybe?

He wasn't supposed to do *that*! He was supposed to be dying to kiss her again!

Instead he just looked all the sexier with that stubble and *she* was dying to have him kiss her even with that.

You're hopeless, Maicy...

Also not aiding the resistance, he was dressed in jeans and a plaid flannel shirt that didn't hide a single muscle and looked so soft she itched to touch it.

The shirt, not him or those muscles inside of it, she told herself, knowing she was lying as she watched him finish the cooking and dish up dinner.

She protested the amount of stew he'd ladled into her bowl as they took the stew and chunks of focaccia to the coffee table, while he continued his threat that she could only have dessert if she finished it all.

"I think you're forgetting that it's *my* wedding cake," she told him.

"Yeah, about that..." he said as they settled in to eat. "Are you still doing okay with all that or was feeling relieved just a passing stage?"

The relief hadn't been a stage. In fact, the further she got away from her wedding day, the clearer it became to her that marrying Gary had been a bad idea. That she really hadn't entered into it because she'd wanted to marry him, but to avoid hurting him the way Candace had, the way Conor had hurt her when he'd turned down her proposal.

The more soul-searching she'd done, the more she'd acknowledged that her feelings for Gary had been nothing more than comfortable affection. And while she had enjoyed his company, making a choice that had just felt practical wasn't really the smart way to go, regardless of what she'd thought before.

Although she was still worried about what it all said about her and wondered if Drake had been right…

But rather than say any of that, she said, "I'm still okay with not going through with the wedding. Actually as time goes by I can see where it was definitely good that it didn't happen."

"Okay," he said, seeming to take her at her word. "Then moving on to your health—if you really are feeling as good as you want me to think you are, why were you having a nightmare about dying alone here? People who are feeling better *stop* worrying about dying."

His interpretation of what she had been dreaming was all wrong but she wasn't sure she wanted to tell him what she really had been dreaming about.

But why should it matter? she thought. And talking—having something to talk about—was better than *not* talking. And kissing.

She'd dreamed that she was walking down the aisle in a soiled, torn, bloodied wedding dress, to a groom who had started out as Gary. And then become Drake. And then morphed into Conor before it was all three of them waiting for her at the altar shouting *Die alone!* as if they were a united front putting a curse on her.

She didn't want to get into the whole thing, so she said, "The dream wasn't about my health…"

She really didn't like talking about this. But if it kept them from kissing…

She took a breath and forged ahead.

"The only other serious relationship I've had was with a guy named Drake. When I broke up with him he showed some temper and said some pretty cruel things. One of them was that I was going to die alone—"

"And you dreamed he was saying that again?"

Him and Gary and you…

"Pretty much."

"So maybe you're *not* so all right with the wedding not happening?"

"It isn't that," she said as she ate some of the focaccia that tasted a little like the box that the mix had been packaged in.

"What is it, then?"

"I'm not sure how to put this… I'm okay not marrying Gary. But because I didn't get there, it's like…I guess it kind of gives more weight to what Drake said before him."

"Drake was just before Gary?"

"He was. I didn't get into any serious relationships until the last—" she did the math "—five years, I guess." And now that she thought about it, Gary had probably been the rebound from the split with Drake. Certainly she'd thought that the relationship with Gary proved Drake wrong and that had made her feel better about the ending with Drake.

Then she realized that Conor might be thinking it had taken her all the years before Drake to get over him and she didn't want that so she said, "Through both rounds of college I had to balance work along with school so there just wasn't time for much else. I dated here and there but nothing serious. When I finished my master's I knew I wanted my own business so those next five years were devoted to focusing on that—with the occasional blind date Rachel pushed me into."

"That's a pretty sparse personal life," he observed.

"I know. Rachel thought so, too, so she gave me a year of an internet dating service for a birthday present."

"You met this Drake on the internet?"

"A lot of people meet that way, you know," she defended because he made it sound as if there was something wrong with that.

"I'm sure," he said defensively himself. "I was just having enough to deal with thinking about you and Gary, now there's *Drake*." He said the name derisively and Maicy again liked that even after all this time the thought of her with another man tweaked a little jealousy in him.

"Drake," she repeated, rubbing it in just a bit. "Drake Astly—"

"I've heard that name. There's an Astly Surgical Equipment…"

"That would be the family business."

"Big money. And a dating service? Somehow that doesn't track. I mean, I get that you were too busy and neglected your personal life—I've done that myself— but wouldn't someone with that kind of bankroll have a lot of options when it came to a social life?"

"Yes and no. He was busy, too, with charities and foundations and fund-raising along with his job. But he was almost forty, his wife had actually decided she not only didn't want kids, she didn't want a husband, either. He'd been divorced for three years, all his friends were married, and he said there weren't as many single women around as he'd thought. Like me, he'd run through all the fix-ups friends and family could arrange for him. He was getting discouraged and on a lark, on one of the weekends when the site was offering a free trial to attract more members, he did some browsing—"

"And found you... Yeah, I could see that selling internet dating for him. And the two of you got serious?" Conor asked before he stood and headed for the kitchen for more focaccia.

Maicy declined his offer to bring her some, too, but on his way to the kitchen, while his back was to her, she spooned the stew she was too full to finish into his bowl.

"We were serious," she confirmed. "We were together a little over three years, we did the whole couples thing with Rachel and her husband, Jake—dinners, movies, regular game nights. We even went on two trips as a foursome. Then Drake wanted to get married."

"Don't tell me you ran away from that wedding, too?" Conor said as he came back and sat down again to resume eating.

"No, I didn't!" she said as if Conor was crazy to suggest it. "I just said no."

"You weren't thinking about how bad it was to be turned down that time?" Conor goaded slightly.

"It was a very different situation," she said, a little defensively. "Drake wasn't down on his luck, he wasn't trying to turn things around. And he was so... He had such a clear vision of what he wanted—and it wasn't at all what I wanted."

"What did he want that you didn't?"

"He sort of wanted me to sign over my life to him."

Conor paused with a spoonful of stew partway to his mouth to frown at her. "He wanted you to sign over your life to him? What was he, a conman?"

"No, nothing like that. It was just that he not only wanted us to get married, he wanted me to sell my business, be a stay-at-home wife and mother, a lady-who-lunched and who represented him and his family name in *important* circles."

"You don't like lunch?" Conor teased, taking that bite of stew.

"I usually eat it at my desk."

This time the look he gave her came from the corner of his eye. "I never thought career would be the most important thing to you."

Because *he'd* been the most important thing to her.

"Things change," she said. "I learned that what's important is to be able to take care of myself—"

"But you were okay taking care of Gary," he reminded. "With him not taking care of *himself.*"

"I'm all right being relied on—"

"Just not relying on anyone yourself."

"I rely on Rachel. But I'm not *dependent* on her and I don't want to be dependent on anyone—which I would have ended up being if I'd given up everything just to be *Mrs.* Drake. He said it didn't matter that I wouldn't have my own income, he and his family had a boatload of money and I didn't need to work. That he didn't *want* a wife who worked. But that's just not for me. Being a stay-at-home wife and mother is great if that's your choice—it's what Rachel wanted so she closed her bakery when she found out she was pregnant. Jake supports them and she's all right with that so I'm all right for her—"

"But for you? You wouldn't be *all right* with it?"

"It's just not something I could do. My mom depended on my dad—why, I never understood, but she

did. And every time he took off she was left hanging—
we were left hanging. She'd have to rush out and get
any job she could while she begged for an extension
on our rent until she could come up with the money.
Then my dad would show up and she'd quit the job to
make a home for him—that's always what she said—"

"And the two of you would be left hanging all over
again when he took off the next time—I know, I was
there for some of that."

And then there was Conor letting her down when
she'd most counted on him—that had cemented her
resolve never to be in a position of helplessness again.

But she skirted around that and said, "So no, I
couldn't be comfortable doing what Drake wanted."

"And that made him mad?"

"He said I was *too* independent. *Too* self-sufficient.
That it made me closed off. That I have such a hard
shell no one can crack it. He said that what he wanted
was to take care of me, that it wasn't about him making
me weak or dependent. That I had a really screwed-up
view of things and if I didn't change it I was just asking to die alone…"

Conor was scowling into his bowl. "He had a lot to
say," he said, his voice deep with disapproval. "You
weren't asking him to change his whole life for you, so
why should he have expected you to change yours for
him? If he wanted you, he should have wanted whatever
life the two of you could work out together."

"Exactly."

Conor paused before saying cautiously, "But *are*
you *too* independent and self-sufficient and so closed
off that you don't let anyone in?"

"Rachel knows me inside and out—that's not being closed off."

Although Rachel *hadn't* jumped in to disagree with Drake's assessment that she was overly independent and self-sufficient. While she'd agreed that Drake had gone too far, and that he had no right to ask her to give up work she enjoyed to live a society life she didn't want, Rachel had actually said that maybe Drake had a point. She, too, had worried that Maicy might never have a husband and family if she didn't bend a little on some of that. It had made Drake's accusation haunt her all the more.

"But Rachel is a friend," Conor pointed out. "Knowing you inside and out as a friend is different from the kind of give-and-take that a marriage is. And if you're only closed off with men—"

"Gary never said I was closed off."

"But could you only do that with him because he needed you more than you needed him?"

She'd never thought of that. She'd just thought that she was proving Drake wrong by being with Gary...

"You know," Conor said then, "you've made sure you aren't in the position your mother was in by getting your education, by owning your own business. I understand why you wouldn't want to throw any of that away and why it would frustrate you if anyone wanted you to. But there should be some middle ground between a guy who wants you dependent on him, and one who's dependent on you. And it's not good if you can't relax unless you feel like the guy is the only one who has anything to lose..."

She *had* felt that way about Gary.

She didn't want to admit it, but it was the truth.

And she really didn't want to talk more about this.

But she had an out because just then she glanced at the window across the room over the sink.

"It isn't snowing!" she said, turning around on the sofa to look through the larger window behind them.

Conor did the same thing. "I knew it had to stop sometime but I was beginning to wonder when that time was going to come," he said.

"You should see if you have cell service," she suggested.

"It's two hours later in Maryland—"

"Still, you could get an update on Declan." And she could have a reprieve from talking about her messed-up love life.

She took both their empty bowls and plates to the sink while he turned on her phone because the battery on his had gone out.

"No, still nothing," he said a moment later.

Maicy had put the dinner things in the sink and was looking through the window there, suddenly feeling uncomfortably shut in.

"I'm going outside," she announced. "I want some fresh air."

She went to the bedroom for her coat, returning to find Conor donning his peacoat, too.

"Maybe I'll have better luck outside," he said, holding up her phone.

She buttoned her knee-length coat all the way up and they went out the back door, where they saw that the sky had cleared of clouds to leave a canopy of stars overhead and an almost full moon.

Conor didn't try for phone reception again, though.

Instead, as Maicy star-gazed, he Maicy-gazed, facing her from the side.

"So tell me one more thing," he said then, not letting her off the hook. "If Drake Astly had been okay with you keeping your business and working, would you have married him?"

Would she have married Drake?

She'd had feelings for him. But like with Gary, those feelings hadn't compared to what she'd had for Conor. And he'd been her first serious relationship after Conor so she'd made more comparisons and that alone likely would have stopped her.

By the time she'd gotten to Gary, she'd decided that her feelings for Conor had been teenage melodrama— the kind of puppy love that feels all-consuming at the time, and isn't intended to last. If she never felt that way about a man again, it just meant she'd finally grown up. She needed to accept that and settle for the way things were now.

"You wouldn't have." Conor answered his own question when she didn't.

"No," she said quietly and for some reason she had the sense that he knew why. She went from looking up at the stars to looking at him to see if she was right. She thought she was because there was a small smile on his handsome face as he studied her.

"I *want* the blame for that if it's because the first time you really got involved with someone after you and me it came up short for you."

"You *want* blame?" she challenged.

"For that I do," he said as he stepped in front of her, blocking her view of the sky and leaving her with the view of his striking features in the moonlight.

"For just one minute don't play your cards too close to the vest and tell me I'm right," he encouraged.

"Maybe," was as much as she would give.

He laughed, drawing her eyes to his mouth, the supple lips that had felt so fabulous last night…

"Good enough," he proclaimed in a voice that had a lower, more intimate timbre.

He went on staring at her with another, more thoughtful smile.

"The first time I ever kissed you was a night like this—outside…"

"Only it wasn't frigidly cold and we were watching fireworks—or at least I was," she filled in.

"I couldn't believe how beautiful you were—more than any fireworks. You were the most beautiful girl I'd ever seen." He ran the backs of his fingers along her cheek. "Still are…" he whispered.

If he'd left the stubble tonight to help him keep from kissing her, it didn't work. Because that was just what he did then—leaning in to capture her mouth with his as he wrapped his arms around her and brought the full length of her body to him.

Unlike the sweet, simple kiss of the previous night this one had heat to it right from the start. And it only got hotter.

Hot enough for the need of his hand cradling her head when that kiss bent her backward.

Hot enough for parted lips to part even more and urge hers to part, too.

Hot enough to send his tongue to entice hers into a sexy joust.

Her hands came out of their coat pockets and found their way under his arms to his back. It felt like an expansive, solid wall that she hung on to as she kissed him as fervently as he was kissing her.

But there wasn't supposed to be any kissing at all, she reminded herself somewhere in the process of opening her mouth even wider, feeling the roughness of his stubble against her face.

No kissing and certainly none of the massage that that big hand of his was doing on her back. None of the headiness that came from her breasts pressed against his chest. None of her melting into him and discovering that the fit was still so perfect...

None of any of it! she silently shouted at herself, torn between what she knew had to be done and what she wanted—which was to go on and on and on kissing him like that and then move on to even more...

It had to be stopped...

In just another minute...

No, now! she argued with herself.

Winning—or maybe losing—that argument, she retrieved her arms from around him, laid her palms to his chest, and pushed her way out of that kiss.

"You didn't see if you could get a signal out here," she reminded, her voice breathy.

"Yeah," was all he said, a little breathless himself and sounding as if stopping was killing him.

Before she could weaken enough to lean into him again, Maicy said, "You should try," and turned toward the cabin's back door.

"You know," he said as she opened it, stalling her rather than turning on the cell phone to follow her instructions, "I think you're taking what that Drake guy said too personally."

Maicy laughed humorlessly. "Everything he said was about me—that's personal."

"Yeah," Conor agreed. "But as much as I hate to cut him any slack for anything, I think I have to."

Then, in a voice that was even deeper, even more quiet, he seemed to confess.

"Take it from somebody who knows—it isn't easy to lose you."

Chapter Seven

Northbridge Hospital.

When Conor woke up in the cabin on Friday morning, the last thing he'd expected was to be sitting in the emergency room's waiting area by sundown.

But there he was. The end of an eventful thirteen hours.

After five straight days of blizzard, Friday had dawned with a clear sky and sunshine that hadn't helped the frigid temperature. But as usual the first thing Conor had done was leave the cabin in search of cell service.

He *had* managed to find that slightly closer than usual, though, only to learn that Declan's condition was the same.

Then he'd called Rickie.

His old friend had had better news for him—the

rockslide blocking the road into and out of town had been cleared.

"I'm right here with my truck," Rickie had told him. "I don't know what the road's like—technically it's still closed between here and Billings. But the snowplow is headed out to start clearing from this end. If I follow behind I might be able to make it far enough to get to you."

Since his friend was willing to try, Conor had agreed to search for cell service every two hours to check in with him for a progress report. Then Conor had returned to the cabin to tell Maicy they might be getting out today.

That had set them both into motion, packing and cleaning and doing what was necessary to shut the rustic shelter down, with Conor hiking out as scheduled to check in with Rickie.

At nearly four that afternoon, Rickie had made it to the foot of the road leading to the cabin.

With that news, Conor had returned to the cabin to outfit Maicy with snowshoes. He'd done a final check to be sure the place was left the way they'd found it—minus the supplies they'd tallied on their list—and then the two of them headed out, with Conor toting his duffel and Maicy's suitcase—minus the ruined wedding dress that was too bulky to pack and so had been left behind.

But when they'd reached the highway and Rickie's truck, Rickie wasn't with it. Instead he called to them from the pile of snow that was covering Maicy's car like a huge dome.

While he'd been waiting for them to get to him,

Rickie had started to dig out Maicy's car. In the course of that he'd lost his footing, fallen and broken his leg.

And once more Conor had been grateful for his field training.

While Maicy had searched the truck for anything he could use for makeshift medical supplies, Conor had stabilized the leg and splinted it with the two planks of wood and bungee cords she found for him.

Then Maicy had come up with the idea of using a ramp she'd found in the truck bed as a stretcher and a plastic tarp as a sheet. Between the two of them they'd cocooned Rickie with the tarp and gotten him onto the ramp so Conor could drag him to the truck and then hoist his pain-ridden old friend inside.

It had been a rough go, but finally Conor had been able to drive the truck into town, delivering Rickie *and* Maicy to the emergency portion of Northbridge's small hospital, where he'd filled in the ER doctor about both cases and—over Maicy's protests—recommended that she have an MRI.

And now here he was once again in the position that he'd come to hate—only hoping that the people he'd handed over to other medical professionals would be cared for the way he thought they should.

Particularly Maicy.

Treating a broken leg like Rickie's followed standard procedures. But with a five-day-old head injury the amount of testing was up to the doctor who took over. To be thorough, an MRI should be done. Whether it would be or not was out of Conor's hands.

It was just so damn aggravating. And since he wasn't Maicy's family, he wasn't allowed in the treatment room to argue for what he believed was in Maicy's best interests. He was as removed from her medical decisions as he was from those of the military men and women he treated before sending them off for their extended care.

As he sat there it occurred to him that the way he felt over having his cases passed on to other hands wasn't the only thing eating at him at that moment, though. Now that the chaos of the day was done and they'd made it into town, he was finding himself also hating that he and Maicy *weren't* at the cabin anymore—as crazy as that seemed.

Sure it was a good thing that they were out of there. No fresh food, limited supplies, no power, no central heat. Primitive plumbing. Cut off from the world unless he'd really worked for a connection—even an unreliable one. Mountain lions, mice and the constant effort to clear away snow so they weren't buried up there—yeah, there was no question that it was good to leave that behind.

But as he sat there it was just setting in that they'd left something else behind, too.

Being alone together like that might have been the only thing that would let them start working through their past. Working through their past and, in the process, maybe reconnecting, too.

Not that they should be. He knew that. Not that he wanted them to be.

But now that it was over it struck him that there had been something nice about being stranded with Maicy.

And now what? he asked himself.

Now Northbridge, where he'd be alone at his family's farmhouse. Where she'd be back at the minister's guesthouse—since the minister and his wife had already shown up at the hospital to invite her to stay.

Now Northbridge, where things had fallen apart for them before.

Now Northbridge, where there were plenty of people to intrude. Not the least of which was the man she'd been about to marry. The man who could have realized his mistake by now and re-ended things with his ex. The man who could be champing at the bit to re-unite with Maicy.

Over my dead body, Stern, you jackass...

Not that he actually thought Maicy would take Gary Stern back. Surely the relief she'd felt at not marrying him would keep her from making the same mistake twice. And the guy had given her a prime excuse not to regardless of what a sad sack he was.

But yeah, as crazy as it seemed, he was suddenly missing the cabin. Wishing they were back there, that he was showering the way he'd done at this time of day, coming out to an evening of just the two of them...

You can't have her, you know. That ship has sailed, he told himself.

Her anger at him seemed to have mellowed at the cabin but he still didn't think she'd forgiven him. He didn't think she'd accepted the whys and what-fors of him turning down her proposal. He'd noticed every gibe she'd fought not to say. He'd seen the look in those gorgeous green eyes when she'd talked about both of her other relationships, the look that said he'd done damage of his own.

And both times he'd kissed her she'd stopped him.

Of course it had to be her who stopped because he sure as hell wouldn't—couldn't—have. Eighteen years ago or eighteen hours ago, he'd never wanted anyone as much as he wanted her. He was trying not to acknowledge that but it was true.

Was it chemistry? Pheromones? Maybe it was forbidden fruit or unfinished business.

She'd been forbidden fruit when they were teenagers. Maicy's mother had been determined to protect her daughter from an unplanned pregnancy and had watched Maicy like a hawk. Her mother had threatened her unmercifully with what she would do if Maicy got pregnant. Maicy had had so much fear of it that she'd been determined to maintain her virginity until they were married.

He'd already lost his virginity just before they'd started dating but he'd been willing to wait for her—difficult as that was when he'd wanted her in the worst way. But he'd known she was worth it. He'd loved her so much that nothing was more than he could take to have her. Plus he'd been certain that they *would* get married, that the day *would* come when he'd get to make love to her, and that had sustained him. For the most part.

But that day hadn't ever come.

Instead things between them had ended in what had seemed like the blink of an eye. Turning the forbidden fruit into unfinished business.

And leaving him wondering for the last eighteen years.

So no, he likely wouldn't have stopped kissing her last night if she hadn't ended it. Unfinished business coupled with how much he still liked kissing her had put willpower at a minimum.

Now here they were in town and…

And he didn't know what.

He only knew that when the minister and his wife had shown up here to offer their guesthouse and wait to take Maicy home with them, he'd nixed the idea of them sticking around, assuring them he would bring her to their guesthouse when she was finished. He wasn't ready to just walk away.

Sure the day was coming—projections were to have the highway to Billings and the airport there open by Sunday. But for now?

There was still tonight. And tomorrow and tomorrow night.

And he knew this town, he knew how gossip traveled, so he knew that by now every person in it had heard about her running away from her wedding. No matter what happened from here on between her and Gary, it wasn't going to be a day at the beach for her to face the looks and whispers. Or maybe worse than that, depending on how the Stern family and friends viewed what had happened. Had Gary and Candace even admitted what they'd done, or had they shifted the blame on Maicy who wasn't there to defend herself? He didn't know, and neither did Maicy.

So for now, if Maicy would let him keep her company, let him be her support system, he wanted to do that. He wanted to be there for her the way he'd wanted to be there for her when her mom died.

And if it provided an excuse to have a couple more days with her?

He couldn't deny that he wanted that, too.

But hopefully being back in town—in separate houses, and with the eyes of the town on them—would help keep things more on track than they had been with the last two nights of kissing. Hopefully being back where their world had exploded would help him remember that it *had* exploded, and there was no turning back the clock.

No, not just *hopefully*. He needed to remember that. To keep in mind that they each had their own lives now and when they inevitably returned to them this whole week would fade into history with everything else.

He had to get back to Declan and make sure his brother was on his feet again. He had to deal with Kinsey and this business with the Camdens. He had to figure out what he was going to do about his own career. And Maicy had her business and her friend Rachel whom she talked so much about and the rest of the life she'd built for herself.

They were just not destined to be together the way they'd thought as wide-eyed kids.

But he could still have the next couple of days, and he still wanted to be the support system he should have been years ago.

And maybe when this was all over with, when she got back to the life she'd built for herself, she might feel as if, in some small way, he'd made up for a little of what had happened long ago.

But kissing wasn't a part of that and he knew he had to not do it again. He knew he had to make sure that he didn't start something that could get out of hand.

Because he sure as hell didn't want to give her something else not to forgive him for.

"Every time I talk about releasing you, your blood pressure goes up," the doctor observed, looking at the monitor Maicy was hooked to. "What about that makes you anxious?"

"It's a long story," Maicy answered, her tone indicating that she wasn't going to tell it.

But Rebecca, the emergency room doctor, pursued it anyway. "Does it have something to do with the man waiting for you?"

"The minister?" Maicy asked. The minister and his wife had arrived just before she'd been called into the exam room. They'd come to assure her that their guest-house was hers for as long as she was in town, and said they'd wait for her to be finished here to take her home.

"No, the man who brought you in—he's a doctor? He wanted you to have an MRI," Rebecca prompted.

"Conor is waiting for me?" Maicy had assumed that Conor would have bowed out.

"I overheard him tell the minister and his wife that they didn't need to wait, that he wanted to be here when you came out, to make sure you're all right before driving you to their house." There was suspicion in the doctor's voice until she said, "And now the blood pressure's going down, so maybe it isn't him who's upsetting you?"

Maicy didn't want to tell the doctor how happy she was to hear that Conor had stayed. "No, it isn't him," she said simply, again offering no explanation.

"I'm new to town. It seems like a decent place, with a lot of decent people. Am I missing something? Is it the thought of being set loose here that's bothering you?"

"No." But because the MD seemed not to want to drop the subject and Maicy wanted out of there, she said, "There's just someone I left behind here that I'm not thrilled with having to see again."

"And you aren't likely to be able to avoid that someone since it's a small town," the doctor concluded for her. "Sorry but I can't admit you just so you can hide out."

Maicy assured her that she understood so the doctor unhooked her from the monitor, produced her release papers to sign and then left her to get dressed.

She put on the jeans and an emerald green turtleneck sweater that she'd picked today knowing it accentuated her eyes. As the day had played out, the choice of the eye-accentuating sweater—and the carefully applied makeup—had just seemed silly and irrelevant.

But if Conor was still waiting for her…

No, being appealing to him wasn't important in the grand scheme of things. It might have been something to do to while away the time in the cabin, but now they were back in the real world. The one in which she'd run away from her wedding.

Having to deal with the aftermath of that was what was making her wish a little that she and Conor were back in the cabin. It wasn't that she was actually missing the place. Or being alone there with Conor. But she *was* having pangs about not being there anymore. And those pangs were helped by the knowledge that Conor was out in the waiting room.

Because yes, the whole time she'd been in this exam room there was a part of her that had been feeling very down at the thought that there wasn't any reason for him to be waiting for her now. Without being stranded in the woods, she'd feared that he would have gone his way, she would be left to go hers and it would be business as usual for them both.

And business as usual did not mean being a part of each other's lives.

*But he waited...*she thought as she went to the small mirror on one wall of the exam room to check her hair.

It was a mess so she took a brush from her purse, straightening it out while telling herself that being soothed by learning that Conor was out in the waiting room wasn't about him. She was just glad she didn't have to walk out of here and face Northbridge alone.

She'd been grateful to have him by her side when the minister and his wife had shown up. It had helped her wade through that first embarrassment as they'd told her with some veiled disapproval that she wasn't the first bride to panic.

And once she left the hospital? She had no idea what might be in store for her.

Gary was much more cemented in the community than she was. He still had friends he kept up with. Plus his family, and family friends. None of whom likely knew that she'd found him kissing his former girlfriend. Most probably, everyone was going to blame her for leaving him at the altar. And even as fiercely independent as she was, it helped to think of maybe having one person in her corner. Even if it was only for the moment.

Though she'd known from the start that their time together was limited, it hadn't felt that way in the cabin. Up there, there was no question that they would have dinner together. That they would spend hours talking. That even good-night didn't mean more than going into another room—knowing when she did that he'd be there when she woke up the next morning.

Now there were no certainties.

Not that she wanted there to be, she told herself.

It was just that…

She closed her eyes, took a deep breath and exhaled before opening them again to her own reflection, forcing herself to be honest.

It was just that it had been kind of nice being with him.

It was weird. She hadn't forgotten what he'd done, but the time in the cabin had reminded her of all the good before that. She did have to concede—only to herself—that she'd ended up enjoying his company in the cabin. And she wasn't altogether happy that it was over. Separate from the fact that she was definitely not happy to be in Northbridge again or to contend with whatever might be coming her way.

"But it is what it is," she told her reflection firmly.

For now, she was glad he'd waited. But only for now. Then she'd be on her own again and she could handle it. She'd handled everything she'd had to handle since her mom had died and she could handle whatever she had to from here on, too.

She hooked her hair behind her ears with a businesslike determination, gathered her things and left the exam room.

It would all be fine, she told herself on the way out.

And the very real pulse-quickening she felt the minute she went into the waiting room and set eyes on Conor in his jeans and another of those muscle-hugging T-shirts of his? The very real feeling that one glance from him made her stronger and better able to face anything and everything?

It didn't mean a thing.

"You stuck around…" she said, crossing to him.

"Sure," he answered as if there was no question. "No MRI though, huh?"

"The ER doctor thought it was too late to bother."

"That's why an MRI should be done—a CAT scan will show new injury, an MRI will show older ones," he explained, clearly displeased.

"But I'm doing okay," Maicy said. "I haven't had a dizzy spell since that one yesterday. She seemed to check me out pretty thoroughly otherwise, so—"

"Yeah, just not what I would have done," he grumbled.

Maicy knew his annoyance was linked to his growing frustrations with his own job. But she wasn't alarmed by the care she'd received. So all she said was, "I just want out of here. I hate hospitals."

Conor nodded. "I still have Rickie's truck—his wife, Jane, came to get him. She'll take him home. He said I should use his truck to get you to the minister's place and me to the farm tonight. Tomorrow Rickie's brothers will come for the truck and me—we're all three going back to the cabin with a plow and a tow truck to see if we can get our cars into town."

Oh yeah, she was definitely having cabin-loss-fever because another twinge hit her at just the mention of the place.

But she was never going to be there with him again. Ever. And she reminded herself once more that the sooner she had her car and could put this entire thing behind her, the better.

"But for tonight," Conor was saying, "let's get something to eat that doesn't come out of a can or a dry mix."

"Sounds good," she admitted, thinking that more than the food, what sounded good to her was that he didn't intend to just drive her to the minister's guesthouse and drop her off. At least they were going to have dinner together one more time.

Sadly, nothing was open but fast food, so dinner ended up being burgers and fries ordered at the drive-thru that they took with them to the guesthouse.

The guesthouse was a one-bedroom cottage not much larger than the cabin, positioned with access from a side street that allowed Maicy and Conor to get to it without disturbing the minister's family. And since the minister had left the key with Conor to give to her, they went directly there.

"I've never been inside this place," Conor said as they went in. By the time Maicy had moved in, when the month's rent had run out on the apartment she shared with her mother, Conor had left for college.

"It's kind of cozy," Maicy said truthfully. "I wasn't allowed to have boys here before, though, so don't be surprised if they come and make you leave," she joked as she turned on lights and raised the temperature on the thermostat.

"What was it like that year you lived here?" he asked somewhat tentatively as they took off their coats. "Were you part of the minister's family? Did you have meals with them and just come here to sleep or—"

"I was *not* part of the family," Maicy said. "I was the babysitter, really, even though they called me the nanny and paid me by the month instead of by the hour. My job was to get the kids up, fed, dressed and to school in the mornings before I went to school myself, then pick them up after school and bring them home or to whatever after-school things were going on. If either the minister or his wife were home in the evenings, they took over. If they both had somewhere to be, I handled evenings. But that was it—it was only about the kids and filling in when their parents couldn't be here. Their *family time* was their family time and that didn't include me."

"You didn't have meals with them? Holidays?"

"I ate with the kids if I was sitting with them, but otherwise, no. They invited me for Thanksgiving, Christmas dinner, their Easter meal—me and anyone else in the congregation who didn't have a family— so I had the choice between here and friends who invited me. But on a regular basis? They're nice people but they're pretty stuffy and formal, and no, I wasn't part of the family—there was no question about that."

"I'm sorry, Maicy. I pictured them treating you like their own."

"It was okay. I wasn't really looking to be part of anyone's family. Not after losing my mom." *And you.* "I liked having my own space," she said honestly. Then, with nothing more to say about it, she nodded toward the café-sized kitchen table, where two chairs waited. "Unlike the cabin, we have a table to eat at here."

"Yeah…" Conor said unenthusiastically. "But I'm kind of missing that place—"

"It's funny, isn't it?" Maicy said by way of admitting it herself.

"You, too?"

"A little."

"Then how about we eat at the coffee table for the heck of it?"

Maicy agreed, only rather than sitting side by side on the sofa the way they had at the cabin, they found themselves on the floor, on opposite sides of the coffee table.

"Be straight with me," Conor commanded as they settled in to eating. "*Are* you really feeling okay even after all we did today?"

"I really am," she said, omitting that she was slightly more worn out than she would have ordinarily been after the exertions of the day. She didn't want him to think she was tired, that he needed to leave. She was very aware that she wasn't in any hurry for that to happen.

"No headaches, no dizziness, no blurred vision, no flashes in my eyes, no memory problems, no nothing," she added. "Exactly what I told the doctor at the hospital. What I was telling her while you were apparently out in the waiting room chatting it up with *Jane*…" She said the other woman's name with heavy insinuation.

He laughed. "I was talking to Jane about Rickie. Whom she's married to."

"I was surprised to hear that. She wasn't interested in him when we were in high school. She was only interested in you…"

"And I was only interested in you," he countered.

Maicy tried to ignore the little wave of warmth that gave her. "It didn't discourage her. I heard that after we broke up—before you left for college—she put the pursuit into high gear."

"Is that what you heard?" he said rather than confirming or denying anything.

Which made Maicy suspicious. "She did, didn't she?"

"It didn't make any difference. She couldn't fill your shoes."

Maicy had heard about him rejecting the other girl, but she'd always wondered if it was true. "So who *did* fill my shoes?" she asked.

He smiled a secret kind of smile before he said, "I plunged myself into school and ROTC training—that kept me as busy as I knew it would," he said, not answering her question.

"For how long? A month before you—"

He laughed. "Longer than that. A lot longer than that."

"To this day you've been pining for me?" she challenged.

"Just a few days ago, you jumped to the conclusion that I have a pregnant wife and now I've just been pining for you?" he said.

"You did say last night that you understood my neglecting my personal life because you had, too," she reminded.

"I may have neglected it, but I've had one."

"That you're being cagey about," she accused.

"I'm not being cagey about it," he said defensively.

"Yes you are. You've heard about my relationships, I want to hear about yours," she claimed, not completely sure that was true. But she thought that it might help her fight his appeal if she had a clearer image of him as a single man involved with other women. A single man who wasn't hers...

"Who filled my shoes for the first time?" she demanded.

Conor made a face. "Really? You want to talk about this?"

"I told you about Drake and Gary."

"You nearly married those two."

"And nothing else counts? Besides, you always wanted a family. Do you expect me to believe you've never come close to getting married?"

Rather than answer that he rewound and answered her earlier question. "I didn't date anyone until my junior year of college—like I said, I devoted myself to school and training."

"And in your junior year..." Maicy persisted.

"There was Michelle. She was on the same fast track to becoming a doctor so we had almost all of our classes together. Eventually she became a...you know, friend-with-benefits. More because it was convenient for us both."

"Convenient..." Maicy repeated. "She was okay with that?"

"It was her suggestion."

"Ah, another Jane in hot pursuit. Only you let *Michelle* catch you."

"There was no pursuit. Just convenient stress release," he said with a laugh.

"Very romantic," Maicy said facetiously. "And after Michelle?"

"There've been a few others," he answered ambiguously. "Another resident when I was doing my residency. A nurse here and there. A lab tech and a social worker—"

"It was the lab tech and the social worker that you got close to marrying," Maicy guessed.

He laughed. "Not close, but... How did you know that?"

She'd heard a slightly more somber note in his voice when he'd mentioned them. But she merely shrugged and smiled coyly to let him know she wasn't giving away her secrets.

"Yes, it was the lab tech and the social worker— they both wanted to get married," Conor confirmed.

"Don't tell me—they proposed to you, too, and you turned them down the same way you turned me down."

"There were no *proposals*," he amended. "There were just ongoing conversations—marriage and kids were what they saw for the future—"

"But you didn't see it for yours?"

"Yeah, I said it was what I saw for my future, too," he said but in a way that hedged. "It just...didn't work out with either of them."

"Why not?"

"With Glenda—the lab tech—we'd only been going out six months when she wanted a firm timeline of when we'd end up at the altar."

"And you weren't ready to guarantee that the relationship would get there."

"I liked her but it had only been six months. And I *only* liked her—I mean, maybe it could have turned into more, but... When I wouldn't give her a firm timeline, a definitely-we'll-get-married, she opted to move on." He didn't say that as if he had any regrets.

"And the other one, the social worker?" Maicy prompted.

"Social-worker-who-became-a-navy-lieutenant. Janice was a social worker here before she joined the navy and was sent overseas as an aide to an admiral.

She came with him on a field visit in Afghanistan. An Afghan national—not much more than a kid— approached the admiral with an IED strapped to his waist. The IED malfunctioned and only killed the kid and injured the admiral."

"And you treated the admiral."

"I did—that was how Janice and I met. He was too badly injured for ground transport and we couldn't get a helicopter in right away, so I treated him. With Janice there the whole time—"

"That is not a meet-cute story," Maicy said.

"It *is* how we met, though. And actually, because we sort of hit it off despite the circumstances and kept in contact even after she and the admiral were evaced, that was the first time I heard about what a patient of mine went on to and got irritated by it."

"When was this?"

"A little over three years ago. The admiral made it but his care didn't follow the course I would have set for him and I think he had a rockier road than he should have had—he ended up losing the arm I'd saved and with different, more cautious care, I don't believe that would have been the case."

"So your job frustrations have been building for that long?"

"They have. After that I started checking up—where and when I could—on what happened to my patients after they left me. And yeah, some of the things I've learned have made me more and more aggravated. But it hasn't mattered up until now because my years of obligation to the navy weren't up—I didn't have a choice except to go on doing what I signed on to do."

"But now you could make a change," Maicy finished

for him. She also realized that he'd effectively steered the subject away from his romances and she wasn't going to let him, so as she picked up the wrappers left from their finished dinner to throw away, she said, "If the social-worker-turned-aide had to stick with the admiral wherever he was, how did the two of you go on to have a relationship?"

Conor laughed. "And here I thought I was getting away from that…" He sighed but continued as she rejoined him with a box of chocolate mints she'd left in the cabin from her pre-wedding days here.

"We just kept in contact," Conor said, taking a mint to eat while Maicy did the same before rejoining him on the floor. "We got together whenever we could. The admiral refused to be sent stateside so that kept Janice not too far away. She had leave time. I had leave time—"

"You must have really liked each other," Maicy said. The same way she'd been able to tell by his voice which women in his life he'd considered marriage with, she could tell that he'd cared about this Janice, and it raised some uninvited jealousy in her.

"I told you, we hit it off," he confessed in a way that confirmed for her that the relationship had been serious. Bothering her all the more.

"And it went on how long?" she asked.

"About two years. Which was why Janice thought it was time to take the next step."

"The next step being to get married."

He nodded but didn't offer more than that.

"So why didn't you?" Maicy asked with some caution.

Another shrug but no answer for a while before he

said flatly, "I just didn't see it and we parted ways." His tone made it clear that he didn't want to say more than that. Then, in a cheerier voice, he said, "And there you have it—nothing as exciting as an AWOL bride."

Maicy mock-flinched. "An AWOL bride?"

"That's what you are, isn't it? Absent without leave?"

"I think I had leave," she countered.

Conor grinned at her. "I think you did, too. I'm just giving you a hard time," he said, looking at her differently than he had been a moment before, his blue eyes softer, warmer, but so intent that he seemed to be committing every feature to memory.

"And you don't have any room to talk," Maicy teased in return. "At least I got close to getting married. But you? Someone who doesn't know you might say *you* have commitment issues."

"But you *do* know me," he said in a deeper, more intimate voice.

"I know how committed I've seen you be with Declan and your family. I know it's commitment to your other patients that's causing you to question what kind of medicine you want to practice, and your commitment to the military that's making it harder for you to consider a change. But with women…" she finished with a goading inflection.

"With women," he went on, still in that quiet, confidential way, "the commitment issue is that once upon a time I made a commitment to some red-haired girl. And even though she called it quits on me, I've never been sure that broke it from my side." He slid out from behind the coffee table and leaned forward, saying as he moved nearer, "Plus the honest-to-God truth about why I never got married is that *no one* has been able to fill that red-haired girl's shoes and replace her..."

No, hearing about him with other women hadn't helped fight his appeal. It hadn't given Maicy a clearer image of him as not hers. Not when he said that. And as irrational and ill-advised and unwise as she knew it was, she just wanted to reclaim him.

So when he raised that left arm from his knee to run the backs of his fingers along her cheek and came closer still, she didn't fight the urge to lean forward, to meet him halfway and kiss him.

And not only did she not fight that urge, she set aside every argument, every warning she'd been fostering, and just let herself be drawn into kissing this man.

Kissing him even more heatedly than they'd kissed under the stars the night before. Even more passionately as lips parted and tongues met again to mingle madly.

His arms wrapped around her and pulled her with him to lounge back against the front of the sofa, holding her close.

Her own arms slipped under his so she could lay her hands on shoulders so much broader than they had been when they were teenagers.

Only unlike kissing him then, Maicy didn't have to be on the alert or worry that they might get caught. She could merely lose herself in that kissing, in that tongue-play, in the feel of all those muscles and sinews that he'd developed, in the feel of the man he'd become.

And in the feel of his hands on her...

On her back where his fingers did a massage that was taking away every last bit of tension, turning her into soft, fluffy, pliable marshmallow.

Then one hand moved to her side, to the outermost

curve of a breast that had come to know his immature touch only in scattered, stolen moments. Breasts that both now cried out to know more of his touch than that.

Her nipples turned into insistent little pebbles and pressed through the lace of a honeymoon bra, through her sweater and into his chest. He must have felt the evidence of her arousal, if the increasing ravenousness of that kiss, if the even wider opening of his mouth, if the even more aggressive plundering of his tongue, was any indication.

There was no timidity in the grown Conor's hand as he brought it to cup her breast then, to enclose it in a grip that was tender and strong at once. A grip that she pressed into, wanting so much to feel flesh against flesh that she nearly tore herself away from that fevered kiss to tell him.

But Conor was in tune with her and she didn't have to say a word because after only a moment his hand slipped underneath her sweater.

He took a little time to test the lace of her bra, to run a fingertip over the edge of the cup, before he lowered it and gave her what she was looking for—the free and unfettered feel of his big, warm hand cupping her flesh.

Oh, yeah, he'd learned a few tricks…

Kneading and caressing, he teased and soothed her breast by turns. He tantalized and titillated. He pinched and rolled and tugged her nipple then cradled it in the tenderness of his palm.

And with each moment that passed came needs in Maicy that were both new and old, all of them more demanding than ever before, and it almost shocked her to discover how much she wanted him to make love to her.

Too much, maybe.

She knew she'd probably regret this later—especially having it happen in the minister's guesthouse, a place that seemed too sacrosanct to do what her body was crying out to do.

So this time she did end that scorching kiss to whisper, "We can't do this...here..."

She should have just said *no* rather than pretending the location was the obstacle. But she couldn't bring herself to refuse him outright. Not when she wanted him so much.

"Come out to the farm with me, then," he said in a voice ragged with desire.

Maicy shook her head. "No," she said more definitively. "There's already enough to answer for..."

"I don't give a damn!" he said, sounding desperate to have her.

Maicy laughed a little wryly, understanding. Still she said, "I do. And this is the—"

"Yeah, I know," Conor complained, "this is part of the church."

"And I'm the guest of the minister," she added with a sinner's laugh. "We have to behave."

Conor groaned. "I'm *really* missing the cabin now," he muttered.

But he gave her breast one last squeeze, readjusted her bra with expertise he hadn't had as a teenager before taking his hand out from under her sweater.

That triggered a moan of regret from Maicy that escaped on its own and prompted Conor to recapture both her mouth and her breast on top of her clothes again.

With some things slightly more in control, Maicy indulged and for a while they went on kissing and caressing as they had as teenagers.

Until her control began to waffle and she knew she had to hold her ground.

So once more she stopped things.

"You have to go," she told him.

He took a deep breath, closed his eyes, let his head fall back and said a "Yeah, okay..." that was full of complaint.

Then he sighed, let go of her and sat up.

"Out into the cold again," he said, getting to his feet.

Maicy stood, too, waiting while he put his coat on again and then walking with him to the door.

Where he grabbed her, pulled her into his arms again and kissed her as if she was his to kiss before he ended it this time.

"Jane said that there's a dance tomorrow night in the school gym to get people out and celebrate the end of the town being blocked off," he said then. "Let's go."

Maicy made a face. "I don't know..."

"Come on. I'll be your shield against whatever comes your way."

She laughed. He was big enough to be a pretty good one.

"We've been even more cooped up than anyone around here. We deserve it. And if anybody should be hiding out in shame it should be Gary and Candace—you should be holding your head up high."

None of that persuaded her.

What did was the excuse of being with Conor.

He kissed her again and then she heard herself say, "Okay."

That made him smile and her drown in the glory of that face and those eyes of his. "Good," he said. "Charge your phone and I'll let you know tomorrow what happens with your car and what time I'll pick you up for the dance."

Maicy nodded, didn't reject yet another kiss and then watched him walk out the door.

Leaving her in the blast of cold air, knowing she was playing with fire.

Chapter Eight

"Gary..."

"Hi, Maicy..."

Alone in the minister's guesthouse on Saturday morning, Maicy had done a lot of pacing, dreading this very conversation but knowing it needed to happen.

Running away from the wedding had effectively canceled their planned commitment, but it hadn't canceled the relationship they'd had. She couldn't just leave things the way they were. There needed to be closure of some kind. And on a purely practical level, there were details that had to be sorted through about what to do with his belongings at her house in Denver, and—most important to Maicy—the fact that since she'd opted to use her grandmother's wedding ring as her own, Gary still had it and she needed that back.

So after fretting over it all, she'd finally shored up her courage and texted Gary.

We should talk. And I need the ring.

Gary had not responded.

But now it was midafternoon and here he was at her door.

"Did you get my text?" she asked flatly.

He pulled the ring box out of his pocket and handed it to her. "Can I come in?"

Maicy stepped out of the doorway so he could enter.

He was a not-terribly-tall, boyishly attractive man of slight build, with pale brown hair. And he couldn't hold a candle to Conor's swarthy good looks or the masculine, imposing presence that commanded any room.

Gary had come up short by comparison when they were all teenagers, and now? He definitely came up short now as he took off his coat.

After meticulously folding it and laying it over the arm of the sofa he looked at her, something sheepish in his plain brown eyes. "I'm sorry."

He'd been so involved in kissing his former girl-friend at the wedding that Maicy hadn't been sure if he was aware that he'd been caught—though perhaps the photographer had clued him in once he'd detached his tongue from his ex's tonsils.

She raised her chin at him but didn't say anything, wondering what exactly he was apologizing for.

"I know you saw us…Candace and me…kissing…"

So that *was* the reason for the apology.

"I don't know how long you were there," he went on. "But when you grabbed the cake box and ran out…"

Had they been making out a long time before that? Maicy wondered.

But she discovered that it didn't really matter to

her. Because standing there, looking at this man she'd almost married, her dominant emotions were still relief that she *hadn't* married him, and true certainty that they shouldn't have ever gotten engaged in the first place.

"I want you to know," he was saying, "that I haven't let you take the rap for the wedding not happening. I didn't tell anybody that you ran out. I said that we talked and both decided that maybe we didn't want to go through with it—"

"So you also didn't own up to what you did," she pointed out without rancor, just glad that while it was still embarrassing, she might not be in line for any scorn.

"I didn't, but…" He hesitated and she could see clearly that he didn't want to say what he was about to. But he did anyway. "Candace and I are back together so… Well, everybody knows that by now, and people are figuring that—"

"You dumped me for her," Maicy finished for him.

He shrugged, looking spineless to her.

"Basically that *is* what you did, I guess." But she'd been thinking more about her own actions and running out on the wedding and having to answer for that.

"It isn't that I *dumped* you… What happened with Candace just…happened. It took us both by surprise. Sparks flew and…"

Sparks…

Maicy had more of an understanding of that than she wished she did. Sparks were definitely flying with Conor no matter how hard she tried to douse or ignore them.

And here she was thinking about Conor even as Gary was talking.

She refocused on him but it took some effort.

"Candace realized that she'd turned me down because she'd been afraid, not because she didn't love me and…" He cut himself off, likely before saying that he loved Candace, too.

"I do care for you, Maicy," he continued when he'd regrouped. "When you and I met in Denver…it was like a little piece of home—comfortable and nice. And it was so easy to be with you."

That's what he'd been to her, too—comfortable, easy, uncomplicated. "But that isn't a reason to get married—for comfort," she contributed. She might have believed that before, but not anymore.

"And I think maybe there was some of that in it for you, too," he said tentatively.

She hadn't thought he'd realized how lukewarm her feelings for him were but she didn't deny it now. "I guess it's just a good thing you and Candace met up again *before* we got to the altar," she said.

"I'm staying in Northbridge," he confessed then. "I'm going back to working in my dad's accounting office. You know I didn't do well in Denver. I guess I'm not a city boy. But I'm really, really sorry for the way things ended…"

"Don't be," she said, meaning it. How could she fault him too much after what had been happening between her and Conor?

"I'll pay you back for what you spent on the wedding. It'll have to be in installments, but—"

Maicy shrugged that off, feeling a bit guilty for having accepted his proposal in the first place when she'd known her feelings for him weren't strong enough for marriage. If the price she had to pay was covering the cost of the failed wedding, she could live with that. "Do you want to come to Denver to get your things or—"

"If I never set eyes on Denver again it'll be okay with me. Could you pack them up and ship them to me? I'll pay for that, too, of course."

"Sure," Maicy said, fine with the prospect of not having him at her house again.

"So are we okay?" he asked then.

"We are," she answered, happy to have this behind her.

With nothing more to say, Gary put his coat back on, buttoning it up. "I heard it was Conor Madison at the Dales' cabin with you. Did you patch things up with him?"

The idea clearly didn't cause any more jealousy in Gary than the thought of him with Candace had caused in Maicy.

We really weren't meant for each other, she thought.

"I don't know that I'd say we *patched* anything up. But we did find some…middle ground, maybe."

"It'd be something if the two of you got back together, too, wouldn't it?"

"That's never going to happen," she said. Maybe too quickly. Too forcefully. She and Conor *weren't* going to get back together, she insisted to herself. Regardless of the sparks, regardless of whatever it was they were doing, *that* wasn't going to happen. She wasn't letting her guard down *that* far.

"Well, I only wish you the best, Maicy," Gary said then.

"You, too," she responded.

He stayed looking at her for another moment, smiling the smile of someone saying goodbye to an old friend.

"Thanks for everything you did for me—giving me a place to live, trying to find me a job…everything," he added.

Especially for running out on the wedding…

It was something that went through Maicy's mind as if he'd said it and made her smile a little, too.

"Sure," she said, walking with him to the door to let him out.

Once he was gone, once the awkward meeting was over, she breathed a genuine sigh of relief—thinking that sometimes things worked out the way they were supposed to.

For Gary and Candace.

There was no way she would put Conor rescuing her into that category.

Even if she did suddenly have the oddest sense that she was a little freer to go to that dance tonight with him.

Free enough to look forward to it.

A lot.

And maybe a little freer to have what everything in her had been crying out for since she'd made him stop last night…

Maicy had arrived in Northbridge only two days before her wedding and had been swept into last-minute details and preparations. In the course of that she'd encountered several people she'd known before, but not so many that being in the small town again had had the air of a reunion. The end-of-the-storm dance did.

It was held in the hastily decorated high school gym and included a potluck dinner to go along with dancing to the music of a local garage band that sometimes played at the town's single bar.

When she and Conor stepped into the doorway of the gym Maicy was met with a better reception than she'd feared. Someone good-naturedly shouted, "It's our runaway bride!"

So much for Gary thinking he'd convinced anyone that they'd just reached an amicable parting, Maicy thought. She shouldn't have believed that anything got past the eyes and ears of Northbridge.

But still everyone laughed at the runaway bride greeting, there was some applause and many shouts of "Welcome back!" and Maicy decided the best thing to do was play along. So she smiled and took a theatrical bow.

And that was it. From then on the incident seemed to be forgotten and the reunion-like air prevailed, making the evening fun.

It didn't even bother Maicy that Gary and Candace came with his family. She was reasonably sure that being there herself with Conor made all the difference in that. And while there were a few comments along the lines of Maicy-and-Conor-back-together-again, they both sidestepped them.

They shared a table with Rickie—who had to use two chairs so he could elevate his broken leg on one of them—and his family, including wife, Jane, and his three kids.

Jane doted on her husband in a way that made it clear that her long-ago crush on Conor was just that—long-ago and over with—so that didn't prove uncomfortable. Plus there was an endless stream of interruptions as people came to say hello and catch up with Maicy and with Conor.

And there was dancing.

Though Maicy did not dance with Conor.

On the way into the school she'd told him that she didn't want there to be anything between them that would set tongues wagging tonight and Conor honored that. They kept a friendly distance from each other, just two single people attending the same function. There weren't any romantic overtures or any exchanges of private conversation. Maicy didn't even pay strict attention when he told Rickie and Jane the things that he'd told her on the way to the dance—that he had been able to speak directly to his brother and while Declan was still very ill, the antibiotics were helping. That Declan had insisted that since Conor had come all this way already, he should go to Denver to at least spend a day with their sister before he returned to Declan's bedside.

She'd also left it to Conor to tell them that both of their vehicles had been dug out of the snow and brought to the farm, where the local mechanic had gone to check them out. That the rental SUV was fine but Maicy's accident had left her car in need of a part the mechanic didn't have. The mechanic had done a temporary fix that he wasn't sure would hold to get Maicy all the way to Denver. But he'd shown Conor how to redo the fix if it failed, so Conor was going to follow her in his rental to make sure she made it safely before seeing his sister. And not even through all of that did he speak directly to her, so everything seemed completely innocent.

Until the last dance.

Just as the band announced it, Maicy's high school frog-dissecting-partner stepped up to ask for his second dance of the night, and Conor inserted himself between him and Maicy.

He was friendly but firm when he said, "Sorry, this one is all mine." Then he held out his hand to her. And she didn't hesitate before accepting it. Despite the ground rules she'd laid down as they'd arrived tonight, she'd spent every minute of what had turned out to be a pleasant event regretting the rules she'd put in place between them. Wishing with everything in her that he would just fold her into his arms and let her have him all to herself.

Which was what finally happened on the dance floor.

Except that he stood military-straight and tall and stiff, and held her at a respectable distance that felt as if there was still a mile between them.

But at least dancing gave her the excuse to focus solely on him, on the fine features of his face, to peer up into cobalt blue eyes that looked at her in a way no one else ever had.

Even as he smiled blandly and said for her ears only, "This is killing me."

Maicy laughed. "What is?"

"You know what is—acting like I hardly know you're here, watching you dance with other guys, keeping my hands off you…" His hand at her waist and the one that held hers both gripped her more firmly— something she felt but no one would be able to see.

"Tonight has been nice, though," she said as if she hadn't been going out of her mind wanting more of him. "It's almost made me sorry that I haven't been back to visit here until now. That I didn't stay in touch with anyone. I've actually been feeling a little homesick for Northbridge tonight."

"You could move back," he suggested.

Maicy laughed. "I wouldn't go that far. But who knows, I might not skip the next class reunion."

"Surprisingly, I made it to mine. I just happened to be on leave and visiting my folks when it happened. But you skipped yours?"

"Oh, yeah."

"You didn't just skip it, you avoided it like the plague," he guessed from her tone.

"They couldn't have paid me to come," she confirmed.

"Why? You never hated Northbridge—in fact, back when you proposed, you said that we could have a good life here if we stayed instead of heading to college."

"I believed that," she said. "But then you left and that last year here, after losing my mom...you..." she added quietly, "all I wanted was to put this place behind me and never look back, and that's what I did. I guess the same way I chose to forget that we'd ever had anything good together before the split, I forgot that there was anything good about Northbridge, too. Tonight I remembered, though—it's not a bad place and neither are the people in it. I was happy here before things fell apart."

"Think you would have been happy if you'd stayed?" he asked.

"Not then." Because she honestly didn't think she would have been happy in the small town without him. But she wasn't willing to say that.

Conor nodded as if he understood anyway. "A lot of people have stayed," he said, taking his eyes off her to glance around the gym before his attention was all on her once more. "They married, had kids... Hard for me to imagine some of the couple combinations that have happened over the years. Harder still to see some of these guys as parents—"

"Rickie especially—I know," Maicy agreed with another laugh. "He was such a—"

"Screw-up," Conor finished with a laugh of his own.

"And now he has your Jane and two *teenagers*—"

"She was not *my* Jane," Conor corrected before he seemed to become more reflective and said, "I keep thinking what if...what if we'd stayed."

"Yeah, me, too," Maicy said. "But what would we have done?" she reasoned, echoing his arguments from eighteen years ago. "You wanted to be a doctor from long before you and I ever got together—and you couldn't have done that here. I know you hated working on the farm. If that was what you'd ended up doing you wouldn't have been happy. And the military...your stepfather had you and Liam and Declan in that mind-set when you were all still in elementary school. There was no question about you all joining the service."

"Yeah, that's all true," he said but with a hint of regret in his voice. "And what about you? You were talking about skipping college—which would have been a waste of that brain of yours. What would you have done here?"

Maicy shrugged at the question. "You were right back then. I would have done just any old dead-end job that I would likely have hated. It took leaving here to learn how to take care of myself, to get me where I am—and I like where I am. I don't think I would have had that same determination if we had stayed."

"Plus there would have probably been kids…"

"It would have been a different life." Maybe better in some ways, worse in others, but definitely different.

Perhaps Conor was thinking the same thing because he only said, "Yeah…"

He pulled her closer—not a lot, just enough to rest his chin on the top of her head. But something about it felt possessive. "I have to tell you, though, I look at Rickie and I'm kind of jealous—"

"You *did* want Jane," Maicy accused, obviously joking.

"No. But I am jealous that he's not going home alone tonight…"

She laughed yet again. "That was not subtle."

He chuckled. "I'm not feeling like there's time for subtlety," he admitted. "What I *am* feeling is that I've spent this whole damn day hating that last night ended and wanting to pick up where we left off."

That was exactly what she'd been feeling.

But before she could say anything, Conor took her elbows and lifted them so that both of her arms were around his neck. Then he locked his hands at the small of her back and looked down at her again in a way that made everything else recede, leaving Maicy with the sense that they were alone in the room.

"I'm just thinking that your car is at my place, that by now the minister and his family are long asleep," he said softly. "We could pack up your things at the guesthouse, slip a thank-you and the key under the main house's door, and you could come with me out to the farm tonight instead of having someone bring you out in the morning. We could have tonight together before we head for Denver tomorrow. Because once we hit Denver tomorrow," he mused, "this is all going to end. You're going back to your life. I'm going back to mine..." He breathed a warm gust of air into her hair before he whispered, "But here we are now..." He paused, then said even more softly, "Give me tonight, Maicy..."

She didn't mean for it to happen but as she thought about that her cheek went to his chest and keeping up appearances was forgotten as she considered going home with him.

She'd been worried last night that she'd wanted him to make love to her *too* much. That she might make the decision in the heat of the moment and regret it afterward.

But this wasn't the heat of the moment.

And they wouldn't be in the minister's guesthouse.

Conor was suggesting that they slip away to his place in the country, where they could have this one last night alone before they rejoined the real world and their real lives.

As she thought about it, she realized that she didn't actually have to ask herself if she would regret making love with Conor because she knew she wouldn't. Instead it suddenly seemed like the natural course of things.

He was supposed to have been her first. But that wasn't what happened. And while, over the years, there had been a part of her that had been glad that she hadn't given up her virginity to someone who had disillusioned and disappointed her so resoundingly, there was another part of her that had regretted that she hadn't. And it had most definitely left her wondering.

Now maybe fate was not only giving her the opportunity to sort through some of the past with Conor, but also the opportunity to know him in the one way that she'd never gotten to explore. The one thing she'd wanted desperately and denied herself.

The one thing she wanted desperately all over again.

And she *did* want him desperately. Not because of the relationship they'd had years ago, but because of the man he was now. The adult Conor she'd discovered herself attracted to in spite of their past, even as she'd fought her attraction.

Tonight, she didn't want to say no. Instead, she wanted this man. The man he was now. Knowing full well that it would only be this one time.

That thought gave her a pretty severe twinge. But she ignored it. She wanted to get back to her life, there was no doubt about that. But before that happened, she also wanted this one last night with Conor, both to put the past to rest and more, to satisfy what the adult Conor had brought to life in her now. And after last night she knew that if she *didn't* go home with him tonight, it was *that* that she would really regret. Forever.

The music ended just then and so did their dance.

Maicy took her head off his chest and gazed up at his face again, drinking in the sight of him.

"What about that 'no exertion because of my head injury' thing?" she teased.

He grinned and that only made him all the sexier. "You can let me do all the work," he answered without skipping a beat, a sly sparkle in those blue eyes.

She laughed once more, paused just to bask in the way he looked at her again, and then said, "Okay."

His grin got bigger, he clasped one of her hands in his and didn't bother to say good-night to anyone, taking her out of the gym, bypassing everyone in the lobby and grabbing their coats to get her out of the school and to his SUV.

Neither of them said much as they returned to the guesthouse, made short work of getting her things and enacted his thank-you-note-and-key-slipped-under-the-door plan.

Neither of them said much as they drove out of town and headed for the farm. But the silence was both peaceful and charged with an underlying excitement. In an odd way, she felt like she was heading for the wedding night she'd always fantasized about. The wedding night that she'd been sure she'd share with Conor, that would make the waiting worthwhile.

When they pulled up in front of the farmhouse she was only vaguely aware that it looked the same as it always had. Her attention was on Conor taking her suitcase from his back seat as she got out of the SUV.

And then they went inside.

He closed the door after them and dropped the suitcase where he stood so he could spin her around to him and catch her mouth with his. But they weren't really picking up where they'd left off the night before because while Maicy had expected a blitz kind of kiss, this was soft and slow and sweet. The kind of kiss that savored that initial meeting of his mouth and hers.

Still, it did the trick. For Maicy, in that moment, the world was shut out and everything fell away so that she could give herself over to everything she'd been wanting.

Making almost no contact, Conor took off her wool coat, letting that drop to the floor, too, before he shrugged out of his and discarded it the same way.

His hands came to the sides of her face then, keeping her in that kiss as it deepened and grew more intense.

Then he stopped, clasped her hand in his and led her up the stairs.

"Upstairs was off-limits," she whispered as if they weren't there alone.

"Not anymore," he said with a smile he cast over his shoulder at her as she took in the very fine sight of him from behind.

When they reached the upper level he brought her into the second bedroom, plain and simple with only a double bed, nightstands and a bureau to furnish it.

"Was this your room?" she asked.

"Back in the day. Now all of our rooms are guest rooms. Mom didn't want to keep the posters or the military and sport stuff, I guess," he said affectionately. "You've been here before…" He swung her around to face him again, his hands at the small of her back. "But only in pictures. And in my fantasies," he added, his smile stretching into a wicked grin before he kissed her again, this one not so slow or soft or sweet, but with lips parted from the start and a wicked tongue coming to dare her to play.

It was a dare Maicy took. He'd worn jeans and a quarter-zip mock-neck sweater tonight, leaving the zipper partially down to expose his throat. It was the open ends of that sweater that she grasped, pulling him into that kiss even further and letting her own tongue introduce so much simmering sensuality that she even surprised herself.

It wasn't lost on him because she heard a quiet rumble in his throat and his arms tightened around her, bringing his hands into a firm hold of her back through the dark gray silk blouse she'd worn tonight with black slacks.

She went on kissing him with the seductiveness of a siren as she kicked off her shoes.

The two-inch-lower height gave him a bit of an advantage that he took, turning the kiss into something more fevered and hungry.

Maicy let go of his collar and lowered the zipper of his sweater. Then she ended that kiss to press her lips to his chest at the lowest point of the sweater's opening.

He laughed, got rid of his own shoes, then let out a sort of growl and swooped her into his arms to lay her on the bed.

Still standing at the foot of it himself, he yanked his sweater off over his head and threw it aside with a vengeance.

The curtains on the two windows in the room were open. Moonlight reflected off the snow, leaving the space bathed in a white glow brighter than any candlelight, and letting Maicy see for sure that there was a vast improvement in Conor-the-man's bare chest over what Conor-the-boy's had been.

He was all broad shoulders and honed muscles that she couldn't wait to get her hands on, so she was glad that he didn't hesitate to join her on the bed.

Straddling her legs, he knee-walked to her hips, his cobalt blue eyes locked on hers as he reached for the buttons of her blouse and began to unfasten them, slowly exposing the lacy black demi-cup bra she'd worn tonight.

He must have liked it because when he slid her blouse off, he stole a glance and gave a little groan of appreciation. The kind of appreciation Maicy volleyed back when she laid her hands to his flat stomach and slid them up his superb torso.

About the time she reached his shoulders he dipped down to kiss her again, a leisurely and oh-so-sexy kiss that locked them together as he stretched out next to her and rolled her with him so they were both on their sides, where he draped one leg over her to pull her up against him.

There were still too many clothes between their bottom halves, though…

That brought memories of make-out sessions of yore when despite exploring hands and the intimate press of bodies, clothes had remained on.

To distract herself from it Maicy focused on that kiss, on the feel of the bare skin she could reach, running her hands from his waistband up the widening V of his back, digging her fingers into the span of his shoulders, feeling the flex of those muscles beneath her touch, and learning the iron strength of impressive biceps before she tested to see what kind of reaction she got from massaging pectorals with slightly taut nibs at their centers.

Slightly taut. Nothing at all like her own nipples that were little diamonds straining for his touch as one of his hands came around from her back to cup a breast in his palm.

Maicy couldn't suppress a sigh at the feel of it, especially when he did something he'd never done before and unhooked her bra, tossing it aside. Leaving her something she'd never been with him before—topless.

Her arousal deepened, intensified, causing her breasts to swell into the hand that was again working magic, kneading and caressing and tantalizing each globe in turn.

For a bit, anyway, until he stopped kissing her, nudged her to her back and found one breast with his mouth while his hand went on tormenting the other, raising the stakes and her yearning along with them.

Oh that mouth and tongue and teeth…

He knew what to do with them all and drove her wild, sucking and flicking and circling and tugging her to distraction until she could barely keep from writhing.

And she couldn't stop herself from finding the button fly of jeans when everything in her demanded more of him.

She closed her hand around him, long and thick and strong and as impressive as the rest of him, and felt his grip on her breast tighten in response to his own pleasure even as he groaned his approval and she put some effort into driving him a little crazy.

A new urgency came over him with that, and before long he got off the bed again, pulling Maicy by the ankles to the end, where he took off her slacks, spent a moment admiring her black lace bikini panties before he slipped those off, too, reveling in the sight of her naked body.

"Oh yeah…" he breathed.

He took a condom from his jean pocket, then dropped his jeans and boxers, and put the condom on while Maicy ogled the magnificence of him that was far greater than anything she'd ever imagined. And something she wanted to know every inch of by touch.

When he came back onto the bed he kissed her again with an all-new fervor, clearly equally eager to explore because as her hands left nothing of him unknown, his traveled everywhere on her, gliding over her skin, sending all inhibitions fleeing, making her pliable and willing before his hand again sought her breasts.

But only for a while before his mouth did, too, freeing his hand to sluice lower, between her legs and into her for a teaser that only drove them both into even more of a frenzy that had to have an outlet.

He nudged her knees apart and rose up over her to find his place between them. To slide smoothly into her.

She never wanted to think that she needed any man to complete her. And yet the moment he was inside of her that *was* how she felt.

Her muscles contracted around him all on their own, holding tight. And she knew he felt it because he moaned with pleasure and surprise and revelation all at once, and he pushed in farther still before establishing a rhythm in and out that Maicy met and matched, her arms around his expansive back holding tight, her thighs and hips aiding the cause.

They moved together and apart, together and apart in unison, both of them striving in answer to what was building, growing between them. Until it reached a peak that exploded in Maicy first and arched her up off the mattress, a high-pitched moan of ecstasy escaping from her just as she felt Conor reach a peak of his own.

Every inch of him stiffened and he plunged even deeper into her as she clung to him, curling her legs around his and pulling him deeper still, their bodies seamlessly together as he brought her to a second, even more powerful crest that was so incredible she tried not to let it pass.

But it did anyway. Slowly releasing her from its hold until they were both drained and spent and collapsed a little.

And once again she was aware of the feel of him inside of her and the thought ran through her mind that she never wanted him anywhere else.

But she chased that thought away and merely enjoyed the weight of him on top of her while they both caught their breath.

Still joined, he wrapped her in his arms and legs and rolled them to their sides again, where he held her close.

He pressed a lingering kiss to the top of her head, sighed a replete sigh, and said, "Are you all right?"

She laughed at the concern in his tone, knowing that now that the deed was done he was worrying about her health again. "Never better," she assured.

"No headache?"

"I did see stars…" she teased, making him laugh.

"You're welcome," he said cockily.

"So are you," she countered, not to be outdone.

"Oh, believe me, I'm grateful," he said, pulsing inside of her.

Then all at once he let go of her and disappeared into what she assumed was a bathroom, before he came back and settled again beside her, pulling her as close as he could get her—only this time he yanked one side of the quilt over them, binding them together.

"Sleep," he ordered. "You need rest."

That was true enough—like with every exertion since the accident, she had tired out faster than normal. But she was loath to close her eyes and miss any of what felt so perfect at that moment.

It was actually Conor who fell asleep before she did, still keeping her near even then, nestled in his arms in a way that was again so, so much better than she'd ever known it could be.

But despite wanting to stay awake and revel in it, she couldn't fight off sleep for long.

And as she began to lose that battle, it occurred to her that the other thing she couldn't fight off was an ache at the thought that this wasn't for forever...

Chapter Nine

It took fourteen hours to make the eight-hour drive from Northbridge to Denver on Sunday. The highway varied from clear to snow-packed, and stopping for checks on the temporary repair of Maicy's engine slowed their progress, too.

The short-term fix lasted, though, all the way to Maicy's mechanic—Rob, the nineteen-year-old brother of her friend Rachel.

Rob either had a crush on Maicy or orders from his sister to rescue her from Conor because he all but shoved Conor out of the way to get to her the minute they arrived at the shop where he worked.

And once he had, he said he would take over from there—both with the car and with getting Maicy home. Then he hovered like a bodyguard, allowing them nothing more than a scant goodbye before insisting that

Maicy come with him to discuss what the car needed. Leaving Conor with no recourse but to watch her be taken from him as she called a thank-you to him over her shoulder.

And that was it.

But how the hell could that be?

That was what kept screaming through Conor's brain even as he called his sister to tell her he was minutes away from her apartment. Even as he called to check on Declan—asleep but still stable. And even through meeting his sister's fiancé Sutter Knightlinger before he dropped his gear in Kinsey's guest room and took a shower.

It was still screaming through his brain as he left the guest room to find his sister saying the kind of heated, passionate goodbye to Sutter that he wished he'd been able to say to Maicy.

Damn, this just wasn't how their time together should end...

"I made a roast for dinner in case you got home earlier." Kinsey's enthusiastic voice cut through his thoughts when her fiancé tossed Conor a good-night and left. "But since it's almost nine o'clock, how about a roast beef sandwich? I've got tomatoes and lettuce and a Havarti cheese with dill in it that'll be great on it!"

"Sure. Okay," he answered her.

"Come and sit at the table while I fix it. Can I get you a beer?"

"Yeah, a beer would be great." He made himself focus on his sister, fighting to clear his head as he nodded in the direction of the apartment door. "Sutter seems like a good guy."

"The best!" she corrected, going on to effusively tell him all the ways in which her fiancé excelled until Conor laughed and cried uncle against the onslaught.

"I get it, I get it—you like him," he understated.

"Oh, sooo much…"

"It's a good thing since you're marrying him. I'm just glad he makes you happy. And that you aren't lonely anymore. You aren't, right?" He knew loneliness was part of what had prompted her to pursue the Camden connection.

"Not lonely, no," she said, adding in a warning tone, "But I still want family, Conor."

"You have family—Declan, Liam and me, and in a few months Sutter and his mother. Then probably kids." It was something he'd said to her before and she was no more receptive to it now than she had been previously.

"I—*we*—also have four half brothers and two half sisters, nieces, nephews, cousins and a *grandmother*," she persisted. "A grandmother, Conor—none of us were born in time to know grandparents on Mom's side, and here we are, with a living breathing one just blocks away from this very spot! How can you not want to know her? Or the rest of them?"

"It isn't that I wouldn't want to know them under other circumstances, Kins. But as it is we're their father's bastard secret family. Our mother—"

"Don't say it!" She stopped him. "You always try to scare me off this by focusing on the worst thing they might say about her. I know you do it for shock value but it doesn't change the way I feel. These people are our flesh and blood. Georgianna Camden is as fully our grandmother as she is to all ten of the others, and I want them to be a part of my life."

"They aren't rushing in for that," he reminded her. "They're having us investigated like we're some kind of scam artists or lowlifes."

"In their position they have to be careful," she defended. "And so what if they're investigating us? All they can find is that it's the truth."

"And then what, Kins? Truth or not, it doesn't change how they feel about the whole thing, about us. About Mom. Do you really want family that hates or resents us?"

"I'm hoping for the best," his sister said stubbornly. "And you should know that I'm inviting every one of them to the wedding—the side of the family that Sutter is related to, and the side we're related to, along with our grandmother."

Conor shook his head. "We're just afraid you're setting yourself up for a fall," he said, speaking for his brothers as well as himself.

"I can take it," she claimed. "Especially now that I have Sutter. But I'd like for you and Liam and Declan to be on board, too," she added hopefully.

"I...I don't know what to tell you, Kins... None of us are going to be on board with mud being slung at Mom—you have to know that."

"I wouldn't stand for that, either. But I've met these people and that isn't how they are. They're good, decent people—"

"The Camdens haven't always been good, decent people," he pointed out. "You know the reputation of the ones who died in that crash—ruthless, underhanded, willing to do *anything* to get what they wanted, to get all they have now. And if Mitchum Camden had been good or decent he wouldn't have cheated on his wife, on his family. He wouldn't have put Mom in the position she was in or had a whole second family on the side. It was Hugh who married Mom and took us on and treated us as his own—*that's* a good, decent guy."

Then he realized he'd been practically shouting. Okay, maybe he needed to tone it down for his sister's sake. What he and his brothers said to each other on this subject might be too harsh for Kinsey, who genuinely wanted to be a part of the Camden family.

She finished making his sandwich and brought it to him, sitting in the chair across from him at the small round kitchen table.

"Mom loved him," she said simply. "She was ashamed of being the *other woman*, embarrassed. She never wanted his wife, his other family, to know about her or us because she didn't want to hurt any of them. But even though she knew it was wrong, she couldn't change the way she felt. She said she wished she hadn't loved him, that she tried to stop and so did he. But neither of them could."

After what he'd felt during this last week with Maicy, much of that struck home for Conor and he didn't have a comeback for it. So all he said was, "I guess we'll just have to see what happens. We just don't want you to get hurt if they aren't interested in connecting. Because you know that could happen—it kind of already did when you showed the grandmother the letter that Mom left us explaining this whole thing."

"And that was hard," Kinsey admitted. "But I came out of their house to Sutter and he was like a safety net, waiting there, ready to cushion the blow. So like I said, having him will help if the Camdens never come around to accepting us, and you guys don't have to

VICTORIA PADE   *191*

worry as much about it not working out. For the first
time since you all left home and joined the military,
I'm not alone in whatever happens."

"I'm sorry that you have been, Kinsey. So are Liam
and Declan. We know finding out about this might have
had a different impact on you if we'd been here to help
out over the years."

"I'm counting Sutter as my reward for the sacrifices,
so you can all stop feeling guilty for that. But I still like
the idea of a big family, here, around me. Including a
grandmother who can become great-grandmother to
my kids. So I'm not giving up on the Camdens and I
think they're going to surprise you."

"For your sake, I hope you're right," he said with
the full extent of his doubts in his tone.

"And when I make out the wedding invitations," his
sister said coyly then, "should I send one to Maicy? Or
maybe she'll be your plus-one if you make it home…"

The first thing Conor and Kinsey had discussed
when he'd arrived had been Declan's health, so Kinsey had already had the update on their brother. Conor
hadn't been too forthcoming with his sister about his
career conundrum, so she didn't know how much that
was weighing on him. But of course the fact that he'd
just spent a week in a secluded cabin with his old high
school sweetheart would intrigue Kinsey even though
she hadn't gotten around to the subject until now.
Though she'd been several years younger, too young
to be close to Maicy when Conor had been dating her,
Kinsey had always liked Maicy. And had seen what
he'd gone through when she'd dumped him.

"Oh, no… I don't know…that all seems weird…" he
answered, struggling for something that would make

sense. Then he settled on, "Nothing's changed just because we were snowed in."

That wasn't true—everything had changed. But now that they'd made it to Denver, everything needed to change back as they returned to their regularly scheduled lives, which didn't include each other.

"Come on, it's me you're talking to. I know how you were about her," his sister said with some authority.

It was authority she'd earned because while he'd put on a brave front eighteen years ago for their tough-as-nails stepfather, and for Declan and Liam, he'd shown some of his feelings over the breakup to his mother and shared even more of them with Kinsey.

"That was almost two decades ago," he said, dodging the issue.

"And now you've just had more than a week with her—most of it *alone* with her. Don't tell me it didn't stir up old feelings."

Old ones. New ones.

Feelings that kept shouting that this just wasn't how their time together should end.

"I don't know, Kins—" he said yet again.

But he was literally saved by the bell just then because his sister's cell phone rang and when she looked at the display she said, "This is Sutter... His mother, the colonel, has bronchitis and—"

"Answer it," Conor encouraged.

She did, leaving him to eat while she had a brief conversation with her fiancé about his mother. It concluded with her saying she would come right over.

Then she ended the call and made a guilt-ridden face at Conor. "I have to go check on her," she said.

Conor laughed. "This is a switch, isn't it? Usually

when one of us comes to see you, you make time stand still for the visit. Now it's you who has something else calling you away."

"I'm sorry."

"Don't be. How many times have we left you hanging? I'm just glad to see your life full enough to have priorities outside of us. Do you want backup?" he offered.

"The colonel saw her doctor yesterday—that's who diagnosed the bronchitis. So I don't think she needs a doctor right now. It sounds like she just needs a nebulizer treatment. But if that isn't enough I'll call you. And I'll be back as soon as I can—we can sit up all night talking."

As much as he loved and missed his sister, it was Maicy he would really like to have the prospect of that with. Although maybe not for *only* talking...

"Don't worry about it," he told his sister. "If you need to stay over there for the night to keep an eye on things, go ahead. The monster storm moved east and now Maryland is socked in with it and their airports are closed. Thank God Declan is doing better because I'll be lucky to get back to him by Tuesday, but that means you and I will still have at least tomorrow to catch up."

"You're sure?" Kinsey said.

"I am. Duty calls—and so do the other people in your life now—so stay there and take care of them. After all the driving I did today, it's better if I just sack out anyway."

"I probably should monitor the colonel's breathing overnight..."

"Go!" Conor commanded.

She did, leaving him alone with the remainder of his sandwich and his thoughts.

Thoughts that were *not* about going to sleep. That instead were all about Maicy and how he was almost glad to have his sister leave so he might have the chance yet tonight to maybe call her or text her. Something. Anything.

To say a proper goodbye to her—that was what he told himself he was contemplating doing.

But was that really what he was aiming for? Just to say the goodbye the mechanic hadn't allowed? For closure for what had opened up between them since the snowstorm had thrown them together?

Yeah, that *should* have been what he was aiming for.

But instead, he was just thinking about how much he wanted to talk to her, to see her. Last night had been better than anything he'd ever fantasized about, better than everything he'd ever imagined it might be. And it had unleashed something in him. He'd thought that if they never left that bed, he could be a happy man.

They'd only made love once and there was no way once had been enough for him. But he'd forced himself to keep in mind that Maicy was still recovering from the accident, that they had the drive to Denver to make, that she needed to sleep. So he'd let her. Snuggled to his side, her head on his chest, one naked thigh over his, his arms around her.

But four times he'd woken up just to reassure himself that she was honestly there. Wanting her so damn bad again. Having to remind himself that he *had* to let her rest, even as he'd basked in her being in his bed, in his arms, where he'd wanted her since he was seventeen.

Their plan had been to get up at dawn and head for Denver. And as was his way, he'd stuck to his plan despite everything in him demanding that he keep her there and make love to her again. But he'd used every drop of willpower his stepfather and the navy had ever drilled into him, and he'd gotten out of that bed.

He'd kept her in his sights through the entire drive from Northbridge, not really thinking about losing her again once the drive was over because it didn't seem— hadn't seemed all through the drive—like that was a possibility. Not after last night.

That had been shortsighted of him. They'd already discussed how getting out of Northbridge had been the cutoff to what was happening between them. The end. The time when they both went back to their separate lives.

But then last night had happened and…

And gut-punched him.

Last night had been more than unfinished business or any kind of ending.

Last night had seemed like a new beginning…

He stood up from his sister's table and took his beer and his plate with him. He rinsed the plate and put it in the dishwasher, then took a swig of beer as he leaned against the counter's edge, still lost in thought.

But what kind of new beginning could last night be? he asked himself.

He was still the guy who had let Maicy down when she'd needed him most.

He still had to get to his brother to make sure Declan came through all right.

He was still in some kind of weird limbo over his

job—a job that would either take him away for long stints or one that would mean nearly starting over.

And Maicy was still where she'd ended up *because* he'd let her down—someone with a business of her own, with a life and friends that held her in Denver.

So what exactly was he thinking was a new beginning?

And a beginning of what?

He hadn't been *thinking*, he realized then. It was only a *sense* that there was a new beginning. It was only feelings that had him in their grip. Feelings about her.

He wanted her.

He wanted her as much now as he had years ago. More...

Yeah, he wanted to make love to her again. That was a given. But that wasn't all he wanted. He just wanted her.

When they were kids she'd been a pretty, good-natured, soft-hearted girl. Fun and funny and a little feisty. Sweet and uncomplicated.

But now?

Now she wasn't merely pretty, she was beautiful.

The soft-heartedness was still there—or she wouldn't have demanded that they save the mouse at the cabin, he thought with a laugh. And she was still fun and funny. But that feistiness had a touch of fire to it, a touch of stubbornness that only gave her personality more depth.

Depth she had all the way around now.

She was strong and resilient and confident. She was organized and efficient and more capable than she'd been as a girl. Braver, even. Brave enough to shoo away a mountain lion.

Thinking about that made him laugh again and realize how much he liked every bit of her. Every aspect just added to the intrigue of her. The sexiness of her. It all just made her one hell of a woman.

A woman who had not only provided a distraction from his concerns and frustrations over Declan but had talked him through them, calmed him.

And she'd been the perfect person to be stranded with. There hadn't been any whining or complaining about the conditions of the cabin, about any of the inconveniences. She hadn't milked the situation or her injury the way someone else might have. Instead she'd been determined to contribute, to do her share. She'd pushed through headaches and dizziness and weakness rather than giving in to them. And she was resourceful—it was Maicy who'd explored their options and devised the plan for how to move Rickie and get him into the truck while Conor had dealt with his friend's broken leg.

She just had so much more substance, so many more layers than she'd had before.

Much of which had come out of him hurting her.

And made it seem like he was the last person who should be in line to benefit from or enjoy any of it...

God, he wished he could wipe that slate clean!

And what if he could? he asked himself. What if they *could* have a new beginning? A future together?

What would that future look like?

Certainly, it would be different from anything he'd contemplated for a long time. It would require major deviations from the plan he'd made for himself. But the clock was ticking on making the decision about what path to take professionally. And that was the first thing he had to sort through...

Could he be satisfied with his life if he stayed in a job that frustrated him more every day? His successes in trauma medicine meant saving a life or a limb in a particular moment. That was something vital, but it was also without a sense of permanence, a sense of complete satisfaction, when he knew the patient had so much further to go before being home free, before they walked out of a hospital under their own steam or returned to their life.

Trauma medicine lacked deeper fulfillment. It was patch up and pass on.

He'd liked that when he'd first started out. It wasn't enough now but he was convinced that the navy wouldn't stand still for him changing his path.

So how to decide?

Take the military out of the equation.

That had been Maicy's advice. Maybe it was time he took it.

So what if he did factor out the military and only considered his medical career?

There was no appeal in doing another residency, a fellowship.

But there was even less appeal in the prospect of sticking with what he was doing now.

And between the two he suddenly knew that he would rather take a few years to step back and retrain than face thirty or forty more, frustrated and dissatisfied and discontent. That he would rather spend those few years in residency and fellowship and then be able to go on in a field he would ultimately prefer for the bulk of his career.

Which left him with one answer.

He had to leave the navy.

But accepting that was no easy task and he chugged the rest of his beer as he tried to sort through it.

Maicy had been right when she'd said that his stepfather had heavily encouraged him and his brothers to be career military. To serve until they were of no more use to their country. That was the plan.

But if changing his medical specialty altered his medical career plan without trashing it, was there a way to alter the plan to serve his country without giving it up entirely?

Looking at things in a clearer light now, he didn't need more than posing that question to find an answer.

He'd seen for himself how short-staffed veterans' hospitals were. If he went to work as a contract physician in a veterans' facility he would still be serving his country and repaying the military for his education, it would just be as a veteran himself rather than as active military.

It wasn't the original plan. It probably wouldn't have pleased Hugh. But it was a workable alternative.

A new plan.

A new plan thanks to Maicy's guidance.

And one load lifted off his shoulders.

Freeing him to think about what his new, civilian life might include. Like Maicy. After all, she *was* the whole reason he'd started thinking about this. As much as he wanted and needed a career change, he wanted and needed her even more. At any cost.

And now that he'd decided to reset his course, he had more to offer her.

An offer he needed to make because he didn't want to say goodbye to her. He didn't want to lose her again. He *couldn't* lose her again!

Maybe he'd been a stupid young fool not to say yes to her eighteen years ago, or maybe he hadn't—he honestly didn't know. But he did know at that moment that no matter what it took, he had to have her now.

If she'd have him…

God, that seemed like a big if.

Especially when he suddenly knew that he was in the position she'd been in eighteen years ago—she'd sorted through the crisis she'd been in the midst of, believed she'd found a solution for it, and had only needed him to say yes.

And he hadn't.

"It would serve you right if she kicked your ass out the door," he told himself.

And it terrified him like nothing in his life ever had that she might.

So what was he going to do?

There was a single answer to that.

He threw his beer bottle into the recycle bin, took his sister's spare apartment key from the hook she kept it on and headed for the door.

Because Maicy saying no was a chance he had to take.

Chapter Ten

"Um, Maicy, some guy just pulled up in front of your house. Some really hot guy…"

Rachel's brother Rob had driven Maicy home, where she'd taken a quick shower and shampoo, twisted her hair into a careless, lopsided knot, then dressed in a soft loungewear T-shirt and flannel pajama pants to go across the street to Rachel's house to have pizza with her friend and her friend's husband.

After eating, Jake had gone to the den to watch television and left Maicy and Rachel to talk and catch up. That was what they'd been doing for the last two hours, sitting in Rachel's living room.

Rachel was curled up on an overstuffed chair that gave her a view of Maicy's house through the front window behind the couch where Maicy was sitting.

"Who would come over this late?" Maicy responded

as she pivoted around to peer out the window, too. Then she said, "That's Conor!"

Whom they had talked extensively about tonight.

"What's he doing here?" she added as she watched him get out of his rented SUV.

"Booty call?" Rachel joked.

"I left my phone at home to charge. Do you think he called or texted? How'd he find me?"

"*Determination* for a booty call?" was Rachel's laughing response as she joined Maicy, kneeling on the sofa beside her to stare directly out the window. "He probably just looked up your address. Why are you sitting here? Go over there!" her friend urged.

Maicy wasn't so sure about that.

Last night with him had rattled her. It had been so good that all of her defenses had disintegrated, leaving her completely unguarded and vulnerable in ways she hadn't been since the day Conor had rejected her proposal. Ways that scared her to death.

Driving back to Denver she'd fought to resurrect everything that had protected her through the last eighteen years. She'd reminded herself in no uncertain terms that she was *not* the wide-eyed, trusting, naive young girl she'd once been. That she did *not* believe in fairy tales and that she had to take care of herself.

She'd told herself that regardless of how things had developed between her and Conor at the cabin, regardless of the support he'd offered in Northbridge and the rekindling of their former connection there, regardless of one mind-bogglingly incredible love-making session and sleeping in his arms more soundly than she'd ever slept before, it was over. Done. Finished. Sealed and filed away once and for all.

She'd actually texted Rachel during the last stop they'd made to check her engine on the way to Denver, asking her friend to alert Rob that she was on her way to his shop and get him to run interference between her and Conor. To do exactly what he'd done—save her from any long, lingering goodbyes between them.

It had been a safety precaution so she didn't give in to the temptation to ask Conor to spend tonight with her—something she knew he was bound to turn down in favor of time with his sister. Because of course his family would be prioritized over her.

Not that she *should* be anywhere on his list of priorities, she'd also reminded herself. But so many lines had been blurred and everything had somehow gotten so confusing and complicated...

"Maicy?" Rachel's voice interrupted her thoughts, sounding confused herself. "Are you going over there?"

Her heart was racing and no, she still wasn't eager to cross the street and be with him again. Why was he there, anyway? Just to say the long, lingering goodbye she'd already taken measures to avoid? To say a *thanks, it's been fun, maybe I'll see you again in eighteen or twenty years and we can have another go-round*?

Or maybe he really was just there for a booty call. But while last night had left her wanting a whole lot more intimacy with him, wanting it as much as she did was a warning that it was exactly what she *shouldn't* indulge in.

The plain truth was that he'd shaken her foundation again.

After he'd turned down her proposal it had taken her a long time to feel like she was standing on solid ground.

A longer time to build the solid base that she'd erected for herself and evolve into the person she was now.

One week with him—including one night in bed with him—and things were suddenly wobbly again.

And coming from that weak-kneed position, she was worried that she might once more be helpless when it came to her attraction to him, that she was just too susceptible to him.

And where would that leave her when he was gone again? Wanting things he wasn't going to give her? Hating herself for it? Hating him again? Angry and hurt and in a state of mind she never, ever wanted to revisit?

"Hey," her friend said, nudging her arm to jar her out of her reverie. "It's okay. If you don't want to see him, you can hide out here. When no one answers your door he'll go away."

Stay here and miss seeing him? she nearly argued.

Okay, she'd gone crazy. She was pretty sure of it since she didn't know which was stronger: her dread at the idea of seeing him, or her overwhelming desire to be near him again.

"No, I have to go over there," she muttered as she watched Conor ring her doorbell.

It would have helped if he hadn't looked so good. Dressed in nothing better than jeans and a gray hoodie, he was still tall and broad-shouldered and all man, and even staring at him from that distance she was impacted by him. Much as she wished she wasn't.

She took a deep breath, sighed and stood up.

As she did Rachel said, "Do you want me to go with you? Or Jake could…"

Maicy laughed. "Conor isn't dangerous." At least

not beyond the effects he had on her. "It'll be okay. I'm sure he's here to formally say goodbye or something. I was just hoping not to do that. I should have known better. I'll call you tomorrow."

She went to her friend's front door but just as she opened it, Rachel said, "Maicy?"

She stopped, casting a questioning glance at her.

"I know you pretty well, right?" her friend said.

"Right."

"Then listen to me when I tell you that you really like this guy. Maybe what you felt for him died and now it's back. Maybe it never went away and you just buried it really, really deep. But the way you are about him is not the way you've been about anyone else. Not Drake. Not Gary. Nobody the whole time I've known you. It's a way I'm scared you'll never be about anyone else. So for once could you maybe try not being Tough-Maicy, let nature take its course just a little and see where it might be able to go from here with him?"

No. That was the answer to that question because if she let herself not be Tough-Maicy she wasn't sure how she would come out of this with her heart intact. So it was Tough-Maicy who was going across that street.

But that wasn't what she said to her friend.

"Sure," she lied.

Rachel gave her a small, sad smile that told Maicy she saw through her. But being a good friend, she didn't say that. She only nodded. "Yeah, call me…"

"Tomorrow," Maicy repeated before she went out the door and crossed the street.

Apparently Conor was on the alert because even with his back to her he sensed her approach and glanced over his shoulder.

When he recognized her he turned to face her. "There you are! Do I have the wrong house?"

"No, this is my place. I was at Rachel's."

"Ah, she's not only your best friend, she's your neighbor."

"Where did you get my address?" she asked as she unlocked her front door.

"Internet. Was it supposed to be a secret?"

He followed her inside and she closed the door behind them, thinking how strange it felt to have him there, in her house.

"No, it isn't supposed to be a secret. I guess I'm just wondering why you went to the trouble of finding it. Is everything okay? Is Declan all right? Your sister?"

"Declan is still in ICU but he's stable. Kinsey is fine but her future-mother-in-law has bronchitis and needed her. I gave her the green light to staying the night. The storm moved east, Maryland airports are closed now, so I'm here until they reopen and Kinsey and I can have a little time together later. Seemed like you and I just got cut off, though, and—"

He was rambling from one subject to another and he stopped himself to glance around at the living room she'd led him into.

"Nice place," he concluded. "Do you have renters upstairs?"

She recalled explaining her plans for the place when they'd talked about Gary. "Not yet. It still needs a few finishing touches before I can rent it. Gary was going to do them after the honeymoon. Now I'll have to hire someone…" Okay, maybe she was rambling slightly, too.

This was just weird. At the cabin, in Northbridge, even at the farmhouse, it had all seemed as if they were on more neutral territory. But this was *her* house. Where she lived her real life. Not only was he not a part of that, she'd been determined that once she got back to her real life, she'd leave her time with him behind.

Plus he looked so good there. So right. So much more like who she'd pictured sharing this house with than Gary ever had. And that was *not* an idea she could entertain!

She didn't invite him to sit but she perched stiffly on the arm of her white sofa and stared at him expectantly. It was not only an inquiry about why he'd come but also an attempt to convey the message that he shouldn't have.

But behind it she was drinking in the sight of that dark hair, that chiseled face, those sparkling cobalt blue eyes that she knew were going to haunt her forever.

"So if everything is all right…" she said to prompt him to tell her why he was there.

"Is that Rob kid in love with you or something? He wouldn't let me near you," he said, still not giving her a clue about this visit.

"He's a good kid. He looks out for Rachel like that, too. He and Jake had to kind of butt heads before Rob would get out of the way. He might be her little brother but he thinks of himself as her protector," she said, telling the truth but omitting the fact that she'd enlisted Rob's protectiveness.

"He thought he needed to look out for you with me?"

"He doesn't know you."

"And you didn't set him straight so we could say goodbye."

"Is that why you're here?" Maicy asked. "Because I didn't think we really needed to have some kind of big, dramatic farewell. I mean, I'm grateful that you followed me all the way from Northbridge and kept the car from stalling, but once we got here—"

"Yeah, I know, that was just gonna be it, we both needed to get on with our own stuff. But I realized that that's not going to do it for me."

Maicy raised her chin at him challengingly, not willing to drop her defenses.

Conor seemed to ignore it and went on to tell her what he was talking about, things he'd thought about earlier that evening, how he'd made his decision to resign his commission with the navy and do another residency to alter his medical specialty.

"I don't know for sure where we stand now, Maicy," he said once he'd spelled it all out for her. Then he amended it to, "I don't know where *you* stand. But I know what I want us to be. I loved you eighteen years ago—maybe you don't believe it, but I honestly did— and because I didn't do what you wanted me to do to prove it, I know I hurt you. I did harm—something I've devoted my life to *not* doing. I can never be sorry enough for that…"

He paused as if that carried so much weight it needed a moment of silence.

Then he said, "But out of what happened, you became the person you are now. And tonight, watching you walk away with that kid, knowing this time together was supposed to be the end… I knew I couldn't just let it happen. I love you, Maicy. I love who you are now more than that boy I was loved the girl you were…"

Another pause. Or maybe time stopped for a split second because that was how it seemed to Maicy as she tried to grasp what he was saying.

"So where I stand is where you stood eighteen years ago," he continued. "In front of you with a new plan for the future. One that has me becoming a civilian and doing a reboot of my career that'll make me a rookie again for a while. But one that could also—once I get Declan on his feet again—put me here, in Denver... with you, if you'll have me..."

Even without an invitation, he moved to perch on the arm of the white overstuffed chair that was at an angle to the couch. Closer to her now, he leaned forward and held out his hands in silent request for hers.

"Don't make me say goodbye to you...not now, not ever again," he said resolutely. "Let me...us...have what we thought we'd have—the rest of our lives together..."

Maicy didn't give him her hands. Instead she stared at his as so many things went through her mind, feeling as if something in her had split and left two halves at odds with each other—half that melted at the things he was saying, half that shied away from it the same way she'd shied away from Drake's proposal.

It was that latter half that was thinking that Conor was right when he said that she wasn't the girl he'd known years ago. And she never wanted to be that girl again—not in any way.

It was that half that *needed* to be strong and independent, to take care of herself because that was what made her feel secure and comfortable. She liked everything that she'd become once she'd risen from the ashes he'd left her in and she would not, under any circumstances, let go of her identity or agree to anything that ever threatened it. And to that half of her, the feelings for him that were fighting to take her over seemed like a great big, looming threat.

But yes, from that other half of her, those feelings for him *were* fighting fiercely to be set free. That half of her that had won out when she'd fallen asleep the night before. And it was begging her to take his hands now and jump at what he was suggesting.

But then what? she asked herself. Then did the soft half come out and stay out for good? The half that left her unprotected, that put her at risk? The kind of risk her mother had taken with her father over and over, getting hurt every time?

Conor wasn't her father, but he *had* let her down once before and devastated her in a way that was similar to what she'd watched her mother go through. It was why she'd convinced herself that she was better off with him out of her life. Was she really going to do what her mother had done and put herself in line for getting hurt again?

Not only didn't she take Conor's hands, she closed her own into fists that retreated from his.

But even as she did, that softer half of her told her that maybe she wasn't being completely fair.

Years before, Conor hadn't been on board with her plan, but it wasn't because he wanted to leave her. It was just that he'd wanted to stick to the original plan, to do what he'd thought was best for them both. He *hadn't* wanted them to break up.

Which, she guessed, made her actions more like her father's than Conor's actions had been because *she'd* been the one to jump ship when he hadn't given her what she'd wanted.

So was it possible that she *could* count on him? That he wouldn't disappoint her again?

She'd had to count on him at the cabin and he'd

come through for her at every turn there—he'd looked after her even in the middle of his own worries and fears and frustrations over his brother.

He hadn't let her down once they'd reached North-bridge, either, she admitted to herself. He'd stayed at the hospital, waited for her, done his best to get her the tests he'd thought she should have.

And afterward, he'd insisted on being by her side for the dance that could have turned into something embarrassing or painful—instead, his support had helped her through that awkward situation and made the whole thing better.

And she'd also been able to count on him helping her get back to Denver—another thing that he could have left her to deal with on her own.

When she honestly thought about it and factored in that it *hadn't* been Conor who had broken his commitment to her years ago, she also had to admit that there wasn't really any question about his loyalty or commitment to anything—to every plan he made, to his family, to everything he did. Even now, when he was dissatisfied with his choice of careers, he was dissatisfied because emergency medicine *didn't* allow him to make the kind of commitment he felt he needed to make to his patients. And as for the military, he'd decided on a course that would still leave him serving veterans and country in order for him to keep on honoring those commitments, just in a different way.

So was this all doubt and insecurity less about him and more about her?

She hadn't figured that out when he interrupted her confusion to say, "I'm not asking what that Drake guy asked of you. I want you to be who you are, I don't want you to change a thing about yourself or what you've built for yourself—I'm proud as hell of what you've accomplished, Maicy. I just want you to let me in so I can be a part of it, so you can be a part of where I'm headed from here."

He wanted her to let him in…

That had been one of Drake's accusations when she'd turned him down—that she wouldn't let him in, that she wouldn't let any man get too close. It was something Rachel thought, too.

But if she was completely honest with herself— which she was being at that moment—she had chosen to be with Drake and with Gary specifically because they weren't the kind of men who could convince her to fully open her heart. She hadn't had the kind of feelings for them that made her too vulnerable. The kind of feelings that had formed any real connection to them. The kind of feelings that had the ability to genuinely jar her when those relationships ended. Instead she'd had only safe, superficial feelings for them.

But is that really what you want? the Not-Tough-Maicy side asked in a voice that sounded a lot like Rachel's.

Safe, superficial feelings for men she could take or leave without any problem?

Not letting anyone get close enough to risk them hurting her?

Being so stubbornly independent and self-reliant that she really would end up dying alone?

But what was the alternative? Tough-Maicy argued. Risk being wiped out the way she had been eighteen years ago?

Because if she opened the door to what Conor wanted,

to what Conor was asking, if she opened the door to the kind of feelings she'd had during this last week and in his arms last night, and it didn't work out this time, it could be just as bad as it had been that other time...

She felt her head shaking no without consciously doing it herself, refusing Conor, refusing the softer side of herself and all the feelings, refusing to let him in...

"Maicy..." He said her name in a soothing voice. He leaned forward enough to put that handsome face in her line of vision.

And whether it was the beckoning tone or one look at him, it somehow altered her focus. It somehow made something in her settle slightly and think more clearly, more rationally.

Clearly and rationally enough to recognize that she couldn't ever again be where she'd been eighteen years ago.

Eighteen years ago she'd been barely more than a child. She hadn't had the ability for true independence, she hadn't had any resources.

But now she did have those things. And she also had the knowledge and the certainty that she could take care of herself, if she needed to. And Conor wasn't asking her to step away from her independence the way Drake had. Conor was honoring her accomplishments and showing a willingness to change his own course to accommodate them.

But he could still hurt her, she thought as she looked at that face that she never got enough of.

Losing him could hurt her really, really badly—it had already hurt just having him leave her behind at the repair shop despite the fact that she had orchestrated that.

"I am not going to let this be another ending for us," he said then, sharply enunciating each word. "Get that through whatever is going on in that head of yours and know this—we're together again because we're meant to be together, and I will do whatever I have to to get us there forever. To keep us there."

She didn't doubt that.

And slowly, little by little, looking into his eyes, those two halves of her began to merge into a whole that was somehow Tough-Maicy with softer edges— the person she was now with only a bit of the girl she'd once been.

And all of her was overflowing with feelings for Conor that she suddenly knew had taken her over regardless of how much she'd fought them.

She loved him. In spite of herself, maybe. Certainly in spite of their history. But she did love him. She couldn't deny it even when she tried to. And she knew she had to take the risk that brought with it.

She inhaled, held her breath, then exhaled, unclenching her fists but still not taking either of those big hands he had extended to her.

"You realize that I owe you a *no*. That you have it coming," she said.

He didn't take her seriously because he gave her a crooked, one-sided smile. "Go ahead, get it out of your system. I'll just keep asking until you think you've evened the score and we can move beyond it." The smile turned more engaging, more enticing. Sexier. "Or you could just be the bigger person and skip that part because you know you really do love me."

"Oh, do I?" she said.

The smile took another turn and became sweet and

boyishly charming. "I hope so. I came over here hoping so…" Then devilish. "You better not have just been using my body last night…"

Maicy laughed, thinking about that body of his. And how much she wanted it again right at that moment.

"Marry me, Maicy," he said then, quietly, earnestly, sincerely. "I love you more than you will ever know and I need you to be my wife."

"Or what?"

"Or the rest of my life will be just going through the motions."

He didn't merely leave his hands offered to her then, he took hers and held them firmly.

"Marry me," he repeated.

Her feelings for him were running rampant, and she was scared all over again by their strength and depth and bounds.

He really could hurt her…

But she also suddenly realized that she had to trust that he wouldn't. To trust him. Because she loved him too much to spend any more of her own life without him.

"Okay," she whispered.

He grinned. "Now tell me you love me as much as I love you," he instructed as if he knew she had to be talked through this.

"You know I do," she said in a low voice, as if it was hazardous to say it too loudly.

The grin melted into a smile that looked relieved. "I was counting on it but I need to hear it."

"I do love you, Conor," she said, still struggling through her own fears to admit it. Then she smiled and added, "Just ask Rachel."

"You told her what you wouldn't tell me?"

"No, she just knew."

He nodded sagely. "I don't care who knows as long as it's true," he said, standing and pulling her to her feet, too, so he could wrap his arms around her and hold her tight.

Those arms that she'd slept in last night and wondered how she was going to go on without.

Now she wouldn't have to...

She slipped her own arms under his and pressed her hands to his broad back as he bent down to kiss her.

And as she closed her eyes and gave herself over to that kiss, to him, to a future and forever with him, it slowly seeped in that she was finally where she truly belonged.

That whatever it had taken to get them there wasn't important anymore.

That all that mattered was that they'd rediscovered each other.

And that neither of them ever again let go.

* * * * *

Don't miss the first story in the
CAMDEN FAMILY SECRETS *series*

THE MARINE MAKES HIS MATCH

MILLS & BOON®

Cherish™

EXPERIENCE THE ULTIMATE RUSH OF FALLING IN LOVE

0817/23

MILLS & BOON®

EXCLUSIVE EXTRACT

Artist Holly Motta arrives in New York to find billionaire
Ethan Benton in the apartment where *she's* meant to be
staying! And the next surprise? Ethan needs a fake
fiancée and he wants *her* for the role…

Read on for a sneak preview of
HER NEW YORK BILLIONAIRE
by debut author Andrea Bolter

"In exchange for you posing as my fiancée, as I have
outlined, you will be financially compensated and you will
become legal owner of this apartment and any items such
as clothes and jewels that have been purchased for this
position. Your brother's career will not be impacted negatively
should our work together come to an end. *And…*" He
paused for emphasis.

Holly leaned forward in her chair, her back still board-
straight.

"I have a five-building development under construction
in Chelsea. There will be furnished apartments, office lofts
and common space lobbies – all in need of artwork. I will
commission you for the project."

Holly's lungs emptied. A commission for a big corporate
project. That was exactly what she'd hoped she'd find in New
York. A chance to have her work seen by thousands of people.
The kind of exposure that could lead from one job to the next
and to a sustained and successful career.

This was all too much. Fantastic, frightening, impossible…
Obviously getting involved in any way with Ethan Benton

was a terrible idea. She'd be beholden to him. Serving another person's agenda again. Just what she'd come to New York to get away from.

But this could be a once-in-a-lifetime opportunity. An apartment. A job. It sounded as if he was open to most any demand she could come up with. She really did owe it to herself to contemplate this opportunity.

Her brain was no longer operating normally. The clock on Ethan's desk reminded her that it was after midnight. She'd left Fort Pierce early that morning.

"That really is an incredible offer…" She exhaled. "But I'm too tired to think straight. I'm going to need to sleep on it."

"As you wish."

Holly moved to collect the luggage she'd arrived with. Ethan beat her to it and hoisted the duffle bag over his shoulder. He wrenched the handle of the suitcase. Its wheels tottered as fast as her mind whirled as she followed him to the bedroom.

"Goodnight, then." He placed the bags just inside the doorway and couldn't get out of the room fast enough.

Before closing the door she poked her head out and called, "Ethan Benton, you don't play fair."

Over his shoulder, he turned his face back toward her. "I told you. I always get what I want."

Don't miss
HER NEW YORK BILLIONAIRE
by exciting new author
Andrea Bolter

Available September 2017
www.millsandboon.co.uk

MILLS & BOON®

Why shop at millsandboon.co.uk?

Each year, thousands of romance readers
find their perfect read at millsandboon.co.uk.
That's because we're passionate about
bringing you the very best romantic fiction.
Here are some of the advantages of
shopping at www.millsandboon.co.uk:

* **Get new books first**—you'll be able to buy
  your favourite books one month before they
  hit the shops

* **Get exclusive discounts**—you'll also be
  able to buy our specially created monthly
  collections, with up to 50% off the RRP

* **Find your favourite authors**—latest news,
  interviews and new releases for all your
  favourite authors and series on our website,
  plus ideas for what to try next

* **Join in**—once you've bought your favourite
  books, don't forget to register with us to rate,
  review and join in the discussions

Visit **www.millsandboon.co.uk**
for all this and more today!